IVAN VYZHIGIN

A volume in the NIU Series in

Slavic, East European, and Eurasian Studies

Edited by Christine D. Worobec

For a list of books in the series, visit our website at cornellpress.cornell.edu.

IVAN VYZHIGIN

A MORAL-SATIRICAL NOVEL

FADDEI BULGARIN

Translated by Michael R. Katz

Introduction by William Mills Todd III

NORTHERN ILLINOIS UNIVERSITY PRESS
an imprint of
CORNELL UNIVERSITY PRESS
Ithaca and London

First published 2025 by Cornell University Press

Library of Congress Cataloging-in-Publication Data

Names: Bulgarin, Faddeĭ, 1789–1859, author. | Katz, Michael R., translator. | Todd, William Mills, 1944– author.
Title: Ivan Vyzhigin : a moral-satirical novel / Faddei Bulgarin ; translated by Michael R. Katz ; introduction by William Mills Todd III.
Other titles: Ivan Vyzhigin. English
Description: Ithaca : Northern Illinois University Press, an imprint of Cornell University Press, 2025. | Includes bibliographical references.
Identifiers: LCCN 2024059697 (print) | LCCN 2024059698 (ebook) | ISBN 9781501782619 (hardcover) | ISBN 9781501782626 (paperback) | ISBN 9781501782633 (epub) | ISBN 9781501782640 (pdf)
Subjects: LCGFT: Satirical fiction. | Novels.
Classification: LCC PG3321.B8 I813 2025 (print) | LCC PG3321.B8 (ebook) | DDC 891.73/3—dc23/eng/20241213
LC record available at https://lccn.loc.gov/2024059697
LC ebook record available at https://lccn.loc.gov/2024059698

Contents

Translator's Note and Acknowledgments ix

Introduction: The Picaresque Adventures of Faddei Bulgarin and His Ivan Vyzhigin by William Mills Todd III xi

Preface to Novel by Faddei Bulgarin 1

1. The Little Orphan, or a Portrait of Humanity in the Manner of the Flemish School 7
2. Mr. Gologordovsky and His Family 13
3. Love 20
4. Matchmaking 24
5. The Ball and Abduction 29
6. Marriage and Parting with the Newlyweds 36
7. A Rich Yid. Sources of His Wealth. 40
8. Meeting a Civil Servant, Returning from a Certain Place, with the Other One Going to a Certain Place. I Leave the Yid. 50
9. An Unexpected Meeting. A Transformation. My Aunt. My Education. 58
10. Examination in Boarding School. A Tempter. My Aunt's New Friend. Something Like First Love. Departure from Moscow. 69

11. I Get to Know Vorovatin Better. An Overheard Conversation. Premonitions. A Police Captain. 81

12. An Emancipated Man. A Lunatic. Deceived in Love. 94

13. A Prisoner of the Kirghiz. A Kirghiz Philosopher, Arsalan-Sultan. I Become a Horseman. 102

14. Arsalan-Sultan's Account of His Stay in Russia 110

15. Consequences of a Hard Winter in the Steppe. The Attack. A Joyful Reunion with My First Benefactor. 121

16. Milovidin's Tale. A Moral Automaton and His Housekeeper. An Old Maid's Family. A Panorama of Moscow Society. A Friendly Quadrille. A Russian Foreigner. Society at the Spa. A View of Venice. 129

17. The Resolution of the Kirghiz Elders Concerning My Reward. The Continuation of Milovidin's Tale. A Duel. The Flight. The Apostate Yid. Arrival in Constantinople. What Is Pera? Betrayal. Slavery. Liberation. 140

18. Departure from the Steppe. The Police Chief Once Again! Collectors of Transit Dues. The Officials' Feast. 154

19. A Business Conversation at a Russian Merchant's. A Tempestuous Man. The End of a Villain. 170

20. A Landowner—the Kind We Need More of in Russia. Judge the Flock by Its Priest. 181

21. The Audacious Landowner—Sila Minich Glazdurin 193

22. A Retired Soldier's Story. Arrival in Moscow. My Aunt's History. I Find My Mother. The Seducer. Murderers. 203

23. The Conclusion of Adelaida Petrovna's Story. Marriage. Reeducation. The Free Life. The Fatal Consequences of Negligence. I Enter the World. Paying Visits. 214

24. A Picture of High Society. Meeting with a Kind Enemy. Oh, Human Weakness! 228

25. Grunya's Story. Friendship with a Clever Actress, or The Shortest, Surest, and Nicest Path to Ruin. 239

26. Deliver Us from Evil! A Lesson in Daytime Piracy. Advice from an Old Soldier. I Come into Money Again. 250

27. False Gamblers. A Letter from Milovidin. He Located His Wife. Petronella's Repentance. Sequestration in Poland, or Check and Mate to Creditors. The Death of Mr. Gologordovsky. Mr. Pochtivsky, His Other Son-in-Law. 261

28. The Young Nobleman. Glupashkin. An Aficionado of Dramatic Art. Disorder in the Robbers' Den. Misfortune. Grunya's Flight. Honesty in Wolf's Clothing, or Don't Judge by Appearances. The Egoist. 272

29. My Intention to Marry. Official Arithmetic. Acquaintance with a Wealthy Tax Farmer. A Feast in the Home of the Merchant Moshnin. His Family. Domestic Theater. 284

30. Failure in Matchmaking. Letters from the Kirghiz Steppe and from Paris. Departure for the Army. War. Distinction. Return to Moscow. 296

31. Retirement. Departure for Petersburg. The Difference between Petersburg and Moscow Society. A Wicked Plan. The Unfortunate Olinka. I Am Imprisoned. It's Possible to Be Happy Even in a Disastrous Situation. 312

32. A Savior. It's the Crime, Not the Place, That Dishonors a Man. A Just Punishment for a Villain. A Secret Revealed. Last Will and Testament. Love and Friendship. The Lawsuit. Solicitors. Secretaries. A Visit to the Judges. There Are Good People Everywhere. 328

33. Usurers. The End of My Lawsuit. Supplement to Pyotr Petrovich's Account. The Fate of Literary Men. Trouble from Hypocrites. Persons Who Curry Favor. Marriage. The Grandee's Kindness. The Course of Affairs. The Incursion of Relatives. Retirement. All's Well That Ends Well. Conclusion. 344

List of Principal Characters *363*

Selected Bibliography of Major Works in English on Bulgarin's Ivan Vyzhigin *367*

Translator's Note and Acknowledgments

I translated the original version of the novel *Ivan Vyzhigin,* first published in St. Petersburg in 1828; it was republished in 1829, again in 1830, and revised in 1831, when it appeared together with a sequel titled *Pyotr Ivanovich Vyzhigin*. Between 1829 and 1832 the original novel was translated into several languages including French, Italian, German, Lithuanian, Polish, and English. The English version (by George Ross) was published in London in 1831 under the title *Ivan Vejeeghen, Or Life in Russia* and was reprinted in Philadelphia one year later. It is available today only as a facsimile reprint. The novel has not been retranslated into English since then.

Russian literature has a long tradition of negative Jewish stereotypes. Nikolai Gogol, Ivan Turgenev, and Fyodor Dostoevsky were all willing participants in that dishonorable tradition. It has been argued that Faddei Bulgarin was "one of the first writers to condemn the Jewish people and make a substantial contribution to the development of Judeophobic discourses in Russian literature."[1] It is therefore essential to alert the reader in advance that Bulgarin was a writer who referred to Jews (*evrei*) almost exclusively as "Yids" (*zhidy*), a derogatory epithet in common use from the end of the eighteenth century throughout the nineteenth and even to the present day. Much has been written about the history of this one offensive epithet (see John Klier's article in the Selected Bibliography). Bulgarin's novel also contains numerous disturbing ethnic and racial stereotypes. No excuses can be made for the author, but I would argue that his *Ivan Vyzhigin* merits the reader's attention in spite of the author's prejudices.

For more on this controversial subject, I refer the reader to Elena Katz's article listed in the Selected Biography, "Faddei Bulgarin's Polish Jews."

---

1. Elena Katz, "Faddei Bulgarin's Polish Jews and Their Significance for the Russian Judeophobic Tradition," *Russian Review* 66, no. 3 (2007): 407.

Special thanks are extended to my long-time good friend and colleague William Mills Todd for first suggesting that I translate *Ivan Vyzhigin* and, later, for agreeing to write a comprehensive introduction.

I also wish to express my deepest gratitude to Aleksandra Baker, lecturer emerita of Russian at Middlebury College, for her thoughtful suggestions and corrections to the draft of my translation; I would like to dedicate this work to her. Of course, any remaining errors belong to me.

Introduction

The Picaresque Adventures of Faddei Bulgarin and His Ivan Vyzhigin

William Mills Todd III

As Richard III and many denizens of *The Inferno* might attest, posterity can be unkind to those who run afoul of a beloved national poet. Faddei Bulgarin (1789–1859) was, by the standards of early nineteenth-century Russia, talented, well read, and impressively polyglot. He became a visionary newspaper publisher, entertaining journalist, friend of enlightened intellectuals, pioneering sociologist of literature, and author of the first Russian novel to earn international attention, *Ivan Vyzhigin: A Moral-Satirical Novel.* But he is remembered among present-day Russian readers primarily for his abuse of their national poet, Aleksandr Pushkin (1799–1837), whom they revere as a martyr to court intrigues, hostile censorship, and Grub Street hostilities. The scorn this episode fostered for Bulgarin's character has, until recently, been extended to his works and literary activity. Michael Katz's excellent new translation of Bulgarin's most successful novel gives us an occasion to reassess both career and work. In doing so, I draw on important recent works which argue persuasively for such a reevaluation as I outline Bulgarin's (mis)adventures, which celebrate the scope and grandeur of the Russian empire, put the quarrel with Pushkin in broad historical perspective, and comment on what Bulgarin achieved with his best novel.

It is a biographical commonplace to casually label Bulgarin's life a picaresque narrative, but it certainly fits this novelistic prototype better than other contemporary alternatives, such as gothic thrillers, novels of manners, "comic epic-poems in prose" (Henry Fielding), psychological inquiries, sentimental epistolary novels, and historical novels in the manner of Sir Walter Scott.

Picaresque novels—mostly translated, sometimes imitations of Western prototypes (such as the anonymous *Lazarillo de Tormes* [1554], Francisco de Quevedo's *The Swindler* [1626], Alain-René Lesage's *Gil Blas* [1715–35], or Daniel Defoe's *Moll Flanders* [1722])—figured prominently among the few fictional titles available to Russian readers of the eighteenth and early nineteenth centuries. Many of these, translated or native, found their way into the world as primitive chapbooks or cheaply printed volumes, pulp literature, dismissed by privileged writers and readers as *lubochnaya literatura*, from *lubok*, the bast strips on which early broadsides were printed. This was the reading material most familiar to the majority of Russia's barely literate public, and it would remain so until the 1917 revolution, when the new Soviet regime closed this vibrant industry down.

Claudio Guillén provides a description of picaresque that is at once concise and inclusive. In his treatment, these narratives offer chains of episodes, linked by the protagonist, often an orphan, a half-outsider who narrates his or her progress through the social layers of a disenchanted, brutal world, a world which no longer fully believes in its values or lives according to them. The narrative becomes the confession of a liar, more victim than agent, who learns hard lessons about this world, armed only with wit, irony, and stoic endurance.[1] This description works, with some variations, for both Bulgarin and his creation, Ivan Vyzhigin.

The future Faddei Venediktovich Bulgarin began life as Jan Tadeusz Krzysztof Bułharyn, the son of a minor Polish nobleman who joined an uprising against the Russian empire, which, together with Prussia and Austria, had occupied and partitioned Poland, which ceased to exist as an independent country after the Third, and final, Partition of 1795. Bulgarin's father was exiled to Siberia, dying shortly after his return in 1798.[2] Bulgarin's mother took her family to St. Petersburg, where through connections her son was accepted into the prestigious

1. Claudio Guillén, *Literature as System: Essays toward the Theory of Literary History* (Princeton, NJ: Princeton University Press, 1971), chapters 3 and 5. The best treatment of the Russian picaresque remains Jurij Striedter, *Der Schelmenroman in Russland: Ein Beitrag zur Geschichte des russischen Romans vor Gogol'* (Berlin: Otto Harrassowitz, 1961).

2. As a result of Bulgarin's poor reputation and lack of canonical status the scholarly literature devoted to him is thin. The following account of his life is culled from Bulgarin's incomplete memoirs, an article by his longtime friend and fellow editor N. I. Grech, two outstanding Ph.D. dissertations, and an edition of his letters to the Third Section (secret police): F. V. Bulgarin, *Vospominaniia: Otryvki iz vidennogo, slyshannogo i ispytannogo v zhizni*, parts 1–6 (St. Petersburg: Olkhin, 1846–1849; N. I. Grech, "F. V. Bulgarin," *Russkaia starina*, no. 11 (1871): 483–523; Donald Andrew Thumim, "In the Spirit of the Government: Faddei Bulgarin and the Formation of the 'Middle Class' in Russia, 1789–1859" (Ph.D. diss., Harvard University, 1995); Yelizaveta Raykhlina, "Russian Literary Marketplace: Periodicals, Social Identity, and Publishing for the Middle Stratum in Imperial Russia, 1825–1865" (Ph.D. diss., Georgetown University, 2018); A. I. Reitblat, ed. and intro., *Vidok Figliarin: Pis'ma i agenturnye zapiski F. V. Bulgarina v III otdelenie* (Moscow: Novoe literaturnoe obozrenie, 1998).

Cadet Corps. Schooling in Russian, a language foreign to him, proved challenging. He began his career in the Russian military in a privileged Uhlan regiment, fighting heroically against the French at the Battle of Friedland in 1807. But subsequent garrison duty in Petersburg proved tedious, and he neglected his duties to frequent the capital's theater world. Feeling disproportionately punished, he compounded the offense by writing satiric verse about his regimental commander, Grand Duke Constantine Pavlovich, an unwise career move which earned him three months confinement in the nearby Kronstadt Fortress and transfer to a less prestigious regiment. He next fought against the Swedes in Finland, suffering damage to his eyes from the severe cold. This pattern of obstreperousness, persecution, and somehow landing on his feet would recur throughout his life.

His military career brought him back to Petersburg and Revel, before he was dismissed from the service for bad conduct. He was able, however, to join the French army without betraying Russia, because the Treaty of Tilsit had made the French and Russians allies. He found himself serving in a Polish unit in Spain, in the bloody Peninsular War, then in Germany, possibly in Russia, again in Germany and France, possibly in Napoleon's legendary Old Guard. The record is unclear, and Bulgarin's memoirs, published in the late 1840s, take him up only to 1811. During the French retreat he was, in turn, made a Chevalier of the Légion d'honneur by Napoleon for capturing an Austrian general, then promoted to captain of the Légion d'honneur, wounded, captured by the Prussians, sent to Holland, then to Pomerania, then returned to France. By 1816 he had returned to St. Petersburg but then moved to Warsaw, making his way back to St. Petersburg in 1819. During the Warsaw years he compiled an impressive collection of books, read extensively, and began to contribute to local journals.

Bulgarin's literary opponents would later fault him for serving the French and Russian emperors—"*Ubi bene, ibi patria*," as Pushkin put it, sarcastically quoting Cicero—but the Napoleonic era was not yet the era of Romantic nationalism, and such shifting allegiances were not uncommon, especially for those whose countries had been swallowed by the major European empires. While the Russian government would at times regard Bulgarin with some suspicion, he was far from punished for his service to the French. He would eventually rise to a distinguished level in the Russian civil service, starting with a high civilian rank equivalent to the captaincy he had achieved in the French military. From all accounts he was loyal to the Russian empire, which had absorbed much of Poland, to the monarch, and to the government, while not denying his Polish origins and remaining nominally Roman Catholic. "Treason," as Talleyrand famously put it to the Congress of Vienna in 1815, "is a matter of dates."

In Petersburg Bulgarin found himself without hereditary wealth or salaried government employment. Professional literary work suited his education, inclinations, and life experience, and he gradually made his way through what passed for professional possibilities in the 1820s, contributing first to Polish-language journals, then to Russian ones, doing some translating, and networking with serious writers and intellectuals, among them the outstanding playwright Aleksandr Griboedov and future participants in the politically high-minded but abortive Decembrist Uprising of December 14, 1825. But literature in Russia could scarcely be called a profession in a full sense, joining vocation, remuneration, and commitment to a set of ethical standards. A number of distinguished poets (Aleksandr Pushkin, Vasily Zhukovsky, Konstantin Batyushkov, Evgeny Baratynsky, Petr Vyazemsky, Anton Delvig, and Nikolai Yazykov), the last four subsequently known as the Pushkin Pleiad, lived for their writing but could not make a living from it and survived mostly from occasional government subsidies, the proceeds of their estates, and civil or military service or by piling up unrepayable debts. The censorship imposed ethical behavior from without, defending religious dogma, the government, morals, and the personal honor of individuals. But bare-knuckle Grub Street hostility often governed relations between publishers, editors, and authors. In the 1820s what income was to be had from literary activity generally fell to the publishers, editors, booksellers, and printers but only to a few writers, such as Pushkin and the official historiographer Nikolai Karamzin. The imperial government was little concerned with stabilizing literary commerce, and it was decidedly ambivalent toward the literary process. The government may have sponsored secular printing, invited artisans from abroad to staff early printing establishments, and called for an educated class of servitors who would become the producers and consumers of secular literature, but it stood poised over the enterprise, capable of interfering with any stage in the process at almost any time, thereby hindering the institutional viability of even a modestly independent press. The state only began to allow private printing in 1783, and the laws changed rapidly in the decades that followed, through all of Bulgarin's life. Private presses were permitted, banned, and reestablished. Once prepublication censorship was clearly established in

1804, ambiguous passages in a text were interpreted in favor of authors, then held against them, then disregarded, then—de facto—held against them again. Censorship agencies proliferated, supervising and often contradicting one another; there were no fewer than a dozen by the end of Nicholas I's reign (r. 1825–1855).

But these rapid changes in the legal process were not, in themselves, the chief problem facing the publisher and the would-be professional writer. Laws, however rapidly they changed, could at least enable people to predict the consequences of their actions. Nor was censorship, in itself, necessarily a principal retarding force. By 1828, in part due to Bulgarin's lobbying, much of the censoring was performed by professor-littérateurs who shared the aspirations of publishers, writers and the public. A number of well-known writers came to hold positions in the censorship. The central problem was the unpredictability, arbitrariness, and vindictiveness of the government. Although during Bulgarin's career censors examined works prior to publication, writers and publishers could be punished subsequent to publication—even when the laws ostensibly protected them—if the published work incurred the displeasure of someone in a high place. The censors themselves were also vulnerable. A work that displeased higher authorities could result in severe reprimands, loss of position, or brief jail sentences. Bulgarin, as writer and editor, would alternately receive diamond rings as rewards, be severely reprimanded for the tone of his polemics, and be sentenced to nights in the guardhouse for his literary efforts, but at least he did not suffer financially crippling suspension or the banning of his periodicals.

The government was one major obstacle to professional authorship; the second was the reading public, or lack thereof. Only in 1897 was mass literacy measured in the Russian empire, at which time—after several decades of increasing educational opportunities—the level of minimal literacy reached only 21 percent of the population—that is, no better than a quarter of the percentage that facilitated profitable publishing in Europe, Japan, and the United States.[3] In the early nineteenth century, not only was the literacy rate most likely far lower, but the populace was not broadly committed to book purchasing or sufficiently educated to respond to sophisticated works. Bulgarin, not differentiating between levels of readership, estimated in 1823 that

---

3. Boris N. Mironov, "The Development of Literacy in Russia and the USSR from the Tenth to the Twentieth Centuries," *History of Education Quarterly* 31, no. 2 (1991): 244, 247.

only one million in a population of forty-five million were readers.[4] Fedor Dostoevsky, writing forty years later, was even less sanguine: he estimated, and his estimate is well supported by publishing statistics, that only one Russian in five hundred could read the literature that he and his rivals were producing.[5] Bulgarin's estimate clearly included the readership for pulp literature (*lubki*), and Dostoevsky specifically had in mind the educated, Westernized elite. In any event, this situation made publishing a precarious enterprise, and the participants in the process, especially periodical publishers, tended to view it as a zero-sum game, which fueled the intensity of their competitive gambits.

As Bulgarin entered Russian literature in the early 1820s, he participated in the debates of the day: about the direction of Russian literature, about its readership, and about specific works, such as Karamzin's *History of the Russian State* (1818–1826) and Pushkin's Romantic narrative poems. He began polemical skirmishes with the friends, colleagues, and relatives of these writers but for a time avoided confronting them in hostile fashion. He even became the first to publish (without the poet's knowledge or permission) part of Pushkin's *Eugene Onegin: A Novel in Verse*, the famous ballet stanzas from Chapter One, taking advantage of Russia's lack of a copyright law before 1828.

The year 1825 proved pivotal in Bulgarin's career. He was given permission to publish, with Nikolay Grech, a private newspaper, *The Northern Bee*, and it would continue to appear until 1864, an exceptionally long run in nineteenth-century Russia. A four-page tabloid, it appeared three times a week until 1831, then six times a week, Monday through Saturday. Unlike the private newspapers which followed, such as the short-lived *Literary Gazette* (1830–1831), which was edited by Delvig and Pushkin, Bulgarin's paper was authorized by the government to print official announcements and political news, which helped build its readership to eight thousand subscribers, even though it cost forty rubles a year to subscribe, a considerable sum for cash-poor landowners and low-ranking civil servants. But Bulgarin and Grech were not allowed to sell and print advertisements, because the government did not want to give them this advantage over state-printed newspapers. Undeterred, the enterprising Bulgarin undertook a program of what film producers call "product placement"—namely, he would favorably mention businesses

4. Thumim, "In the Spirit of the Government," 59.

5. F. M. Dostoevskii, *Polnoe sobranie sochinenii v tridtsati tomakh*, 30 vols. (Leningrad: Nauka, 1972–1990), 5:1.

and publications in his articles for bribes, a practice which increased his reputation for venality. Legend has it that Mikhail Lermontov's doting grandmother paid Bulgarin to give the subsequently canonical novel *Hero of Our Time* (1841) a positive review. Bulgarin used his lively page four columns (*feuilletons*), not unpredictably, to publicize his own books and those of his associates while denigrating those of his literary and journalistic rivals, but the feuilletons were also notable for their insight into contemporary mores and for their cultural commentary.

Among the official announcements he published at the end of 1825 were those concerning the suppression of the Decembrist Uprising, in which a number of his friends and many members of noble families had taken part. Many of them considered this cooperation with the government a betrayal, but the record shows that Bulgarin did not denounce his friends and that he himself was briefly held in suspicion during the official investigation of the uprising.

It is an historiographical challenge to assess Bulgarin's role in the government dispassionately. It is known that he was on active service in the Ministry of Education between 1826 and 1831, but that he was generally on leave during this time. During these years he was, however, actively providing reports and memoranda to the Third Section of His Imperial Majesty's Own Chancellery, the imperial gendarmes, through his friend M. Ya. Fon Fok, chief assistant to the head of the section, A. Kh. Benckendorff, who had known Bulgarin since their days in the Cadet Corps.

For subsequent scholars Bulgarin's service to the Third Section is inevitably colored by what has transpired in Russian history since the 1820s: the rise of terrorist opposition to the tsarist government in the second half of the nineteenth century and its harsh repression; Soviet-era purges of many groups, including cultural figures; current Russian suppression of potential political opposition to the regime. Increasingly harsh measures of surveillance, intimidation, and punishment are easily projected upon the early years of Nicholas I's reign, when it is true that the Decembrists were harshly punished (and five of them hanged). In the Soviet period both official and dissident scholars would come to view the police tactics of those years in negative terms; official historiographers because they saw persecuted intellectuals as the forebears of Soviet ideology, dissident scholars because they saw them as models for opposition or as martyrs. Roman Jakobson's 1931 essay "On a Generation That Squandered Its Poets" is but one in a long series of martyrologies written by and about victims of autocracy and totalitarianism.

Abram Reitblat's superb edition of Bulgarin's letters and memoranda to the Third Section, which span a thirty-year period from 1826 to 1856, together with Reitblat's introduction and detailed commentary, give us a chance to reevaluate Bulgarin's activity as he became a literary and journalistic opponent of subsequently revered figures in Russian cultural history. Quite frankly, these writings fail, in venom and deadly effect, to match the murderous denunciations of later periods, in part because the Third Section was minuscule by comparison with subsequent organs of state repression, and in part because its mission was largely to report on the state of public opinion, not to arrest, interrogate, and punish dissidents.[6] Bulgarin was most active during the first years of the section's existence; his reports and letters are general surveys of public opinion in Petersburg, Poland, and the Baltic provinces; arguments for relaxed and rational censorship; analyses of the reading public; and other comments on cultural institutions. Their "poetics," as Reitblat puts it, feature anecdotes, quotations, moral conclusions. Their ideology presents a politically harmless version of the European Enlightenment. Culturally Westernizing, it defends literature and a public sphere, while remaining supportive of an enlightened monarchy. The reports and letters are generous in defense of Bulgarin's friends, such as Griboedov, and harsh in their analysis of his opponents.[7] They show a Bulgarin more the victim of censors, government, and "aristocrats" (Russian and Baltic German) than victimizing. In style, topic, and tone they are of a piece with his newspaper feuilletons and with his first and most successful novel, *Ivan Vyzhigin*, which was written at the height of his government activity.

Bulgarin's analysis of the Russian reading public is particularly insightful, capturing the deep cultural divisions in Russian society. Submitted in 1826, it was widely distributed within the government and was read with approval by Nicholas I himself. Bulgarin's typology distinguished between (1) "noble and wealthy people," superficially educated in French culture and superficially oriented toward the thinking of the French Encyclopédistes of the eighteenth century; (2) the "middle stratum," consisting of service gentry, landowners living on their country estates, impoverished gentry, clerks, wealthy merchants, factory owners, and non-noble townsfolk—the true "Russian public," it

6. The best study in English of the Third Section remains Sidney Monas, *The Third Section: Police and Society in Russia under Nicholas I* (Cambridge, MA: Harvard University Press, 1961).

7. Reitblat, *Vidok Figliarin*, 16–18.

read mostly in Russian, followed the development of Russian literature, and remained loyal to the monarchy during the Decembrist Uprising; (3) the "lower stratum," consisting of petty clerks, literate peasants and townsfolk, rural clergymen, and religious sectarians—it read religious books and amusing moral tales and could be politically dangerous but was loyal to "Mother Russia"; and (4) scholars and littérateurs, very few in number.[8] Bulgarin and Grech oriented their successful newspaper toward the interests and cultural level of this middle stratum.

Bulgarin's next daring foray was into fiction, a succession of novels. His success in taking a type of writing previously suitable for his "lower stratum," a *lubok* genre, may be judged from a citation issued by the Moscow Society of Lovers of Russian Literature, which proclaimed Bulgarin and Pushkin "the two leading lights of our literature." Pushkin took umbrage at this coupling and refused to join the Society, which would later erect a monument to him in Moscow (1880). Bulgarin and Pushkin squared off, each trying to lay claim to the fragile beginnings of a profession of letters which the poet-historian Karamzin had tentatively crafted a generation before, when he delicately synthesized journalistic activity, prose fiction, and government service without loss of noble dignity and the ability to speak truth to power in the refined language of the educated, Westernized gentry.[9] Their quarrel had many dimensions—prose literature vs. poetry, unquestioned loyalty to the state vs. loyal opposition, new vs. old nobility—which made it all the more bitter.

The quarrel centered on charges of elitism or "aristocracy," a pejorative for both Pushkin and Bulgarin, but they understood it in very different terms. For Pushkin the court aristocracy was a malignant growth on Russian history, consisting of scheming courtiers elevated to high rank by the eighteenth-century emperors and empresses. For Bulgarin it was the educated Westernized gentry, habitués of urban salons and familiar associations in which he was not welcome; it included Pushkin and his poet friends. For Bulgarin and his close associates to label their opponents "aristocrats," therefore, infuriated Pushkin. More than this, it constituted a cunning and largely successful play in their competition with the Pushkin Pleiad for the small educated public. Bulgarin

---

8. "O tsenzure v Rossii i o knigopechatanii voobshche," in Reitblat, *Vikok Figliarin*, 45–48.

9. For a more complete analysis of this conflict, see William Mills Todd III, *Fiction and Society in the Age of Pushkin: Institutions, Ideology, and Narrative* (Cambridge, MA: Harvard University Press, 1986), chapter 2.

had mastered Karamzin's refined middle-style Russian and could persuade his readers that he was using it in the service of morality and patriotism. His reviews of Pushkin's work, especially Chapter Seven of *Eugene Onegin*, could persuade readers that Pushkin's talent was exhausted, while his periodicals and associates praised Bulgarin's own works. As Bulgarin wrote disparaging pieces about Pushkin's ancestry, talent, and lack of patriotic fervor, Pushkin retaliated with a series of incisively devastating portrayals of Bulgarin as a police agent, equating him with the reformed criminal François-Eugène Vidocq, whose memoirs (perhaps ghostwritten) had appeared in 1828. Under a pseudonym Pushkin cast aspersions on the virtue of Bulgarin's wife, dismissed Bulgarin's works as inferior *lubki*, and threatened to write a picaresque novel about Bulgarin himself. Bulgarin's sallies appeared in periodicals with impressive circulation and Pushkin's in a much less widely circulated Moscow journal. By the time that the government had put a halt to these unseemly exchanges, it was clear that Bulgarin had won the battle. Pushkin would, in the eyes of posterity, win the war but for the present Bulgarin's opponents had to content themselves with unpublished epigrams (by at least a dozen poets), letters, and obscure articles.[10]

Ivan Vyzhigin had, indeed, made Bulgarin the "leading light" of Russian prose. Marketed, like his other volumes, by subscription, it sold out its first printing within a week, a second printing soon thereafter, and a second edition a year later, in 1830. The seven thousand copies sold made it the most successful novel of its time, excluding *lubok* ones. Not that it had much competition that year, as Jurij Striedter reports that of the sixty-nine novels published in Russia, only nine were not translations.[11] Bulgarin happily noted that his sales exceeded those of Karamzin's *History*, the previous greatest success in Russian prose. His profit was, by the standards of the time, considerable.

The temptation to view Bulgarin's success as the opening of a new era in Russian literature must be in large part resisted. *Ivan Vyzhigin* was, it is true, the first nineteenth-century novel to enjoy commercial success with the educated Westernized public. Within a few years it would be translated into French (1829, 1860), Polish (1829, 1830), German (1830, 1843, 1868), English (1831), Swedish (1830–1831), Dutch

10. For Russian texts of the epigrams and satiric poems, see Thumim, "In the Spirit of the Government," 391–97.

11. Striedter, *Schelmanroman*, 254n37.

(1831), Czech (1842), Moldovan (1852), and Italian (1853). But its sequel, *Petr Vyzhigin* (1831), lost money for its publisher. The price of Bulgarin's novels and of his collected works remained well beyond the reach of the broader public served by the *lubok* trade and beyond many members of the "middle stratum." Donald Thumim's careful analysis of all of Bulgarin's subscription lists shows that Bulgarin's readership belonged more to his first category of readers ("noble and wealthy people") than to such constituents of the "middle stratum" as non-noble townspeople and rural landowners. In a telling commentary on the fleetingness of fame, only 15 percent subscribed to more than one of his editions.[12] Bulgarin, no less than Karamzin and Pushkin, negotiated his way among the feebly institutionalized possibilities of Russian culture: government patronage, the reading public with its susceptibility to fashion, and the literary market, which could produce high profits on relatively small editions that won fashion's approval. The success of *Ivan Vyzhigin* did not surpass that of Pushkin's *Eugene Onegin*, which Pushkin published in separate chapters at a large profit, then in complete editions in 1833 and 1837.

Pushkin was shot and killed in a duel in 1837. Bulgarin continued to write and co-publish his newspaper for another two decades, but those years brought a steady decline in his success, commercial and critical. The Third Section paid less attention to his complaints; his high rank, wealth, and occasional praise from the emperor did not insulate him from reprimands, the vicissitudes of the marketplace, and his own inability to complete encyclopedic and historical projects. Monuments were erected to Pushkin; beginning in 1880, his works came to be published in millions of copies; the Academy of Sciences Institute of Russian Literature (Pushkin House) bears his name; many museums keep alive the memory of his life and work.[13] Bulgarin, by contrast, has been largely forgotten. His works disappeared from print after his death until a one-volume collection of them appeared in 1990. He has been neglected by historians of Russian literature, domestic and foreign, although some critical studies have begun to explore parallels and contrasts between his works and those of such canonical authors as

12. Thumim, "In the Spirit of the Government," 207–20.

13. On Pushkin's afterlife and canonization the best places to begin are Marcus C. Levitt, *Russian Literary Politics and the Pushkin Celebration of 1880* (Ithaca, NY: Cornell University Press, 1989); and Stephanie Sandler, *Commemorating Pushkin: Russia's Myth of a National Poet* (Stanford, CA: Stanford University Press, 2004).

Nikolay Gogol and Dostoevsky.[14] Only recently have his works (essays, correspondence with the Third Section, his historical novel *Dmitry the Pretender*, and *Ivan Vyzhigin* been reprinted. But readers with Russian can now easily find a very generous selection of his works on multiple websites, including in the "classics" section of the generously populated online Russian Library. He would have appreciated this tardy modicum of canonization. In the last decade two major collections of scholarly articles have begun to restore his place in literary history.[15]

Toward the end of *Ivan Vyzhigin* its hero, whose autobiography the book purports to be, considers becoming a writer and is talked out of it by his wise friend Virtutin (Mr. Virtue), who points out the difficulties faced by Russian authors in terms reminiscent of those used in one of Bulgarin's feuilletons for *The Northern Bee*. This is a nice touch on Bulgarin's part, to make his own profession one of the last stages in a rogue's progress. But Virtutin's warnings came true for the author himself, and his last years were not happy ones, although his four children were able to make their way in the world. Whether this fate realizes the novel's rhetorical pattern of vice punished and virtue rewarded, I leave it to the reader to decide.

Readers who come to *Ivan Vyzhigin* for the first time but with a knowledge of other nineteenth-century classics—the brilliantly experimental *Eugene Onegin* (Pushkin), *A Hero of Our Time* (Lermontov), and *Dead Souls* (Gogol) or the profound psychologically and philosophically engaged novels of Ivan Turgenev, Dostoevsky, and Leo Tolstoy—will find Bulgarin's greatest novel a new experience.

This was his first novel, but he could bring to it a decade of writing feuilletons, sketches, critical articles, stories, and, yes, memoranda for the Third Section. These taught him to convey scenes vividly, to give snippets of dialogue, to sum up a personage in a few paragraphs. As a successful newspaperman, he had a "nose for news," and this helped him to make his novel's episodes entertaining and memorable. His own adventures had given him a sense of scope, and he used this to good advantage, to convey a sense of the vastness of the Russian empire and its expansive conquests to the west, south, and east.

---

14. For a survey of Bulgarin's literary afterlife, see Thumim, "In the Spirit of the Government," chapter 6.

15. A. I. Reitblat, ed., *Faddei Venediktovich Bulgarin: Ideolog, zhurnalist, konsul'tant sekretnoi politsii. Stat'i i materialy* (Moscow: Novoe literaturnoe obozrenie, 2016); A. I. Reitblat, ed., *F. V. Bulgarin—pisatel', zhurnalist, teatral'nyi kritik: Sbornik statei* (Moscow: Novoe literaturnoe obozrenie, 2019).

Writing in the aftermath of the Karamzinian development of a relatively smooth, non-ecclesiastical, non-bureaucratic middle style, Bulgarin's novel in the original Russian is remarkably accessible and "readable" to this day, and Michael Katz's translation successfully conveys this. Bulgarin in this regard surpassed earlier Russian writers of picaresque fictions, such as Vasily Narezhny—whose *Russian Gil Blas* (1814), like Bulgarin's *Ivan Vyzhigin*, combined social satire, picaresque movement through levels of society, and Enlightenment moralizing. Bulgarin avoided censorship, which Narezhny, whose novel was crippled and ultimately suppressed by the censors, could not. Narezhny, a Ukrainian, is best remembered in his native country, but his novel and stories live on in Russian literary history for their impact on a brilliant Ukrainian writer of the next generation, Nikolay Gogol; for their realistic descriptions; and for their stylistic range. In an act of restorative justice a two-volume collection of Narezhny's works, including his picaresque novel, appeared in 1956, decades before Bulgarin returned to print.

Bulgarin's literary, ideological, and cultural orientation is evident from the novel's dedicatory epistle: addressed to a friend and military comrade (who had reached ministerial rank), it celebrates hard work, a quiet life, service to morality, and the past enlighteners of Russia (Peter I and Catherine II, Griboedov, Denis Fonvizin, and Gavrila Derzhavin). It gently defends satire. Readers may wish to compare it to Pushkin's dedicatory verse in *Eugene Onegin*, which celebrates many of the same virtues, including an avoidance of the proud, aristocratic world. Most of Bulgarin's readers were in no position to assess how well he embodied these virtues in his own life.

Bulgarin's great contribution to the novel in *Ivan Vyzhigin* is its plotting, which is highly intricate. Many characters disappear only to reappear, sometimes after many pages, or tell their stories, which then turn out to bear obliquely on the main plot, which takes Vyzhigin from the bestial life of a kidnapped infant on a remote estate to the imperial capital, St. Petersburg. I will not comment further in order not to spoil the plot's play of surprise and suspense for first-time readers. Suffice it to say that Bulgarin's readers were probably grateful for his summarizing chapter titles.

The novel's characterizations may disappoint admirers of Russian fiction, which is justly celebrated for its wealth of "round" characters (E. M. Forster in his *Aspects of the Novel* opined that there may be too many such characters). In this novel a character's essence is quickly imparted, if not by a significant name (and Katz has helpfully provided a list of them), then by physiognomy or by ethnicity. Bulgarin's antisemitism is remarkable, even by the poor standards of Russian culture, for its vicious presentation of its Jewish characters and their culture. Other subject peoples of the Russian empire, such as Poles and Ukrainians, fare only somewhat better. The nomadic Kyrgyz, who rescue Vyzhigin in one of the novel's episodes, are treated condescendingly, as noble savages who might become civilized by the empire. This celebration of Russian superiority is reinforced by the novel's vilification of the European-oriented urban elite.

There are few exceptions to the rule of *nomen est omen*. One involves the ambiguous surname of the novel's protagonist. In the novel it is given to the foundling in recognition that the scar on his shoulder had been burned off in childhood (from *vyzhigat*, to cauterize). But in popular Russian speech a *vyzhiga* is an inveterate rogue. Such essentializing devices as talking names, ethnic otherness, and unattractive appearance, familiar from comic and satiric genres of the eighteenth century, do seem to contradict Bulgarin's enlightenment view that people are born good and subsequently fall into error from the circumstances of their life.

Bulgarin subtitled Ivan Vyzhigin "a moral-satirical novel" but took pains in his dedicatory epistle to suggest that he had pulled his satirical punches. Historically vague in its setting (the late eighteenth century, to judge from wars and cultural figures mentioned), the novel becomes more a satire against vices than against specific persons or profound injustice. Its moral rhetoric and genre make it something of a literary comfort food, not a slap in the face of contemporary Russia. Its values are those of the European Enlightenment, but enlightenment without tears: civil liberties, the rule of law, honest behavior. Its protagonist, as he moves through his many adventures, comes to embody these virtues, toward which we generally see him striving. More sinned against than sinning, he acquires culture and morals from the good examples which occasionally appear before him. His temporary failings are occasioned by bad companions and circumstances.

This novel opens a window, a wide one, onto what Russians in Bulgarin's esteemed "middle stratum" were reading between the late eighteenth century and the 1917 revolution. It enjoyed a momentary sojourn in the realm of elite culture (Bulgarin's first and fourth sets of readers), then disappeared, as it failed to satisfy the often maximalist aspirations of competing ideological groups: religious nationalists, Westernizing liberals, populists, advocates for socialist transformation. Now that a new official nationalism again summons Russians to restore the scope and grandeur of their reduced empire, it merits attention for its definition, through inclusion and exclusion, of that empire. That same scope and ambition, captured in its intricate plot and expansive novelistic space, make it an engaging experience for readers without access to Bulgarin's Russian.

IVAN VYZHIGIN

Preface

A Letter to His Excellency Arseny Andreevich Zakrevsky[1]

Twenty years have passed [written in 1829], since I saw you for the first time on the battlefield in Finland, when the unforgettable Count Nikolai Mikhailovich Kamensky[2] was leading us to victory and, together with us, was overcoming innumerable obstacles, including climate, geography, and the brave enemy. Twenty years is a great deal of time: one-fifth of an entire century! Since then much has changed in the world. Regarding the world with a philosophical eye, I'm consoled in my insignificance only by the fact that with the reversal of fortune, certain worthy people, whom I knew previously, have attained elevated levels through their merit and constant striving for the common good. My joy is impartial. I'm not looking for anything; I don't desire anything, aside from the respect of honorable people and the favor of the public, which I try to gain through my hard work and my quiet life. From the number of people to whom this book is dedicated, I chose

---

1. A Russian statesman and minister of the interior from 1828 to 1831.

2. A Russian general (1776–1811) who outlived his father, Field Marshal Mikhail Kamensky, by two years. His father played a prominent role in Catherine's wars and in the Napoleonic campaigns.

to place before Your Excellency my intentions in publishing this work to the world. I'm writing not to the minister, whom I respect, but to a man whom I love dearly. You haven't had a change of heart during your twenty years; in the Cabinet of Ministers you're the same generous man with other people who are seeking the truth, just as you were on the field of battle with your military comrades. I hope that you'll accept this letter from an old soldier who's exchanged his saber for a pen, to pursue truth, at least as he sees it.

"To love one's fatherland means to wish it well," I wrote then. "To wish it well is the same as wishing for the eradication of abuses, prejudices, and bad habits, and the establishment of good morals and enlightenment. There are many cases where laws can have no influence on morals. Well-intentioned satire promotes the perfection of morality, presenting vices and eccentricities in their genuine guise and showing in its magic mirror what to avoid and what to pursue. That's the goal for which my novel *Ivan Vyzhigin* was written. In it readers will see that all that is bad comes from a lack of moral education, and that for everything that is good people are indebted to faith and enlightenment.

All the great lawmakers of Russia have understood the goal of well-intentioned satire and have themselves often resorted to it for assistance in eradicating vices and prejudices. Peter the Great ordered that many useful foreign books be translated into Russian. The translator of Puffendorf's[3] works omitted all the caustic aspects of the morals and customs of the Russians of that era and replaced them with ingratiating praise. The wise reformer of Russia was angered by this distortion of the original and ordered the entire book translated again and dedicated to him. "It wasn't to vilify Russians that I ordered this satire on our morals," said the sovereign, "but for their improvement. Let them know how we were then, how we are now, and how we should be. If everything written in the book is untrue, lies will not defame us; but if the author is telling the truth, we will try to become such that his words will seem like lies."

Peter the Great, in spite of his indefatigable concern for the civic well-being of Russia and her defense from envious neighbors, couldn't establish a literature that demands a great deal of time to mature; he merely sowed the first seeds. Those seeds produced nutritious fruit no earlier than the reign of Catherine the Great. In the period between

3. Samuel Freiherr von Puffendorf (1632–1694) was a German jurist, political philosopher, economist, and historian.

these two famous reigns, there began the flowering of Russian literature; her first fruits were the satires of Prince Kantemir,[4] who, by rights, should be recognized as the first secular Russian author.

Catherine the Great gave life and support to the newly developing literature and used it to refine Russian morals. The imperial hand that signed the *Nakaz*[5] and strengthened Russia's prosperity by wise laws and great political planning was also able to control the instrument of well-intentioned satire. By command and under the wise monarch's special patronage, in 1793 a journal was published under the title *The Colloquy of Lovers of the Russian Word*,[6] which included acerbic articles about Russian morals. There vices were mercilessly attacked, as were prejudices and superstitions of that time, especially those prevalent among the nobility. The empress herself had the kindness to place her own articles in this publication; as a result of the low rate of literacy at the time and ignorance of literary decorum, many Russian readers didn't understand the true purpose of these satirical articles. Therefore the wise monarch ordered there to be published in the journal an explanation which I will cite as a curious reminder of Catherine's cast of mind concerning satirical works in general, as well as evidence for those today who don't understand the usefulness of moral satire.

> When I was writing, I wasn't thinking about anyone in particular. If one doesn't write about weaknesses common to human beings, there's no sense in writing about anything else. If weaknesses and vices aren't censured, virtue cannot be praised either; by coming to know the former, the latter also becomes known. If someone recognizes himself in my book in a wanton or unworthy portrayal, it was he who made himself subject to it; common sense commands him to reform himself and not to get angry. Does anyone demand that the mirrors in his furnished quarters be destroyed so that he won't have to see his own ugly countenance? Don't be annoyed, reader, but reform yourself; then, being in the world with me, I'll amuse you and, with your reformed weaknesses, you'll earn general esteem as well as my own.[7]

---

4. Antiokh Kantemir (1708–1744), a distinguished Russian statesman who was one of the leading writers of the classical school.

5. A statement of legal principles written and promulgated by Catherine the Great, permeated with the ideas of the French Enlightenment.

6. It contained various works in verse and prose of several Russian writers.

7. See Part I, p. 9. This excerpt is printed in italics in the original. [Bulgarin's note]

That's what I shall reply to those who will attempt to misinterpret the goal of my novel!

I know that the sincerity of my *Vyzhigin* won't please those people who consider every truth, proclaimed loudly, as willfulness; who ascribe every denunciation of abuse to evil intention; who consider enlightenment, the sole means for the well-being of people, as evil; like robbers, who wish for the establishment of general darkness, the numbing of the mind, profound silence, so that their actions would be concealed. One can ascribe to them words uttered by the immortal author of the comedy *Woe from Wit*:

From *evil* ways to turn *them*.
You'll have to take all books *and* burn them.[8]

But, no! Our wise government takes care of enlightenment, the establishment of morality, and, in spite of the understanding of inveterate old believers and champions of ignorance, gives free rein to intelligence. Well-intentioned people of all social classes sense, in full measure, the intentions of our wise rulers and are prepared with all their might to facilitate the common good. The Decree on Censorship, confirmed from above on April 22, 1828,[9] is the sturdiest monument of love for enlightenment and truth, worshipped by us, of the just monarch—a reminder, worthy of our age and of mighty Russia! All we have left to do is to pray to the Almighty that those who carry out our sovereign's noble intentions understood his great designs: then our happiness will be complete, and the golden age of the Derzhavins and Fonvizins will arrive again in our Russian literature. . . .

Our aristocracy doesn't read Russian and is unfamiliar with our literature; our ladies even speak their native language infrequently, and many think that it's a significant barrier to the advancement of our literature. No, it's not a barrier but an obstacle; however, it is unable to restrain its aspirations. Fonvizin's *The Minor* and *The Brigadier*,[10] Kapnist's *Slander*,[11] *Recruitment*, and *An Unheard-of Marvel*[12] were presented in

8. From A. S. Griboedov's famous comedy in verse, also known as *The Misfortune of Being Clever* (1823).

9. By His Majesty the Tsar.

10. Denis Fonvizin (1745–1792), one of the founders of Russian comedy, wrote two satires, *The Minor* (1782) and *The Brigadier* (1768–1769).

11. Vasily Kapnist (1758–1823) was a Russian poet and playwright (his satire was written in 1798).

12. *Or an Honest Secretary*, a verse comedy in three acts by Nikolai Sudovshchikov (1770–1812) in 1802.

the public theater, by the will of Russian crowned heads. "The Grandee" by Derzhavin[13] was published by permission of Catherine the Great. And so, could there be barriers when the autocrats act in the spirit of their time—for the good, that is, for the enlightenment of their subjects? Thank God, we still have honest Russian grandees, who, by their merits, have obtained the right to approach the sacred steps of the throne: they will also cleanse the path to truth. Such thoughts console the heart and open the mind.

I consider it my duty to say a few words about my novel in relation to literature. Scholars and pedants, wishing to keep minds in the grip of fictitious rules devised by them for each genre of literature, put together particularly confining frameworks and demand that all writers compose by their standard. To deviate from these rules is considered literary heresy. But where did these rules come from? They were developed from the compositions of writers who wrote not knowing any other rules besides the standards of taste of their own age and their nation, not knowing other patterns besides nature. Other times had other morals. But the scholars, their minds locked in chains of prejudices, absolutely demand that in all times for all nations, poems should be written as in the time of Homer and Virgil, odes according to the rules of Pindar and Horace, tragedies like Racine's, comedies in the style of Molière, moral novels in the form of riddles. According to the rules it is necessary for the hero of the novel to act like Bayard,[14] to speak in maxims like an orator, and to represent a model of human perfection . . . and boredom. When my composition was almost finished, I received a little book from a splendid French journal, *Revue Britannique* (no. 29, 1887), and to my great satisfaction found an article under the title, "Why Are Heroes of Novels So Affected?" In answer to this question, the author says: "It's from the perfection with which they're presented. They're angels, not people." The author adds: "They present to us a novel's heroes as some kind of theatrical divinities; as a result, they're so cold. Many people think that to present them as weak, indecisive, and subject to their circumstances means to debase them. But we are people, we have our weaknesses; therefore the very failings of humanity move us more deeply." Such was my own frame of mind concerning the heroes of my novel. My Vyzhigin is a good creature by nature, but he's weak in

13. Gavrila Derzhavin (1743–1816) was one of the most highly esteemed classical Russian poets. This poem was written in 1794.

14. A magic bay horse in legends, renowned for his spirit; he possesses the supernatural ability to adjust his size to his riders.

moments of error, subject to circumstances—in a word, he's a man like many of those we often see in the world. That's how I wanted to depict him. The events of his life are the kind that can happen to anyone, without the addition of invention. I don't know whether the simplicity of the story's events will please my readers. May they forgive the faults due to the goal and because this is the first original Russian novel in this style. I boldly affirm that I didn't imitate anyone, didn't copy anyone, but wrote what was conceived in my own head. Let my literary opponents abuse Vyzhigin: they'll have the exclusive pleasure—they'll hurl abuse but receive no reply.

I didn't even touch on our literature with the instrument of my satire, because it still requires assistance, not disapproval; it has yet to mature and hasn't been burdened with ailments harmful to morality. We don't have so many writers as to constitute their own class in society, as in other countries. Writers in our country don't write harmful things; they don't have twisted views of literature or write insults about literature; the abuse of worthy writers carries no weight with the public and serves only to embarrass such biased and immature critics. I left those critics in peace: after all, you don't beat a fallen man!

As far as moral portraits in my novel are concerned, it would've been possible to increase their number and present them much more vividly. But I considered it better to follow the rule of our inimitable writer of fables, I. A. Krylov:

It would be easy to make this fable more intelligible,
But I am afraid of provoking the geese.[15]

These are the motives and rules, that guided in the composition of *Vyzhigin*. Your Excellency's approval will be a guarantee of the good opinion of well-intentioned people and the sweetest consolation for the misguided views of others.

Faddei Bulgarin
St. Petersburg
February 6, 1829

15. A quotation from the fable "The Geese" by Ivan Krylov (1769–1844), Russia's outstanding fabulist.

CHAPTER 1

The Little Orphan, or a Portrait of Humanity in the Manner of the Flemish School

Until the age of ten, I grew up in the home of the Byelorussian landowner Gologordovsky, reared like a homebred wolf cub and known by the name the *Orphan*. No one cared for me, and I cared even less for anyone else. Of all the inhabitants of the house, not one caressed me, except for the good old dog, who, like me, was left to provide for itself.

There was no corner of the house assigned to me for my lodging, no food or clothing provided, and no fixed activity. I spent my summer days in the open air and slept under the shed attached to the barn or in the cattle yard. In the winter I lived in the huge kitchen, which served as a meeting place for the many servants, and I slept on the hearth among the warm embers. In the summer I wore only a long shirt with a rope tied around my waist; in the winter I covered my nakedness with whatever came my way: an old woman's jacket or a worn-out peasant's coat; these items were furnished by compassionate people, who didn't know what to do with their old rags. I had no footwear, and my feet became so hardened that neither the soft grass nor the mud nor the ice felt any different. I never used to cover my head: the rain washed away the dirt, and the snow cleaned away the ashes. I ate leftovers from the servants' tables of various houses and feasted on eggs, which I gathered from the area around the henhouse and in the barn; I drank the residue in the milk pails, which

I licked up with unusual skill; and I munched on vegetables pilfered from the garden at night. I had no direct overseer: everyone ordered me around at his or her discretion. In the summer I was supposed to herd the geese in the pasture and guard the ducklings and chicks from dogs and hawks. In the winter they used me instead of a device for turning the spit in the kitchen: that was a most enjoyable chore for me. Every time the cook turned his or her back on the hearth, I'd stick my hand on the juicy joint and suck my greasy palm the way a bear licks his paw; sometimes I very craftily tore off a piece of ham from the roast or snitched cutlets from the frying pan. My primary duty was to run errands for all the lackeys, servant girls, and even the young lads. They would send me to the tavern for vodka, stand me on guard in various locations with no explanation, ordering me to whistle or clap my hands if the master or the steward or even, at times, other lackeys and servant girls approached. At their first word, "Little Orphan! Run over there, call so-and-so," I would run as fast as I could and carry out their orders precisely, because the smallest mistake would occasion an inevitable beating. When they placed me on guard and told me not to look around (which occurred frequently in the summer), I stood as if rooted to the spot, not daring even to raise my eyes, and moved only when they released me from that post. Sometimes, although very infrequently, they would reward me for my attentive service with a hunk of black bread or some old ham or cheese; and no matter how hungry I was, I would always share it with my beloved dog, Shaggy.

Seeing how other children were caressed and kissed, I wept bitter tears; I don't know why, probably from feelings of envy and irritation. Shaggy's affection and licking relieved my grief and made my loneliness more tolerable. Observing how other children hugged their mothers and nannies, I hugged my Shaggy and called her mommy or nanny, caressed and kissed her, pressed her to my chest, and tumbled in the sand with her. I wanted to love people, especially women, but I couldn't nurture any feeling other than fear toward them. I was constantly beaten and pushed around–from annoyance, for amusement, or from boredom. When I would meet a lackey or a servant girl who'd received a scolding or a beating from the master or mistress, they'd vent their irritation on me, driving me away with an insult or a box on the ears, with the words, "Get away, you *orphan*!" If out of curiosity I sometimes wanted to watch how the team of horses was harnessed, to elicit laughter from the bystanders the coachmen would strike me on the head with the whip or lash my feet and make me jump with a yelp from the blows.

I didn't dare get close to the hunters or within range of their whips. Even the herdsmen would make fun of me: as a joke they'd drive me with a lash into the midst of their flock and amuse themselves, watching how I tried to evade the cows and sheep. The master's two sons would divert themselves shooting arrows at me and chasing me with their little lapdogs, but my Shaggy would always defend me.

I rarely saw the master himself: after meeting me once in the courtyard, he forbade me from even approaching the windows of the manor house and stamped his foot so terribly, saying, "Get away, you little beast!" that I dared not show myself to him again and would hide in the kennel as soon as I spotted him from a distance. I had no opportunity of seeing the mistress and her two daughters except through the fence in the garden or in their carriage, and I recognized them only by their apparel. I was deathly afraid of the steward and his wife because they had whipped me several times as an example to their own son, who was refusing to learn his letters but loved to rob birds' nests and throw stones at the master's ducklings and chicks. The destruction of domestic fowl was attributed to the hawks and to my negligence. As a punishment for this good-for-nothing lad, they would make him watch how I was whipped and listen to an admonition, which consisted of the words, "Watch out, Ignashka,[1] if you keep on misbehaving and refusing to learn your lessons, you'll be whipped too, just like this *orphan*. Do you hear how he's screaming? You'll be singing the same song!" As a reward for my dramatic performance of this moral lesson, the steward's wife would give me a hunk of bread and cheese or a pitcher of milk, which I swallowed together with my tears, understanding neither the cause of the punishment nor the kind reward.

This is all I recall from my early childhood, which was etched in my memory only as a period of sorrow and suffering. At last, fate intervened to lighten my heavy load or at least to include me in the number of rational creatures. The change occurred in the following manner.

One of the servant girls, Masha, a cheerful and good-looking young woman who used to place me on guard in the garden more often than the other girls, after meeting me once on an autumn evening in the courtyard, called me over, patted my head, and said to me, "Take this paper, *little orphan*; keep it firmly in hand and go to the village. There, in the village elder's house, ask where the officer lives; then give him the paper and come back. But don't tell anyone that I sent you, and if

1. A diminutive form of the name Ignaty.

somebody tries to take away the paper, don't give it up, swallow it. Do you understand, *orphan*?

"I do."

"Well, repeat everything I just told you."

I repeated the instructions word for word, and she was so pleased that she almost kissed me, but refrained merely because I was so dirty.

"Do you know which house belongs to the village elder?"

"Of course, I do. It's the third house past the tavern."

"Good. And do you know what an officer is?"

"Well, he's the gentleman who wears red patches on his jacket, who goes around on horseback, and who comes here in the evening . . ."

"Enough; I see you're clever and quick; if you carry out this task, you'll have lots of bread, meat, and everything else you want: do you hear?"

"I do," I replied. With these words I whistled for Shaggy and ran out of the gate at full speed.

It was several miles to the village along the main road, but by a path I knew over wattle fences and through vegetable gardens, it was not even half that distance. After reaching the village elder's house, I met the officer whom I recognized at the entrance, greeted him, and handed him the note. He looked me over from head to foot, smiled, and ordered me to follow him into the hut. There, after reading the paper, he seemed very satisfied with it; as a reward for the apparently good news, he gave me a piece of sweet pie. It was the first time in my life that I tasted that delicious delicacy, and I couldn't control the excitement at the unfamiliar sensation; right in front of the officer I began to devour that whole pie, even as I expressed my joy by loud laughter and leaps. Just then another officer came in, and they were both very amused by my wild antics at the taste of sugar, wine, and various treats.

"Who are you?" asked the officer to whom I'd been sent.

"An *orphan*," I replied.

"Who are your parents?"

"I don't know."

"What's your name?"

"*Little Orphan*."

"Poor little creature!" said the kind officer, patting my cheeks. "I'll take care of you. Isn't it true that he's a handsome lad?" said the officer, turning to his comrade.

"It is," the other officer replied. "But it's a pity they treat him like a pig."

The attentions of these kind officers moved me to such an extent that recalling other children who, before my own eyes, were caressed by their mothers and fathers, I began to cry bitterly and hastened to embrace the feet of the officers, those who had treated me like a human being for the first time in my life. Up to that time the hand of man was raised against me only to beat and shove me; therefore I felt these attentions deeply, which I'd first envied from afar, never having experienced them myself. My tears and gratitude, as I understand now, made a strong impression on the officers. They doubled their tender treatment and gave me various snacks for the road.

"Now, go home, *little orphan*," the officer said to me, "and tell the person who sent you, 'Good,' but don't say it so others can hear you. Do you understand?"

"I do. I'll grab hold of Masha's skirt, pull her aside, and tell her that that the kind gentleman says, 'Good.'"

"Excellent, splendid! This lad's clever beyond his years," said the officer. "I shall make a man of him. Good-bye, *little orphan*!"

In general, all secret commissions lie near to the heart of those who initiate them and become a source of happiness for those who fulfill them, when they are carried out successfully. The same thing happened to me. When I arrived at the manor house, I crept quietly into the kitchen and, seeing that Masha glanced at me rather anxiously and was looking all around, I didn't show that I wanted to speak with her and left the kitchen. Masha followed me; when I told her the reply to my commission, she also patted me, praised my cleverness, told me not to tell anyone about what had happened, and promised to reward me the following day. I spent the most pleasant night of my life, under the shed, on the straw, with my dog Shaggy, who warmed me with her own body heat. I dreamt all night of the officers who'd plied me with pies and sweets.

In the morning, while I was straying, as usual, near the kitchen to find something to eat, I saw Masha, who called me over and ordered me to follow her in to see the steward. Thinking that I might have to undergo another whipping to set an example for the good-for-nothing son, I wept bitter tears and got ready to run away to the officers in the village. But Masha reassured me that nothing bad would happen, so I followed her—trembling, however, from fear. They washed me, combed my hair, and properly speaking, scrubbed and scraped me; they dressed me in clean linen, covered me with a caftan, and then led me into the rooms where the master lived. I was exactly like a sheep in the hands of a shepherd; I was shaking with fear, not knowing if I would be sheared or slaughtered. I was left in the entrance hall and told to wait. I was extremely surprised that the lackeys and the lads who passed me in the hall neither beat me nor made fun of me as they usually did. This fact encouraged me, but when the door to the room opened suddenly, and I saw the master, mistress, and his sons and daughters, all of whom welcomed me, my courage deserted me, and my recollection of the master's order not to approach the windows of the house came to mind. A chill coursed through my veins; I trembled, cried out from terror, and wanted to run away as quickly as possible, but they stopped me. Fortunately, I noticed that the officer was there among the group assembled. I threw myself at his feet, embraced them with my little hands, and wailed pitifully, "Don't let them whip me, kind sir; I'm really not to blame."

"Poor orphan!" said the officer. "He's so distraught and frightened! Get up, my little friend," he said. "They won't beat you but will feed you some pies."

The word *pies* produced a magical effect on me. I stood up, wiped my tears on my sleeve, looked around, and noticed that the master was frowning and stroking his mustache; the young ladies held their handkerchiefs to their eyes, the mistress turned away from me, and the sons stuck their tongues out and made faces at me from behind their mother's back.

"Mr. Kanchukovsky," said the master, turning to the steward. "I shall take this boy to serve my elder daughter in the house in the role of an *English jockey* on her part of the estate. Send for the Yid,[2] the tailor, in town and have a uniform made for him according to the drawing which my daughter will send.

"Yes, sir," said the steward with a deep bow.

"I like the boy," Mr. Gologordovsky said grandly. "I'm surprised I didn't notice him in the house before."

The women began caressing and stroking me.

"What's his name?" the master asked the steward, but like me, he couldn't answer that question. They sent to inquire among the other servants, but it turned out that in response they supplied me with the name *Ivan*. From that time forth they stopped calling me the *little orphan*, and I became known in the household by the name of *Ivan the Englishman*, thanks to my jockey's clothes. I'm neither the first nor the last person in the world to take my name from my apparel.

2. See Note on Translation regarding the repeated use of this derogatory epithet.

Chapter 2

Mr. Gologordovsky and His Family

When Byelorussia belonged to Poland, Mr. Gologordovsky manifested his deep attachment to Russia and even maintained that he was descended from an ancient Russian family that had settled in this area during the reign of Mstislav the Brave.[1] But when this country was joined with Russia, Mr. Gologordovsky suddenly became a supporter of the ancient Polish state and began to trace his lineage to the chamberlain of the Polish King Popiel, who, according to legend, was eaten by mice on Lake Gopło.[2] Mr. Gologordovsky very much regretted those blessed times when a strong Polish nobleman could oppress the poor gentry with impunity, yet still call them his brothers and equals and beat them with rods while they lay stretched out on a carpet (as distinct from the peasants), and when he could decide to send them to prison and confiscate their estates. He especially regretted the change of customs at the *Sejm*[3]—that is, during the sessions of nobles. In the good old days the wealthy landowner would

1. Mstislav (died c. 1280) was prince of Tmutarakan and Chernigov and one of the most popular and active princes of Kievan Rus' in the decades preceding the Mongol invasion.

2. A legendary ninth-century ruler; as a consequence of his bad rule he was deposed, besieged by his subjects, and supposedly eaten alive by mice in a tower in Kruszwica.

3. Polish diet or parliament.

bring along wagonloads of poor but high-spirited and armed gentry, compel them to choose him and his friends for various positions, and would beat and defeat his opponents. Those days were called the period of *golden liberty*.

After losing such important privileges from without, Mr. Gologordovsky was limited to ruling his estate from within, in the old style. Besides his numerous household servants, who were his own serfs, he had in his service a number of gentry who hoped to ennoble their low standing with high-sounding titles. Mr. Gologordovsky's household was organized the same way as ancient feudal barons and ancient Polish nobles organized theirs. His principal servants were his confidential agent, or plenipotentiary, for the management of lawsuits, of which there were always two or three dozen pending in the courts; the commissary or chief steward, who managed all his property; the steward or bailiff; the housekeeper, who presided over the table and domestic servants; the stable master who saw to the stables and grooms; the head chef, or commander of the pots and pans, and other cooks, of course; and the chief housekeeper, who managed the maids, linens, and the pantry, which in Polish households was called the locked chest and contained all the sweets—preserves, confections, sugar, coffee, various spirits, and liqueurs. In addition to these servants always ready to serve, there lived in the house the music master, who taught the young ladies and young gentlemen music and led the orchestra consisting of twelve men, who during the winter served as footmen and in the summer raked hay and worked in the garden; the chaplain or domestic priest, a Jesuit, who had under his command three tutors and oversaw the education of Mr. Gologordovsky's children; in addition, there was a French tutor and a French woman living with the young ladies. The gardener, a German, was also an advisor on agricultural matters. The master himself had a personal valet, a low-ranking member of the Polish gentry, his favorite and his confidant in secret affairs; and the mistress had a maidservant who served a similar function, also from the lower Polish nobility; although she fulfilled all the duties of a chambermaid, in accordance with her birth and merit, she enjoyed great respect in the household and was addressed as *Pani*—that is, Mademoiselle. The young ladies also each had a *Pani* from the lower nobility, who was in charge of their wardrobe and serf girls, of whom one with each young lady bore the title of wardrobe mistress. The hunt formed a department in and of itself and came in part under the jurisdiction of the master, who was a great hunter. There were several Polish nobles among the sportsmen who were referred to as the *streltsy*[4]—that is, chasseurs. The most important of these superior servants, such as the confidential agent or plenipotentiary, the commissary, the bailiff, the stable master, the housekeeper, the music master, and the head tutor, all lived in the house with their wives and children; in addition to their salary, they received provisions for their own table or board; they were attended by the house servants and had their own horses fed at the master's expense. All the other free servants received board as well, but the serfs were fed only in part from the master's table; in addition, they had a general table of their own. But since the free servants drank up part of their board, and the serfs never ate their fill, each one snatched and stole whatever he could, by hook or by crook.

In addition to all these feudal attendants, there lived in the house for company and for the amusement of the master and mistress several noblemen and noblewomen—entertaining people, friends, and distant relatives, male and female, who were referred to as "residents"—a rank which corresponded to our companions and inhabitants. They received no salary but enjoyed taking their board; they fed their own servants, and several of them even had the right to keep horses. Among these residents were the unmarried creditors of Mr. Gologordovsky, a few widows of former servants whose wages had not been paid for the last twenty years or so, and several orphans with their own capital under the master's guardianship. In a word, in Mr. Gologordovsky's house there were almost as many mouths and stomachs to feed as there were working hands on the entire estate; as a result, the working hands were extremely tired and worked exhaustively to fill the stomachs of the large number of idlers. It's true that Mr. Gologordovsky himself, his family, and his guests ate and drank well, but his huge table had a so-called *gray end*, where tasty dishes and fine wines never reached, and where those seated experienced in full measure the inconvenience of the lack of proportion between expenses and income.

Mr. Gologordovsky, as a sign of his Polish lineage, sported a large mustache, which he frequently stroked, especially when he was discussing important matters, such as the votes of nobles, his lawsuits, and his quarrels with the neighbors. He considered them all beneath him, in spite of the fact that many of them were wealthier and of more use to the fatherland through their merit and actions. Mr. Gologordovsky's

4. A military corps instituted by Ivan the Terrible in the sixteenth century.

pride was founded on the antiquity of his family, which he proved not with historical documents attesting to their heroic deeds but with legal records that contained, over the course of four hundred years, complaints of robberies committed by his forebears as well as decisions condemning them to the gallows. Families only one or two hundred years old were called *upstarts*, and he didn't consider it necessary to have anything to do with them or even to associate with them in friendly fashion. He felt special contempt and hatred for those who'd earned their own fortunes by honest means and hadn't inherited them from their ancestors. He received all into his house without any exception but treated lavishly only those people he needed, including civil servants, capitalists, and moneylenders; he was particularly generous to those nobles who had *need* of him, and he agreed to show them clear preference, to listen without objection to their stories, and to hear their abuse of his enemies. The mornings when it was not possible to hunt Mr. Gologordovsky would spend reading legal papers; they were compiled by his confidant, and for his own amusement he would add slanderous digs, personalities, and invented claims. After that, he walked around the courtyard to relish the deep bows made by all his servants. Amusing himself after dinner with various (not very subtle) jokes about his dinner partners, he would go to take a nap to allow the vapors from the wine to dissipate, which had thickened in his head after lunch and dinner. The time until evening was devoted to various amusements invented by the ladies; Mr. Gologordovsky participated in these entertainments only as a spectator. The evenings brought the appearance of Iosel, a Yid who leased all the mills and taverns on the estate. This Iosel was the general solicitor for the entire household, the secret confidant of the masters and servants, a walking newspaper or source of political events, and scandalous anecdotes; within a distance of twenty miles or so, he was the reporter of all that was good and bad. The Yid was in possession of two powerful talismans for the subjugation of hearts: money and vodka. Everyone needed him, from the master to the last shepherd in the village; everyone owed him money, and they all had a greater desire to borrow than to repay. Mr. Gologordovsky spent the major portion of the evening with this Yid, while he drank his punch, gathering from him all the news of the capital and the provincial town, where the Yid had his correspondents. Together they devised projects for the sale of grain, spirits, and timber, for borrowing money and avoiding repayment of old debts. He conferred with the Yid about launching new lawsuits, the pursuit of existing suits, and about the endless course of those that had been dragging on. The Yid suggested various measures for increasing their income without any outlay of funds; for example, to make the peasants' horses carry larger loads, to dig canals on a neighbor's estate, to cut down woods and burn charcoal, and so on and so forth. In a word, the Yid tenant was considered the most important person on the estate after the master himself and was more indispensable to Mr. Gologordovsky than the head on his own shoulders, if it had been possible to move the mouth to some other part of the body. Without regarding such a close relationship, the Yid, knowing Mr. Gologordovsky's character, swore an oath that he respected Mr. Gologordovsky as the only true master and grandee in the province. Thus, enjoying his confidence, the Yid, like a true vampire, sucked the blood of all sleeping humanity on Mr. Gologordovsky's estate; he grew rich and, just as a swamp absorbs all the life-giving moisture into itself, he sucked the surrounding sources of wealth dry and spread poverty and barrenness all around.

Mrs. Gologordovskaya considered her origins much higher than those of her husband. She used to say that she never would have married him if she hadn't been compelled by a particular circumstance, in which a Russian colonel in the Hussars had played an important role. However, she lived very amicably with her husband, and he attempted to please her in every way. She selected her own society, chose appropriate amusements and entertainments, and her husband had the honor of being invited to share them with the family. Mrs. Gologordovskaya never asked her husband for anything: in shops she bought everything she needed or fancied, even though it was unnecessary; she sent the merchants in to see her husband, who was supposed to pay his wife's debts, even though he paid his own debts only with great reluctance. However, although she didn't get involved in running the household, Mrs. Gologordovskaya was a very kind mistress; she treated the servants cordially, without any concern for their needs and without listening to their reasonable requests. She believed from the bottom of her heart that her kind word and smile were more valuable to each than good food, clothes, or wages. She dearly loved to read tender romances, and even more loved to converse with men about love, but most of all she liked to get dressed up. Some serf girl seamstresses, who had been taught in Warsaw or Petersburg, were constantly occupied cutting out patterns and sewing; almost every week packages and trunks would arrive from the capital filled with caps, hats, headdresses, patterns, and various items of clothing. Every day she would dress up like a doll, even though there were no guests; in spite of all his feudal pride, at home Mr. Gologordovsky wore a greasy dressing gown, partly in the old Polish fashion, as if he were the first of his wife's most obedient servants.

The Gologordovskys' daughters, Petronella and Cecilia, were pretty, pleasant in conversation with men, bold as dragoons, lively, and cheerful. They were excellent dancers and musicians. They spoke French very well, sang wonderfully, dressed with good taste and elegance, following their mother's example, and read tender romances along with her. They both had very kind hearts and preferred not to drive through the village where they might notice the poverty of the inhabitants. The elder, Petronella, was eighteen years old, while Cecilia was sixteen.

Two sons—one aged twelve, the other fourteen—were genuine monkeys with their mischief, cunning, wrath, gluttony, and secrecy. They were continually playing tricks on their teachers, their sisters, and the servants. The greatest pranks were ascribed by their parents to the excellent abilities and inventive intelligence of their children, on whom they rested all the hopes of their family and whom they treated as if they were the heirs of the Mongol empire. The name *Infanta*, given to the elder son as a joke by a passing officer, was retained forever. The servants, who didn't understand the significance of this title, failed to provide any other name for this wild child, and this fact pleased the parents greatly. They predicted that both sons would achieve the rank of general, earn millions of rubles, and marry princesses, as an appropriate reward for the qualities, thanks to which everything is lost and nothing is gained in this world.

As for the other inhabitants of the household, there were so many of them that I can't even recall all of them in these entertainments; when I later visited Mr. Gologordovsky's house, many of them were no longer there. The Jesuit father, being a Jesuit, was an enigma to everyone except the mistress, whose confessor he was. The steward was the personification of a whip or a machine for compulsion: everything trembled in his presence, except for the Yid and the master's favorite hounds that he dared not disturb. The butler and stable master were silent creatures, a kind of instrument for digesting edible provisions. Their entire job consisted of watching, with eyes wide open, the crowd of bustling servants who were always bowing to the master and mistress, constantly "yes-ing" them, eating for four people, and getting drunk on wine every evening. The legal agent belonged to the kind of people who could, without any remorse, be hanged first and tried afterwards, knowing for certain that you could find twenty reasons for it during every week of his life. His soul consisted of hooks and eyes to latch onto whatever desirable objects he might notice with his eagle eyes. He knew not right from wrong, black from white. He considered laws no more than words whose veracity depended on the interpretation, whether from the right or the left. In a word, this agent was a professor of chicanery and, after the Yid—he was Mr. Gologordovsky's principal advisor. The commissary . . . the poor commissary! His job consisted of overseeing the entire estate, checking the accounts, and collecting the income, but since everything was in disorder and the income was collected before it was due, if and when that was possible, and since there was no real auditing of the accounts, he spent eleven months a year drinking out of grief, and in the twelfth month he composed a general statement at random, or, better said, he made a summary of funds received, copied it onto a sheet of clean paper, and presented it to the master together with a note that it had been collected during the previous year (although not in full). This very much pleased Mr. Gologordovsky, who assumed that he really had such a large income as was indicated in the *summary*.

The most important person in the house was the housekeeper or house manager, not because she knew all the mistress's secrets and enjoyed her unlimited confidence, but because all the fortifying beverages came under her supervision: the rum, cognac, and liqueurs, both bitter and sweet. The entire house treated her kindly, including even the young ladies, who received preserves and sweets from her. The esteemed housekeeper loudly proclaimed her hatred for strong beverages, and while she stretched herself out on her bed with her bright red face and nose glowing like the burning end of a candle every evening before dinner, this was because she was suffering from toothache and was frequently compelled to apply spirits to her tooth. At least that's what she said. There's no doubt that Mr. Gologordovsky put great faith in this remedy: he frequently placed his hand on his cheek and visited the pantry or the medicine chest so often that the floor was worn with his footsteps all the way to the door.

These were the people among whom I was the last, by the destiny of fate! During my childhood, they all seemed extraordinary, higher beings, bright suns! Subsequently, I learned their real worth and mention them now only so the reader won't be surprised why they kept me in the house like a wild beast. However, we'll have the chance to meet some of the people mentioned here, and therefore a previous acquaintance with them won't prove to be superfluous.

Chapter 3

Love

All military men love being stationed in Poland in spite of the peasants' poverty, the Yids' slovenliness, and the difference in languages and religion of the gentry. To tell the truth, the men are cordial; they love and are glad to live joyously; Polish women are extremely nice and are more attached to foreigners than their husbands and brothers would wish. A military billeting, especially for the artillery and cavalry, is very pleasant for landowners, Yids, and women. The landowners find a convenient outlet for their agricultural produce, the Yids for their merchandise, and the women always find admirers and sometimes husbands, in spite of the exhortations by their Catholic priests, the nationalist preaching of the landowners, and the anxiety of military life. Every prolonged billeting of a regiment in any district generally ends with a couple of marriages and several dozen anecdotes, propagated by old maids at the expense of young ladies. As a result of these anecdotes, modest people are at first appalled, then they don't believe them, and finally, they consign them to obscurity until another opportunity arises.

In general, Polish women are obliging: they know how to please and they love tenderly, with all the enhancements of romantic passion, although constancy isn't one of the main traits of their character: once in love, who thinks about such abstract matters? Besides, there are no rules without exceptions: is it possible to refrain from loving Polish women merely from fear of their inconstancy? Polish women feel to a full extent that women are created for love, and they spend their entire youth in such pleasant dreams. In the Polish language there even exists a special verb, made up to designate the sweetest and, in other respects, the most vacuous activity in life: *romansowac*.[1] This word denotes tender, respectful love, mutual pleasure based on morality and decency; it can't exist anywhere except in Poland, where the free interaction of both sexes is not only permitted but also even considered necessary. Only Italy surpasses Poland in the freedom of women. In Poland, no one thinks it strange or improper if a married woman or a young unmarried woman converses alone with a man, strolls with him, arm in arm away from other people, accepts small gifts or entertainments from him, although she's not engaged, married, or related to him. Tender looks, sweet words, sighs, verses dedicated to her, music, even letters, don't attract any unwanted attention from her parents or from strangers. They say openly that a certain man is in love with so-and-so and is courting her (*umizga się*);[2] that a certain woman is in love with so-and-so, and none of this detracts from a woman's reputation. Tender lovers swear each other mutual oaths, make promises, build imaginary castles for future happiness, and afterwards separate with coolness and composure, without any temptation. It's appropriate to recall the saying "Every city has its customs; every village has its ways." Meanwhile I can honestly assure my readers that in spite of the free and easy relations, nowhere in the world are there so many virtuous young women as in Poland: believe it or not. I won't even mention married women, because . . . because it's not relevant to our current subject.

A certain Lieutenant Milovidin was stationed in Mr. Gologordovsky's village with his regiment of military hussars. He had all the good and bad qualities of a young cavalryman: he was brave and honest, and he knew service, but was frequently out of order as a result of his emptyheadedness and excessive passion for amusements. While not being particularly mercenary-minded, he gambled for high stakes and often lost his last kopeck at cards merely from boredom or having nothing better to do; with a natural inclination to temperance, from sheer bravado he would just as soon drink Tokay wine as he would drink water, and he would imbibe champagne as he would kvass. His principal occupation

1. "To carry on an affair with, to make love to" (Pol.).
2. "To woo, make passes" (Pol.).

was flirting. Handsome, clever, witty, raised in a circle of high Moscow society, an excellent dancer, musician, and painter, schooled in the works of French literature, gifted with an unusual memory, Milovidin was a spoiled child of fortune, a love object to all young women within a twenty-five-mile radius. They organized fêtes for him, he was invited everywhere as a guest, and what was most surprising, men—that is, landowners—not only didn't get angry with the favors shown him by women but even loved to love him. Milovidin was a *good fellow* in the full sense of the term: candid and, with all his wit, openhearted. He didn't argue with the Poles about politics, he drank with them to the health of previous patriots, and he abused bureaucrats for all he was worth. As a result he enjoyed the trust of the old landowners and the friendship of younger ones, who wished to make it look like the clan of Milovidins had originated in Poland, or at least in Livonia.[3] A high distinction that few Russians receive in Poland!

His heart was so capacious that he could love fifty women at the same time without tiring of love and without exhausting himself with sighs and sufferings. At this time, of all the women he knew, he preferred Petronella Gologordovskaya, who, to put it simply, was head over heels in love with him. Now you needn't guess, dear reader, from whom and to whom I was sent with a letter to the village! Now you understand why I was immediately promoted to the rank of English jockey and recruited to perform special commissions for Mr. Gologordovsky's eldest daughter. Without doubt, dear reader, you've guessed why I occupied that rank of *messenger of love*. Exactly: my entire duty consisted of standing behind the young lady holding a plate and of carrying letters from the master's house to the lieutenant's quarters—a task which I fulfilled with particular care, precision, and alacrity. For that I was loved by my mistress and, consequently, by the entire Gologordovsky family. The term *orphan* was no longer used as a sign of degradation; on the contrary, it expressed gentleness and compassion and was uttered with sympathy and special tender feeling. The servants, always following the example of the master and mistress, embraced me as much as they had despised me previously. This change in my fate produced a rapid change in my intellect, which from nature had been well established. In half a year I understood everything that formerly seemed mysterious to me; I surpassed all the other servant boys who were raised in the house in

3. Livonia is a historical region on the eastern shores of the Baltic Sea, a former part of the Russian empire.

efficiency, and I became, as they say, a rogue or a sharp lad. I was obligated to love for this entire fortunate change.

After the pleasant days of love and enjoyment came the storm. The regiment received orders to move to another province, and this unexpected occurrence cast all the women of the district into despair. The doctors made their way from one house to the next; the apothecary's laboratory was set in motion; messengers galloped along all the roads at full speed, some with prescriptions, others with love letters. It seemed as if some sort of plague or other contagious disease was raging through the neighborhood. In reality, spasms, migraines, the vapors, nervous attacks, and vertigo overcame the entire female sex. My mistress especially, Petronella Gologordovskaya, went into a complete collapse. She took to bed, swore she would die from love, and refused to take any remedy prescribed by a doctor for her fever arising from a cold. As a matter of fact, her condition was dangerous. Unceasing tears and sobs, insomnia, and inner agitation could severely aggravate a mild cold contracted in the garden during late-night chats with her beloved. She didn't want to take anyone's advice or consolation from her parents, sister, or friends and calmed down only a little when Milovidin gave her his solemn word to return as soon as possible, promising to crown their tender love with marriage. Milovidin's vanity was touched by such a strong declaration of passion by the lovely Petronella; all his life he'd never seen people fall ill and die from love, and being a witness and object of this scene, worthy of being included in the most tender chivalrous romance, Milovidin softened and decided to reward the sufferer with his hand in marriage. But this promise was given in secret, without the knowledge of her parents. They agreed to continue their correspondence through the Yid agent; Milovidin threatened to pull off his nose and ears if he betrayed them; meanwhile, during his absence, he entrusted Petronella's aunt on his mother's side to arrange the match. The lovers foresaw difficulties in obtaining consent from Petronella's father, who was nursing the hope that some itinerant prince, even an Asian one, or some other dignitary, would ennoble his family line with a union with the Gologordovskys. Of all human follies, love is the most powerful; our lovers hoped to overcome Mr. Gologordovsky's pride and obstinacy or, at any rate, to surmount them by force.

Chapter 4

Matchmaking

Winter passed drearily. Mr. Gologordovsky had to travel frequently to the provincial town on matters pertaining to his various lawsuits, which hadn't ended in the most satisfying manner. The legal expenses compelled the household to undertake some retrenchment and forced the family to remain in the village during the sessions of the nobility, which drew all the other gentry to town for a few weeks. This circumstance resulted in melancholy for Mrs. Gologordovskaya and her younger daughter; the elder daughter was already suffering from an ailment of the heart. In vain the Jesuit father preached about the vanity of this world: they listened to him with sighs, then interrupted him to launch a conversation about society balls and apparel. Mrs. Gologordovskaya regretted only that her absence during the sessions would afford visitors from other provinces and military personnel an unfavorable opinion of women's taste in regard to apparel, and that without her daughters, they would not be able to dance mazurkas and French quadrilles. After this lady's preface, she launched into a critical survey of all the women in the entire province, from age sixteen to thirty-five; in conclusion it turned out that only Mrs. Gologordovskaya and her daughters were lacking in moral and physical defects, and that all other women had been badly treated by nature. The freeloaders or residents, and the trusted mademoiselles, as well as the wives of the confidential agent and the commissary, even the Jesuit father, all confirmed Mrs. Gologordovskaya's opinion, which provided some consolation in her grief. If as much as one-tenth of Mrs. Gologordovskaya's opinion concerning women was correct, men should seek wives not only in another province or in another empire but on another planet. Fortunately, all mothers thought the same way about themselves and their daughters, and therefore one had to accept all women's defects, only if considering them as part of a compound number.

Milovidin remained constant. He replied to every ten letters he received from Petronella with one letter, very tender yet amusing, written on pink, green, or blue paper. This was still the fashion in the provinces. Although I couldn't read these letters, I was able to surmise their content by the effect they produced on the young lady's mood: she would reread them a hundred times, always beginning in tears but ending with a laugh. Milovidin would describe his new acquaintances to her, his various adventures, characters, and anecdotes, which consoled the young lady in her separation and amused both her and her sister. The Yid faithfully carried out the duties entrusted to him: he fetched the letters from the post office and dispatched the replies with great precision. In spite of the fact that I was now of no use to the young lady, she continued to love and favor me. Sweet recollections were associated with me; besides, Milovidin had recommended me to her protection.

Spring arrived: all nature revived, but the roses didn't blossom on Petronella's lovely cheeks. She became more dejected with every passing day, and she couldn't even look at the little birds perched in pairs on the branches. Everyone knew the reason, but no one except her sister, the faithful Masha, and the Yid ever mentioned her beloved or tried to bolster her hopes.

Once, on a pleasant spring day at sunset, the entire Gologordovsky family was enjoying a snack in the garden. Roast chicken with salad, accompanied by sour cream, and a bottle of rare Hungarian wine, a gift of the Yid agent—all this put Mr. Gologordovsky in such a cheerful state of mind that the aunt decided to take the opportunity to carry out her commission. She signaled the young ladies to withdraw and began a conversation, at first from afar, about the happiness of wedlock where the attraction of hearts is mutual; then she touched on Petronella's pitiful condition, pining away from love, and she finally declared outright that she was authorized by Milovidin and her niece to beg her parents' consent to their marriage; then she pulled out a letter of her bosom. Mrs. Gologordovskaya was silent during her cousin's speech; she sighed, looked up at the sky, and shook her head. On the contrary, as soon as the aunt began speaking, Mr. Gologordovsky began to show his impatience and irritation. First he doubled his sips of wine, then his face grew red, and finally, after draining the entire bottle, he grew furious, banged his fist on the table so hard that the dishes jumped, and exclaimed stridently, "Enough!"

However the aunt wasn't frightened by this storm and she replied calmly, "I don't see anything that could hinder this match."

"A great deal, madam, a very great deal," replied Mr. Gologordovsky. "You don't see it because you've never looked at my family archives and you've probably never noticed the family portraits in the dining room."

"But isn't Milovidin a member of the gentry?" the aunt asked. "Both his father and grandfather were generals."

Mr. Gologordovsky smiled bitterly

"Madam," he said, "I asked Milovidin about his family line before you did and learned that his nobility begins only with his great-grandfather."

"Don't you think that's enough?" asked the aunt.

"It's not enough for entering into a union with a family that counts its noble status for fifty generations. So you see, madam, my nobility relates to that of Mr. Milovidin as fifty does to three; there's *little* difference between them." Saying this, he smiled craftily.

"But in our day the old and new gentry have the same right to distinction, and the same period of service results in a higher rank," said the aunt.

"That's not our business, madam," replied Mr. Gologordovsky. "You know the old proverb: 'A nobleman in one garden is equal to a general in another.'"

"So, Milovidin is equal to you," said the aunt.

"Not at all," objected Mr. Gologordovsky. "It means that only gentry of equivalent rank are equal among themselves, without regard to the difference in ranks. Besides, antiquity of family origin alone is insufficient to merit becoming my son-in-law: he has to be wealthy—extremely wealthy, to uphold the dignity of the two united families. Milovidin is poor as a church mouse."

"It's true that Milovidin's father spent all his money in the service," said the aunt. "But he has a rich and childless uncle who's determined never to marry. He loves his nephew very much, supports him in the service, and intends to make him his heir."

"How do you know that?" asked Mr. Gologordovsky.

"I have seen the uncle's handwritten letters to Milovidin," replied the aunt.

"That's all castles in the air; you should be ashamed, madam, for debasing my family to such an extent that you dare propose a union with a man who lacks both name and property," said Mr. Gologordovsky imposingly and stood up from where he sat. "I beg you not to speak of this again, if you wish to keep my friendship."

"Very well," retorted the aunt, flushing from annoyance. "But allow me to make one observation: do you really want to be the death of your daughter as she pines away from love or to force her to marry against her heart's wishes?"

"Don't worry about that, madam," said Mr. Gologordovsky. "Young women don't die from love and can even be very happy in a marriage contracted against their will. Your own cousin serves as proof of that: my beloved spouse was also in love with an officer before her wedding, and she fainted three times before pronouncing the fatal 'Yes' at the marriage altar. All this was finally overcome, and I hope that Mrs. Gologordovskaya doesn't complain about her unhappy fate, although her husband doesn't wear spurs or a uniform. Isn't that true, my dear?" asked Mr. Gologordovsky, kissing his wife tenderly for the first time since I'd been admitted to the room.

"Yes, it's true," his wife replied with a deep sigh.

"Tell the servants to harness my wagon and saddle my riding horse," said Mr. Gologordovsky. "Dear ladies! Would you care to join me for a short ride? I'll show you something new: a tavern, which I'm now building on the edge of my land under the nose of my neighbor Mr. Protsessovich. I've named the tavern *The Thorn*, and it will be a real thorn in my dear neighbor's side. Isn't that so, Mr. Commissary?"

"Absolutely," replied the commissary with a deep bow.

"I shall sell vodka much more cheaply in my tavern than it's sold by Mr. Protsessovich, and thus I'll draw away all his peasants. Isn't that true, Mr. Commissary?"

"Yes, indeed," replied the commissary. "If he decides to drive his peasants away from my tavern, I'll haul him into court and bring an action against him. Isn't that true, Mr. Plenipotentiary?"

"Yes, indeed, it's the absolute truth," replied the agent. "We'll haul him into criminal court, *pro expulsione et violentia*.[1]

1. "For expulsion and violence" (Lat.).

While Mr. Gologordovsky continued speaking in such a manner with his servants, all of whom stood at a certain distance when the match was being discussed, Mrs. Gologordovskaya went to her room to dress, and the aunt joined the young ladies and accompanied them into a dark alley. She relayed the conversation that had just taken place. I don't know what occurred among them, but to my own surprise, I didn't see any tears in the young lady's eyes when she returned to get into the carriage. On the contrary, she seemed to be more cheerful than usual.

Chapter 5

The Ball and Abduction

Mr. Gologordovsky wanted to celebrate his wife's birthday and, at the same time, his recent victory in a lawsuit over some twenty-five acres of land. This lawsuit had lasted about thirty years, and it cost each side sixteen times more than the object in dispute. But since the main point consisted in winning, a public declaration of joy served as the reward for all the trouble and expense incurred during the course of the suit, together with the humiliation of his opponent. A week before the celebration, invitations were sent to relatives, neighbors, and even distant acquaintances in the province. The Yid agent brought in two other Yids as contractors for providing wines and spicy treats for the feast. These alleged contractors, as I learned subsequently from the steward Kanchukovsky, were selling goods belonging to our commissary, who didn't want to sell them under his own name because he feared being paid with a pledge or a promissory note, which he couldn't refuse to take from Mr. Gologordovsky. But since there was no spare cash in the house, and the grain was still unripe, the wheat and rye crops were sold for so much an acre or, as it's called, sold *on the stalk*. Our agent got the power of attorney from the alleged contractors to receive the grain after it was harvested and threshed, and three dozen calves after they were born, on condition that they would be fed for a period of eight months. In this way Mr. Gologordovsky, selling his grain while still in the bowels of the earth, and the livestock while still unborn, received a large supply of wine and delicacies for the table, which would all be consumed in the course of one day. All the hunters from the village were dispatched into the woods to furnish game: each was supplied with one pound of gunpowder and three pounds of shot on the condition that each one would return with sixty head of game. For every two pounds of powder, allowance was made for missing three shots, and for the rest, they had to pay the master at the rate of ten kopecks in silver for each shot missed. The Yid agent provided Mr. Gologordovsky with a list of all the peasants who owned hens, chickens, eggs, and butter. The servants of the house were sent to these peasants to collect those items by any means, fair or foul. Those who surrendered them by their own free will were promised a reduction of so many days of work on the master's land; those who refused were compelled to recall the existence of Mr. Kanchukovsky and threatened with punishment. In the Polish provinces that usually entailed lodging several servants, typically the most unruly ones, those who would eat and drink in the peasant's house until they paid their dues or complied with the landlord's demands. Sometimes these punishments were inflicted for not working diligently, rudeness to the Yid, and for other reasons.

Preparations for the ball during the last week resulted in extra commotion and bustle in the house. The villages were a scene of pilfering, an enemy invasion! The hungry servants behaved like true marauders. They looked for hens in trunks, butter hidden among the linen, and eggs in the women's bosoms; they grabbed what they could and where they could and managed to offend the poor inhabitants and the women by all possible means. It's a misfortune, a genuine misfortune, when people of lower standing, with neither education nor morality, attain power! They try to retaliate against other people and think that they inspire respect from them when they make others tremble. The peasants and their women were continually running to the manor house to complain that impossible things were being demanded of them; they swore that the Yid had made false statements about them; that they didn't possess what was being requisitioned. Futile complaints! Mr. Gologordovsky believed the Yid more than he believed his own wife and children; he referred the complainants to Mr. Kanchukovsky, whose look alone was enough to scare them away from the courtyard.

Work continued day and night in the kitchen; to prevent stealing, guards from the stables were assigned to the kitchen doors, but they themselves stole hunks of meat, chickens, and eggs and carried them to the tavern at night. All the servants were employed in cleaning and straightening the rooms. For the first time in a year, cobwebs were swept away and spiders were banished from the family portraits. The oak- and alder-wood armchairs were covered with fresh canvas. Mahogany furniture, which fitted out two rooms in the entire house, was polished with olive oil instead of varnish. The floors were scraped anew, because it was impossible to wash them. All the mirrors in the wing belonging to the higher servants, residents, and companions were carried into the master's rooms, which in addition to all the other changes and repairs, were decorated on the eve of the holiday with branches of pine and fir. The house musicians rehearsed and practiced in the barn continually, where the Jesuit father, a great chemist in the opinion of the whole province, prepared fireworks for surprising Mrs. Gologordovskaya; two hunters worked under his supervision. For the guests' horses, a separate stable was provided and a provision of *guests' hay* was prepared—that is, a dozen cartloads of sedge and marsh grass which was impossible to grind on a millstone, let alone with the horses' teeth. Guests' oats were a mixture of chopped hay and chaff. The rules of hospitality specify that guests, their servants, and their horses are all to be fed; but since the landlord's obligation is limited to the entertainment and treatment of the gentry, if the servants and horses go hungry, all the blame usually falls on the steward, in case any of the guests should think about his servants and horses. However, with *essential people*, such as provincial and district officials, another procedure is followed: their horses and servants are entrusted to the special care of the butler and the stable master.

At last the day of the feast arrived. A number of guests arrived before morning mass. Carts and carriages of various kinds occupied all the space between the stable and the farmyard. Almost every family brought along a dozen horses: six for their own carriage, four for the wagon in which the servants rode with trunks and boxes, and a pair of horses with the cart transporting the suitcases, bedding, and cooking utensils for meals prepared along the way. Unmarried guests came with six horses, rarely only four. Some families came with a larger number of horses because the number indicated the importance of the owners. I really think it's not inappropriate for Mr. Gologordovsky to feed all these horses with chopped hay and chaff. This custom of going visiting with an entire herd of horses at the host's expense, is the same as the arrival of a Tatar horde, and if the landowners didn't prepare forage for the guests' animals which is but the shadow of the real thing, then two such gala balls in the village would use up their annual supply of oats and hay. But since no gathering can occur without livestock, the main thing is to know how to cope with it successfully.

After the church service came breakfast or, better said, *vodka drinking*, because the women ate very little and the men drank more than they ate. Vodkas of various colors and flavors were continually circulated and sampled, decanters passed from hand to hand until they were all emptied. Then the men went into the garden to join the ladies. Meanwhile the tables were laid in the dining room as new guests were continually arriving, and four servants continued serving vodka and snacks in the garden.

At two o'clock in the afternoon, when all the food had been placed on the table, the musicians, led by the music master, assembled on the stairs leading out to the garden and played a Polish tune. This was a signal that dinner was served, and all the guests gathered in the main avenue of trees. Mr. Gologordovsky offered his arm to the most distinguished female guest, the wife of the provincial marshal; the marshal himself accompanied Mrs. Gologordovskaya, and thus the two couples proceeded into the dining room. The remaining guests followed the hosts in pairs, and they all took their seats around the table, just as they entered—that is, the women sitting next to the men. It's true that Mr. Gologordovsky placed the most esteemed guests closer to the head of the table, in spite of the fact that they entered the hall later. Before they were seated, he called them forward from the crowd and asked them to sit closer to the lady of the house, arranging the seating with various jokes and facetious sayings.

Dinner was splendid, and although more than a hundred guests sat down to eat, the food was ample. With regard to the wine, the following order was established. Ordinary table wine, say French wine, was served in decanters set before the guests; the better wines of different qualities were carried around and poured out by the lackeys under the supervision of the butler and the stable master. The first, with three lackeys was on the right side of the table; and the other, with the same number of lackeys, on the left. On each side the first lackey held the bottle of the finest wine; the second, average wine, and the third, the most ordinary wine, belonging to the class of best wines in name alone. The butler and the stable master, by previous agreement, understood from Mr. Gologordovsky's directions which wine was to be served to which guest; for example, when Mr. Gologordovsky said, "I beg you, dear sir, to do me the honor of trying my wine; I assure you it's worth it," they were to pour the finest wine.

"Try a drop of wine, it's really not too bad," meant to pour the second choice.

"You're not drinking at all; hey, pour some wine for this gentleman!" signified the third choice.

It seems that Mr. Gologordovsky knew well the tastes of his guests, because they all drank a decent amount and even anticipated the landlord's urging. However, I consider Mr. Gologordovsky's conduct very admirable: why treat a guest in a manner he won't understand, when he's completely satisfied with the name and the quality of his wine? Some people drink champagne and Hungarian Tokay because they like the taste; others drink it only because they wish to say: "We drank champagne and Tokay!" Who doesn't know the proverb? "Don't cast your pearls before swine."

At the end of dinner they carried in a large goblet decorated with monograms and inscriptions. Mr. Gologordovsky filled it with wine, drank to the health of his spouse and, amid loud cries of *Vivat*![1] and peals of music and drums, he emptied the goblet, bowed to his neighbor and said, "It's your turn." With exactly the same ceremony the cup was passed from hand to hand. Finally, when all the neighbors refused to drink any more, saying *the day was not yet over*, the host stood up and, followed by all the guests, each taking the arm of one or two women, they tottered off into the garden where coffee and sweets awaited them. As soon as the gentlemen had left the dining room, the lackeys, both those of the house and those belonging to the visitors, the musicians, and even the servants, rushed in like vultures and set upon the remains of the feast, not heeding the threatening voices of the butler and stable master; they tore everything to pieces and emptied all the bottles. In the kitchen an even greater uproar occurred when the servants got their dinner. The visitors, without standing on ceremony, helped themselves, taking possession of the saucepans and satisfying their appetites whetted by the journey. Recalling now all the details of this feast, I'm convinced that half of all the provisions consumed would have been completely sufficient for the masters and servants, but some order would have been necessary and that was missing entirely from Mr. Gologordovsky's household.

---

1. A cry wishing someone long life and prosperity (Lat.).

After dinner several of the older gentlemen went to have a rest; a large part of the guests seated themselves at card tables, where some inveterate money-grubbers, or simply enthusiasts, kept the bank in a game of faro. All of these gentlemen—who at the dinner table had complained loudly about hard times, the decline in grain trading, and their lack of funds—squandered gold, silver, and stacks of paper money at the card tables. Several, having lost their last kopeck, right there, in the heat of the moment, sold their horses, carriages, domestic livestock, and copper vessels from their distilleries and, in the hope of regaining them, continued losing money. Young people and old philanderers chatted with the ladies; enflamed by the wine, they made declarations of love and entertained the women with nonsense and amusing stories. At last, when it started to get damp, the women withdrew to their rooms to change clothes and prepare for the dancing. At eight o'clock the lamps were lit, the music began, and Mr. Gologordovsky opened the ball by dancing a polonaise with his wife. Dancing continued until midnight; then supper was served.

Supper was just as abundant and lavish as dinner, but the drinking took a different course. Almost all the guests became completely drunk. They drove the musicians away into another room, and the gentlemen began declaring their friendships for one another, followed by embraces, kisses, and promises to forget all their quarrels and mutual differences. The women were summoned to serve as witnesses to these reconciliations and had to vouch for making good on these promises by both sides. When the well-known toast, "Let's love one another" (*Kochajmy się*),[2] was pronounced, the guests drank an entire goblet, sinking down to their knees or embracing each other. Finally they turned to the women and began drinking toasts out of the women's shoes to each one of them in turn. A gentleman, sinking to his knees before a woman, would remove her shoe, kiss her foot and hands, and place his glass in her shoe, sometimes pouring wine into the shoe itself, and then pass it to someone else.

Suddenly a salute from two dozen muskets and several small cannons was fired and alarmed the merrymaking guests. Everyone rushed to the windows and in the middle of the courtyard saw the flaming monogram of the lady in whose honor the affair was being held. A merry *Vivat*! rang out again in the hall; a flourish was sounded, and

2. (Pol.).

the enormous goblet appeared once again on the scene. Several dozen rockets and Roman candles were launched into the air to the spectators' delight. But from a lack of skill, or from carelessness, several of the rockets landed on the straw roof of the barn; since the wind was rather brisk, the roof burst into flame and in a few minutes the entire structure caught fire. It was hard to imagine the confusion aroused by this unexpected turn of events. The inebriated men were concerned; the servants didn't know what to do. Everyone started giving orders, but no one was inclined to follow them. They didn't even know how to operate the fire hoses, so each one went running toward the blaze carrying a bucket, an ax, or a pike, but no one dared to approach the flames. They sounded the alarm, sent into the village for help, but it seemed they were not eager to come to the master's rescue. The guests hastily ordered their horses harnessed and packed up their belongings. The house servants tried to save the table silver and dining room linen from plundering. Confusion, disorder, shouting, noise, and commotion were enough to stupefy even the most cold-blooded people: everything was turned upside down in the house.

I felt terrified and didn't know what to do. I stood on the porch, looked at the fire, and was about to start crying. Suddenly Masha appeared. "Vanka! I've been looking all over for you. Follow me."

We ran headlong through all the rooms into the young lady's bedroom. Masha put on my head a braid-trimmed cap that had been stored in the young lady's wardrobe, gave me a bundle and a box to carry, tossed on her cape, and ordered me to follow her. We ran through the garden, climbed over the broken fence, and wound up in a field next to a grove. There stood a carriage drawn by four horses. In the darkness I couldn't see who was already in it. Masha got in and sat up front; a tall lackey with a mustache lifted me up on top of a suitcase in the cart, and he himself sat on the coach box next to the driver. The horses turned and trotted slowly to the main road, which was only about a mile away, and then set off at full speed. As exhausted as I was by the hustle and bustle of the day, I couldn't close my eyes. The fire was constantly glowing in my imagination; I was worried about the well-being of my young mistress, assuming that most likely everything in the house would be consumed in the fire, and that was why Masha had fled the scene to save herself, along with me. I thought that this carriage probably belonged to one of the guests. It seemed that I heard whispering coming from the carriage, but I couldn't tell from their voices who was speaking. Finally at daybreak we arrived at the first post station.

Chapter 6

Marriage and Parting with the Newlyweds

When I climbed down from the suitcase and went to the carriage, I almost cried out from astonishment, after seeing Milovidin and my young mistress, Petronella Gologordovskaya, wrapped up in her cloak, resting her head on the shoulder of her dear friend.

"You recognized me, Vanka!" said Milovidin with a smile.

"Of course. How could I not know you?"

Meanwhile Kuzma, the lackey with the mustache, who had gone to the post station with the order for fresh horses, returned and announced the station master's response: there were no horses to be had. After hearing these words, Milovidin jumped down from the carriage and ran headlong into the cottage, and I rushed in after him. The stationmaster was sitting in his dressing gown at the table, leafing through a book where orders were recorded.

"Horses!" Milovidin shouted menacingly.

"There aren't any; they're all out," replied the stationmaster coolly.

"If you won't provide horses this minute," said Milovidin, "I'll harness you to the carriage with all your offspring and servants. Do you hear?"

"You're welcome to make jokes," replied the stationmaster with his previous calm. "Would you care to rest a while and have some coffee? In the meantime, the horses will return home."

"The devil take you and your coffee! I need horses!" cried an angry Milovidin.

"There aren't any!" answered the stationmaster again.

"You're lying; no one travels on this road, and I didn't encounter anyone on the way," said Milovidin.

"Be so good as to check the book here."

"I don't want to waste time; instead of counting the pages, I'll beat the living daylights out of you," said Milovidin, and he took a step closer to the stationmaster.

"It won't help you to get angry," replied the latter. "Be so good as to read the regulations on the wall: you'll see that for insulting a postmaster of the fourteenth rank, you're subject to a fine of one hundred rubles."

"If you want the money," said Milovidin, "I'll pay you three times that amount and treat you in such a way that you'll never in your life collect another fine. But I want to discuss the matter with you civilly. How much must we pay for the established fare to the first station?"

"Sixteen rubles," replied the stationmaster.

"So, I'll pay you double—that is, thirty-two rubles—and in addition I'll give you three rubles for coffee or tobacco: that makes thirty-five rubles altogether; provide us with some horses, or, so help me God, I'll give you a beating!"

"I can see that there's nothing to be done with you," said the stationmaster. "I'll have to give you my own horses." After saying this, he stuck his head out of the small ventilation window and shouted to the drivers, "Hey, lads, saddle the gray horses, and hurry up, as though for a courier."

"You wretched rogue!" said Milovidin, as he received his change.

"What can one do, Your Honor?" replied the stationmaster. "One has to make a living somehow."

"That's one of the misfortunes of this country: everything is done *somehow*," said Milovidin, as he was leaving the cottage. Meanwhile they harnessed the horses, and we set off.

We galloped along the main road for three days and three nights without any special adventures. There were difficulties at each posting station because our order didn't contain the words *Traveling on Government Business.* But by means of threats, abuse, shouts, and bribes, Milovidin overcame the inflexible stubbornness of the stationmasters, who, for the most part, considered it their responsibility to dispatch couriers as quickly as possible and detain others as long as possible.

On the fourth day at dawn, within sight of a town, we turned off the main road; after passing through the woods for some two or three miles, we stopped in front of a peasant's cottage in a village. That's where Milovidin's friend Lieutenant Khvatomsky was quartered. He came running out of the cottage, helped Petronella down from the carriage, and escorted her into his rooms. They summoned two priests at once, Russian Orthodox and Catholic, who had been brought there intentionally and were awaiting Milovidin's arrival. He showed them his permission to enter into legal marriage and the agreement, or indult,[1] of the Catholic bishop, with a so-called window, or blank space, for inserting the names; two hours later both ceremonies had been completed, the Russian Orthodox marriage in a church and the Catholic ceremony in the priest's house. After resting and dining with Khvatomsky, the newlyweds headed into town at twilight, where Milovidin's apartment was located. To thwart any misunderstandings, he didn't want to appear before his squadron except with a legal wife; this precaution, without doubt, does credit to his character.

Before leaving to collect his bride, Milovidin put his quarters in good order as best he could in order to receive his wife. He occupied two rooms in the home of a rich Yid. But since cleanliness isn't a characteristic of wealth among Yids, he fixed up the apartment at his own expense. He covered the walls in bright wallpaper and the floors with cloth; he created an alcove in the back room as a bedroom, and that space was hung with carpets. The windows were adorned with pink curtains. From one of his female acquaintances, the wife of a landowner, who lived apart from her husband, by decision of the Consistory Court,[2] Milovidin borrowed a piano, a dozen chairs, a pair of card tables, and a mirror. Several pairs of pistols, Turkish sabers and daggers, Persian fittings for a horse, and two rifles were hung in the living room instead of pictures. A pyramid of pipe stems with huge amber bowls and gold embroidered covers also served to decorate the room. In a word, considering the place and the circumstances, Milovidin's rooms were splendidly furnished, with no less luxury than those of Mr. Gologordovsky himself. In addition, on top of the piano lay a large sheaf of music, ordered intentionally from Petersburg; in the bedroom there were several dozen new illustrated French novels on a shelf. Milovidin hadn't neglected anything to make his quarters comfortable.

1. Special permission in canon law granted to do something otherwise prohibited.
2. A type of ecclesiastical court.

Petronella expressed her astonishment upon entering his apartment for the first time. After surveying the surroundings, she threw her arms around her husband's neck and wept from joy and gratitude for his thoughtfulness. The next day Milovidin visited the colonel, the paymaster, the quartermaster, and a few more married officers to introduce his wife to their spouses. Over the course of the next week, they made regular visits throughout the neighborhood, and everywhere Milovidin received congratulations concerning the beauty and kindness of the lovely Petronella.

Soon guests from all sides began to visit him. Milovidin loved living grandly: he organized dinners, evening parties, and suppers, which usually ended with drinking bouts and card playing. Time flew by, as did his supply of money. At first he purchased wine and provisions for cash, afterwards on credit, and at last, when the Yids saw that he wasn't paying his debts, they stopped trusting him; he had to pawn his belongings.

Petronella's parents didn't want any letters from her and returned them to her unopened. Milovidin's uncle also grew angry at him because he'd deceived him, saying he was marrying a wealthy bride, and for marrying without the consent of her parents; he refused to provide him with any funds. Milovidin got involved in playing cards on credit: he associated with gamblers who cheated and swindled him out of his last funds. His situation became critical. Six months after his wedding, he had sold everything he could; there was nothing left to pawn, no money available to bet on cards, and no one to borrow from. Milovidin decided on a last resort: to go to his uncle with his wife in the hope that her charms would soften the stubborn old man. After he received a leave of absence, he sold his last saddle horse; with that money he redeemed his carriage. He collected the remains of his property, linen, saddles, and arms and pawned them to his Yid landlord to raise money for the journey. Mrs. Milovidina didn't want to part with her dresses or with Masha. Her husband was forced to submit to her wishes; and so, after loading the carriage with boxes, taking with them Masha, a lackey, and a cook, my master and mistress set off for Moscow. They left me in their apartment to take care of their things in hock and ordered the Yid to feed me at their expense.

Chapter 7

A Rich Yid. Sources of His Wealth.

A month after the Milovidins' departure, the regiment was transferred to other quarters. I stayed with the Yid and the remaining items, since none of the officers wanted or was able to redeem them or take the locked trunks along with them. Left alone without supervision or protection, according to the natural order of things, I became a servant for the one who fed me—that is, the owner of the house, the Yid Moishe. He was considered one of the wealthiest people in town. His wife, Rifka,[1] a short, portly woman decked out in pearls and scabs,[2] traded in silk goods, sugar, coffee, and dried fruits, or *groceries* in a shop. At home Moishe traded in wines, porter, and various provisions for the dining table, spicy herbs, Dutch herrings, cheeses, and all sorts of accessories pertaining to gastronomy. But as a Yid, he couldn't live without dealing in spirits, so, in addition to his other business, he kept a tavern in his house, primarily for peasants and the lower class.

The niggling sale of vodka is the Yid's primary function in the Polish provinces. By this means and for a tenth of the actual cost, he acquires all the household provisions and heats his home for next to nothing.

---

1. The Hebrew form of the name Rebecca.
2. Presumably from a case of smallpox.

Besides, by means of the vodka, he ferrets out of peasants and servants all their secrets, requirements, connections, and the relationships of the masters, which makes the Yids the real rulers of the landowners; he subjects to Yid control all matters and circumstances in which precious metals and paper money play a role. As a matter of fact, the landowners are pleased merely by the sound of the precious metals and the sight of paper money, while in essence they all belong to the Yid.

In Moishe's writing desk there were three large registers or books of debts. In the first one women's debts were recorded, a result of Rifka's trading; in the second, the landowners' debts and those of men in general, the so-called *Panie*, for beverages and food supplies; the third book contained the debts of unfortunate peasants who would come into town to sell products of the earth by necessity, keep only enough to pay the money owed to the landowner, and drink up the rest—in addition, going into debt. To give the reader an idea of how the Yids treat peasants, I'll relate a story about how Moishe balanced the account of one of the rich peasants, an event of which I was the eyewitness.

This peasant arrived in town on the eve of market day with two wagons loaded with rye and wheat, and he brought two cows with him to sell. He stopped over at Moishe's house to spend the night. The sly Yid, seeing that the peasant was about to sit down to dinner with three of his comrades, served him a glass of his very best vodka. The peasant really liked the vodka, and the Yid gave him another glass at no cost. When the peasant became lightheaded, he sold him a pint of it for cash. The Yid had been waiting for this. He knew his guest's temper and his generosity; therefore, as soon as the peasant drank, he sent word to his comrades and invited some well-known town drunks, who have the knack of insinuating themselves with strangers. As the guests' faculties diminished due to the vodka, the Yid kept adding more water to the vodka, and although the company recognized this and expressed its dissatisfaction in rude terms, the Yid patiently tolerated their rudeness and continued his operation until the majority of guests had fallen asleep at their places, while the rest of them managed to straggle out onto the street.

The next day when the peasant, who was suffering from a severe headache, returned to the shed where his horses and cows were standing, the Yid demanded payment of his debts, accumulated during the course of several months. The peasant begged him fervently to delay the settlement until a later time; but the Yid, an astute psychologist, knew the rule: *in corpore sano, mens sana*;[3] he wouldn't agree to the delay and hoped to use his debtor's lightheadedness from the fumes of the wine after his lack of restraint the day before, as well as his feeble state of mind. The Yid brought out his record of debts, written in Yiddish, took a piece of chalk, sat the peasant down at the table opposite him, leafed through the pages of the book, and began his calculations.

"Do you recall," said the Yid, "how you stayed here three days with your load before the summer feast of St. Nicholas?"

"Of course, I do," replied the peasant.

"The first day you took a pint of vodka in the morning. Isn't that correct?"

"That's true."

"Well, then I'll note that," muttered the Yid and made a mark on the table with his chalk. "Afterwards, when your brother-in-law came with Nikita, you had another quart," and with these words the Yid made two marks. "At dinner, you had another two quarts." The Yid made two more marks, regardless of the difference in size. "After dinner—"

But the peasant, who was already scratching his head and mopping his brow, interrupted the Yid. "*Pane* tavern keeper," (that's how Lithuanian peasants dignify Yids), "I really don't have the strength to continue: give me some vodka—I have a terrible headache."

That's just what the Yid wanted to happen.

"Hey, Sorka,[4] Rifka!" cried the Yid. "Serve the *hospodar* some vodka" (the title the Yids give peasants when they want to deceive them).

The peasant drank a large glass, grimacing and shuddering, and things took a different turn.

"After dinner," continued the Yid, "you had a pint."

"I did."

The Yid made a mark.

"And when Ivan came in, you had another pint."

"No, I didn't, Ivan did," replied the peasant.

"Fine, you didn't," said the Yid while making another mark. "In the evening, did you have a pint?"

"I did."

The Yid made a mark.

"And the next morning?"

"No, I didn't, but Ivan did," replied the peasant.

3. "A healthy mind in a healthy body" (Lat.).

4. A nickname for Sarah.

"You didn't?" asked the Yid, and made another mark. "For dinner the next day you had a pint."

"No, only half a pint," replied the peasant.

"Fine, only half a pint," said the Yid and made another mark, which represented a quart. The accounting continued, during which Moishe's wife, Rifka, and daughter Sorka kept plying the peasant with vodka, while the Yid made his marks; it didn't matter whether the peasant had consumed it or not, or how much he drank. At last, when the peasant's head started spinning and his eyes became clouded, the Yid took a piece of chalk from his bosom that had a split in it and with this instrument, proceeded to draw two lines at a time instead of only one. When the table was covered with marks, the Yid called in as witnesses some of the peasant's neighbors; after counting up the marks, it turned out that the unfortunate peasant had to surrender his best cow to the Yid, as well as all his wheat, although in fact he owed him only about a tenth of that amount.

Moishe behaved in almost the same way with landowners, but more skillfully and more fondly. However the same split piece of chalk and the doubling of spirits and wine were also used in accounting with the gentry, as they were with the peasants. The Yid, knowing that the Polish *panie* and Russian officers didn't like to keep account books and would get very bored during lengthy computations, would choose a favorable time for the calculations and would approach the debtors with their accounts when they were in an extremely merry or very despondent mood. Moishe's wife, Rifka, who also sold provisions on credit and, instead of interest, would receive as a gift from the landowners' wives whole tubs of butter and entire flocks of domestic fowl, would choose the time for reckoning with her debtors when they were in great need of credit—that is, before balls, gentry elections, and weddings. In this kind of trading, it was impossible to cheat in the same manner as her husband did in the sales of wine and vodka; but shrewd Rifka, taking advantage of her customers' needs and their vanity, would give them short measure and short weight, charge twice as much, and in addition, managed to wheedle presents from them, under the pretext that she herself had received the goods on credit and was obligated to pay interest. Besides that, her trade brought her certain advantages: through the wives, Moishe had influence on the husbands—that is, on the landowners' fiscal speculations. They were even glad that if they wished they could pay for silks and lace, wine, rum, port, sugar, and coffee in wheat, flax, hemp, and other agricultural products, because in that case, the

Yid would pay cash for the remaining stock at a price he himself set, half the price at the exchange or at the ports. In these provinces landowners in general have no idea about trade; they receive their commercial news only through the Yids. In the entire province there are hardly any people who subscribe to newspapers, and that's merely for notices about lawsuits and a supply of absurd rumors about politics.

All of this Yid trade based on deceit was called *lawful*, and therefore Yids engaged in it openly—obtaining much more, however, in a concealed manner, by means forbidden by law and conscience. Moishe came to like me for my modesty and thoughtfulness; he regarded me as his own servant, because Milovidin, after retiring and settling in Moscow, gave up his possessions and me, for he had no means to redeem either his own things or me from pawn.

Moishe employed me for his most secret commissions and promised me mountains of gold if I would decide to become a Yid. Although I had no conception about religion whatever, having been reared like a little wild animal, the very term *Yid* frightened me, and, while not refusing outright, I kept postponing circumcision, offering various excuses. In the meantime, I resolved to escape this misfortune.

One day Moishe was visited by two agents of wealthy gentlemen, who were returning from Riga with money received for the sale of grain and hemp. These agents were, it seems, on intimate terms with Moishe: they gave him all their masters' gold for safekeeping, which Moishe promised to return the next day; besides, he gave one of them silver money of equal worth as a pledge to the one inexperienced in such matters.

That night Moishe locked himself away upstairs in his own room, summoning me and his son, Yudel, to him, announcing that we had work to do all night. He emptied a large pile of gold coins onto the table, made Yudel pick out of the pile the heaviest and largest; he spread a cloth on the floor for me, sprinkled some black powder on it, and had me rub selected coins on the cloth, pressing them firmly to it. Moishe himself sat down at a table on which stood two wax candles and a magnifying glass on a stand. Yudel passed the gold coins to him; he looked at them through the magnifying glass and clipped them with a pair of slender crooked scissors. I don't know how many gold coins passed through our hands, but by dawn I'd changed the cloth three times, and Moishe had collected an entire teacup full of gold clippings. The agents received their coins back promptly, without measuring their weight; in return for their indulgence, each one received a few coins; besides, the Yid took no money from them for feeding their horses or for their food and drink; he even provided each with several bottles of wine for the road. That evening Moishe burned the cloths and then in his small room melted the clippings in a stove built for that purpose. Our night's work produced a lump of gold the size of a man's fist. We always engaged in this practice of clipping gold from coins whenever well-known agents and commissars of wealthy *panie*, merchants, or gentlemen happened to stay overnight with us and entrusted Moishe with their gold.

One evening Moishe ordered me to prepare for a journey the next day. Rifka placed a pair of Moishe's best clothes in a small trunk: a black half-silk homespun coat, which fastened with small hooks from the collar to the waist; a black silk cloak with large tassels in front; a pair of gray stockings, new shoes, and a round broad-brimmed hat; she included enough linen to last for the two weeks he planned to be away. She filled a separate basket with edible provisions: one bottle of Shabashovka vodka, so called because of its high quality and because it's consumed only on the Sabbath, when they sing a joyous *Majofis*;[5] two kosher cheeses made from goat's milk; two large radishes; two dozen onions; a dozen herrings; two loaves of bread; a string of Yid pretzels or bagels; and a small piece of roasted goat. This supply was intended to serve five men for a period of two weeks. Moishe was escorted by the following people: the Yid Furman, his brother-in-law Iosel, his nephew Khankel, and poor me. The suitcase and basket were put into my hands; when I remarked to Rifka that the provisions wouldn't be sufficient, she grew angry and yelled at me. "Shut up, you *goy*![6] All you think about is your belly; you never stop to consider that each and every crumb costs money: we have to save money; we live in difficult times!"

"But you have plenty of money," I said through my gritted teeth; my head was partly obscured by the basket. She suddenly grew furious.

"How dare you say that we have plenty of money? *Hörst du*?[7] Oh, you! Have you seen and counted our money?" The Yiddess trembled with rage, threatening me with her fists; most likely, she'd have struck me if I hadn't assumed a dignified air and cried out in turn, "Why are you angry, *Pani* Arendarsha? If you touch me, I'll pick up and leave!"

Moishe came running when he heard all the shouting; when he learned the cause of the squabble, he yelled at his wife and led her to

5. A Yiddish song of joy, sung without words.
6. A gentile (Yiddish).
7. "Do you hear?" (Yiddish).

another room, where they argued and she calmed down. Rifka, upon her return, patted me on the head and gave me a large pretzel, saying, "Don't be angry, Vanka! For you I'll put a piece of smoked goose in the basket; if our Yids want such delicacies, let them buy them with their own money."

One of our neighboring landowners was staying in our apartment. In the evening just before Moishe's departure, the landowner ordered a glass of punch for himself and for the owner, told him to sit down, and began conversing with him. In general a majority of small landowners consider that Yids are well informed about all matters, even about politics; instead of paying to subscribe to newspapers, they use the money for lunch and wine, and the time they would have wasted on reading they spend in conversation with the Yids about world events. This landowner's door happened to be open to the doghouse where, by the light of a night lamp, I was supposed to pluck feathers for the Yids' mattresses, merely to prevent me from being idle for a single moment and, according to the Yid's standard, not to eat my bread for free. Every word was audible: while they were talking about trade, the economy, war, and the governor, I paid no attention to their conversation; but when they mentioned Moishe's trip, I began to listen, curious to know where we would be going and why.

"It's strange, Rebbe Moishe,"[8] said the landowner, "that you, who carry on such extensive trade, should've thought to rent the tavern on an estate some twenty miles from your place of residence. I know that you also make tar and potash there, but you could have all that a stone's throw away, so to speak. I and every other landowner would be glad to do business with you."

"Particular circumstances, most honored sir," replied Moishe, "require me to rent a place far from home. All my wife's relatives live in that part of the country, and from *pure benevolence*, I established them all in taverns. It's easier to get rid of the tar and potash there because the estate lies near the border. I don't receive any profit from all this; I go there twice a year merely to make sure everything's in order, to settle my accounts, and to pay my rent; my wife's relatives receive the profit, which I bestow on them."

"That's praiseworthy, very praiseworthy, Rebbe Moishe," said the landowner. "That model is worthy of imitation, and between us, and to

8. A traditional Yiddish title or form of address, corresponding to sir, for a man who is not a rabbi.

do justice to it, the outcry raised against the Yids is excessive; even one such example of *disinterested love for one's relatives* puts their behavior in a more favorable light."

They called me in to supper, so I didn't hear the continuation of the conversation. The reader will soon see what *disinterested love* for one's relatives and *pure benevolence without profit* are all about.

The next day a long carriage covered in oilcloth smeared with tar and mud was brought around to the door; three skinny horses were harnessed with ropes and the remnants of a gentleman's old harness; they piled featherbeds and pillows into the carriage, loaded the trunks and boxes, and we set off on our journey. Moishe, Iosel, and Khankel, all wearing soiled gowns and nightcaps, sat on featherbeds, practically one on top of another; I was placed at their feet, on a trunk containing clothes. Since it was autumn, I was given some sort of old woolen coat bought at the market and a hat that had been left in the tavern by a drunken lackey; this hat was very annoying; it fell down over my eyes with every bounce of the carriage.

I won't describe our journey, which wasn't interesting in any way and lasted two and a half days. On the third day we turned off the main road and around noontime we arrived at a small tavern located a certain distance from a poor village, consisting of ten huts. The owner of the tavern seemed to be delighted by our arrival and immediately dispatched three peasants bearing letters in different directions. The Yids began gathering at nightfall—some riding bareback, others in carts. Meanwhile a Yiddess cooked up some food for the twenty or so assembled people. As usual, toward evening there was also a gathering of peasants in the tavern, who'd come to smoke tobacco, drink vodka on credit, enjoy some dried fish and sea roach, and, in the light of a torch, talk about their master and his steward.

The Yids paid no attention to the peasants; they locked themselves up in another room and chatted loudly among themselves for some time—for the most part, all speaking at once. Finally, when the noisy conference was at an end, the agent drove the peasants out of the tavern without ceremony, saying that he had to make up the beds for his guests. He provided some vodka and tobacco for the discontented peasants to take home, those who didn't want to leave the tavern; they went back to their village singing. Around midnight some gentleman arrived on horseback; he spent about half an hour alone with Moishe; I heard them bargaining through the doors; at last they shook hands, and Moishe counted out several dozen silver rubles and banknotes. The gentleman, after drinking a glass of vodka to the health of the *honest* company, lit a pipe, mounted his horse, and galloped off into the forest. The Yids had supper, and then they left, too. Moishe and his fellow travelers lay down on feather beds without undressing, while I stretched out on some straw. Sometime before dawn the agent woke us up, and we set off on two carts and one horse along a narrow road into the forest. I drove the cart in which Moishe and Iosel were seated, while the landlord and Khankel went off in the other cart. We drove for a long time through the woods before dawn and finally heard the creaking of wheels and the noisy cries of drivers. Moishe was overjoyed and ordered me to hurry on. We soon encountered a string of some fifty carts, loaded with barrels of tar and potash. Only one Yid accompanied them; the drivers were all peasants. After talking to the Yid, Moishe ordered me to turn the horse around and follow the caravan. After traveling back a little more than a mile, we met a detachment of Cossacks stationed at the frontier; with them was the same man I'd seen before in the tavern. He wasn't in the military and was dressed very simply. After seeing us, he left his party and galloped up to our carts with his Cossack officer.

"What are you carrying?" asked the officer.

"Potash and tar," replied the Yid in the cart.

"Are you the owner?" asked the Cossack officer.

"No, sir. There he is, Your Excellency, Your Honor," he said, pointing to Moishe, who had climbed down from the cart and was standing there bareheaded, making deep bows.

"You rogues are probably transporting contraband!" shouted the gentleman in civilian dress.

"How is it possible, sir, that honest people would be carrying contraband?" asked Moishe, making a low bow. "God keep us from that! We're poor Yids, trading tar and potash. You're free to inspect our carts."

The gentleman dismounted, took an iron rod from his saddle, removed a hammer from a leather sack, and began to knock it against the barrels, listening to test the sounds it made; finally he searched the peasants, and exclaimed as if in irritation, "There's nothing to be done! They're right—devil take them!" During the search the Cossack officer remained on his horse and diligently observed the actions of the gentleman in civilian dress, but seeing that everything was in order, he left us in peace and went on his way with his detachment.

Moishe couldn't contain his joy. When the Cossacks had disappeared from view, he snapped his fingers and sang a cheerful tune, repeating frequently, "*Atrapirt, atrapirt*!"[9]

On arriving safely at the tavern, the casks were unloaded into the storehouse; the peasants were released, paid in part with money but more in vodka, tobacco, and herring. After having dinner and a nap, Moishe locked himself away in the storehouse with Iosel, Khankel, and me. I was very surprised when he began to work on the barrels. There was tar and potash in the middle, but the two ends had double bottoms, and the space in between was filled with valuable goods—silk, linen, cambric, lace, fancy goods, and the like. They were also transporting a brazier, stamps, black and red ink; they heated the tin, and while I fanned the coals, Moishe and his comrades began to stamp and seal the goods, just as I would see it done later on in the customhouse. At night several large Yiddish wagons arrived, onto which the goods packed in bales and trunks were loaded and sent home with Iosel and Khankel; Moishe and I went back in the same carriage in which we'd journeyed to the tavern.

Moishe, as mentioned above, had planned to be away for two weeks but stayed only one, because the carts with the goods from abroad had arrived early. There was joy and elation in the house; the next day, which was the Sabbath, Rifka baked pies with honey and poppy seeds, and made *kugel*;[10] she roasted a goose, made noodles and *tzimmes*;[11] and she even treated me to some kosher wine.

Moishe announced to his agents that he wished to celebrate the fortunate conclusion of one of his affairs by doing some *good* deed. When he paid out money on a pledge, he usually charged two kopecks on the ruble per week; now, for the period of one month, he intended to charge the poor and needy only *one and a half* kopecks. The agents sent word of Moishe's beneficence to all gamblers, spendthrifts, and drunkards, and Moishe had to put up with his wife's reproaches and even her abuse for this unnecessary generosity, which, in Rifka's opinion, could result in their ruin.

9. "Evaded, got away with it."

10. Baked pudding or casserole, most commonly made from egg noodles or potato (Yiddish).

11. A traditional and delicious dish that usually includes carrots and other root vegetables and dried fruit, such as prunes or raisins (Yiddish).

Chapter 8

Meeting a Civil Servant, Returning from a Certain Place, with the Other One Going to a Certain Place. I Leave the Yid.

Winter arrived and, with it, an increase of activity in Moishe's house and, for me, extra work. Strings of carts and passengers stopped at our house, and I was assigned to the guests' rooms, the same ones previously occupied by Milovidin. Besides having to light the stoves, carry in water, and sweep the floors, the Yid ordered me to eavesdrop behind the doors to hear what the gentlemen were saying, especially the civil servants. I was told to find out if they were looking for someone or searching for something, and to pay attention to whether the words *counterfeit* or *contraband* were ever mentioned. Although I didn't understand the true meaning of these words, and sensing that they concealed some Yid trickery, I would have had no desire to serve the Yid faithfully if he hadn't bribed me with the promise of reward and if hunger hadn't compelled me to become the instrument of his Yid scheme. But I was so bored with this kind of life that I resolved to run away at the first opportunity, wherever my legs would carry me. Only one thing was holding me back: the lack of winter clothes.

Once when it was starting to get dark, some carriages stopped in the marketplace just opposite Moishe's house. He went out immediately, ran up to the four-seater on runners, made a low bow, and offered the passengers an apartment, praising all the comforts of his house, the low cost of fodder, and all the conveniences, recommending himself as a man well known for his honesty and helpfulness. The beautiful exterior of Moishe's house, compared with others, seems to have been more persuasive than the owner's words, and the carriages, to the delight of the entire Yid family, drove up to the porch.

Rifka came running out with her daughters to greet the guests, while they directed me and the maid to prepare the guest rooms: to wipe away the dust, sweep the floors, and clear the table of any remains of refreshments which Moishe had offered to the magistrates that morning, who were talking about the *substitution of pawned goods*. We'd barely finished when the guests entered the room. I remained at the door to take a good look at them. First came a short, lean, pale man, wrapped in a fur coat. His eyes were flashing, like those of a fox; he looked around, went into the next room, and started to take off his coat. He was followed by two boys and two girls, aged from ten to fourteen, wrapped and bundled up like snails. The lady herself, also lean with a malicious glance, moved very slowly, like a toad. She was followed by a number of maids, nannies, and lackeys carrying bundles and boxes. The first words of greeting she uttered to me and to the maid were, "Get out of the way, you creatures!" After returning this politeness with a low bow, we left the room and, once behind the door, returned her compliment in similar terms.

In the common room I learned that the travelers were using rented horses and were on their way from the province to Moscow, where this gentleman named Skotinko was a public prosecutor. They brought in candles, heated the samovar, and Mr. Skotinko's cook began preparing supper. Meanwhile Mr. Skotinko himself summoned Moishe to a conversation and to report on the news.

About two hours later, when it was already dark, a cart drove up to our porch, covered with matting and drawn by two horses. The landlord and landlady didn't rush out to greet the guest. A tall gentleman entered: he was portly and red-faced; when he learned that the best rooms in the house were already taken, he settled in a small room, where the owner's son Yudel slept. The entire luggage of this gentleman consisted of a small leather suitcase and a leather pillow, which his lackey, dressed in a bare sheepskin coat, carried in under his arm. The gentleman's own worn-out fur coat explained the secret of the leather suitcase. Rifka treated the lackey to vodka and learned that the gentleman was named Plutyagovich, and that he was traveling from Petersburg to take up a position as prosecutor from the same provincial town that Mr. Skotinko was coming from. The magistrate's clerk, who at this time was standing next to the buffet drinking some sweetened vodka, smiled slyly and said, "There's a meeting of raptors for you!"

Mr. Plutyagovich, after learning that his predecessor was staying in the same house, immediately went to make his acquaintance. They seemed to like each other, because Skotinko invited Plutyagovich to have supper with him, and they spent the entire evening engaged in conversation.

Meanwhile Plutyagovich's lackey, having supped on a piece of stale bread and some kvass, lit his pipe and seated himself next to the hearth where the servants were cleaning up the remains of Mr. Skotinko's tasty supper: they were also joking among themselves, looking proudly at Plutyagovich's lackey. When they learned that Plutyagovich was going to take the place of their master, they softened their tone and treated the poor fellow to some vodka.

"What's your name, neighbor?" Skotinko's valet asked him.

"Farafont," replied Plutyagovich's servant.

"You look out, Farafont," said the valet. "Keep your ears to the ground, and you'll be just fine. Don't get too friendly with the petitioners, and don't let anyone in the door for free; make them pay to see the master as if they were about to watch some dancing dogs. Why feel sorry for them?"

"I'd be glad to make them pay, but will they be willing to do so?" replied Farafont.

"Of course, they will, if you squeeze it out of them," replied the valet. "Learn to declare loudly, 'He's not home, he's busy, he's unwell, he's not receiving, he's resting!' And if they ask when they can come back, or if they can wait, or if he might take a message, tell them, 'Everything on earth is possible, if you're only careful.'"

Hearing this, all of Mr. Skotinko's servants burst out laughing. Farafont said, "But what if some gentlemen arrive without previous notice, someone whom the master wishes to see, I'll get nothing from them."

"Nonsense!" replied the valet. "You'll do very well. Bow to them, open the door, follow them with a candle, and wish them a happy holiday. Oh, brother Farafont, it's a good life with the prosecutor; and with the governor, it's paradise, all beyond measure! We wept as we left the city. We don't know how it will be, but it was fine there. And you, in Petersburg, what sort of life do lackeys of civil servants lead there?"

"It depends on the place, brother," replied Farafont. "Some of us show off, while others wipe away tears with their fist. My master was only a department head—an unimportant spoke in the wheel. He himself was glad to extract a kopeck or two from both the innocent and the guilty, but he didn't always succeed. I'd only receive a tip when my master sent me with a copy of a document to the petitioner, or if there were some business in the house, and the petitioner would drop in and talk to us. But this is all nonsense: only small crumbs left by experienced hands."

"But now your master will be an important man," said the valet. "Oh, Farafontushka, Farafontushka, I'd give a great deal to trade places with you! But the master's calling. Farewell!"

All this time I was warming myself next to the fire; overhearing these conversations, I envied the fate of the other servants. Realizing that the Yid had no right to detain me, I decided to ask one of these traveling gentlemen to take me along with them.

Plutyagovich, returning to his small room, summoned Moishe, who, after learning that he occupied an important place in the province, had already altered his attitude toward him. He kept bowing and excusing himself before the new prosecutor for not having a better room for him; to make up for it, he kept offering him whatever he had in his house at no charge. Plutyagovich sat down on his bed, lit up a large wooden pipe, and began interrogating the Yid. I stood behind a partition, looked through a crack, and heard their entire conversation.

"Listen, Moishe; be frank with me, and perhaps I'll be of use to you."

The Yid removed his skullcap and bowed. Plutyagovich continued, "Here I am, going to occupy Mr. Skotinko's place, who, as he says, has been dismissed for no good reason, a result of the intrigues of evil-minded people and for the fearless and meticulous performance of his duties."

The Yid smiled slyly and nodded his head. Plutyagovich continued, "Mr. Skotinko frightened me, saying that the position is very bad, that there's no extra income, besides the salary . . ."

Here the Yid interrupted Mr. Plutyagovich and cried loudly, "*Hörst du?* Only a salary! Oy, *vez iz mir*!"[1]

Plutyagovich continued, "Mr. Skotinko says that while living there, he spent all his father's and his wife's money, and now he's fleeing merely with the respect of honest people and a conscience at peace."

1. "Oh, woe is me" (Yiddish).

At these words the Yid burst into loud laughter, grasping his sides, and he kept it up for so long so that Plutyagovich tried to stop him.

"*Hörst du*," said the Yid. "Mr. Skotinko is talking about conscience! Where did he acquire one: somewhere along the road? After this we have to expect that wolves will start guarding the sheep, Yids will go to the monastery to save their souls, and landowners will forbid peasants from getting drunk on vodka. I tell you, sir, Your Excellency, that I knew this Mr. Skotinko when his father was a tanner, a skinner; meanwhile a poor clerk, he ran barefoot through the streets and stole pretzels and bagels from other Yids. He's from the same town where I was born. Now Mr. Skotinko is as rich as the devil. He has real estate and property, so much gold and silver that he probably can't count it. He has both ranks and orders! *Oy vey, oy vey*! Mr. Skotinko has sucked his opportunities dry: not one legal leech had ever gotten so fat!" Here the Yid remembered that he was talking to a candidate for the same position, and he corrected himself. "Excuse me, sir, Your Excellency, but a master like Skotinko hasn't been living among us with a conscience like a net: clean water passes right through it, but fish are caught. His position is a mine of ready money. Don't believe a word he says: Mr. Skotinko lies even when he's telling the truth—that is, he speaks truth to deceive. I'll tell you once again: Skotinko used to be as poor as a church mouse, but by serving as a counselor and a prosecutor in many different provinces, he's amassed so much wealth that although he may look like a dried lizard, he's really hairy as a Siberian beast."

"Why's he hiding himself from me?" asked Plutyagovich.

"He wishes to be known as an honest man, as is the custom of all so-called profiteering bribe takers . . . excuse me . . . Mr. . . ." replied the Yid.

"It's a pity," said Plutyagovich. "I'd have liked to learn something from him—that is, about service—do you understand?"

"Of course, I do," replied Moishe, "but you don't need teachers for that. As soon as you arrive in town, hire the Yid Isaac as an agent. He served in that position under Mr. Skotinko: he'll help you in every way; he'll seek out petitioners, negotiate with provincial civil servants, and accept bribes in your name—it goes without saying, without bills or receipts. I'll provide you with letters to my relatives and to Isaac: rely on them for everything; they won't cheat you—just help us in our dealings with Yids."

"With pleasure," said Plutyagovich. "I'll be yours; prepare everything for tomorrow; meanwhile farewell."

Moishe left the room, and I went after him, coming out from behind the partition.

The next day, Mr. Plutyagovich departed very early, while Skotinko remained behind because he felt unwell. The former hurried so he wouldn't lose a single day of reaping a profit; the latter had no reason to hurry since he had achieved his goal.

Mr. Skotinko's children, lads, went to play in the shed; since I'd become accustomed to the games of the masters' children at Gologordovsky's house, I got involved in the games. I helped them to hitch a billy goat up to a little cart, fashioned a swing for them out of old reins, and cheerfully put up with the unpleasantness of being pelted with snowballs when I served as their target. Rifka called me away from the games to work, but Mr. Skotinko's sons begged their father to order me to play with them, and the Yiddess had to agree. Although I was younger than Mr. Skotinko's children, I was much cleverer than they were and therefore took advantage of their partiality for me, persuading them to beg their father to take me with them. After dinner Mr. Skotinko called me to him.

"Under what conditions are you in service to the Yid?" Mr. Skotinko asked. "I told him the story of Milovidin's marriage and his departure for Moscow; falling at his feet, I asked him to rescue me from the Yids, promising to serve him faithfully for my whole life. Mr. Skotinko looked at his wife, and she rendered a verdict in my favor. Skotinko summoned Moishe at once.

"By what right do you hold this lad?" he said sternly. Moishe faltered three times before being able to utter one word in reply.

"His master, Mr. Milovidin, owed me some money and left his belongings with this lad as collateral."

"Do you dare take a Christian subject as a pledge?" replied Skotinko. "Don't you know the law which forbids Yids to keep Christian servants? Do you know the law against usurers? Show me at once the document that gives you the right to hold this lad. Where's his passport?"

The Yid was frightened. "*Hörst du*!" he said softly. Then, bowing from the waist, he said, "I have no papers: the matter was agreed upon by word of mouth."

"So, you're harboring people lacking passports in your house," said Mr. Skotinko. "Hey! Bring some paper and ink; I'll demand satisfaction from you now. I'll write a declaration and, on my arrival in the capital, I won't delay in presenting a petition. Meanwhile I'll take the lad with me, under my recognizance."

"Your Excellency," said the Yid, "is it worth our quarreling over such trifles? You want to take the lad: by all means. I won't argue but give me a statement so that I can give an account to Milovidin when he inquires. And, so that you don't get angry, I won't take a kopeck for your night's lodging and for everything you ate and drank here; besides, I'll load into your carriage half a dozen bottles of Hungarian Tokay, the likes of which you've never tasted. Are you satisfied?"

"Fine," said Skotinko. "But does the lad have any warm clothes?"

"No, but I'll provide that for him, too. It will all be ready by tomorrow."

Mr. Skotinko sent us out of the room and ordered us to prepare for the journey.

"Damned scoundrel!" exclaimed Moishe, when he met Rifka. "This scrounger is taking away our Vanka." Rifka was furious, but Moishe said something to her in Yiddish, and she calmed down and even patted my head. Moishe led me upstairs to his room, sat down in an armchair, and said, "Vanka! You're a good fellow; you'll probably remember all the good things that we did for you."

"What good things?"

"Haven't we provided your food and drink and your clothes?"

"Didn't I work from morning to night?"

"*Hörst du*! Everyone has to work. But tell me, haven't you been treated well here?"

"Not very," I replied bluntly. "Much work and too little food."

"Don't lie, Vanka! It would've been much worse elsewhere. At least we didn't beat you; other masters make their servants work and don't feed them; they beat them and order them not to cry."

"I can't complain about that: you didn't beat me."

"Therefore you should be grateful to us; here's a *whole* half-ruble piece for your service; and if someone should ask you about us, tell them you didn't see anything or hear anything bad in our house, and that we're poor folk, always in need of money."

"But what about the gold coins?"

"What gold coins? Are you crazy? You never saw any gold coins here."

"Fine, if you say so," I said, just to get rid of the Yid.

"You saw yourself how we love Christians and help them: we supply vodka and bread on credit to the peasants and give alms to poor people."

"Dry bread, which is fed to the livestock, if there weren't poor people asking for it."

"Vanka, Vanka, don't lie! Here's another whole half-ruble. Isn't it true that we're good people, kind and of modest means?" I kept silent. Moishe put the money in my hand, kissed me, and said, "Isn't it true that you'll speak well of us?"

"I will, I will!" I said, running downstairs to my new masters. The Yid procured a used sheepskin coat, hat, and gloves for me; Rifka gave me a string of bagels, some of which we ate, and others we fed to Mr. Skotinko's son's dogs, by virtue of his authority over me. I spent the night in pleasant dreams about my adventures. The hope of meeting my kind Milovidin filled me with joy: I didn't want anything more in life.

The next morning everything was ready for our departure; I was told to take a seat in the back of the carriage, together with the valet, and we set off.

Chapter 9

An Unexpected Meeting. A Transformation. My Aunt. My Education.

We arrived in Moscow without any further adventures. A house had already been rented and furnished for us by Mr. Skotinko's steward, who'd been sent ahead several months before. Mr. Skotinko had many acquaintances in Moscow among civil servants, who gathered at his house together with their wives once a week to have dinner and twice a week to play cards. Soon after his arrival, Mr. Skotinko engaged a Frenchman as a tutor for his sons and a Frenchwoman for his daughters. In addition, every day they had other teachers who came to the house to give them lessons. I was assigned to serve the sons; I had to keep the classroom clean and remain in the room during the lessons to carry out the orders of the teachers and the young gentlemen. Besides that, I served at the dinner table and fulfilled Mrs. Skotinko's commissions in various shops; I also carried her notes to her acquaintances around town, went to the pharmacy to collect her medications, and in addition fed the birds and dogs, which were much favored by my mistress. I was, as it's been described, a chamber-boy. I was dressed as a Cossack and was called the *Little Cossack*.

Gifted by nature with a good memory and imitativeness, in a few months I learned to read and write Russian from the cook and the first four rules of arithmetic by sitting in on the master's sons' lessons; in half a year I learned by heart many French and German words and became familiar with geographical and historical names. The teachers, after taking notice of my understanding and curiosity, would examine me for their own amusement to see what I recalled from the lessons I'd overheard, and they explained what I'd misunderstood. Thus I became a learned man among the lackeys. I was content with my lot, compared with my situation in the Yid's household, and although servants were kept and fed very poorly in Mr. Skotinko's house in general, more from neglect than miserliness, I enjoyed many advantages, making up for other deficiencies. I got the remains of the children's breakfasts and suppers; they gave me money for spice cakes in fancy shops, in the pharmacy, and at other places I frequented on the mistress's errands; besides, I played a game of pitch and toss with the neighboring boys and postilions, and, partly through luck, and partly skill, I almost always won. I even managed to amass a small amount of capital, which was sufficient for supplying me with treats and relieving my hunger in case of need. Thus I spent a year and a half in Mr. Skotinko's house in Moscow, without worrying about the future or expecting any improvement in my lot. My most flattering hope consisted of coming to occupy a position of valet for one of Mr. Skotinko's sons or to return to my previous master, Milovidin, whose kindness and generosity had made a lasting impression on my heart and mind. Fate decreed otherwise.

Once I was waiting in a fashionable shop for the completion of some repair work for my mistress. Suddenly a magnificently dressed lady entered the shop and began inspecting various items. Glancing at me by chance, she stopped and examined me closely, with some special attention. She wanted to return to her inspection of the items on sale, but by some involuntary power, her gaze continued to focus on me. At last she was unable to overcome her inner feelings and approached me.

"Whose boy are you, my dear?" the lady inquired politely, stroking my cheek.

"I myself don't know," I replied. "Now I'm one of Mr. Skotinko's servants."

"Who is this Mr. Skotinko?"

"A wealthy gentleman; he came to live in Moscow a year and a half ago, and I entered his service along the way."

"So, you're a free man and not a serf?"

"I really don't know who I am. I grew up in Byelorussia, in the home of Mr. Gologordovsky . . ."

At these words the lady interrupted my account, left the shop, and ordered me to follow her. She sent her lackey to fetch her carriage; he'd been standing on the steps waiting for her; meanwhile she continued talking with me.

"What's your name?"

"Ivan."

"How old are you?"

"I don't know."

"You say that you grew up in Mr. Gologordovsky's house," said the lady. "Who are your parents?"

"I don't know. I'm an orphan . . ." All this time I was looking at the lady's face and noticed that she blushed and her eyes filled with tears.

"Ivan," she said in a soft voice. Then, after a brief silence, she said, "Vanyusha! Do you have a mark on your left shoulder?"

"How do you know, Madame, that I have a large scar on my shoulder?"

At these words the lady covered her eyes with her handkerchief and remained silent for a brief time. At last she kissed my face, inquired about the whereabouts of Mr. Skotinko's house, gave me a silver ruble, instructed me not to tell anyone about our meeting and her questions, and returned to her carriage, saying that we'd see each other again soon.

I followed the kind lady with my eyes to her carriage and returned to the shop. Since I was a handsome child, I was frequently admired by strangers, especially women who would stop me on the streets, but not one adventure produced the same powerful impression on me as this meeting. My heart was pounding; the lady's splendid face and dark eyes constantly appeared in my imagination; her tender voice sounded in my ears. I returned home despondently. I dreamed about that kind lady all night; I woke up several times and wept from sorrow and annoyance that I hadn't encountered such a sympathetic, polite lady before. I had no idea of any other feelings.

The next day, at twelve noon, a carriage with six horses and three lackeys in livery pulled up to our gates. One of the lackeys entered the hall and asked to tell Mr. Skotinko that Prince Chvanov wished to speak with him about a very important matter. Mr. Skotinko, who was sitting in his dressing gown, immediately put on his frock coat and asked the prince to come in; he waited for him in the hall. The prince was about seventy years old; his face was marred by wrinkles and red splotches; his bald head was covered with a paste made of powder and pomade; the remains of his gray hair were curled and tied in a braid. He hardly moved his legs, and his lackeys supported him under his arms very carefully as if he were made of glass and could shatter into pieces from the slightest touch. Mr. Skotinko received the prince with deep bows and escorted him into the living room, but the prince wished to speak with him alone, so they went into the study where they remained for about an hour. At last Mr. Skotinko emerged from the study and summoned me. I thought that he wanted me to fetch something, but I was astonished when, pointing to me, Mr. Skotinko said, "Here he is," and the prince began stroking my head, patting my cheeks, and muttering something in a foreign language.

"Vanka," Mr. Skotinko said to me, "you will leave immediately with His Excellency. I have no further claim over you: here's your new benefactor."

I was so surprised at these words that I made no reply and stood there without moving. The prince stood up, shook Mr. Skotinko's hand, and slowly made his way to the door, leaning on my shoulder. In the hall Mr. Skotinko said, "Well, farewell, Vanya; you're no longer my servant. Go with His Excellency."

The valet handed me my cap, and I went out with the prince. I was almost frightened when he ordered me to sit next to him in the carriage. I was in such confusion that I dared not raise my eyes or catch my breath. Fortunately the prince was silent all along the way and dozed. My heart was pounding when we stopped in front of a splendid house. Not knowing one's fate is sometimes worse than certain misfortune.

As soon as we entered the rooms—which were sparkling with gold, bronze, and marble and adorned with carpets and paintings—the prince sat down on a sofa and summoned his butler. Meanwhile I stood in the doorway and watched everything with curiosity. The butler entered.

"Take this lad," said the prince, "and go with him to the tailor and seamstresses; buy the best linen for him, fashionable apparel to suit his age, and dress him like a doll, like a prince's son; have his hair cut, wash him, clean him, and dress him as best you can, and then take him to see Adelaida Petrovna. Do you hear?"

"I do, Your Excellency."

"Have him ready by six o'clock. I'll be there this evening."

The butler signaled to me, and I followed him out.

Without further questions, he seated me next to him in a cart and took me to the tailor. He left me there, ordering him to fulfill the prince's directive immediately and saying that he'd return in several hours. The tailor's wife went running out to buy me some linen. The tailor found some magnificent ready-made clothes, a jacket, and fine-twilled, violet woolen trousers with gilded buttons. The shoemaker brought in a pair of shoes. My hair was given a bowl cut, Russian style.

The barber combed it and curled it. The tailor's wife soon returned with the linen and an embroidered shirtfront: she washed me herself and couldn't refrain from kissing my red cheeks. I almost didn't recognize myself when I looked in the mirror and proudly perceived that I was more handsome than all of the children of Mr. Gologordovsky, Mr. Skotinko, and the boys I'd seen in these gentlemen's houses. The butler returned shortly and was also astonished at my transformation. We got in the cart again and journeyed to the place indicated by the prince. I asked no questions, merely admired my new appearance.

On arriving at a small, clean, wooden house, we stopped, and the butler led me by the hand into the rooms. The lackey opened the door into the dining room, and I almost fainted with joy when I saw the same lady who'd interrogated me yesterday in the shop. She also shouted for joy and rushed to hug and kiss me, led me to another room, and dismissed the butler. When we were left alone, the lady sat down on the sofa, sat me next to her, told me to take off my jacket, examined the mark on my left shoulder, and began to cry. I cried, too, thinking that the kind lady must have had a reason for her sorrow.

"Vanya," she said to me. "You'll no longer be a servant. You're my nephew, my sister's son. You must call me *aunt* and tell no one who you were previously. From now on you'll be a young gentleman, just like the children of Gologordovsky and Skotinko."

"Oh, no, auntie!" I said. "I want to be much better than they are. They treat poor boys and servants badly, play pranks, deceive their parents, and don't study properly."

My aunt kissed me instead of replying.

"Would you like anything, Vanya?" she asked.

"I'm hungry, auntie."

She rang for the servants. A maid appeared, and my aunt told her to feed me, explaining who I was, and ordered her to give me to a separate room and arrange everything for my comfort.

My aunt, Adelaida Petrovna, was about thirty years old, but by her face, she seemed much younger. She was a beauty in every sense of the word. Her black hair, soft as down, lent her pale face a special hue; a fresh rosy tint colored her cheeks. Her features were regular and animated by the sweetness of her smile and her sincere kindness. Her dark eyes, overshadowed by her long eyelashes and tender brows, attracted one's gaze like a magnet attracting iron. Her full pink lips and white teeth invited a kiss on her lovely mouth. She was tall, and her bearing was beautiful. In a word, my aunt's appearance was attractive, and her polite and pleasant behavior added charm to her beauty.

My aunt spoke French and Italian, played the piano extremely well, and sang like a nightingale. She lived comfortably; the house was fairly spacious and extremely well furnished. She had the following servants: two lackeys, two maids, a cook, a coachman, and a caretaker for menial work. She kept a pair of beautiful horses in her stable. Her house didn't lack for anything. She entertained many guests, with very few women among them, and they were mostly actresses and foreigners. She gave a musical evening every week attended by various virtuosos and celebrities, mostly older people. Young folk and middle-aged men came only with their relatives, very infrequently. In addition, my aunt received guests for tea every day, and some were invited to stay for dinner or supper.

Prince Chvanov came daily and was something like a papa in the house. The servants obeyed him as if he were their master, and my aunt submitted to him, although at times unwillingly, as I observed. Sometimes the prince argued with my aunt in private; she always wept on such occasions and would sometimes even faint. Then the prince would kiss her hands, beg her forgiveness, and their friendship would be restored to its previous basis. But I observed clearly and came to understand that my aunt didn't care for the prince's visits; she always frowned when his carriage drove up to the porch and always smiled pleasantly when it left together with him.

My aunt was one of those women who regard beauty as one of the greatest goods, dressing up as the most important necessity of life; her principal pleasure was the gratification of men and the envy of women. She spent a great deal of her time planning what to wear and how to appear in public in all the glory of her beauty and wealth. Even her favorite pastime, music, served merely as a pretext for attracting to her house people of good society who, merely on that account, presented themselves as connoisseurs of this art. She was the widow of an Italian named Baritono, who at one time was engaged in giving music and singing lessons. I didn't know anything about my aunt's origins, and she never talked about her relatives or her own birthplace. She called herself a Russian and frequently attended mass and vespers in a Russian church, but only on major holidays. At the time I joined her household, she was particularly friendly with a young gentleman who served in Moscow, Semyon Semyonovich Plezirin. He carried out all of my aunt's commissions, escorted her to the theater, to concerts, and for strolls, and a few times a day he would call at her house, but always when old Prince Chvanov wasn't there. Plezirin would only appear at the musical evenings in the presence of the prince and then would address himself to my aunt with cold politeness, as if there were no close friendship between them, only a musical bond. My aunt's other confidant was the French Abbé Pretatout; he was about forty-five years old, with a pleasant appearance and a very cheerful demeanor. He was a family friend of Prince Chvanov, lived in his house with bed and board provided; he received a salary, or, better to say, a pension for the education of his son (who was already serving in Petersburg); he supervised the prince's library, looked after his paintings, and was a confidant in all private matters. Abbé Pretatout also visited my aunt almost every day but never encountered Plezirin. My aunt maintained strict order in everything; every meeting was set for a specific time. There were four entrances to her house, each to a specific room and on a different side: one from the street, another through the gate, a third from the courtyard, and a fourth from the garden. Her guests entered and left without meeting each other, if that's what my aunt preferred. All of her visitors were tenderly attached to her, and I was very surprised that those same people who were so friendly with her in her house didn't even greet her on the street or in the theater, when they were with other women; they would always turn away, as if not noticing my aunt. The women would regard her with a smile or sullenly and, seeing her, always exchanged whispers among themselves. But my aunt was so kind that nothing angered her. She treated her own servants very kindly, and got angry with her maid only on occasion, when, helping her to get dressed, she did something awkwardly, reluctantly, or too slowly. But she always made up for her momentary lapses of temper with a polite word or gift, and therefore the maid was devoted to her, even more than the other servants. In a word, my aunt was beloved by everyone who knew her; and I, who got to know her last of all, loved her more than anyone and was the first object of her tenderness and care.

I had my own room with a clean bed and chest of drawers filled with clothes and linen. My aunt and her servant fed me and caressed me from morning to evening. Every day my aunt took me out to walk with her and complimented my external appearance enthusiastically. All of her acquaintances and friends pampered me and gave me sweets and toys. Three months passed since my fate had changed, and I could hardly come to my senses. Sometimes I dreamed of my previous situation: I would wake up screaming and begin to weep, fearing a return of my cruel existence. I would always relate my terrible dreams to my aunt, who would console me with assurances that my misfortune would never be repeated. At last, little by little, I began to forget about my previous situation. That's even forgivable during one's childhood. How many grown-ups in their good fortune forget what they were before? And even worse, how many avoid those who drew them out of their misfortune? At least I didn't resemble them in this regard: I adored my aunt.

Once Plezirin arrived very early, not at his usual time. They served coffee, and my aunt called me into her room.

"Vanya, it's time for you to get educated," she said. "By my calculation, you must be at least twelve years old. Semyon Semyonovich has found you some tutors. You'll study French and German, learn to play the piano, and to dance. Would you like to do that?"

"How could I not like to do that, if it would please you, auntie?" I replied.

"Remember that if you study diligently, you'll always be as well-dressed as you are now, and you'll always eat well; but if you know nothing, you may fall into misfortune again." I began trembling from these words, and in a quivering voice, I replied, "I shall study diligently, auntie!"

"Good, Vanechka," she replied, and turning to Plezirin, she added, "I told you before that he must have a surname: it must be decided today. Come up with one."

Plezirin got to thinking, paced the room several times, and said, "You told me, Adelaida Petrovna, that you recognized your nephew by his astonishing likeness to his late father, and you confirmed the accuracy of your guess by the mark left on his shoulder, a result of a small growth in his infancy."

"Exactly," replied my aunt.

"And so, your nephew should be called *Vyzhigin*:[1] it's a name to remind him of the fortunate change in his life as a result of that mark . . . and . . ."

My aunt didn't allow him to finish. "Splendid, splendid!" she cried. From now on, Vanya will be called Ivan Ivanovich Vyzhigin. Do you hear, Vanya?"

"I do."

"Well, what's your name?"

1. "The seared" (Rus.).

"Ivan Ivanovich Vyzhigin."

"Very good," said my aunt. "And who are you?"

"I'm Adelaida Petrovna Baritono's nephew."

"Excellent," said my aunt. "Now remember that your father was a civil servant from the nobility and was called Ivanov; he even managed to amass a sizable estate; unfortunately, he was ruined and died when you were still a child; and your mother, my sister, was also of the nobility and married out of love; she died only one day after you were born. Since your father left no living relatives, it doesn't make any difference what your name is: Ivanov or Vyzhigin."

I remained silent and listened.

"Now, Vanya, go to your room," said my aunt. "Your lessons will begin tomorrow."

Plezirin, who loved to make jokes, bowed to me, saying, "Good-bye, Ivan Ivanovich Vyzhigin. I hope you'll love your godfather and regard him with favor."

My aunt started laughing and said, "I'll allow you to love him, but I forbid you from resembling him—otherwise you'll deserve to be called a *mauvais sujet* (a scoundrel)."

I'd been familiar with this French expression for some time because the children of Mr. Gologordovsky and Mr. Skotinko were called that in their absence by their teachers; therefore I considered it my duty to reply, "Don't worry, auntie, I won't try to resemble Semyon Semyonovich."

The next day my tutors appeared. The German, Herr Biersaufer, a stuffy old man sprinkled with tobacco, whose ruddy face revealed the glories of Bacchus. Monsieur Felix, a young Frenchman, a worker from a pomade factory, who by imparting grammar to beginners taught himself to become a tutor. Herr Schmiernoten, also a German, a teacher of music and singing; although he knew the theory of music very well, he played the piano so poorly and roared so loudly and clumsily that everyone in the house covered his ears when he felt like singing or playing after his lessons. I learned how to dance in dancing school, taught by a lame theatrical dancer who had broken his leg while playing the part of some monster during a performance of some magic ballet.

My language teachers followed opposite methods. When I'd learned to read, the German began to beat the rules of grammar into my head, while the Frenchman cared little for grammar and made me memorize long lists of words and expressions. Since French was spoken in our house almost constantly, all of our guests, vying with one another, examined me to assess my progress in learning the language. The result was that I soon started jabbering away in French and understood all their conversations, to my aunt's great delight. When I had begun to understand what I read, Monsieur Felix began to teach me grammar: that is, he explained what gender was, both nouns and adjectives; he taught me to use *les articles* and to conjugate auxiliary verbs. Within a year I could already speak French as well, and almost as confidently, as our acquaintances, but in German I barely made it to the declensions.

I learned to play the piano much better than my music teacher, and I sang so well that at our musical evenings I would perform solos. Dancing for me was a real pleasure: in the course of a year I learned not only the waltz and the quadrille but also the minuet, the allemande, and many other fashionable dances. When I turned fourteen, after one year of education, I was, in my aunt's words, *un jeune homme accompli*,[2] a chatterbox, smart, bold, even daring: all of these qualities were said to be marks of genius. A counselor of my aunt's friends advised her to send me off to a fine boarding school to make me a *learned man*. Prince Chvanov took it upon himself to pay for my education. But since my aunt didn't want to part with me under any circumstances, on my name day, when, according to my aunt's calculation, I turned fourteen, I was enrolled as a day student in Monsieur Lebrilliant's school, where the children of the best Russian families studied. I was supplied with books, given a splendid briefcase, and began attending class conscientiously, observing that my successes in my studies afforded my aunt gratification and also resulted in more presents for me.

I had promised my aunt to be better than the children of Gologordovsky and Skotinko, but inasmuch as the same reasons result in the same outcomes, from overindulgence I acquired the same vices. People embraced and praised me to my face; I became haughty and imagined that I was superior to everyone else. They never refused me anything, and this roused my desires because whims are conceived according to the possibility of fulfilling them. At the boarding school the older children (having observed the activities of their parents) played cards, treated each other to breakfasts, and those among us who could spend more money enjoyed more respect from their comrades. When I was short on cash for my amusements, I thought up essential necessities; not daring to confess to my aunt what we did in secret, I asked for funds

2. An accomplished young man (Fr.).

to buy books, paints, compasses, and paper; thus I learned to lie and deceive. My aunt and her well-to-do friends fulfilled my desires without contradicting me, and so I came to regard it as an unpardonable sin if a servant delayed in carrying out my orders; as a result I became rude in my treatment of them, arrogant, and capricious. I treated my poor comrades impertinently, my wealthy comrades—haughtily, considering myself richer than the former and better than the latter. I wasn't afraid of the teachers and governors and therefore didn't respect the proprietor of the boarding school, who was afraid to lose Prince Chvanov's patronage and my aunt's gifts, so he flattered me, turned a blind eye to my pranks, and paid no attention to the teachers' complaints.

So without willing it, I became just like those children whom I had previously considered so unbearable. I even lost my desire to study because my head was constantly occupied by something else. Fortunately, my exceptional memory and natural grasp of things replaced diligence: hearing the lessons in passing and never bothering to memorize them, I knew better than the others everything that was being taught in the school, except mathematics. The study of math requires fixed attention, repetition, and exercises; and since those were not to my liking, I resolutely declared to my aunt that I had no inclination or ability for mathematics. She conferred with Mr. Plezirin and Abbé Pretatout, and they agreed to end my math lessons, and all of my progress in that field was limited to arithmetic.

Chapter 10

Examination in Boarding School. A Tempter. My Aunt's New Friend. Something Like First Love. Departure from Moscow.

The age of childhood passes swiftly. I grew, living in luxury in my aunt's house, studying, playing pranks in boarding school, and having no time to notice what was going on inside our house; therefore I have nothing to say about it. The date approached for my solemn examination in school and my graduation from the upper class in which I was one of the best students. The oldest of us was no more than seventeen years old, but we all considered ourselves worthy of occupying the most important positions in government; we regretted the time we lost not for studying but for earning an officer's commission.[1] With impatience we awaited the examination, about which our parents were notified two weeks in advance. Preparations began: each pupil was given a certain number of questions and answers beforehand to learn by heart; the teachers conducted rehearsals daily, training us by various signals what to reply if any of the spectators asked about something not covered in the previous questions. For example, each button on the language teachers' coat and vest stood for a different part of speech and the various rules of grammar. All of their movements had special significance. The piano teacher's nose represented a bastion, his

1. In the Russian army, no commissions were awarded until the candidate had served time in the ranks.

mouth a moat, his teeth palisades, his chin a sloping bank, his eyes a fortification, his neck a bridgehead, and so on. The head of the geography teacher represented the universe. The crown of his head denoted the zenith, his chin the nadir, his cheeks turning circles, his nose the ecliptic, his beard the first meridian, his mouth the ocean, his eyes the stationary stars, and so on. In addition to the teachers, students also learned how to assist their comrades by means of signals. Monsieur Lebrilliant prepared certificates for each student to show to their parents, relatives, and guardians. A good or bad testimonial of learning and behavior didn't depend on the success and conduct of the student, rather on the distinction, wealth, generosity, and degree of attachment shown the children by their parents and relatives. Those from whom M. Lebrilliant hoped to obtain the greatest benefit received the best testimonial, but since no one supposed that there were pranksters and idlers in the school, the bad testimonials were awarded to those children whose parents were absent or to orphans, whose guardians were usually unconcerned about them, and to two poor boarders, who were being educated free of charge by M. Lebrilliant, so that he might become known for his generosity and magnanimity. All of the students who were supposed to receive awards—purchased, of course, with their own money—and good testimonials were informed about this in secret beforehand, so that they could invite as many of their relatives and friends to the ceremony as possible. At last, after all these preparations, the solemn occasion took place.

The hall was crowded with visitors, civil servants, ladies, and scholars who were friends of M. Lebrilliant. The event was opened by a speech in French, which I delivered with the greatest confidence. The address was composed by Abbé Pretatout and corrected by the teachers, including the calligraphy teacher. For the preference shown to me, my aunt gave M. Lebrilliant's wife a piece of silk and some lace, which she'd received as a gift from Prince Chvanov. The examination of the older students went fairly smoothly, thanks to the agreed-upon signals. Many of the official visitors asked us difficult questions, which we knew in advance—and the inexperienced parents were astonished at our knowledge. But there were several obtuse students, who'd learned by heart neither the assigned questions nor the agreed-upon signals, and as a result, there were several extremely awkward hesitations and exchanges. For example, they asked the son of the chief secretary, "What sort of occupation or profession yields the most money in the government?" In vain did the teacher of statistics keep sticking his hand in his side pocket, which, by our agreed-upon signals, indicated *trade*—the young man, having heard from his parents discussion of the same question, thought he was giving the proper reply, said, "Lawsuits!" Everyone began laughing, and the lad's father covered his face with his handkerchief, as if he were wiping away perspiration. Another student, son of a wealthy and arrogant solicitor, was asked, "What *auxiliary verbs* are there in Russian?" He remained silent. His father, not satisfied with his silence, said in annoyance, "Vanya, have you forgotten what you learned before you left home?"

Someone whispered into Vanya's ear, and he replied, "*We* have two active verbs: *to lie and to take*."

A burst of laughter once again resounded from all ends of the hall, and the proud solicitor blushed from anger. M. Lebrilliant, to avoid further temptation, began to interrogate the students himself. He asked questions so skillfully that they were answered successfully, to the greatest satisfaction of the mothers and aunts. Here are some examples of M. Lebrilliant's pedagogy.

"What is the name of the capital of Spain?" asked M. Lebrilliant. "Isn't it Madrid?"

"Madrid," replied the pupil.

"Splendid. And on which river is it situated? Isn't it perhaps the Manzanares?"

"Madrid is situated on the Manzanares River," replied the pupil quickly and loudly.

"Very good, very good indeed; have a seat. Now tell me, Mr. N. N., is it fair to call the Volga the longest river in European Russia?"

"The longest river in European Russia is the Volga," replied the pupil immediately.

"Very good. Splendid. Tell me, Mr. N. N., who was the Roman emperor when Augustus was the first to assume the imperial distinction?"

"Augustus," replied the pupil.

"Very good," said M. Lebrilliant.

In this way all of the pupils gave satisfactory answers to M. Lebrilliant's questions, and their tender parents agreed unanimously that the teaching in the boarding school was first-rate and if the children sometimes answered inappropriately, it was only because the teachers didn't know how to ask the questions as well as the learned M. Lebrilliant.

The examination lasted two hours; afterwards we were given our awards and diplomas amid the sounds of trumpets and kettledrums, and they sent the pupils off with their parents. The men—that is, the friends of the proprietor, the teachers who helped to examine us using the agreed-on signals, and the domestic friends of wealthy parents—all stayed to have dinner with M. Lebrilliant, to whom, the day before, baskets had been sent from various houses with bottles of wine. There were no classes for three days afterwards because the teachers were resting after the feast.

Although I'd already finished the course of study taught in the boarding school, at Abbé Pretatout's advice I was to continue attending lectures in the school while they discussed what was to become of me. I heard from the next room how the abbé gave my aunt instructions on this matter.

"Let Vanya continue at the boarding school," said the abbé. "It will cost you nothing, because the prince will pay for it. It's not necessary for his education but so that he doesn't learn at home what he doesn't need to know. Youth is inquisitive and quick on the uptake, and our Vanya has always been clever and quick-witted beyond his years. Do you understand me? We'll soon find a position for him."

"Let it be as you advise," replied my good aunt. "From my love for him, I'm ready to do anything."

As soon as my classmates left the boarding school, I considered myself better than everyone else and stopped studying. During class I read books supplied by a common acquaintance at the school, Luka Ivanovich Vorovatin. He wasn't acquainted with my aunt, and it was my comrades who introduced me to him. He lived opposite our school and was on friendly terms not only with M. Lebrilliant but also with all the teachers and tutors; therefore, in our free time from classes, they allowed the boarders to visit him and sometimes stay there until midnight. Luka Ivanovich taught us to play all sorts of card games, even faro. He let us smoke pipes; allowed us to drink wine, punch, and vodka; and amused us with accounts of his amorous adventures. He had a small library of forbidden books, and everything obscene which fell into his hands, in prose or verse, was preserved in his little collection of manuscripts. Several portfolios were filled with prints and drawings, which he, most likely, never dared show anyone except us, so inexperienced, and his friends, who were as depraved as he was. In his conversations with us, he was constantly making fun of men's spiritual and civic obligations, the burden of ties to one's own relatives, and respect for one's parents—in a word, everything that good men consider sacred.

Luka Ivanovich carefully observed our inclinations, gradually developed our passions, aroused our desires, and constantly maintained that the goal of life was enjoyment and that in aspiring to any goal the surest and safest method to achieve it was always the easiest. According to Mr. Vorovatin's rules, children had only one obligation in life with regard to their parents—namely, to pretend to be the kind of person their parents wished them to be. He considered frankness with one's parents and other adults a vice and foolishness. Mr. Vorovatin cloaked his diabolical rules under the sobriquet of the *new philosophy*; and under the name of the *laws of nature* and the *rights of man*, he sowed in our inexperienced hearts ideas of unbelief and the concept of animal equality. We thought his ideas exceedingly pleasant because we found in them everything that could flatter our vanity and support our imaginary claim of independence. We considered ourselves eighteenth-century philosophers; everyone who disagreed with Mr. Vorovatin and us we called barbarians and ignoramuses. Vorovatin knew all sorts of scandalous anecdotes about the best families in town; by exposing our parents' weaknesses, he eradicated in our hearts all seeds of attachment and respect for our elders.

He lived by playing and by all sorts of other schemes: he lent money to wealthy heirs, won it back from them, traded in promissory notes and purchases bought on credit in the shops, and served as a procurer and agent in all the love intrigues for young and old, men and women. The entire town knew Vorovatin, and although he didn't show himself in decent families on the days they received visitors, he was very often summoned for advice and assistance by the wealthy and people of rank.

Luka Ivanovich was around forty years old, short, and lean. He had reddish hair and a pale face covered in wrinkles, the premature results of debauchery. He was always squinting, and his somber look aroused some sort of unpleasant impression. Vorovatin boasted that he'd already managed to foster an entire generation in the rules of his new philosophy; as a matter of fact, the greatest scoundrels and debauchers in the capital were his friends from their youth. Not one of them had escaped from under his wing free of charge: he helped them to squander their money and was the first to take advantage of their ruined circumstances. Devout people referred to Vorovatin as a *demon*, young people as a *fine fellow*, and inexperienced youth, as I already said, as a *philosopher*. In police records he was known as a *cheating gambler* and a *crook*.

Luka Ivanovich was especially attached to me, predicting that I'd become a great philosopher and would attain a high degree of wealth and fame. In my presence he never spoke ill of my aunt, knowing my devotion to her; however, he forbade me to mention our friendship to her, saying that he was a personal enemy of both Prince Chvanov and Plezirin, who could smear him to my aunt, and that she, due to her feminine naïveté, might dissolve our friendship. Vorovatin even gave me money for cards and for my other needs; he referred to me as none other than his younger brother. I was a sort of second landlord in his quarters; I came whenever I pleased, did what I wished, and even if he wasn't at home, I ordered around his servants, treated my comrades at his expense, and regarded his property as if it were my own. Is it a wonder that this behavior of Vorovatin's forced me to believe that he loved me for my own personal qualities? And this same idea made me feel attached to him. I was even proud of his showing me such preference. There were no secrets between us; according to his wishes, I related all my adventures to him, the misfortunes of my childhood, the meeting with my aunt, and finally showed him the lucky mark on my shoulder by which she became convinced that I was her nephew. It seemed that from the time of my candor, Vorovatin came to love me even more tenderly. He was the first person to whom I opened myself up.

Meanwhile a personage who had occupied an important position in Petersburg began visiting my aunt's house very frequently; he retired and settled in Moscow to enjoy the fortune he'd acquired (I don't know whether it was honestly or not) during his long years of service. Mr. Grabilin was about fifty years old but was hale and hearty in spite of his years. He was proud, bold in words and deeds, and capricious, and his behavior often caused my aunt to shed tears. He became the master of the house, appointed his own servants, and forbade my aunt from receiving guests without his permission, except for a few elderly musicians. Grabilin didn't respond, turn around, or reply if he wasn't addressed as *Your Excellency*. Semyon Semyonovich and Abbé Pretatout didn't dare appear in our house; only Prince Chvanov kept coming as before. My aunt referred to him as her godfather and benefactor, and Grabilin dared not oppose the prince; on the contrary, he took advantage of this situation by forming a fast friendship with him. The two old men spent time together, sometimes talking about politics; meanwhile, my aunt would slip away to her neighbor, a friend who lived in the other half of the house, where she was sure to find Semyon Semyonovich or another one of her acquaintances. The matters of state in which the two old men no longer took part interested them so much that in the heat of their quarrels and gossip, they didn't worry at all about my aunt's absence. However, since Grabilin's appearance, everything had changed in my aunt's house; even the musical evenings were cancelled and in general a mood of gloom prevailed, instead of the former joviality.

I was particularly bored. Grabilin treated me with arrogance; he hardly deigned to look at me, criticized every immodest word, every free action, and he didn't like it when, as was my habit, I would intervene in the conversations. I avoided his presence, and under the pretext of studying at boarding school, I almost came to live at Vorovatin's.

Vorovatin introduced me to several homes where, without any further connections, I was invited to dine, sup, and dance. Most often I visited a close female friend of Vorovatin's who had a lovely daughter. Matryona Ivanovna Shtosina—a widow aged about thirty-five, cheerful and whimsical—loved the amusements of society and card games. She had a rather large circle of acquaintances among clerks of various kinds of visiting gentry from the provinces. Her husband was some sort of civil servant in a profitable position and, after his death, had left her a house and a considerable income. Almost every evening she hosted guests, men and women, who played cards and talked about business affairs in general. They began with commercial card competitions but always ended up playing faro and other games. Her daughter, Grunya,[2] who was in her fifteenth year, was known for her beauty. She was a pensive girl and spent most of her time alone in her room, reading sentimental novels; she knew *The Sorrows of Young Werther* and *The New Heloise* by heart.[3] I had the opportunity of chatting with her fairly often while her mother was gambling at cards. I very soon became closely acquainted with Grunya, and after some quarrels about morality and philosophy, we agreed to initiate a correspondence between us on various philosophical matters to improve our French skills and increase our intelligence. But intelligence doesn't like to mingle in the affairs of young gentlemen and young ladies. Our philosophical letters soon assumed the tone of the affectionate Saint-Preux and the tenderhearted Julie,[4] and without knowing why or when, we expressed our love for one another and dreamed of our future bliss. Of course, Vorovatin was my confidant in this love affair. He would encourage me, enflaming my

2. A nickname for Agrafenya.

3. *Die Leiden des jungen Werthers* is an epistolary novel written by Johann Wolfgang von Goethe in 1774. *Julie, ou la nouvelle Héloïse* is an epistolary novel by Jean-Jacques Rousseau, published in 1761. Both were extremely popular with young Russians, especially women.

4. The main characters in Rousseau's *Julie.*

inexperienced heart with hopes and descriptions of being loved, and he advised me how to behave with Grunya.

In misfortune a youth matures quickly, while a man grows old. It's only in contentment and overindulgence that the young mind grows weak and gets stuck in mediocrity. But a child, left on his or her own, either perishes or deploys all his moral powers with unusual alacrity. I've already said that since my childhood I'd been regarded as clever beyond my years. My physical constitution also developed extremely early, surrounded by all the comforts of life; at the age of seventeen, I seemed like a youth of twenty. Passions seethed powerfully in my bosom; thousands of desires disturbed my thoughts, but no one passion controlled me exclusively. Sometimes, looking at a man of high rank, with all his stars and ribbons, or at a general in a dazzling uniform, I suffered from ambition for several days and made plans to attain honors. At another time, a splendid equipage, rich attire, or a magnificent house extinguished all sparks of ambition and gave birth to my desire for wealth: I pined in contemplation of the means to acquire an immense fortune in the shortest possible time. Sometimes a desire for fame aggravated my soul—and I conceived of projects that would be spoken and written about throughout the world. At last the sight of a charming woman walking arm in arm with a gentleman would excite in my breast a wish to possess such a treasure—and I began thinking about love and marriage. My passions combined with the impressions I received, without leaving any trace in my heart. But at long last, my friendship with Grunya, the daily correspondence with her and our frequent meetings, revealed a new walk of life and devoured all the other buds of passion. I tried to convince myself that I was in love—that I had to be in love, that it was impossible not to be in love. Grunya was beautiful, clever, or at least engaging to me by her conversation, which revealed a familiarity with French novels. She loved me, and in my imagination I added all possible perfections to her actual good qualities, and I created an ideal, which I was pleased to call Grunya. Forcing myself to think about my love, I dreamed about Grunya constantly, and on all occasions I sought an application for my passion. If, during my strolls, I heard some peasant driver singing a song, "Eyes, my eyes, my lovely eyes!" I immediately began thinking about Grunya's dark blue eyes. If I heard someone say about a woman, "Ah, she's so nice!" I would say to myself, "My Grunya is much nicer!" If it was said of someone that he was happy with his wife—I thought that I would be much happier with my dear Grunya. In a word, Grunya was always in my heart and in my mind, and I tried to keep her before my eyes and on my tongue: for this, if I couldn't be with her, I was always with Vorovatin, with whom I could speak about my love.

By the time they reached their fifteenth year, provincial girls were more grown up; Grunya loved me more with her heart than her imagination. Her mind worked hard only to search for romantic names for me and for expressions of tenderness. Her heart was completely occupied with me. She would spend the night without sleep and in tears if she hadn't seen me for one whole day. When I couldn't visit her, at least I had to go past her windows and make the usual signal with my hand that I was pleased with her and had received her letter. When we were alone together, our greatest happiness consisted in looking each other in the eye, holding hands, and repeating a thousand times previously uttered expressions of tenderness, which seemed to us, or at least to her, a novelty. Grunya loved to stroke my chubby, rosy cheeks with her hand while I played with her soft curls. It goes without saying that I swore a thousand times not to marry anyone but her, and she swore not to marry anyone but me. But when and how—we didn't think about that at all. It seemed very ordinary to marry and live like songbirds. I awaited permission with impatience to forsake my boarding school and to cast off the role of student. I decided to ask my aunt about it.

Once, after dinner, when my aunt seemed more cheerful than usual, I approached her intending to carry out my plan.

"Dearest auntie," I said. "You're paying money to the boarding school in vain. I know everything that they teach there by heart, and I'm only wasting time, listening to what I already know. I speak French like a Frenchman, my German is tolerable, I dance gracefully, in history, geography, and other subjects I know as much as the teachers; besides, thanks to you, I've become a good musician. What else do I need? I can't be and don't want to be a teacher; I'm already too educated to be a man of the world. You know so many distinguished and important people: review all of them in your mind and tell me who knows more than I do? Wouldn't it be better if I stayed home and devoted myself to improving my mind by reading and at the same time, sought my happiness in the civil service or elsewhere? Consider it, auntie, and please, don't listen to that bear of a man, Grabilin, who only advises you to send me off to boarding school so that he can get rid of me." I noticed that my aunt blushed at those last words.

"Do as you like, Vanechka," she said. "I don't want to force you. I can see for myself that you're brighter than everyone I know."

"And so, tomorrow will be the last day I go to boarding school," I said.

"The last day," repeated my aunt, "but there's no need to tell Grabilin about it. You'll stay in your room when he comes to visit me or else leave the house."

"Splendid!" I rushed to kiss my aunt and that very day informed M. Lebrilliant that I would no longer be attending his boarding school. Since my fees had been paid for the half year in advance and we didn't ask for a refund of the money, he was satisfied and provided such a glowing testimonial on a large sheet of parchment that if one were to believe half of what he said, I could be considered on a par with the seven sages of Greece.[5] My aunt and I sincerely believed everything stated in the testimonial: she—because she loved me so dearly, and I—because up to then I hadn't met a man who'd earned my respect through his knowledge and intelligence.

Readers, you've probably noticed already that up to this point no one has been mentioned who gave me lessons in religion, morality, or the enhancement of the heart. At first I was in the very lowest rank of society, but after that, I was suddenly raised to a level occupied only by children of high rank and wealth. In the first condition no one worries about the moral nature of a person; people are content with having their servants taught the mechanical use of their corporeal functions, just as poodles are taught to carry something in their mouths; in the other condition I mentioned, they're raised to turn a boy into a man who in everything resembles the people who, by birth or fortune, have the right to live in so-called high society. But since in higher circles there's no talk of religion or philosophy, and no attention is paid to learned people, or to the sciences, or the behavior of one's acquaintances—the French language, dancing, and a knowledge of society's customs constitute all of social refinement. For this alone money is paid to French tutors who do only what's required of them. I must solemnly confess that in no way is M. Lebrilliant responsible for the fact that after I'd completed my education in his boarding school, I had no conception of the obligations of a man and a citizen. No one asked him about that, and a well-bred person need not bother himself with matters that no one asks about. To fulfill one's duty according to one's conscience is largely a concern

5. The title given by classical Greek tradition to seven philosophers, statesmen, and lawgivers of the sixth century.

of the middle class, who, in society are called in French "bad company," *la mauvaise compagnie*!

I barely had time to enjoy my freedom for a month before grief darkened my sweet idleness. One evening when Mrs. Shtosina was playing cards, as usual, I sought a chance to chat privately with Grunya; the servant girl, walking past me, whispered to me that I should proceed directly to the young lady's boudoir. I found Grunya in tears. She told me that her mother was taking her to Orenburg[6] to receive the inheritance of some property left by her husband's cousin. This respected cousin was first secretary of the Department of Salt, and afterwards he became superintendent of the barter trade with the Kirghiz. All his life he was known as a very poor man, and several times he even received financial support from the government because of his insufficient income; but after his death, when they began to seal up his property, they found pawnshop tickets and promissory notes worth more than half a million rubles. During his lifetime, one never heard anything about his relatives, and even Mr. Shtosin avoided him each time it was necessary to assist him; but as soon as the inheritance was revealed, several dozen relatives turned up, who, in memory of the dear departed man, began taking each other to court. Mrs. Shtosina's departure was set for a week hence and her return—at an undetermined time. After weeping together, Grunya and I repeated our oaths of eternal love and loyalty and agreed to write one another with every post, until I could find an opportunity of joining her in Orenburg. I promised this to Grunya, not thinking how I could fulfill my promise. The next day I immediately told my friend Vorovatin everything that had happened; he swore to help me, even to take me to Orenburg; on his advice, I should abduct Grunya, marry her, and as an heir of the wealthy Kirghiz superintendent, I should demand my share in a legal process, if Mrs. Shtosina didn't want to turn over the inheritance of her own free will. Grunya, on her father's side, was the real heiress of the fortune.

Meanwhile, Grabilin somehow found out that I'd left my studies in boarding school; just as he'd previously driven me out of his house to go to school, now he tried to drive me into the civil service. I resolved to use his dislike of me to my own advantage.

It would be futile to describe the tears, sobs, swoons at my parting with Grunya. These are boring things and well known to all. As soon

6. A city on the Ural River, about nine hundred miles southeast of Moscow, very close to the border with Kazakhstan.

as she left for Orenburg, I began to search for a means to make haste after her. Vorovatin, feeling sorry for my sadness, resolved immediately to escort me to my beloved and even advised me to leave without seeking my aunt's permission. But I didn't agree to that, and a month after Grunya's departure, I managed to wheedle my aunt's permission in the following manner.

"Auntie!" I said. "I've been promised a good position at the Mint in Moscow. But since some experience is necessary, one of my acquaintances who works in the Department of Mines wants to take me with him to Orenburg. He'll spend no more than four months there to conduct his business, and I'll go there as his clerk. When I return to Moscow, I'll have the right to claim a position in the civil service, and my protector promises that I'll be immediately accepted on his recommendation due to my previous work. Will you agree, auntie? Isn't it better if I'm obligated for my happiness to my own work and to myself rather than to your friends, who, it seems, don't like me very much? You know that without the rank of officer, I can't really appear in good company."

For a long time my aunt wouldn't agree to part with me, but when I told Mr. Grabilin this story, conceived by Vorovatin, he prevailed on my aunt to release me. One of Vorovatin's friends had assumed the role of an official in the Department of Mines for my aunt, and he gave her his assurance that he would take me under his protection, promising her all possible advantages in the service. My aunt prepared me for the journey and filled my purse generously. Even Grabilin gave me a gift of fifty rubles in silver. The kind old man, Prince Chvanov, who by then had an incurable habit of visiting my aunt daily, also gave me some money and a letter of recommendation to the governor. After bidding farewell to my aunt, I climbed into the carriage with Vorovatin's friend, while he himself waited for us beyond the gate. I was like a man in a fever from the struggle of conflicting feelings: love for my aunt, sorrow and grief that I was leaving her, and the joyous hope of seeing Grunya again, marrying, and acquiring wealth and independence. The distraction of the travel calmed me to some extent, but unintentionally I kept thinking more about my aunt than about Grunya.

Chapter 11

I Get to Know Vorovatin Better. An Overheard Conversation. Premonitions. A Police Captain.

"How much money do you have?" Vorovatin asked me at the first posting station.

"A hundred and fifty silver rubles."

"Splendid little capital," cried Vorovatin. "Very few people at your age have that much money in hand. You're richer than I am, Vanya. Justice demands that you pay half of our traveling expenses."

"I never thought otherwise," I replied. "I wanted to settle with you when we reach our destination."

"It's all the same," said Vorovatin, "but since you're not used to handling money, why not give it to me for safekeeping?"

"It's quite safe in my suitcase."

"It would be better off in my locked trunk," replied Vorovatin.

"As you wish!" I said, and immediately turned my money over to him, keeping a few silver rubles for incidental expenses. For several stations Vorovatin was silent and brooding; finally he started a conversation in a serious, cool tone of voice.

"Can it be that your aunt never told you about your father?" asked Vorovatin, fixing a penetrating look on me.

"Nothing except what I've told you."

"That's strange, very strange," grumbled Vorovatin.

"I don't think it's strange," I said. "If there'd been anything curious about my late father's life, my aunt would most likely have told me. Do you know anything more?" I asked, looking him in the eye. "You'll do me a great favor if you can tell me something on that account."

"How should I know?" Vorovatin replied drily.

"If it disturbs you so little, why don't you believe me?"

"You still don't know women's ways and schemes," said Vorovatin. "When you've suffered at their hands, you'll be more skeptical."

"I haven't the slightest reason to doubt my aunt; she loves me like her own son, has done everything for me that she could, and is prepared to sacrifice everything on my account."

"That's exactly why," retorted Vorovatin, "it's hard to believe your aunt never said anything to you about your father's financial situation, about his future hopes, and his various adventures."

"Although you've given me much advice on the subject of insincerity, I haven't yet learned to follow your instructions," I said with some irritation. "I repeat: my aunt's told me everything she considered necessary about my father's financial situation and about his lineage; as for his adventures, I suppose, if she was silent, it was because they were not that interesting. Besides, when I return to Moscow, I'll ask her about this subject, which up to now I've considered of little interest, in more detail."

"It's too late now," said Vorovatin, with a feigned smile.

"How so?" I asked.

Vorovatin suddenly started laughing with a terrible laugh and said, "We'll see what we shall see!"

He directed the conversation to other subjects and tried to distract me, but I felt sadness in my heart: I was gloomy and silent. From that time forward my trust in Vorovatin disappeared and I began to be afraid that he might damage my relationship with Grunya by telling her about my origins. However, he then began to make peace with me and bolster my hopes of marriage and the acquisition of wealth.

We stopped to spend the night at a posting station in a small town. Toward evening a middle-aged man arrived in a post chaise, also to spend the night. I saw from the window that Vorovatin greeted the new arrival warmly, but he treated Vorovatin deferentially and didn't replace his cap until he was told to. They moved aside to a corner of the house where there were no windows and began conversing; since the wind was coming from that direction, I was able to hear part of their conversation by stepping into the corner room.

"You're in too much of a hurry, Pafnutich," said Vorovatin. "You should've waited until I'd spent some time in the place and devised the means. You know we can't tie a stone around his neck and toss him into the water."

"It's not my business how we get rid of him," replied the new arrival. "But the countess wouldn't give me any peace and drove me forcibly on my way. They say that the count's returning to Moscow . . ."

Here the wind slammed the gates closed, and I couldn't hear the end of the conversation because of all the creaking and banging.

"Am I to blame," asked Vorovatin, "that the countess doesn't want to send him packing from this world? Whenever conscience gets in the way of business . . ."

The driver, who was in the courtyard, called loudly to his comrade, and once again I wasn't able to hear the end of Vorovatin's speech. After that the stranger said, "I was ordered to stay with you until the conclusion of this business, and to help you in any way I can; afterwards I'll return to the countess near Moscow."

At these words Vorovatin and the stranger went out of the gates; I remained standing next to the window in consternation and apprehension at what I'd heard. There was no doubt that Vorovatin was intending some evil deed; knowing his cast of thought, I was sure that neither the fear of God nor his conscience would hold him back from committing a crime. But who was the unfortunate victim against whom he was plotting? Who was the countess who was impatiently awaiting news of the unlucky target? Who was the count? Who was this new arrival? This secret, in which I foresaw someone's demise, tormented me, but I felt that it'd be futile to ask Vorovatin and tell him that I'd overheard part of his conversation with the stranger. I was even afraid that the discovery of his plot might make him angry with me and even result in his reprisal; so I decided to remain silent, observe, and, if there was an opportunity, to thwart the execution of his evil intention. Tormented by these thoughts, I paced the room in a state of great spiritual distress. My heart was pounding violently, my head seemed heavy, and my mouth was dry. I went into the stationmaster's room to get a drink of water and inadvertently saw the stranger's order for fresh horses. From it I learned that Vorovatin's confederate was a tradesman heading from Moscow to Orenburg.

To distract myself, I set off on a stroll around town. But in our lesser towns there's little to divert the traveler. This is what I saw as I wandered from one end to the other across bridges: ragged boys, hungry dogs, cattle, and domestic fowl, affably trampling in the dirt in the middle of the street. Old women, their hands on their hips, stood near the gates of log houses, gossiping about their neighbors or quarreling with one another. Grown men crowded in front of a pub where old men were seated; young men with balalaikas and Jew's harps strolled in front of the windows from which sweet young girls' faces would peek. In a few places I could hear mournful songs; to liven the picture, in two places peace-loving citizens were pulling each other by the hair in a circle of good friends and neighbors, and some respectable fathers, intoxicated by the blessed gifts of tax farmers, linked arms with dozens of boys, singing dance tunes. It was a festive evening.

The town was nothing but a large square, surrounded by a broken wattle fence; three-quarters of the enclosed space was pasture. In the middle of the area there was a wide street or, better to say, a post road: along both sides, beyond the gutters, stood small wooden houses and shacks. To the right and left there were a few streets with huts half sunk into the ground and large empty spaces with the remains of wattle fences and railings. In the middle stood a square with a stone church and a half-ruined brick building, which at one time had been intended for legal proceedings. On paper this town occupied a great deal of space; all the streets, demarcated in nature by excavations and the remains of gutters, presented a beautiful perspective on the plan. It was a pity that piles of manure and rubbish had replaced a large number of houses, splendidly designed by a provincial architect. My readers, of course, have seen many such towns. Since as the name exists on maps and plans preserved in the public archives, and since the locations of the houses have been marked out and even the facades projected, it seems that half the project has already been completed. However, no one is to blame: "Man proposes, God disposes" (*L'homme propose, Dieu dispose*)! It is as impossible to populate a town without particular local advantages as it is to set the exchange rate.

Returning to the posting station, I found Vorovatin in an extremely cheerful mood. He was waiting for me to have his own supper; meanwhile he was treating the stationmaster to vodka, interrogating him about the life of each of the local landowners, the provincial officials, and all the area news. Vorovatin did this at each station, by comparing the stationmasters' words with the tales of drivers, tavern owners, and inns along the highway; he collected these observations and wrote them down in his notebook. When I once asked him about the reason for his curiosity, Vorovatin replied callously, "How can you know in advance the people with whom you'll have dealings in life? But when you know their way of thinking and acting, there may be an occasion when this knowledge comes in handy. I consider people like apothecary drugs: you have to know their qualities to make use of them. In social life, as in the economy of nature, nothing's lost if the clever man knows how to use man's various qualities and passions. Poison in the hands of a wise man may serve to cure disease, and the greatest rogue or fool may sometimes be of use to the clever man in his dealings."

Vorovatin said this to me and finished, as he usually did, with a laugh, adding, "Make a note, Vanya, of this advice in your calendar. It's one of the important rules of my philosophical school."

At the time I took this as a joke, but after the conversation I'd overheard between Vorovatin and the stranger, these questions made a bad impression on me; I knew they might be leading to some evil purpose.

There are people who think that you can drown your sorrows in drink. I've never believed that during the course of my life. For the first time ever, I tried to eat and drink against my will, but the wine tasted like bile, and the food was bland and heavy as a stone. The perceptive Vorovatin noticed that I wasn't quite myself but couldn't guess the reason why.

"It seems you're angry at me, Vyzhigin?" he observed.

I remained silent.

"Could my question about your father have distressed you to such a great extent?" he asked.

"It wasn't your question; I find your distrust of me very unpleasant," I replied.

"Well, excuse me, my dear fellow," cried Vorovatin, embracing me. "Know that I asked solely out of my love for you. I was told in Moscow that your father left an estate, but that your aunt appropriated it for herself. God knows what else she did; I merely wanted to find out whether you knew about it."

"In that case you should've communicated your doubts to me without beating around the bush. After considerable thought, I feel there's a great deal in my short life that I don't understand. Perhaps the strangest of all, for example, is that on Gologordovsky's estate a gentleman's son was tossed, like a kitten, to the whims of fate, and no one looked for him or worried about him until that accidental meeting with his aunt. But whether that was done to deny me my legal rights to property—I can't believe that, after receiving so much proof of my aunt's affection for me. She's ready to give her life for me, not only all that she has; and if it was to her advantage that I not know about my relatives, then she never would have acknowledged herself to me."

"You argue like a book," replied Vorovatin. "But I've experienced so much in life that I'm prepared not to believe anything, except what's bad."

"I feel sorry for you," I said, "and hope to avoid such bitter experience for myself."

"You must agree, however," said Vorovatin, "that it's astonishing, or, better to say, incomprehensible, that your aunt recognized you in a shop, without having seen you since infancy!"

"I'm not arguing: this must seem astonishing, but merely because I never explained all the circumstances to you. My aunt has two very striking portraits of my father: one was painted in his childhood, precisely at the age she encountered me in the shop; the other was done when he was twenty-five, the year he married my late mother. I saw these portraits and confess that it'd be hard to find a closer resemblance between my father and me anywhere in the world. Here even two drops of water aren't as much alike as a comparison. My aunt says that besides that, my voice, gait, smile, even my manners are becoming more and more like my father's day by day, and that whoever's seen my father even once in his life, either in his youth or by looking at his portrait, would, at first glance, recognize that I'm his son. And so, you see, it's not at all astonishing when my aunt, having these two portraits in her boudoir and seeing them every day, was struck by my likeness to my father at our first meeting and, knowing the mark on my shoulder, she was convinced that I was indeed her nephew. My own emptyheadedness and carelessness are more astonishing: it never occurred to me to ask my aunt about my parents."

Vorovatin listened to me attentively, looking me straight in the eye, and sank into deep thought. At last he stood up from the table and said, "Enough about this. The matter's closed; now it's time for sleep."

I couldn't close my eyes for a long time. For the first time I began to regret that I'd deceived my aunt, taken it into my head to fall foolishly in love with Grunya, set off for distant places in search of amorous adventures, and become involved with an immoral man. Reason can be compared to the sun, passion to fire. A man who's inside a house surrounded by smoke and flames isn't able to see the sun. But when the fire goes out, the beneficial light of the daytime luminary is more pleasant and perceptible. Reason spoke up within me, and I felt that the steps I'd taken would lead me into unpleasant circumstances, especially in Vorovatin's company. I decided to return to Moscow at the first opportunity, to enter the civil service, to be more careful in my choice of acquaintances, never to fall in love again, and the main thing—to get rid of Vorovatin. It's thus in bad circumstances that we conceive of wise plans which are forgotten once the misfortune or danger passes.

I'm not superstitious, but certain prejudices (if one can call them that) have taken strong root in me, and neither age nor experience nor reason can obliterate them. The major ones are belief in premonitions and in physiognomy. That day was the first in my life when I started to believe in these so-called prejudices. This is the condition I was always in when some sort of misfortune threatened me. My heart beat louder than usual and ached as if it had been wounded; my blood circulated the wrong way in my veins and, upon reaching my heart, produced an unpleasant feeling. Everything bitter that I had seen or experienced in my life presented itself to my imagination and combined to form a gloomy picture of my future. In this picture I always saw myself in the most unfortunate position. My sleep was restless, disturbed by the most terrible dreams. Some sort of physical weakness accompanied this ailment in my soul, and every penetrating glance at me, every question aroused my suspicion; every sound or loud exclamation, every appearance of some new, unexpected person generated instant terror. People who were closest to me, whose love and friendship I never doubted, became unbearable. With every moment I expected a blow of fate, like a condemned convict awaiting his execution. I confess it rarely happened that after such a state of mind, I didn't fall into some calamity, or at least something very unpleasant.

As for physiognomies, I learned my first lesson from Vorovatin's features, which I began to observe assiduously from that day: I weighed all his words and actions and examined his facial features closely. From then on I couldn't refrain from judging people by the impression made at our first meeting. Subsequently I read the works of Lavater and della Porta about physiognomy,[1] but I always stick to my own system and judge not by the facial features but—how to say it?—by the play of the physiognomy and the man's actions. If a man looks at me sullenly or

1. Johann Caspar Lavater (1741–1801) was a Swiss writer, theologian, and physiognomist who attempted to elevate physiognomy into a science. In the early 1600s the Italian scholar Giambattista della Porta (1535–1615), considered the father of physiognomy, was instrumental in spreading ideas about the link between character and appearance throughout Europe.

doesn't look me straight in the eye when he's speaking, or if he filters his words through his teeth or deliberately organizes his speech during our conversation; if he speaks to me in questions, always asking my opinions, or silently agrees with me, or contradicts me only to force me to explain myself more fully—I confess, I don't trust him. A false smile and artificial laughter serve as indicators of insincerity. Grimaces made involuntarily with the mouth, constant movement, or biting the lips are all bad omens. An uneven gait in which we see some sort of vulpine wiles, a compression of the whole body toward the center, or a hunching up like a cat before prey, stretching the head forward like a snake that is about to pounce—for me these are infallible indications of a bad person. Loud outbursts of joy and kissing every acquaintance upon meeting seem very suspicious to me. I shall conclude my brief digression admitting that I'm sometimes mistaken in my intuitions but never about a man's physiognomy. I won't describe all the physiognomic signs now: readers will observe them subsequently in the portraits of the many people I have met during my life. As far as premonitions are concerned, I should say that they always happen to me after some lapse or careless act, when I could expect well-deserved or undeserved enmity on the part of my enemies. This was not the cause but the consequence, not an admonitory genius like Socrates but an informative one. However, anyone who has to deal with human selfishness and passions should often expect misfortunes, even though he didn't do anything bad, and even though, on the contrary, he may have done something deserving praise and reward. This is the way of the world: he who does no evil must be subject to a test and suffer evil at the hands of others. The difference between a good man and an evil one in this case is that, amid the greatest calamity, a good man finds consolation in his conscience and in the opinions of honest people; while for the evil man, there's neither joy nor hope of life in the hereafter, where the strong cannot oppress the weak. But let's return to the story.

Not being very good at pretending, I couldn't adopt a cheerful countenance, but in order to avert all suspicion, I told Vorovatin I was feeling unwell. I don't know if he believed me or not, but he doubled his kindness and attentions to me and treated me with a father's tenderness, which to some extent reconciled me with him. To allow me to get some rest, we stopped for several days in a provincial town situated in a beautiful location on the banks of the Volga. Vorovatin had an old acquaintance there, a police captain, with whom he spoke very frankly.

In their conversation I heard some things that I'd had no idea about previously. Since they made such a powerful impression on me at the time, I will provide the reader with some details.

Savva Savvich was considered one of the smartest police captains in the whole province. He was of gigantic height and had served at one time in the police dragoons; he'd kept his military bearing and habits, stood straight as an arrow, and turned quickly with his entire body. His advanced age and hard drinking had weakened the roots of his hair to such an extent that he'd lost almost all his hair, except for a few tufts on his temples and the back of his head. His long nose and the extremities of his gaunt face were covered with reddish blotches; his small, gray feline eyes shone from under his thick gray eyebrows. He always wore his official uniform and a Cossack leather shoulder belt. He never wore his sword unless he was going out on official business; his everyday weapon was a Cossack whip with a lead bullet woven into one end. He usually sported a leather cap with a stiff crown, which afforded him a military appearance. His voice was like a bear's roar. All his paperwork was handled by an old scribe, who'd spent three-quarters of his life with one leg tethered to his writing table. In addition, Savva Savvich ordered him to remove his boots, so that he couldn't go scurrying off to a tavern frequently. But the crafty scribe found a way to imbibe without getting up from his seat. The willing servants would bring him vodka in apothecary's glass bottles, several doses every hour since Savva Savvich would search for the bottles in the stove and even behind the wallpaper. On holidays the scribe was allowed to get drunk; then he was carried home stiff as a board, laid out in a cell, and doused with water. In his travels around the province, Fomich (that was the scribe's name) had full permission to drink hard for several days in a row, but only after he'd finished his business, because afterwards his hand would shake so violently that he'd be unfit for work. Savva Savvich called Fomich a *man of gold* and attributed his proclivity to drink excessively to his unusual gifts, which, in the opinion of old-fashioned men, couldn't flourish unless watered with vodka: therefore, one could conclude that Savva Savvich was also a genius. However, he was very knowledgeable about business—especially in interrogations, investigations, and general searches—except that he was unable to write his thoughts down on paper as easily as he could pour vodka down his throat; he couldn't find in either capital a pair of glasses, by means of which he could read hastily written documents even by syllables, just as if they were printed, and he could never remember the dates of various ukases.[2] Fomich served as his stand-in in all this. For his good work the inhabitants of the district, called Savva Savvich a *gray wolf*, and his faithful co-worker Fomich was nicknamed the *snare*.

The police captain came to spend the evening with us, and when the samovar was brought in, he wetted his throat with punch made with Kizlyarsky vodka and felt an inclination to have a frank conversation. He began, as usual, with his favorite exclamation. "Enough about this. The matter's closed; now it's time for sleep."

"Enough complaining about fate, Savva Savvich," Vorovatin objected. "I know that government jobs pay very well; the devil himself couldn't make you stay here if it weren't profitable."

"But where would you advise me to go?" the police captain replied in irritation. "We have nothing to live on but our old reserve; the income from today's jobs can't provide any money. Just think that we have to feed the provincial folks, just as children feed their old father. What difference does it make if I have 9,218 serfs, if they're in emaciated bodies!"

"What!" I cried. "You have 9,218 serfs, and you're complaining about fate!"

The police captain smiled and answered, "These souls, brother, are not really mine, don't you see, but government souls, under my jurisdiction; but 'he who milks the cow has a right to drink the milk.' It's impossible to expect that from the government take, there won't be a few crumbs left over, so-called *accidentia*.[3] But we live in bad times, bad times!" He added, "Education, legislation, and no money to be had! Bootlegging is disappearing, deserters and vagrants are coming into our province, though unfortunately, not many of them; so there's no one to latch onto. It's clear that the Day of Judgment is at hand! Even theft has become rare and murders are almost unheard of. For our kind, the smart dealers, times have changed: it's a plague! There's no business and no profit. Meanwhile they keep writing to us from the higher offices: 'nightingales don't live on fairytales,' 'coats cannot be lined with bows,' and so on and so forth. A calamity, a real calamity! From all sides we're swamped by education; even government officials are walking around with books and making jokes at one another's expense; in the capitals, they say, they even make fun of industrious people, not only in theaters but even in newspapers, and why? It's merely because

2. A written order or edict, usually issued by the tsar.
3. Extra dues or fees in government offices.

we want to eat our daily bread in exchange for our labor. Even landowners have wised up these days: not that they're educated, but they all want to become smart operators, as soon as any calamity occurs; they go right to the provincial powers or even to Petersburg. It's better to feed the wolf, they say, than the wolf cubs. To tell the truth, I pester them a fair amount for this and handle them with iron gloves. If I find even one deserter in our district, I force him to admit that he's been sheltered by all the wealthy landowners and even the peasants (their masters' fault), and immediately turn the entire district upside down. If I happen to find a dead body, I drag it around to thirty different places so that afterwards I can conduct an investigation everywhere. On paper a stolen horse spends the night in twenty different stables. But all this is bitter bread, a hard-earned kopeck! Drive around, run here and there, write, interrogate, bang my head against the wall, a hundred times in one place, fifty in another, and ten in a third. These are bad times, brother! Education, legislation!" Savva Savvich drank down his grief, banged his glass on the table, and sank into thought.

Vorovatin was amused by his friend's frankness and compelled him to speak once again. "But what about the trade fairs, Savva Savvich, passports, penalties for official arrears and private debts, distraints, and gentry guardianships, lines for repairing roads, and supplies, and so on and so forth?

"The devil has overturned it all and mixed it up," Savva Savvich replied angrily. "Few gamblers come to the fairs, and those who do are as poor as church mice and in no position to pay fees for permission to cheat the landowners, who nowadays go to the two capitals[4] to be ruined, because it's in fashion. There's little income to be had from passports; there's little work in the capitals; trade is going badly, and few peasants leave the countryside to work in transportation or to find other work. It's true that we're well paid for our labor in prosecuting government arrears and private debtors, but today the orders are very strict, and governors and prosecutors oppress our brethren if we lose sight of government interests. There's not a word about private business. In my opinion, if you're in debt, just sit there quietly or pay us back on time. We'll never prosecute for debt or for paper or correspondence. Provincial and local courts write to each other amicably and let

4. Moscow was the original capital of the Russian Empire; Peter the Great built a city on the Gulf of Finland, later called St. Petersburg, and moved the capital there in 1703. They were both considered as capitals of Russia.

the moneylender read, if he will, the court orders about prosecution for debt in the legible handwriting of the court clerks. That is an object which, thank God, is left untouched; it's not yet been overturned. The roads, brother, and the means of conveyance—that's nothing! We repair only the post roads, and only when some important personage is to travel on them; as for other roads, though the devil may break his neck, that's not our business! Today regiments are stationed on the frontier, so that loads are infrequent. As far as gentry guardianships are concerned, don't make a mistake, my friend, by assigning us any revenue. Of course, everybody may earn something from an orphan's property, but today the gentry are masters at fleecing their charges. However, if anyone were placed under supervision for bad management, then without doubt a rat would die of hunger on that estate; profit is bad with a bad manager. No, brother, times are bad—times are very bad. Education, legislation, and no money to be had!"

"No, Savva Savvich," said Vorovatin. "Now you've fallen silent: there was a time when you boasted about your loot, like a skillful marksman standing over his downed prey, but now . . ."

"But now," said the police captain, "one has to be careful; honesty is called for." He repeated his favorite saying. "Times are bad, times are very bad! Education, legislation, and no money to be had!" Vorovatin left the room, and the police captain turned to me and said, "I've heard that you're a relation of Mr. Vorovatin's?"

"Yes, sir."

"Have you served anywhere?"

"No."

"It's time, sir, it's time; especially if you want to enter the civil service. The official language, sir, is like an ocean! You can't drink it all, but one must drink a lot of it very early. To tell the truth, the only ones who succeed are those who began their service with office drudgery. I advise you not to lose any time."

"Yes, sir."

Then Vorovatin came back into the room, and the talkative police captain, seeing that his friend had become silent and thoughtful, began in turn to torment him with questions. I allowed them to go on about various common acquaintances without paying attention, but one circumstance struck me powerfully.

"Listen here, friend," said the police captain to Vorovatin, "you're still in debt to me."

"For what?" asked Vorovatin.

"What? Have you really forgotten that by your request I allowed the tradesman Nozhov to escape from prison; he'd been accused of escaping from Siberia where he'd been banished. You sent me only three hundred rubles and promised me twice that amount: meanwhile Nozhov's at liberty, and I haven't seen or heard of your money. That, brother, is not acting like an honest man."

"Hey, my dear Savva Savvich," said Vorovatin, embracing his friend. "Do we really have to count such trifles? You did a *good* deed. Nozhov was unjustly slandered, and I, from my love for fellow man alone, sacrificed my own money to save him. I thought that when he returned to Moscow, he'd repay me and give me enough money to repay you, but he fell ill and died a month later from despair, a victim of human malice."

"Something's not right here," said the police captain coolly. "Nozhov has been known to the police for some time for various offenses; there's no end to rumors about him and I recently learned that our merchants spotted him in Moscow last winter. No, no matter what, you still owe me money! I myself had a narrow escape as a result of that damned affair: I had to endure two examinations, three reprimands, and in addition to all the expenses, I had to pay a fine. Furthermore, thank God the prosecutor's wife liked my Moscow sleigh, or else it would've turned out even worse."

"Okay, okay, we'll settle the debt," said Vorovatin. "But for now, let's go to sleep. My head aches."

Savva Savvich grimaced, but to console himself, he emptied what was left in the bottle and went home. We went to bed at once. I couldn't sleep all night, thinking about Vorovatin's connection with such a notorious villain as Nozhov and about the conversation I'd half overheard. At break of day, when I finally fell asleep, I had a terrible dream about Nozhov, who was trying to chop off my head with an ax. I cried out, jumped out of bed in a frenzy, and woke Vorovatin. He was frightened and concluded from my restless night that I was ill with a fever. He decided to treat me and would have me drink some sort of remedy with vodka. I didn't obey him, and that ended his concern with my health.

To get rid of the police chief, who'd reminded him about his debt, Vorovatin decided to leave town at once. On learning that Savva Savvich would be out of town for several hours, Vorovatin sent for horses; before noon we galloped away toward Orenburg.

Chapter 12

An Emancipated Man. A Lunatic. Deceived in Love.

We arrived in Orenburg about ten o'clock in the morning and stopped at the house of the tradesman Ivan Karpov, who kept a sort of inn for acquaintances and people who'd been recommended. We were shown to two clean rooms with walls covered in colorful wallpaper, while Vorovatin's servant, a kind of automaton or machine for removing boots and brushing clothes, settled opposite, in the owner's quarters. After changing his clothes, Vorovatin headed immediately into town, saying that he'd return late that night; he recommended that I have dinner and get some rest after our trip. Left alone, I went to see the proprietor to learn something during our conversation about Matryona Ivanovna Shtosina and her daughter, my dear Grunya, for whom I'd first decided to set out on this journey. Our proprietor, a handsome man of about fifty, tall, broad-shouldered, ruddy, could serve as a model for a sculpture of Hercules. He was cheerful and talkative, like all full-blooded and convivial fellows. In answer to my first question—was he a native of the place or a newcomer?—he related his history to me in a few words.

"I, sir, was born near Moscow and was a serf of General Volokitin's wife, a wealthy widow who owned several estates. They say that I was not bad-looking in my younger days; that was the source of all my misfortunes, which ended happily, thank the Lord. The general's wife, who came to spend the summer in our village, saw me at work and immediately took me into her household. I was sixteen years old at the time, my mother's only son. My father was no longer alive. I was given a German-style haircut, dressed in a caftan with galloons, and turned over to an old footman and a housekeeper to teach me how to serve. With many tears I exchanged my sheepskin coat for embroidered livery. Household servants always seemed to me to be dogs on a leash, and I never envied their existence. However, I lived very well in the manor house. The mistress caressed me, patted my cheeks, stroked my head, and sent me treats from the dining table. The maids regarded me slyly, while the footmen and even the butler treated me as if I were the master's son. I didn't understand the reason for all this kindness and distinction; then the old housekeeper, my tutor, explained to me that I would soon be called upon to fulfill a role that was not at all to my liking. This duty compelled me to be constantly in the mistress's presence, and that seemed to me to be worse than death. A chill ran through my veins upon hearing this news. One glance at the mistress forced me to quake in my boots! Just imagine a short, fat, old woman, around fifty years old, her face smeared with red and white makeup, looking just like a horse rug, with slanted eyes and red hair mixed with gray who, instead of teeth, had a few loose yellow bones sticking out of her mouth. Her voice was like the creaking of an ungreased wheel of a cart; she was constantly shouting or swearing at the servants, or else summoning and caressing her dogs. Having heard the tale of Baba Yaga,[1] it seemed to me that she couldn't have been better or worse than the general's widow. The housekeeper explained to me that the former valet, Filka, was leaving the next day to go to Moscow to live there legally, and that I would have to take his place tomorrow. This Filka was a young man, around twenty-two years old. He'd spent six years in his position (because the mistress chose valets of that age), and although he was not bad-looking, he was so wasted away, probably from sorrow and boredom, that he resembled a corpse. He was extremely grateful for his deliverance and could hardly await the next day to set off on his journey. But I preempted him. As soon as it was dark, I secretly took a horse from the stable, jumped on it bareback, and galloped out on the highway as fast as the horse could carry me, not knowing where I was headed or why. Each time I recalled my mistress's 'charms,' I spurred

1. A supernatural being who appears as a deformed or ferocious-looking old woman.

the horse on harder, as if she was chasing me. No one's ever run faster from a beating than I ran from her kindness.

"Finally, toward dawn, I galloped into a provincial town and immediately found the police chief, whom I knew by sight, because he often used to come to our village to collect money—I don't know if it was for himself or the treasury. I candidly told the police captain all that the housekeeper had said and declared my unwavering decision to enlist as a soldier, rather than return to my mistress. The police captain and his wife laughed until they cried at my tale, but it was impossible to help me, because I was complaining verbally without offering any proof. They led my horse to the stable, arrested me, and sent the general's widow word of what had become of me. Afterwards I learned that the widow had paid the police captain handsomely for not divulging my testimony; they whipped me for stealing a horse and running away, then banished me to an estate belonging to the widow in the province of Saratov, where there was a distillery, with orders to guard me strictly and punish me as often as possible. Fortunately my mistress didn't know that the manager of the distillery, also one of her serfs, was my cousin. He felt sorry for my plight, ordered his clerk to teach me to read and write and to learn my numbers, and made me his assistant in keeping the books. No one in the distillery, except for my cousin, knew about my adventure, and since my cousin kept people under strict control, I was respected as his assistant.

"Ten years elapsed and my mistress passed into the other world, and my misfortunes ended. The estate went to her son, whom she never wanted to see when she was alive, because once, when he was home from the regiment, he took it into his head to pursue one of her wards or, more accurately, one of her maids, chosen from orphans of different classes. The young master knew the reason for my banishment and, on his arrival at the distillery, summoned me, welcomed me, and, on my uncle's recommendation, made me the manager; he awarded my uncle jurisdiction of the whole province and gave him his freedom, too. Since I knew the business and had the fear of God in me, I earned the master's kindness. At last, after some twelve years, our kind master died childless; in his will he granted me my freedom, together with the other deserving household servants. By being thrifty, and by the generosity of my kind master, I had amassed a small amount of capital and intended to settle in Orenburg, where I had spent time before on my master's business. I had also managed to find a fiancée.

"Now it's almost fifteen years since I've been living here. I married and built myself a small house, and with God's help, I run a market with the Kirghiz.[2] God has blessed me with good children: my elder daughter's already fourteen, the middle one is twelve, and my young son is in his tenth year.

"That, sir, is how I wound up here! No one can foresee what will happen at one's birth; only God knows where and when one will come to rest his bones. But would you like something to eat? Today's a holiday, and we can treat you to a pie made from buckwheat and with fish from the Urals."

I didn't want to part with my kind host and asked permission to dine alongside his family, which he agreed to, saying, "If you don't stand on ceremony, do as you please."

Fortunately, destiny and nature distribute their gifts to people without regard to birth or pretensions. How many wealthy people would consider themselves fortunate if, instead of sallow or pale children, they had healthy, rosy-cheeked children such as my landlord's? His wife, a woman of about thirty-five, fresh, nimble, obliging, was a cheerful sort, just like her husband. These kind people took a liking to me when we first met and treated me like an old friend; the elder daughter would glance at me furtively, blush, and drop her large black eyes whenever they met mine. This girl seemed to me much better than Grunya, but since I'd come especially for her, I decided at last to ask my landlord about Grunya's mother.

"Mrs. Shtosina lives in our town," replied the landlord, "and lives happily. She has a daughter, young and frivolous, who attracts officers like honey attracts flies. Two months ago a young officer was living with us who wanted to marry this young lady, but, after losing his money, he thought better of it, realizing that her house was nothing but a trap, where people are robbed daily, and Mrs. Shtosina's daughter is a lure for simpletons. This officer told me a great deal about both the mother and the daughter, but I don't like to repeat what's bad, and it's better if you don't know it either."

Dinner ended, and I dared not ask my landlord any more questions. I returned to my room with a heavy heart and lay down on my bed. I couldn't fall asleep for a long time, thinking about my bitter fate and

2. A Turkic ethnic group native to Central Asia.

the disasters of my first friendship and my first love. I consoled myself by thinking that the officer's stories might not be true and might have been the result of the man's irritation at his losses at the card table; I decided to make sure that this was true.

Vorovatin returned earlier than I'd expected. He was gloomy and thoughtful. After a light supper he went to bed, having said that he was feeling unwell. From boredom I followed his example, although I didn't feel sleepy at all.

Around midnight, just as I was starting to doze, a sudden noise in the other room startled me. I got out of bed, crept on tiptoe to the door, opened it halfway, and peered in . . . There was Vorovatin, sitting at the window, wearing only his shirt, with a bare chest. His face was deathly pale; his reddish blotches had assumed a violet color; his eyes were wide open, and he seemed to be avidly drinking in the rays of moonlight; his hair was disheveled and standing on end; he was moving his lips, as if trying to say something; all of a sudden he began to scratch his breast and tear his hair, gnashing his teeth. I froze in terror and dared not utter a single word; I was unable to budge from where I stood. Vorovatin howled in a terrible, unearthly voice and began to speak loudly but extremely rapidly and unintelligibly. He finally calmed down and then began to speak slowly and distinctly.

"What right do you have to warn me, threaten me, advise me? You're a priest—God be with you! Counsel those who seek your advice. I came to see you when I was ill, and you, knowing a few secrets of my soul, decided at our first meeting to appeal to my conscience. No, Father Pyotr, no, you've wasted your words on me. I'm well, healthy, and might live another twenty or thirty years."

After a brief pause, Vorovatin continued, "Really, it's time to come to my senses. How many gullible young men have I brought to ruin in the depths of debauchery? Like a fallen angel, I teach atheism to the thoughtless, while I myself fear a righteous God's vengeance. Is it possible that, after increasing the number of the condemned, I can save myself from ruin? No, it's time to change my mind. Ruining the inexperienced through false play, handing them over into the hands of usurers, instilling into the hearts of those I led astray hatred for all the natural and legal obligations of man, extorting money—up to this moment I haven't acquired the riches that have been my object my whole life. I barely have fifty thousand rubles in cash. That's not much, not much at all. Listen, Father Pyotr! As soon as I amass a hundred thousand, I'll swear an oath to you that I'll become an honest man, settle down in some remote village, where I'm unknown, and live quietly, without trying to deceive or ruin anyone. I'll start to fast, go to church, pray, and upon my death, I'll leave my money to a monastery. Right now I have three matters on hand; as soon as I finish them, I'll be very close to having a hundred thousand. First of all, I have to get rid of that damned Vyzhigin. But that's not my business, and I wash my hands of it. Let Nozhov deal with him as he likes. That's his business. I've fulfilled my commission: I've dragged him off to the frontiers of the empire. Father Pyotr, why are you looking at me so dreadfully? Stop talking to me about hell, the last judgment, and the fire everlasting! It's terrible, very terrible. I teach others not to believe in it, but I myself can't hear it without trembling. Get away, Father Pyotr, get away from me! It's dreadful, dreadful! There's the fire, the blood, blood!" At these words Vorovatin's whole body began trembling, and he fell from the window onto the floor, moaning painfully, as if his soul was separating from his body. Suddenly he began shouting and closed his eyes. I myself almost lost consciousness and began shaking like an aspen leaf. Not daring to disturb Vorovatin and afraid to wake him, I gathered my last strength, reached my bed, and threw myself on it in exhaustion, as if after an attack of illness.

Now I was convinced that there was some conspiracy against me and that the conversation I'd overheard between Nozhov and Vorovatin concerned me. But who was this Nozhov? What had I ever done to him? What did I do to Vorovatin? What countess was seeking my destruction? I had never angered any woman in my whole life. Could it be Grabilin's machination? Of all the visitors to my aunt's house, he was the only one who didn't like me. But the countess! Unfathomable!

With such reflections, I fell asleep toward dawn, from mere exhaustion. Assuming that Vorovatin was still suffering a fever, I intended to use the time of his illness to arrange my escape and to hide it from him and his friend Nozhov, who at this time no doubt was also in Orenburg.

To my astonishment, the next day Vorovatin got out of bed completely healthy and cheerful: on the contrary, I felt heavy in all my limbs and had a general lack of energy. During tea Vorovatin proposed that I go hunting the following day; I refused, fearing some evil plot. He told me that Mrs. Shtosina was out of town and would return in a few days; meanwhile he advised me to stay at home, adding that he saw by my face that I was unwell. I promised not to go out, but as soon as he'd gone, I got dressed and resolved to find out about Mrs. Shtosina myself, no longer believing Vorovatin about anything. In any case, I wanted to say farewell to Grunya and afterwards to look for a way to get back to Moscow. I was hoping for some assistance from my kind landlord.

At ten o'clock in the morning I was already standing next to the house occupied by Mrs. Shtosina, and from her neighbors I learned that she hadn't left town at all. There was a gate from the street into her garden, and I went in there to gather my strength and prepare for my meeting with Grunya, about whom I'd been forewarned. Crossing a dark alley with quiet steps, I saw a gazebo at the end of it. Through the branches of the trees and lattice of the gazebo, I noticed something white. As I made my way through the bushes, I heard Grunya's voice; she was talking with some man.

"I congratulate you, Grunya," said the man. "An admirer from Moscow has arrived, and he's fortunate, as Vorovatin says: this young man has run away from his relatives, a distance of several hundred miles, for an amorous rendezvous, hoping for your love and your hand in marriage. This is no joke, dear Grunya, and he certainly has powerful reasons to expect that his feelings will be reciprocated."

"Stop playing the fool, *mon cher* Alexandre,"[3] Grunya replied. "Vorovatin is intentionally arousing your jealousy with his vacuous tales. It's true: I knew this Vyzhigin in Moscow. After I perceived his foolish love for me, I relieved my boredom at his expense. But this dissolute urchin, who's no more than seventeen and hasn't even finished school, has already taken up gambling and philandering: in a word, he's a worthy disciple of that infamous rogue Vorovatin. Do you really think I could be in love with him? My mother ordered me to be polite, because he would always lose at her card table—and that's our entire connection. It annoys me that even as a joke you're jealous of that schoolboy."

"But they say," the man objected, "that this Vyzhigin has a handsome face, that he's clever beyond his years, extremely cunning, that he sings well and plays both the piano and the guitar—in a word, he's capable of turning the head of . . ."

". . . Of some foolish country lass," replied Grunya. "How could I even think of preferring his pretty, half-girlish mug to this sweet little mustache and these warlike eyes?" The man didn't even allow Grunya to finish when I heard the sounds of kissing.

Wounded vanity, anger, and disappointment overcame me. I came running out of the bushes like a madman and confronted the astonished lovers.

---

3. "My dear Aleksandr" (Fr.).

Grunya cried out and covered her face with her hands. The hussar jumped up from his place, struck his saber on the ground, and exclaimed threateningly, "Who are you, and how dare you enter without permission?"

I didn't say a word in reply to the officer, but I turned to Grunya and said, "You liar, you fraud! You call me a schoolboy, depraved; you say that you never loved me, that you were merely amusing yourself with my innocence. But I have here in my hands proof, if not of your love, then of your deceit, your coquetry. Here, look at this lock of your hair; your letters in which you professed endless, boundless affection; you swore to be mine forever. I'll expose your worthless character. I'll broadcast it everywhere and spread your letters far and wide. Are you curious, Mr. Officer?"

Grunya dissolved in tears, threw her arms around the officer's neck, and cried, "Defend me from this rascal, or I shall die in despair! He's a ridiculous liar . . . If you love me, defend me!"

It seems that the officer didn't worry all that much about Grunya's tender feelings; enjoying the present moment, he thought neither about the past nor the future. He threw himself on me like a madman, tore the letters and the lock of Grunya's hair out of my hands, and seizing me by the collar, dragged me out of the gazebo. Resistance on my part resulted only in extra blows: the strong officer tossed me out of the garden gate; after giving me a kick, he locked the entrance. I was in turmoil; shame and despair crushed me completely. I started running home, wanting to shoot both the officer and Grunya. Thousands of terrible thoughts followed one after another. But arriving back at my apartment, my whole body suddenly felt weak. It seemed like my brain was being seared with a red-hot poker and that all my blood had turned to fire. I soon lost consciousness, and beside the dreadful heat in my head and my thirst, I had no awareness of being in the land of the living.

Chapter 13

A Prisoner of the Kirghiz. A Kirghiz Philosopher, Arsalan-Sultan. I Become a Horseman.

I don't recall how long I was in that unresponsive condition, but I came back to myself in a dream. I dreamt that I had fallen into the water and lay on the bottom of a deep river. The cold forced me to wake up. I opened my eyes, wanted to move, but felt that I was wrapped up in something wet and binding. A sound, similar to that of a *gudok*,[1] struck my ears. With the greatest effort I turned my head away from the wall toward the light, and everything that appeared before my eyes aroused my amazement. I was lying in a tent, on strips of felt, completely naked; I was covered with an old dry sheepskin with the wool turned outward. A man wearing a colorful robe and a high black sheepskin hat sat next to my bed; he was playing a *gudok* and singing in a mournful voice, shaking his head in time with the music and making dreadful faces. From this man's narrow eyes, dark complexion, prominent cheekbones, and scanty facial hair, I recognized him as a Kirghiz. He was extremely pleased when he noticed that I'd opened my eyes and was making an attempt to escape my swaddles; he jumped up from where he sat, turned on his heels several times, and began to shout with all his might while playing the bells hanging on his belt. In answer

1. An ancient Eastern Slavic musical instrument with three strings, played with a bow.

to his shouting several Kirghiz, including three women, came running in. One of them, a tall figure dressed in a silk robe and wearing a small skullcap trimmed in gold, approached my bed and said affectionately in rather precise Russian, "What would you like? Are you feeling better?"

"I'm cold," I replied, "and I'd like to eat or drink something hot. Tell them to release me and give me some warm clothes to wear."

"Well, you must feel better if you want to eat," said the tall Kirghiz. He sent the women out and ordered two Kirghiz to take off the sheepskin, to wash me, rub me with some strong ointment resembling bile, and cover me with robes, which command was immediately carried out. I tried to stand up on my own two legs but fell back onto my bed from weakness. Meanwhile a young woman brought me some broth made from local millet; after eating this fortifying soup, I felt that my blood had resumed its proper course and that my strength was returning. Sleep began to overcome me after I'd satisfied my hunger, and the tall Kirghiz, noticing this, ordered everyone out of the tent, saying, "Don't worry; get better. God is great in heaven, and in the steppe there's no lack of good people."

I fell asleep at sunset and awoke at sunrise; first I raised my head, then I stood up and was very glad that I could stand on my own two feet. With difficulty I managed to walk out of the yurt. Seeing the sun and the cloudless sky, I threw myself down on my knees and with tears in my eyes, I thanked God for my deliverance from such a serious illness and for saving my life.

A strange sight greeted my eyes. The yurts were pitched on the shores of a lake; the boundless steppe was visible all around me; and among the scanty bushes, a large herd of sheep, horses, camels, and horned cattle was feeding. Men and women were busy with work: some were milking the cows and mares; others were spreading out felt to dry in the air; still others were lighting fires and carrying water; and some were slaughtering sheep and colts. The talk and cries of people were mixed with the neighing of horses, the lowing of the cows, and the bleating of the sheep. I guessed that I was in a Kirghiz encampment but couldn't understand how I'd wound up there. My last recollection was meeting with Grunya and returning to my apartment. After that, it seemed to me that I was no longer alive and then I'd risen from the dead in a Kirghiz tent. A tall Kirghiz in a silk gown stood next to a yurt, which was larger and more beautiful than all the others. He was smoking a pipe and looking around. Having noticed me, he ordered one of the Kirghiz to bring me to him. Guessing that he must be the elder, I bowed to him and asked his permission to sit down on the ground because I was still feeling weak.

The elder ordered that felt be brought and placed under me, and he himself sat down on a carpet opposite and said, "You should know, Ivan, that you are now my slave. I'm the headman of a renowned division of the Kirghiz horde. My name is Arsalan-Sultan. Serve me faithfully if you want to live a happy life; if I observe any desire on your part to run away, I will sell you in Khiva or have you slaughtered like a sheep."

This speech of welcome did little to console me after my recovery, but there was nothing to be done. I replied with feigned indifference, "I will serve you faithfully, and although up to now I've not been of any service to you, I still dare to ask one favor, as a pledge of the future: tell me how I came to fall into your hands. I was so ill that I don't recall what happened to me."

"If you like, I'll tell you. I was in Orenburg on business, about three weeks ago. After leaving town and turning off the road to return to the steppe along familiar byways, I saw two armed people who were taking something out of a cart. I had only four Kirghiz men with me to lead my camels; the rest had gone on ahead. Fearing that the Cossack mounted patrol might hear the sound of gunfire, I didn't want to attack these bandits, who were arguing between themselves about what to do with you. One—a tall, stocky cutthroat—wanted to chop off your head; the other, pale and lanky, advised him to throw you into the field and avoid shedding blood, saying that even without their aid, you would soon give up the ghost. I heard their conversation from a distance, thanks to the wind. They were terrified when I galloped up to them and were extremely happy when I announced that I didn't want to start a fight so close to town, and that I intended to save them from further trouble by taking the person about whose fate they were quarreling along with us. The villains agreed and gave you to me on the condition that I not allow you to write to Russia to ask that a ransom be paid. I promised, and they returned to town. You lay in a fever, unconscious, wrapped in a blanket. At once I ordered the slaughter of two extra sheep and had you wrapped naked in the damp sheepskins, added you to my baggage, and loaded you onto one of the camels. The damp sheepskins and some powder from the dried legs of the *tilegus*,[2] which I always carry with me because it helps to cure the bites of rabid dogs, sustained life in your body. When we arrived back in the village, at my wives' request,

2. A bird resembling a partridge.

I summoned the most skillful shaman and ordered him to predict your future and play his *gudok* all during your illness, changing the skins for fresh ones of various animals sometimes two or three times a day. My wives fed you millet broth and an herbal potion. At last God and His Prophet deigned to spare you for the honor and glory of serving me, Arsalan-Sultan. I pitied your youth! Now your life belongs to me, and you must renounce any hope of seeing your native land ever again. But tell me, who were these bandits who wanted to kill you, and why were they so embittered?"

After first thanking Arsalan-Sultan for the care he'd taken of me and renewing the assurance of my fidelity, I told him how it was that I'd left Moscow with Vorovatin to see Grunya; how I met Nozhov and how I'd overheard his words; and finally, how I learned about Grunya's betrayal; then how I came down with a fever as a result of the powerful emotional upset. I declared to my new master that I had never suspected anyone of intending to murder me except for Vorovatin and Nozhov, but I couldn't say what inspired them to hatch a conspiracy against me because I myself didn't understand the reasons. I didn't want to believe these villains made an attempt on my life on account of several hundred rubles, which Vorovatin had in his possession, having taken them from me for safekeeping.

"It's a pity," said Arsalan-Sultan, "that I didn't wipe those heartless villains from the face of the earth; they were merely testing their strength and courage against a sick young man. If I come across them another time, I shall leave their bones to dry in the steppe and leave their skulls as a nest for snakes, which is better than they deserve. Listen, Ivan, until you get stronger, I won't give you any work to do. My wives will give you food and drink, and then we'll see what you're suited for."

Arsalan-Sultan's family consisted of three wives and four children: three daughters aged five to seven and one son, a lad of my own age. All three wives were young and pretty. If you accept as a rule that narrow eyes and prominent cheekbones aren't unattractive, Arsalan-Sultan's wives would be regarded as beauties in any European capital; and he himself, although he was older than forty, could have been called a Kirghiz Apollo. His son was born from his fourth wife, who was no longer alive, but the young Gayuk received kindness and tenderness from each of his three stepmothers, which doesn't always occur with stepsons in more sophisticated societies. My new master was content with his family. His wives got along well with each other, had cheerful natures, and tried to please their husband as best they could. They were very friendly in their treatment of servants and they loved me like their own brother. I am much obliged to them for my recovery.

Autumn arrived, and we began to break up our camp and go in search of winter quarters. Arsalan-Sultan sent messengers to friendly neighboring encampments with news of our impending move and the direction that he intended to take us in the steppe. Upon the return of the messengers, all the baggage was packed in piles, the tents were struck, the camels and packhorses were loaded, and at a given signal they all assembled in marching order. Each family formed a separate division. Children, old women, young girls, elders, and sick people sat on the camels, but all the men capable of bearing arms and all the young women rode on horses, wearing their best clothes, as if dressed for a special celebration. At both ends and alongside the caravan rode troops of horsemen armed with pikes, spears, sabers, and some long rifles. The herds made up a separate group in sight of the caravan. When everything was ready for the departure, Arsalan-Sultan ordered the shaman to begin his prediction regarding the success of this enterprise. The shaman stepped forward, withdrew a knife from his belt, drew a circle around him in the sand with his knife, and then, placing the knife on his own throat, began to sing in a loud voice. His singing was accompanied by terrible grimacing and jumping, which soon led to his complete exhaustion. He fell down like a dead man, his breathing scarcely discernible, and he seemed to be asleep. The whole village looked on in silence and reverence at this alleged magic. After a quarter of an hour the shaman began to stir as if speaking in his sleep. Arsalan-Sultan and the other elders listened attentively to his words and concluded that our journey would be successful. They placed the exhausted shaman on a camel, and after a signal was given, we all moved forward.

I was stationed next to Arsalan-Sultan on a spirited steed and dressed in Kirghiz style. By special kindness shown to me and at the request of his wives, he made me his arms-bearer, or better to say, his military escort. My duty consisted in holding his horse when Arsalan-Sultan dismounted, to serve him koumiss, to fill his pipe, clean his musket, serve him dinner, and entertain him with stories and songs. After the first stage of our journey, Arsalan-Sultan moved some distance away from his people, summoned me to him, and said, "You've had a look at our life, Ivan, and I hope that you won't want to exchange our steppe for your stuffy towns, where people gather to deceive each other and invent needs which make them slaves to all sorts of stupidities and compel them to crawl and fawn before all those who have the power to raise them in the eyes of fools and convey riches to them, of which they know neither the worth nor the measure. What does a man need? He needs to have his belly filled, to be clothed, and then left in peace. You'll find all this among us. Without hard work and worry, we have food and clothing from our herds. We don't torment ourselves with concern about the future, and we're always ready to repel any enemy or rapacious neighbor by force; we prefer using our arms to playing dirty tricks, lies, and deceit, which your city residents use when they fight wars among themselves. You evaluate the beauty of your towns by the breadth of their streets, the spaciousness and the size of their buildings. Our mosque is the open sky, and our town is the boundless steppe, where no one is crowded and no wall or fence interferes with our freedom. I've been in Moscow and Petersburg, I saw all your wonders, and I was surprised, looking at those clever people, playing with their toys and trinkets, sacrificing their health and serenity merely to be shut up always in a splendid cage, whether on the road or at home, and to fill their bellies with odoriferous poisons. I've come to love you, Ivan; I'd like to make you a daring horseman; I'll teach you how to manage a horse and a musket. If you should come to like some Kirghiz girl, I'll be your matchmaker and will help to set up your new household."

I thanked him for his kindness to me and said, "In my situation, there's really no choice to make; in any case, I would rather be a warrior than a servant."

After this, Arsalan-Sultan ordered his horsemen to show me their artistry. He tossed some Russian coins on the ground, and his swift riders picked them up while galloping at full speed; they galloped standing on the saddle, stood on their heads, stabbed stones wrapped in dry grass and thrown into the air with their lances, snatched one another's caps, and wrestled on horseback. Their agility and the art of the Kirghiz on horseback and in all martial exercises enchanted me, and I asked Arsalan-Sultan to begin teaching me the art of a horseman immediately.

"Confess, Ivan," he said to me, "that this amusement is much more suitable for a man than your sad dancing to music, jumps and turns, which your youths perform at so-called society balls. I've seen your amusements and dozed off from boredom. I noticed, brother, that at first you didn't agree willingly to become a Kirghiz warrior, but I'm sure that with time, after you've rid yourself of those town fumes, you won't part from us."

Meanwhile we arrived at our night quarters. Before some lazy driver would have unharnessed our horses, our camels were unloaded, the yurts were pitched, a fire was made from dry bushes to warm our kettles. The women busied themselves preparing food and milking the cows and mares; the men formed a guard and patrol. At the fires, cheerful songs and the sounds of reed flutes could be heard. The sky was clear and strewn with stars, and the air was mild. Arsalan, while waiting for supper, sat on his saddle in front of his tent and summoned me to him.

"Ivan," he said, "you speak many languages, and therefore you know better than I do how to learn them. But since we have neither books nor schools nor teachers, I must advise you to learn Kirghiz as soon as possible. Ask for the name of every object and use the words you know boldly, without being ashamed of being laughed at. Necessity will teach you faster than a paid tutor. To learn the language quickly, I advise you to fall in love: that's the best and fastest means. That's the way I learned Russian. I will tell you that tale sometime. But know that to be a brave horseman, it's not sufficient to know how to manage a horse, handle arms, and speak the language of our people: you must also know how to read the heavens like a book. I myself want to teach you that art."

At these words I interrupted Arsalan and said, "What! Do you really want to make me a shaman or a seer?"

Arsalan smiled. "I believe the shaman's predictions no more than you do," he said. "But that's not the point. Living in the steppe—where, fortunately, people are not so attached to one place like trees—we have to be able to read signs so that we can make our way day and night. By day the kurgans, tombs erected above the graves of our deceased brethren, act as our guides, as well as bushes, lakes, rivers, hills, and even the color of the steppe. At night, it's the sky. Do you see that bright star? It's the *Temir-kazyk* (iron pole).[3] It's always visible in the place from which winter and cold winds come. That's where the sun rests. To the right of that star the sun rises; it stands opposite it at midday, and it sets on the left. This star serves us instead of that little case with an arrow that you call a compass. There's the *Chuban Zhuldus* (shepherd's star),[4] which indicates the time when we drive the herd from the field back to the encampment and back again. There's *Arkar* (the wild sheep):[5] these stars hide during winter, and their return in the spring signals

3. The North Star.
4. Capella.
5. The Pleiades.

the reappearance of fresh grass. But I don't want to confuse you now with all these names. Learn to know the heavens and the earth and you will never lack for anything but your courage." The night passed propitiously, and at sunrise we struck our tents and continued our journey.

We continued in the same fashion for about ten days; we stopped at the foot of a hill dividing the steppe from the north, and we made our camp close to a small river. Since the old men were foretelling a harsh winter from various omens, we began to build double-felt yurts ahead of time and prepared a large quantity of firewood, reeds, and dry bushes. As for provisions, we prepared primarily dried meat and a beverage of fermented rye flour, similar to the residue in a distillery.

Meanwhile, at Arsalan-Sultan's orders, I was trained every day in military matters and horsemanship. They began by tying me to an unbroken horse and releasing me into the steppe—to drive my town cowardice out of me, as they said. They provided me with meat in no other way except by placing it on the ground; I was supposed to procure my dinner by grabbing it while seated on my horse, first at a walk, and then at a trot, and finally at a full gallop. I was also supposed to secure, on the point of my lance at a gallop, flour cakes baked on the coals, a great delicacy; up to then they wouldn't let me eat any game until I myself could catch it and knock it over with my whip. They wouldn't let me mount a horse except at full speed. Thus by the time the first frosts arrived, I had become a skilled horseman, by following one rule: "Little strokes fell great oaks."

Chapter 14

Arsalan-Sultan's Account of His Stay in Russia

When it snowed, the Kirghiz spent the majority of their time in their yurts, sitting around fires and listening to their storytellers. Our herds and flocks were still out in the open and grazing on the grass below the snow cover. Besides driving the herds from one place to another, guarding them and preparing food, more meat during the winter, we had no other work. The Kirghiz, in their inactivity, live in their imaginations. Their tales are filled with marvelous, supernatural events, and they always have as their subject some horseman who wanders through the steppe, does battle with tyrants and those who oppress the fair sex and with magicians; he steals beautiful women, robs rich caravans, and finally returns to his village and rests on his laurels. Love always serves as the beginning of these tales; their songs also breathe tender passion and heroism. Understanding the Kirghiz language well enough to sense the sameness of these stories, I soon grew bored of them, so one evening I asked Arsalan-Sultan to tell me his real adventures. He fulfilled his previous promise. In his story all the ideas belong to him because with the passing of time, I couldn't maintain the originality of the Kirghiz style. Arsalan spoke Russian with some minor mistakes—just like our well-born lords and ladies, who from the cradle receive a foreign education. He told me the following tale.

"It is ordained that man, gifted with intelligence and an immortal soul, should surpass all senseless creatures in malice and cruelty, and not being content tormenting and consuming other animals, he constantly aspires to the destruction of his fellow man. You see, Ivan, that in our encampment we live amicably and harmoniously like brothers, but don't think that love and friendship are shared by all our people. No! All tribes, all hordes, fight among themselves. And an insult perpetrated against a Kirghiz in another settlement or in another horde must be avenged by his whole encampment or horde. This general revenge, or *baranta*,[1] although a common custom, is stronger than any law, because people are usually more eager to submit to their evil propensities and personal advantage than to the laws of wisdom.

"My father was beloved by the khan and was even his relative, but our khans are powerless and my father couldn't defend himself with his protection from the vengeance of a powerful sultan who ruled the tribes of the Chizlyk and Dert-Karik, the bitterest enemies of Russia. The pretense for this quarrel was that my father had received gifts from the Russian court; as a matter of fact, the quarrel was caused by my mother's preferring my father when two suitors had already been courting her. Frequent attacks and insults caused by enemies of the encampment dependent on my father forced him to migrate from the depths of the steppe to the Russian frontier and to seek assistance in the form of gunpowder and arms from the Russians. As proof of his loyalty and devotion to Russia, my father left me and several other young boys as hostages, wishing me to see the world, observe the orderliness in civilized countries, and after a while, be useful to my fellow countrymen by my new knowledge.

"At the time I was about your age, Ivan, they sent us to Moscow, where they appointed an officer—that is, an official—who was obligated to look after us at government expense, to accompany me everywhere, to point out all the curiosities, and to supervise our behavior. This official, who had lived for a long time in the Orenburg area, knew our language slightly. From Moscow they sent us to Petersburg, where the government provided a Tatar translator and a Russian teacher.

"I confess that the splendor of luxury and the appearance of general contentment at first made a great impression on me and aroused the desire to remain in the city forever, or to build a city in my own territory

1. Retribution (Kirghiz).

and to establish the same kind of order there. My curiosity couldn't be satisfied: I wanted to see and know everything; I wept from irritation when I didn't understand what I saw or heard. Empress Catherine II was willing to receive me. I was dressed elegantly and brought to the palace in a carriage harnessed with six horses. I looked at the people proudly from the carriage windows and assumed that the entire capital was absorbed with me because everyone stopped and looked at me with curiosity. Making our way along one street, we were forced to pause because the crowd was blocking our way and asking the officer about me. Suddenly music began to play, and monkeys were visible at the open windows of a house we were passing. The people, without waiting to hear what the officer would say, ran to see the monkeys, and we continued on our way. This was the first blow to my vanity, and I formed a low opinion of the crowd who preferred to look at the monkeys, rather than at a sultan's son. At the time I didn't understand that it's just as difficult to maintain the constant attention of any people as it is to harness the wind, and that people always recall only what they fear.

"The empress received me very graciously; she showed me much kindness, gave me presents, and sent me home, having instructed the notables of the court to introduce me into society so that I could be a better judge of the advantages of enlightenment.

"With the empress's words, I became fashionable, like a new hairdo or a new style of dress. There wasn't a single ball in town, grand dinner, or special evening where the *handsome Kirghiz* wasn't in attendance. That's how the notable ladies referred to me, because at court it was said, 'This princeling is not as homely as the Kirghiz are usually described.'

"Distinguished ladies and gentlemen were charmed by my simplicity, and I was amused by their loquacity and their foolishness, with which they mistook big things for small ones and small things for big ones. Once I found a worthy family in tears and sorrow: everyone was weeping, from the father to the nursing infant.

" 'What's happened to you?' I asked the lady.

" 'Ah, dearest prince, you knew our uncle . . .'

" 'What happened? Has he died?'

" 'Oh, if he'd died, that would've been only half the misfortune, because he's already begun to squander his estate, which my children are supposed to inherit, but he . . . ah! He's fallen into disfavor with his powerful protector!'

" 'What was the cause of his sudden fall from grace?'

" 'His immodesty and talkativeness. My uncle's protector took pride in and bragged about concocting a new sauce for fish, but my uncle confided in a friend in secret that he'd invented it; and that was the end of his friendship with his protector!'

"I couldn't refrain from laughter, and this reaction was ascribed to my ignorance and savagery. Another time I came upon a friend in despair, a young, educated man. He wanted to shoot himself, to run away to us, to the Kirghiz steppe, to hide from the world.

" 'What catastrophe has struck you, my fine friend?" I asked him with sympathy and sorrow.

" 'Dear prince—I was cursed by my father!'

"I was horrified.

" 'What? Cursed by your father? Did you commit some crime to disgrace your father?'

" 'I didn't play into his hand at cards!'

" 'What? And he cursed you for that?'

"He did, and he banished me from his favor!'

"I began laughing heartily.

" 'Be reassured, my fine friend, such a curse won't rise to heaven but will remain at the card table until some amusing fellow turns the tables on him, to amuse good people at your extravagant father's expense.'

" 'The matter at hand is not in heaven, but here on earth,' my friend replied. 'As a result of this curse, I was deprived of financial support. My father's glad that now he's found an excuse to cut me off.'

" 'Why does your papa hoard his money?'

" 'Because he supplies food and drink to a crowd of casual acquaintances, who laugh behind his back at his foolishness; he boasts of his fine wines and dishes, as if it were the result of his intellect, virtue, and merit and constituted the worth of a man.'

" 'As you like; but to me you do seem ridiculous with your unreasonable habits,' I said to my friend.

" 'It's funny to some, sad to others,' he replied.

"Strangest of all is the opinion of people received into the higher circles of society. There they never ask about intellect, spiritual qualities, or a person's behavior. The first question is always, how many serfs does he own? The second question is, what rank does he hold? The third, what's his family background? And the fourth question, what connections does he have? If the answers to all these questions satisfy expectations, or if even one point is sufficiently powerful to override the others, then even if the man's a rogue, a liar, a thief, and an oppressor—all doors are open to him, he's greeted with a smile and bid farewell with another invitation. And money? Oh, for money an uncouth peasant, who for several years before then has sold spirits to lackeys and drivers, who has grown rich through cheating, is received in his master's house better than a poor warrior who has no protector other than his own service. And dinners! Your dinners have driven me mad! Just like dogs who fawn over those who feed them, your enlightened people, for a savory dish or a fine bottle of wine which they could have enjoyed at home, crowd into the house of every rogue, every thief, and don't merely forgive his dishonesty but even defend him from justice. By the way, about justice. In your courts, some people play blind man's bluff and at random latch onto the innocent and guilty; others sell justice by the pound, like some remedy at an apothecary, according to the prescriptions of secretaries and clerks.

"In a word, I have become convinced that your civilization consists in the art of speaking and writing about what's advantageous to *others*, while doing what's useful for *oneself*. Words and deeds are in such contradiction that if someone says about himself, 'I'm honest,' that means he's a liar; and if someone says, 'I'm rich,' that means he's poor, that is, in debt; and he who confesses and cries out that he's 'poor' is wealthy and wants to become even richer. When someone shouts about general welfare, it's a sure sign that he's seeking his own advantage; and he who preaches freedom demonstrates that he wants to subjugate others. After observing all these contradictions over the course of four years, and comparing your enlightenment and the advantages of city life with our own ignorance and our nomadic existence, I felt a strong desire to return to the steppe and forget about everything I'd seen and heard, like a bad dream. I was about to ask for permission to leave, when suddenly one circumstance detained me—it was love!

"According to the custom in Russia, they rented an apartment for us, the savage Asians, in a distant part of town, so that we could freely practice our religious rites and prepare our food in our own manner, without attracting the attention of curious bystanders. Once, while strolling along a quiet lane, I heard sobbing and a woman's pitiful cries coming from one cottage. Feeling an involuntary impulse, I went running into the house. A sorrowful sight astonished me. A young girl, as beautiful as an angel, held an old woman, who had fainted, in her arms and was weeping desperately, not knowing how to help her. Without saying a word, I ran into the entrance hall of the house, found a bucket of water, returned to the room with a full ladle, and sprinkled the old woman's face; I began to rub her temples and the veins on her arms, and finally brought her to her senses, carried her over to the bed, and asked the girl's permission to fetch a doctor immediately. It seemed the girl didn't notice me at first, being so preoccupied by her mother's condition, but she finally turned her magnificent blue eyes, still glistening with tears, to me and, blushing, thanked me in a soft voice. My Kirghiz apparel confused the girl; she regarded me stealthily, from head to foot, and didn't know what to say.

"'Don't be afraid of me, madam,' I said. 'I'm a Kirghiz, born in the wild steppe; but we Kirghiz also have hearts, and we know what compassion is for an unfortunate fellow human being. Be frank with me, as with a person who regards any opportunity to be useful to someone suffering and unfortunate as a rich prize. I see that you're in need: that's clear from your lodging. Oblige me by accepting this modest gift for your sick mother.'

"Without waiting for the young beauty's response, I tossed a pile of money onto the table and quickly left. The young girl wanted to detain me by grabbing my hand and imploring me to take my money back, but without listening, I pulled my hand away forcefully and ran back home.

"I've seen many Russian beauties, but never have they produced such a strong impression on me. But the image of that poor girl was imprinted in my heart and in my memory. Day and night she was present in my imagination, and I suffered for more than a week, not knowing what to do with myself, not daring to return to her house, fearing that she'd give the money back to me and thus deprive herself of the assistance. In vain I tried to forget the beauty: she'd taken possession of me like life itself, like a soul, and my Asiatic blood boiled as if a flame burned in my heart. Neither the diversions of society nor reading, which I loved a great deal, nor solitude could console me. At last I decided to see her again.

"I went to visit her one evening. Some sort of incomprehensible timidity kept me standing at the entrance; I paused beneath a window that was closed and shuttered, and I heard voices which I didn't recognize arguing in the room.

"'You should be ashamed, sir, ashamed!' said the woman. 'How dare you propose such disgrace to me in exchange for your protection, which I despise. Look at my daughter: she's unable to utter a word from a surfeit of indignation; she doesn't wish to debase herself with reproaches. We're poor, defenseless orphans, and that's why you're so impudent;

but if my husband were still alive, in spite of your wealth and rank, he'd compel you to reconsider.'

"'Enough, mother, enough; don't get angry,' someone else replied in a trembling voice. 'It's much better to give your daughter to me for her education than to marry her off to some clerk or noncommissioned officer. And you, my beauty, don't be shy, come and let me kiss your rosy cheeks!'

"'Leave me alone!' cried the beauty, and I heard the sound of an overturned table. The thought of offended innocence inflamed me with rage; I burst into the room like a madman and saw that a decrepit old man dressed like a dandy was pulling the girl by the arm, wanting to kiss her against her will. I seized him around the waist and dragged him like a sack of hay into the courtyard and tossed him with all my might into the mud. Two lackeys standing near the corner of the house came running at their master's shout and threw themselves at me. But despair and thirst for revenge doubled my strength. I took hold of a piece of firewood in each hand, fell upon my enemies, and drove them out of the gates. The old philanderer ran to his carriage, which was standing on the street corner, and called to his servants. Soon I heard the carriage take off down the street; I locked the gate and returned to the room.

"Tears of gratitude were my reward. The mother thanked me for the kindness and protection I'd shown them; the daughter remained silent, but her silence was much more eloquent than the old woman's words. The mother told me her history. Her husband had served as a commissary in the navy and was an honest man. After his death, he hadn't left them any other inheritance except the right to receive a small sum from the treasury for the prize, which had been won by the crew of the ship on which he served. His successor presented some claims against the deceased and illustrated the Russian proverb that 'the dead and absentees are always guilty.' The matter was brought to the attention of that lecherous old man—who, upon seeing Sofya, proposed that with her dishonor she purchase a favorable decision and his protection for the future. Of course, she proudly refused, with the disdain characteristic of noble natures, but the old man didn't desist in his pursuits and even began to threaten the poor mother with prison for consuming government property, unless her daughter ceased her stubborn refusals. When I found the mother in a faint, it was when she'd just received this news.

"The mother and daughter lived by the work of their hands, embroidering garments for fashionable shops; but the vile old man, to drive the unfortunate victims to extremities, deprived the poor family of even this means of support, paying the shops so that they'd no longer buy anything from Sofya and would cease placing any further orders. Poverty, one of the greatest misfortunes amid the general affluence of civilized people, soon visited this virtuous family, and if I hadn't come to their aid, Sofya would have gone to work weeding gardens to feed her ailing and weak mother, because, except for the clothes they were wearing, they had nothing left to sell. Never in my life had I shed tears, yet I wept at hearing the old woman's tale of woe.

" 'Allow me to intervene in this matter,' I said. 'If I don't find justice among the notables, I will find it higher up.'

" 'Let it be, kind Prince,' the old woman replied. 'Until the grass grows, the horse will starve.[2] We're planning to drop the search and settle with our relatives in a remote little town. If you have acquaintances, ask them to prevent that gentleman whom you saw from pursuing us. His name is Firyulkin, and he holds the rank of general. Don't go see him, because he may take revenge on you for your impetuousness. In the meantime, take back your money: we can't accept such a large sum as a gift.'

" 'You'll return the money after you receive what you deserve from the treasury; as far as Mr. Firyulkin's concerned, don't worry about him: I'm not afraid of him.'

"After staying with these unfortunate people for a while, I returned home, even more in love with Sofya than before.

"The next morning I went to the office where Firyulkin worked and waited for him on the staircase. He was alarmed when he saw me, and his expression would've changed completely, if it could have. But he didn't have a drop of blood in his body.

" 'What do you want, dear Prince?' he asked, stammering.

" 'To speak with you privately.'

" 'Very well, but this is not the place. Please come to my house tomorrow morning around nine o'clock. I'll receive you with pleasure.'

"The next day at the appointed hour I was at Firyulkin's house. The lackeys had instructions to admit me, but since there were a few petitioners in the hall and the secretary was busy in the study, the valet led me through Firyulkin's dressing room to the inner rooms. As I passed, I paused involuntarily to examine some items that I'd never seen before.

2. Literally, "Until the sun rises, the dew will ruin your eyes [and blind you]" (Russian proverb).

"'What are these two sacks tied up with strings?' I asked.

"'Those are my master's calves,' replied the valet.

"'And what's this skull?'

"'That's his hair.'

"'And these bones?'

"'They're his teeth.'

"'And what's all this makeup on the table among the brushes, powder, and pomade?'

"'That's to add color to my master's face.'

"'What a fine fellow!' I said mockingly. 'He has neither a body nor a soul.'

"'Excuse me,' replied the valet. 'He has three thousand souls. That's more important than one of his own.'

"I understood the valet's clever observation and concluded from this that Firyulkin must be a disagreeable man in all respects, if the servants had so little respect for him.

"I was called into the study. Firyulkin took me by the hand and very politely asked me to take a seat.

"'Let's forget about the past,' he said. 'You were very rude to me, but I forgive you because you don't know the rules of our communal life. Among us you can murder or shoot a person, but you mustn't touch him with your bare hands. However, there's no reason for you to get angry with me. I was in search of game, the same way you were, and I didn't know that pigeon had already been shot down by you.'

"'I beg you to speak plainly, without beating around the bush,' I said, raising my voice. 'I've only seen the poor girl you're persecuting twice in my life, and I decided to defend her out of mere compassion.'

"'Compassion in the Kirghiz steppe!' Firyulkin said craftily.

"'There's more of it there than in your gilded palaces and in your law courts,' I answered, annoyed. 'But however that may be, if you don't cease your persecution of Sofya, and if you don't resolve the matter of her father's bequest according to the law, I swear to you by my life and fortune that I shall fall at the feet of our impartial empress and lodge a complaint against you; meanwhile I shall inform all the notables and the court about our meeting at Sofya's house.'

"'Be quiet, be quiet; don't get angry!' said Firyulkin. 'Even without that I'd be pleased to oblige a Kirghiz prince: I give you my word of honor that I'll forget about your Sofya's existence, and tomorrow I'll issue a verdict in favor of her mother, because the matter's already finished. The one condition is—not a word to anyone.'

" 'Here's my hand!' Firyulkin kissed me and quickly left his study.

"I hurried to Sofya with this joyful news and was showered with caresses and expressions of gratitude. The next day the verdict was issued, and the money was paid one week later. Firyulkin didn't appear in the part of town where Sofya lived ever again. He kept his word: I think it was for the first time in his life.

"I stopped thinking about a return to the steppe. Sofya loved me; I was happy and lived my new life.

"We hid our love from her mother because she'd never have agreed to give her daughter in marriage to a Muslim. I didn't know how to proceed. Her mother's death gave her the full right to decide her own fate. The kind old woman, weighed down with age and sorrows, died about half a year after we first met. Sofya remained an orphan and declared that she was prepared to follow me not only into the steppe but also to the ends of the earth, the uninhabited wilderness.

"It was necessary to take some precautions. Sofya went first to Orenburg, while I, having asked permission of the empress, set off after her. I didn't know whether my father would allow me to marry a poor orphan, so I left Sofya in the neighboring village with my acquaintances, while I went alone to see my father.

" 'Father!' I said. 'You've experienced love and surely won't condemn your son if he chooses a wife according to his heart's desire, and not according to financial calculations.'

" 'I would like you to marry the daughter of the sultan, my benefactor,' my father said to me. 'But if you've already chosen a bride and don't want any other for your wife—it's your choice. It's you who will live with her, not me!'

"I told him about my adventure, and later that same day Sofya was in his warm embrace. Our elders were angry that I chose to marry a foreigner; our young girls were displeased, but my brave horsemen agreed that Sofya deserved to become a Kirghiz. The khan himself was eager to see my wife, and he applauded my choice."

Arsalan fell silent and covered his face with his hands. I saw his tears. At last he said, "I spent ten happy years with Sofya. Gayuk is the fruit of our love. But my wife died unexpectedly! According to the custom of our people and the will of the khan, I had to marry again. I now have three wives. They're all good women; you know them. But I loved only Sofya and will never be consoled for her loss. Ivan! Believe me, in the steppe the Kirghiz know both love and friendship, although they don't know how to speak eloquently about them. Now you know why I love

Russians. Sofya connects me to you. That's why in spite of our custom, even though you're my slave, I treat you as an equal. I was happy with a Russian woman; Russian blood flows in my Gayuk's veins, and although I witnessed many absurdities in your homeland, it's a characteristic of all enlightened peoples; so I learned from reading books. You're to blame only because you imitate foolish foreign ways. I found many good people in Russia, worthy of living with us in this steppe—and their memory is dear to me. Go to sleep now, Ivan! I feel sad; I'll get on my horse and dispel my grief in the steppe. Remembrance of past misfortunes consoles a man, while memories of former, irrevocable joys fill his heart with sorrow. Farewell . . . Onward, my steed!"

Arsalan jumped on his stallion and, galloped off into the steppe by the moonlight. I also felt sad: I loved the good sultan with all my heart.

Chapter 15

Consequences of a Hard Winter in the Steppe. The Attack. A Joyful Reunion with My First Benefactor.

We live in constant delusion and see objects as a reflection, only in a magical mirror of passions. But if delusion is excusable in a man, it's only in the case when he's distracted by feeling and doesn't see the faults in his parents and his homeland. No matter how much the noble Arsalan tried to extol the steppe, neither the eloquence of his educated intellect nor the enthusiasm of this wild child of nature could induce me to forget Russia. Winter doubled my sadness. Living in a crowded yurt with Gayuk and a few of his comrades and finding my sole pleasure in conversations with Arsalan, I was bored during the long evenings and thought about my homeland, my kind aunt—who, most likely, was in despair when she discovered that I'd disappeared without a trace. The crude diet, lack of cleanliness, smoke in the yurts, and savage cold in the steppe, where we had to patrol and guard the herds, were distressing and forced me to feel more strongly what I was missing. Finally the cold increased to an incredible degree. Our herds couldn't get to the grass under the snow, which had in any case lost its nutritional value. Storms covered the cattle with snow and the piercing cold winds hampered the breathing of the animals. At last, misfortune arrived, terrible for a nomadic tribe: a cattle plague.

The shamans tried their predictions and remedies in vain: our herds and flocks continued to diminish, and there was no way to stop the plague. Even healthy cattle, stumbling among the snowy mounds without food and lacking the strength to rake aside the hard, deep snow, succumbed to exhaustion. This situation was accompanied by a shortage of edible provisions and firewood. Despair permeated all our hearts. Instead of cheerful songs, one could hear the whistling of the winds and the moaning of dying animals. Women and children hid their tears in front of their husbands and fathers, but their feigned indifference couldn't conceal the general sorrow.

Arsalan displayed more courage than all the rest. He inspired us to work by his own example. He himself was present during the general work and encouraged the despondent; he dug up food for the horses from under piles of snow; he rode with us to collect reeds and twigs of young trees; and he surveyed the herds and selected new pastures for them. Fearing that the plague might deprive us completely of our provisions, we slaughtered a large number of sheep and buried the meat in the ground, using our dry goods with the greatest frugality. Fortunately, the wealthy Kirghiz had kept a supply of brick-tea, which we drank several times a day, preparing it first as a soup with milk, butter, and salt, and afterwards, when there wasn't any milk or butter, simply with salt and some sheep's fat. This beverage helped me to maintain my strength. Arsalan-Sultan saved the rye flour he'd procured in Orenburg and served it only as a delicacy. The Kirghiz don't eat bread, but they cook a kind of kasha from the rye flour and bake flat cakes on the coals. Only Arsalan had any rice, and that in a small quantity. It was reserved for women and the sick. Although we still weren't experiencing real famine, with the loss of our cattle that misfortune would threaten us in the spring.

At last, winter passed, the snow melted, the earth began to turn green, the plague ended, but we remained poor. Without external assistance famine would overtake us before the end of spring. We foresaw all of this, but no one knew what to do about it. Some people started talking about entering Russian service, on salary; others wanted to beg assistance from the khan. Arsalan intended to overcome our misfortune using force. Once he invited the elders to confer, and when they were all seated on the floor and had lit up their pipes, he uttered the following remarks. "It's my obligation to take care of you. I do what I can, but it was beyond my power to end the frost or stop the plague. I don't wish to conceal from you that we're now threatened by an even greater misfortune. Our enemies, having learned of our weakness and need, will attack us and exterminate everyone or else make us their slaves. Only desperate courage can save us. In obvious danger it's better to prevent misery by resistance than fearfully await the strike. I received news that a wealthy caravan is crossing the steppe and that the enemy of our tribe, Sultan Altyn, escorts this caravan with his best horsemen. Let's mount our horses and ride out to meet him, defeat him, take the caravan, and by one bold deed save ourselves both from the enemy and from famine. That's my intention. Announce this to my bold warriors. He who's not afraid of death and who wishes to save our people from abuse and catastrophe, let him come with me. I won't accept anyone except volunteers."

Several elders wanted to object, but Arsalan stood up and said, "I won't force anyone to go with me. If someone doesn't approve my plan, let him remain here in the village and, after my departure, say whatever he thinks appropriate. But now I ask you to repeat my words only to your families, without any comments. If I learn that someone dares to sow discord, remember than Arsalan-Sultan has a dagger, a lasso, and a whip. Farewell!"

Everyone left in silence, and Arsalan ordered me to remain.

"Well, and you, Ivan, will you go with me or stay with the women?"

"Of course, I'll go with you, through fire and water!" I cried.

Arsalan sat down on the ground, fell into thought, and after a brief silence, said, "Think it over carefully, Ivan; we're going to our certain death. I see no other means of deliverance to our desperate predicament except for an attack. But we'll be confronting brave and powerful enemies: they probably have twice as many men as we do, and if we don't win, we'll surely perish. As the commander, I must set an example and conceal the danger from my fellow countrymen. But I wish to be candid with you. I feel sorry for you. I grant you your freedom. Take my horse and return to your own people. Why should you have to share my bitter fate?"

I rushed to embrace the kind sultan. Touched to the point of tears, I said, "No, Arsalan-Sultan, I won't desert you in such danger! A Kirghiz doesn't surpass a Russian in magnanimity. You saved my life; you treated me not as a slave but as a son, like a friend; you taught me how to manage arms, so I would be unworthy of freedom if I were to run away from you in such cowardly fashion when you march to your death. I'll go with you; I'll fight alongside you; I'll shield you with my body; I'll perish together with you or else be with you to celebrate a victory."

Arsalan kissed me and said through his tears, "So be it!"

The next day at dawn, a hundred excellent horsemen were ready for action. In addition, almost twenty men were with our reserve horses and several camels, loaded with provisions. To my surprise, I witnessed no tears from the women and didn't hear any wailing when the men said farewell to their beloveds. Those who were unable to conceal their grief didn't show their faces. The others, folding their arms in silence, watched our preparations for the campaign. This quiet sorrow and despondency had a greater impact on the warriors than any loud expressions of grief. Arsalan appeared on his spirited steed in a rich fur coat. He turned to the crowd of women, old men, and warriors who remained behind to defend the village, and said, "Farewell!" Then he rode off into the steppe at a gallop. The horsemen followed him, waving to their loved ones.

After we had gone a certain distance from the village where we could see nothing but the smoke from our encampment, we halted to allow the beasts of burden to catch up with us since we had to keep them in sight. We spent our first night's lodging in the steppe, amid the kurgans; we released the horses in the steppe; we stationed guards all around, lit the fire, and gathered nearby on our felt pads.

The next day we set off for the Syr-Darya River and continued in single file, guided by the kurgans and the path of the sun, verifying our direction at night by the position of the stars. We marched a long time without meeting anyone in the steppe, and at last, on the seventh day toward evening, we saw some smoke in the distance. At first we thought that it was a village, but the scouts who went ahead reported that it was the bivouac of a caravan. We stopped, and Arsalan decided that night to reconnoiter and determine precisely if this was the same caravan that constituted the object of our search—and if so, to attack in the morning and be done with it.

Eight of our best horsemen approached the caravan on three sides. Four of them hurried and crept among the reeds on a small lake close enough to hear the sentries' voices and look the enemy in the eye. Meanwhile we stood ready for action and resolved to attack at the first sign of alarm to come to the aid of our scouts. But the search proved successful. They reported that this was indeed *our* caravan, but that the protection was ample, and that it would be dangerous to attack at night because they had made a kind of fortification out of the packs of goods, and their riders, armed with muskets, kept vigilant guard. We withdrew a few miles to one side and made our camp behind a hill so that our fires couldn't be seen. Arsalan gathered his warriors in a circle and made the following disposition. Our forces were divided into three detachments. He himself chose fifty horsemen to remain with him in the rear. One detachment of twenty-five would launch a false attack on the front of the caravan, and the other detachment, of equal strength, would attack from the flank. After this, the main detachment would attack the rear of the caravan and try to cut off a part of it and defend their plunder with the horsemen of the two smaller detachments, which were then to try and rejoin the main one, withdrawing from both flanks and luring the enemy's riders farther away. I was assigned to the main detachment together with Arsalan's son, Gayuk.

Before dawn, the two smaller detachments set off, while we stayed behind and extinguished the fires so that our smoke would not be visible during the day. Around noon, we heard the clatter of horses' hooves in the distance and the calls of the camel drivers. Arsalan, wrapped up in a gray horse cloth, climbed the hill to take a look at the caravan. Once he was out of sight, we mounted our horses and slowly followed his tracks. As soon as we heard shots, we began galloping after the caravan, and when we spotted it, we attacked with loud cries. The enemy, choosing not to waste its gunpowder on our two detachments, and seeing how small they were, responded with pikes and were separated from the caravan. We took advantage of this circumstance: we struck at the others, crushed them, took possession of the larger part of the caravan, drove all the loaded camels into one group, and resolved to defend our plunder to the last extremity. Sultan Altyn, seeing our success, ended his pursuit of our small detachments, which pretended to flee, luring him farther into the steppe. After returning to the caravan, Altyn attacked us with fury, seeing his personal enemy Arsalan-Sultan in the crowd. Arsalan couldn't restrain his rage either; he grabbed a spear, separated from his troops, and attacked Altyn. Rising up on his trusty steed, Arsalan drew near his opponent and was ready to strike, but just at that moment, a shot rang out and Arsalan's horse fell and knocked his rider under him.

With fiendish joy, Altyn jumped off his horse; seizing his Turkish scimitar, he threw himself at the prostrate Arsalan, ready to chop off his head. I was several paces away from Arsalan and, seeing the danger he was in, I grabbed a loaded pistol from my belt, cocked it, and fired—Altyn fell down dead next to his enemy, who in the meantime had managed to extricate himself from under his horse. Arsalan seized Altyn's saber and cut off his head with his own weapon; he put it on the end of a pike and rode back toward his own warriors. As soon as Altyn's troops saw their leader's head on a pike, their fierce bravery vanished instantly and was transformed into childlike timidity. They retreated at a gallop with pitiful cries, leaving us the entire caravan as plunder, which consisted of a hundred camels loaded with valuable Asiatic goods, a large flock of sheep, and a number of horses loaded with baggage and provisions. In addition, we took ten merchants from Bukhara as prisoners, along with fifty drivers and twenty slaves.

As soon as our enemies had galloped out of sight, we proceeded on our way in the direction of friendly villages to avoid pursuit. Arsalan didn't even have a chance to speak to me during all this commotion, but on the march he took me by the hand and turning to his horsemen, he said, "I owe my life to this person, and you owe him for the victory and the spoils! He's already free, but his merit exceeds all reward."

My comrades surrounded me and overwhelmed me with their gratitude and hugs. One of the poets who'd been with us, of whom there are a great number among the Kirghiz, immediately composed a song of praise to me. My comrades learned it by heart and sang it in a chorus during our march.

We proceeded at a quick pace and changed our direction frequently so as to avoid pursuit. After ten days of marching we returned to our village, exhausted with fatigue, but in victorious triumph. The entire village rushed out to greet us and received us with boisterous cries of joy. Arsalan related my valor to the entire gathering: the ecstatic Kirghiz took me off my horse and carried me around our encampment in their arms with songs and music, improvising verses and songs in my honor. Three yurts were granted to me, and I was offered the right to choose the most beautiful Kirghiz women as my wives. I didn't avail myself of this last privilege, but I confess that I was pleased with the honors shown me and considered remaining among the Kirghiz forever.

A few days later, they began dividing up the plunder. All the silks, pearls, and other valuables were put aside to sell to the Russians, and the money was to be used for the common needs of the village, except for a few items which were divided among the families, as well as the livestock, horses, and camels. The cash and slaves were divided up among the warriors who took part in the expedition. They allowed the Bukharan merchants an opportunity to buy their freedom. By general agreement, they granted me four shares of the plunder and the right to select four prisoners as my slaves. Among the prisoners we captured, most of whom were Persians and Afghanis, there were two Russians. Of course, I chose them as part of my share, intending to free them at the first opportunity.

In the confusion of our hurried march I didn't have much opportunity to pay attention to my fellow countrymen and didn't even have the time to interrogate them properly about their condition; I learned merely that one of them was from the gentry and the other was a retired soldier. When they were given to me, I lodged them in my tent and that same evening invited them to have supper with me so that I could learn more about everything concerning them. One of them was thirty-five years old, good-looking, even handsome. In spite of his long beard and long hair, his features seemed familiar to me. The retired soldier, about forty-five years old, was cunning and quick.

"Who are you, my dear countryman?" I asked the first one.

"I'm from the gentry and a retired officer."

"What's your name?"

"Milovidin."

"Aleksandr Ivanovich Milovidin," I cried, jumping up from my place, throwing up my hands.

"Do you really know me?" he asked in astonishment.

"Know you? I'm surprised I didn't recognize you at first sight. But you've aged, changed, grown thin, and then there's your beard, these rags! Aleksandr Ivanovich, take a look at me. Don't you recognize your *little orphan*, your Vanka, whom you took from Gologordovsky's house and left with the Yid at Slonim?"

Milovidin threw himself on my neck, exclaiming, "So it's you, it's really *you*?[1] What a strange turn of fate!"

We wept for joy and hugged in silence. The retired soldier stood a few paces away and wiped his eyes with his fist. At last we calmed down, and I, after sending the soldier to the other tent, remained alone with Milovidin to narrate my adventures to him.

Milovidin, after hearing my story, rejoiced that I was so well brought up and was positioned in society in such a way that I could be his friend and comrade. That same evening we swore a mutual oath never to be separated and to share all our sorrows and good fortune. From that moment on, we agreed to address each other informally and to be called brothers. Since it was late, we went to bed, and Milovidin promised to tell me his adventures the next day.

We rose before dawn, and Milovidin began his tale. Here I must warn my readers that everything I said about Gologordovsky and his family, everything I said about love, marriage, and Milovidin's relations to that

1. Milovidin switches from the informal *ty* (you) to the formal *vy* in one sentence.

family, I borrowed from his tale and placed in the first chapters of my autobiography for the proper order of the narration. It goes without saying that I was so young and naïve in Gologordovsky's house that I was unable to understand everything described here in such detail. And so, I'll begin Milovidin's tale from his departure from Slonim to Moscow with his young wife.

CHAPTER 16

Milovidin's Tale. A Moral Automaton and His Housekeeper. An Old Maid's Family. A Panorama of Moscow Society. A Friendly Quadrille. A Russian Foreigner. Society at the Spa. A View of Venice.

"After arriving in Moscow intending to appease my uncle and obtain some help from him, I spent several days hiding from my acquaintances; through an old friend of my father, I tried to enter into negotiations with my former benefactor. My uncle refused even to see me. All the efforts of my father's friend to reconcile us were in vain. Here's the reason for this unprecedented stubbornness: my uncle—a cold man, indifferent to everything, difficult and lazy—was a slave to his habits. He'd served for thirty years in the same office, where his job consisted of the following: to write on the bottom of the official papers *A faithful copy of the original, Stepan Milovidin*. He spent almost every evening at the English Club, where his greatest pleasure was to drink cranberry lemonade, play whist, and listen to the gossip, which, upon his return home, he would share with his housekeeper, Avdotya Ivanovna. This woman was the widow of a retired collegiate registrar; twenty years ago she'd rented lodgings in the same house as my uncle, and, after learning that he'd taken seriously ill and there was no one to care for him besides his servants, she deliberately moved into his apartment with the assistance of the police inspector; she subjugated the servants to her will, quarreled with the patient and the doctor, meanwhile never leaving the patient's bedside; she poured medicine down his throat and pestered him until he recovered. Whether it was out of gratitude or cowardice, he didn't have the nerve to drive her out of his apartment, and seeing her petulant attachment to him and her tremendous zeal in overseeing the housework, he left to her everything relating to the management of his house. My uncle soon felt the superiority of female housekeeping over that of an elderly bachelor. His linen was all in good condition, his tea and coffee tasted richer, and some favorite dish of his always appeared at his dinner table. Habit soon overpowered my uncle to such an extent, that he couldn't do without Avdotya Ivanovna; everything that she didn't prepare with her own hands seemed disagreeable to him.

"Avdotya Ivanovna's broad, pock-marked, Kalmyk face was undoubtedly unable to tempt my uncle; but he'd become so accustomed to it that he found it necessary to glance into her feline eyes every day, as a fop looks into a mirror. Similarly his ears became used to her shrill voice, like that of an old soldier to the beat of a drum; and he couldn't fall asleep easily unless during the course of the day he heard her abusing the servants, neighbors, and peddlers. My uncle's laziness and indecisiveness required some sort of excitement, and soon Avdotya Ivanovna overpowered him to such an extent, that he became a complete automaton in her hands, unable to arrange his own sleeping cap without her advice, patiently listening to her abusive tirades, and doing everything with her permission, except for signing documents *A faithful copy of the original.*

"My uncle considered himself lucky that he'd found a person who thought for him, wished for him, feared for him, and hoped for him. He gladly turned over the running of his estate to Avdotya Ivanovna so that he'd have nothing to do with the elders, stewards, and creditors, who were always trying to wheedle something out of him and then deceived him. He was grateful to fate that she allowed him to visit the English Club on the condition that he'd bring all the gossip home to her—he'd return trembling after losing at the card table, having missed some amusing scandal, and coming home without any news. Someone else in his place would have thought up something to appease the naughty woman, but my uncle had become so unaccustomed to mental exercise, that he'd suffer a migraine for three days if he had to think for three minutes about something besides filling his belly, trumps at whist, and his own *A faithful copy of the original.*

"Avdotya Ivanovna had a daughter by her husband, a retired collegiate registrar; she was in her third year when her mother took over my uncle's house by storm. It goes without saying that since then this daughter, Liza, was educated at my uncle's expense, and Avdotya Ivanovna would immediately demand that her daughter speak French, play German tunes on the clavichord, sing in Italian, and know all the European dances. All of this was provided for Liza with money, but since foreigners don't import intelligence for pay, Liza remained the same blockhead, just as God had created her.

"My father, being a general in active service, was always in the army; I lost my mother during my infancy, and until the age of ten I was brought up by one of my mother's relatives, an old maid, together with two dozen monkeys, parrots, dogs, dwarfs, Kalmyks, and all sorts of other marvels. The greatest justice ruled in this menagerie: all of us, that is, people and beasts, were equally loved, fed our fill, caressed and beaten, depending on our benefactress's disposition. Usually she was in a good mood when she heard news of the termination of a proposed marriage, whoever it was, or any bit of scandal about a married couple. She was furious when she heard about weddings, births, christenings, and happy marriages. Naturally, the happiest days for us were during the fasts, when there were no weddings. During her happy days, all of us—dogs, monkeys, Kalmyks, dwarfs, and me—were fed the same sweet biscuits and almonds, and on the bad days, we were all beaten with the same bunch of birch rods. We were taken in turns for an outing in the carriage: one day she took me, the next day a monkey, and so on and so forth. It's not for nothing that it's said, 'Equal fate unites hearts': our man-and-beast society lived in great harmony and accord, except for one mean Siberian tomcat and one stubborn old monkey, who would never join our circle and for that reason would always receive beatings from me and the Kalmyks, while we in turn were beaten by our *benefactress*. I think that I myself might have been transformed into a Siberian tomcat or a monkey had I lived longer in that household.

"Fortunately, my father, after his arrival in Moscow, took me away from there, having quarreled with my benefactress for praising the married state in her presence and affirming that he'd lived happily with my mother. My father had spent part of his paternal inheritance while in military service; my uncle, however, while signing *A faithful copy of the original*, managed to multiply his portion tenfold: he undertook to pay for my education and support me in the service. I was sent to a French boarding school, as is the custom; on holidays my uncle invited me to dine with him. Avdotya Ivanovna, to everyone's surprise, not only wasn't jealous that my uncle divided his assistance between her daughter and me; on the contrary, she loved me very much, caressed me, gave me presents, and treated me like her own son.

"When I entered the civil service after the death of my father, Avdotya Ivanovna not only made my uncle provide me with everything I needed but even made him give me more money than had been apportioned. Finally, the reason for her tenderness was revealed. Avdotya Ivanovna intended for me to marry her daughter, Liza, and as soon as I married another woman, she forced my uncle to believe that I'd been guilty of the greatest crime, had shown myself to be ungrateful, and finally, depicting me as nasty and depraved, she forced him to disinherit me and deprive me by legal means of any inheritance. A friend of my father's provided me with a copy of this pernicious document, with my uncle's signature: *A faithful copy of the original.* It was the verdict of fate, since my uncle would sooner have resolved to extinguish the sun than his countersignature; he had always regarded the copy as more important than the original.

"After learning about my arrival in Moscow and my misfortune, several of my father's friends joined together to alter my uncle's intention. They approached Avdotya Ivanovna and threatened her with hellfire and criminal court, finally managing to force her to provide me with twenty-five thousand rubles in my uncle's presence—on the condition, however, that I voluntarily renounce the entire inheritance, which was estimated at a million rubles. Since I was desperate, I agreed to everything, certain that I wouldn't gain anything by resistance. The money was handed over to me, and I left my uncle in peace to think with the head and feel with the heart of Avdotya Ivanovna, to play whist, drink cranberry lemonade in the English Club, listen to gossip, and sign *A faithful copy of the original.*

"You were educated in Moscow, my dear Vyzhigin; but you don't know our ancient capital, because you were too young and inexperienced. That den of thieves, and of Vorovatin, the corrupter of youth, and the refuge of old admirers of the fair sex at your aunt's house, are two undistinguished points on the Moscow horizon. As far as the French boarding school at which you studied is concerned, these establishments throughout Russia are as like each other as two sheets of white paper. Petersburg can be compared to a beautiful young coquette of high society, seeking delight with all the decencies and all the calculations of educated society. Mother Moscow resembles an elderly, rich widow, who, after having lived in high society, has withdrawn into the heart of Russia, to a provincial town located in the midst of her landholdings, to play the leading role in her neighborhood, without severing her ties with the capital. Moscow, my dear friend, has succeeded in weaving out of all the foreign wonders and customs its own fabric, an original tapestry in which foreigners recognize only the threads of their own factory, but the pattern and embellishments belong to our native Moscow.

"The best Moscow society is composed, in the first place, of so-called old men, who've served their time and settled in Moscow out of exhaustion or for some other reason, for some temporary rest, in anticipation of their eternal rest. This venerable rank constitutes a living chronicle of the last half-century or, better to say, living citations in contemporary Russian history. Members of this status also form an Areopagus,[1] or supreme court for judging all contemporary occurrences. They hold their meetings at the English Club and in the salons of respectable elderly ladies of the first three classes. The distinction by ranks among them is observed with absolute strictness, as in a disciplined regiment under arms. Politics, warfare, internal administration of the state, appointments to public offices, legal proceedings, and especially the awarding of ranks and granting of honors, are all subject to review by this clamorous Areopagus. It's this class that gives society balls, dinners, suppers, and evenings for important people visiting Moscow, first-class local officials, and the best members of the gentry.

"In the second place are officials in active service in Moscow courts of law, who are distinguished from officials in Petersburg and other towns merely because they live in greater luxury, have more influence on affairs, and don't waste their time on peripheral matters—for example, literature or the sciences—the way some young officials in Petersburg do.

"In the third place, there are officials who are not in active service, or their mothers' little pets: that is, the rear rank of the phalanx, protected by blind fortune. Of these lucky ones, most are unable to read the Psalter, printed in old Slavic characters, although they're all included on the list of Russian antiquaries. They're called the 'archival youth.' These are our *petits maîtres*,[2] fashion-mongers, betrothed of all brides, in love with all women whose noses aren't located on the back of their heads, and who know how to pronounce *oui* and *non*.[3] They set the tone for

1. The earliest aristocratic council of ancient Athens.
2. Dandies or fops (Fr.).
3. Yes and no (Fr.).

Muscovite youth on the promenades, in the theater, and in salons. This rank also provides Moscow with philosophers of the latest fashion, who are full of everything beyond measure except for good sense; masters in rhyming and desperate judges of rhetoric and the sciences.

"In the fourth place, there's an enormous crowd of all sorts of retired officials belonging to old families and those who have obtained distinguished ranks, of whom some are spending their property at leisure, while others play cards and all sorts of tricks; still others simply live from day to day at the expense of Moscow hospitality.

"In the fifth place come provincial landowners, who arrive to spend their winter in Moscow, to devour their rural reserve and admire their daughters dancing at balls during the Assembly of Nobles or at evening parties, until some suitor, attracted by the dowry (about which the talkative aunts know well how to spread the news all around Moscow), demands their charming hand in marriage, never having done a day's work in his life.

"In the sixth place are visitors from the capital and from the army, come to seek rich brides, which Moscow has been long known for. These gentlemen usually begin from on high and end up with wards and merchants' daughters, with whom calculations are much more accurate.

"These are the chief divisions of our Moscow society, which, in spite of its diversity, constitutes one whole similar to an endless masquerade or a Venetian carnival. There's no sense for me to tell you all the good and bad about this mixture now. You'll see it yourself in time. I'll merely say that there aren't as many good people anywhere else, in spite of their eccentricities, as there are in Moscow.

"The most prominent feature of Moscow is its hospitality or its passion to provide food and drink to anybody and everybody. Dear Vyzhigin! If by any chance our planet were to be subjected to ten years of bad harvests, and if provisions were sold only for gold, even then no one in Moscow would go hungry, except for the household servants, who in general are not that well fed, most likely for the purpose of making it easier for them to carry out their tasks. Although I'm not a statistician, I can vouch for the fact that more is eaten and drunk in Moscow in the course of one year than in all of Italy in two years. To force their guests to eat and drink to excess is considered the primary characteristic of a warm welcome. To drink and eat one's fill is a form of pleasure, which not even educated men can refuse. But I've gotten carried away about our beloved Moscow and digressed from the tale of my adventures.

"After receiving twenty-five thousand rubles, I proceeded the same way as I did with any money passing through my hands: that is, I looked only at the beginning of my capital and didn't want to see the end of it, so as not to be too alarmed as it shrank. I rented a nice apartment and a carriage with four horses. I engaged an excellent cook, chose one day a week to entertain my friends to dinner and an evening, and went to pay visits in town. My wife won a large following among the men, as I did among the women. The former found my wife *astonishingly* charming, while the latter called me *terribly* agreeable; soon we made the acquaintance of the best families in town and began to live as *decent* people should: that is, plying others with food and drink, receiving a surfeit of invitations to dinners and suppers, dancing everywhere it was desirable, getting dressed up, playing cards for high stakes, and therefore going into debt that we couldn't pay, and so on and so forth.

"All capital in the hands of a spendthrift has two ends. At one end are pleasures and whims; on the other, if there's no repentance, there are delusions, which frequently lead to crimes. I came to my senses with my last one-hundred ruble bill and was awakened by the piercing cry of my creditors. A bankrupt man, like a corpse, is always surrounded by a swarm of creeping moral vermin and bloodsuckers, wishing to destroy his moral existence. There appeared a multitude of fake gamblers, moneylenders, and all sorts of operators to lure me onto a path of vice. They proposed to convert my house into a den of iniquity, hoping that I'd attract wealthy people from the upper class of society, and that my wife, a beauty, would console the losers with affectionate glances. Others wanted me to allow my name, for a certain percentage, to be used for dishonest purposes, and so on. I confess that I often broke the laws of strict morality, out of thoughtlessness and a propensity for extravagance, but I never debased myself by deceit or violated the laws of honor. I drove away all of my tempters and resolved . . . I didn't resolve anything; I merely refused to host gatherings in my house, having obtained my carriage from a coach maker on credit and decided to pay more frequent visits in Moscow than previously, hoping to stumble across some good luck. I convinced my creditors to wait, promising to pay my debts as soon as my situation improved. Seeing they'd nothing to take from me, they agreed. Fortunately, there was no one among them who, to console themselves for their losses, wanted to send me to prison for nonpayment of my debts and have the pleasure of having to feed me at their own expense.

"Although my financial ruin didn't occasion a great deal of noise, nothing is hidden in Moscow, and soon the news spread in whispers throughout the capital. I've already said that in Moscow there are more good, or at least condescending people, than in any other place. They talked it over, argued, criticized, and abused me behind my back but then fell silent.

"One elderly wealthy lady, who found me *terribly* nice, offered me her friendship and assistance; her husband, considering my wife *astonishingly* charming, in spite of his age and gout, had a very tender heart and couldn't stand by callously and let the lovely Petronella go in need of fine clothes. We became friends, formed one happy family, and once again lived in clover. My wife began to dress more elegantly than before; I began to invite my acquaintances more often and to treat them more generously, to gamble for higher stakes; and, after paying off my old debts, I began to rack up new ones.

"The relatives of Count and Countess Tsiterin were very displeased at our close friendship. To distract and divert the old couple, they asked their doctors to advise them both to travel abroad to take mineral waters at one particular celebrated spa, thinking that my wife and I would remain behind in Moscow out of decency. But where there's passion or need, decency plays no part. The elderly couple decided to visit the spa out of a love for life, but they proposed that we accompany them. We accepted this proposal with pleasure. To free us from the boring company of the old countess on the trip and abroad, I feigned illness; meanwhile, though I moaned and limped at home, I sang and danced around in different places. We had a rather nice time in Carlsbad.[4] Society at the spa consisted of withered coquettes searching for their lost freshness in the mineral waters; gamblers; ministers and grandees of royal courts, deprived of their places and powers, who, at the beginning of their disgrace, usually resort to the mineral waters, as if to the waters of the Lethe,[5] to expunge the memory of their former majesty; young married beauties, who, out of love of virtue, search for relief from the confines of painful conjugal fidelity, far away from their homeland; young and old scatterbrains in search of adventures throughout the wide world; and finally, a multitude of nervous, consumptive folks of

4. Karlovy vary (in the Czech Republic) is one of Europe's most fashionable and famous spas.

5. A river in Hades whose water, when drunk, made the souls of the dead forget their life on earth.

both sexes, who, according to the accepted rule, consider treatment at a spa a distraction and a pleasure, and consequently both healthy and sick try to commit more stupidities, to the benefit of doctors, innkeepers, gamblers, and nymphs.

"I fell into my element and, feeling bored in the company of my friends, the count and countess, I rewarded myself outside of home for suffering boredom. My wife, with whom I lived in harmony meanwhile, looked for distractions of her own; there was neither jealousy nor concern between us. But, dear Vyzhigin, sooner or later a thoughtless and depraved life leads to the abyss. Listen and learn!

"Among the attractive visitors to Carlsbad, I liked Countess Sensibili most of all; she came from Vienna with her two small children to make use of the curative waters at the spa to treat her hypochondria. Her husband, an Italian of noble birth, held a distinguished position in the Austrian territories in Italy and was unable to accompany them. Some sort of languor was spread over the countess's face, and a deep sensibility was expressed in her gaze and communicated to those whom she looked upon with her large black eyes. After meeting her several times in the home of an elderly Austrian baroness, I gained her favor and received permission to call on her. I considered her an Italian, but just imagine my surprise when I learned that she was a Russian princess, although she didn't speak a word of Russian. Educated in Petersburg by a French woman, she never heard a word of French in the home of her parents, who were native Russians. In that house a preference was always shown to foreigners; from her childhood the young princess became accustomed to hearing that Russians were barbarians, incapable of anything besides paying their quitrent[6] and engaging in petty trade, and that only foreigners were *real people*, from whom Russians should take an example of how to live in the world. The princess was told that the Russian language could be used only among the common people, and that it was so crude that a well-brought up lady might suffer a sore throat from pronouncing the challenging endings on Russian words. The princess' governess swore that she'd suffered a whole week from both toothache and a swollen tongue as a result of trying to pronounce the Russian word *poshchechina*,[7] in spite of the fact that it was uttered so readily by Russian maidservants. The unfortunate princess (I say *unfortunate* because I consider all those who don't

6. Payment made by Russian serfs in lieu of feudal service.

7. "Box on the ear" or "slap in the face" (Rus.).

know and love their native countries as unfortunate) was extremely glad when her mother, after her husband's death, left Russia and traveled far and wide through Europe, finally settling down in Florence. There the old lady married a young French bourgeois, for whom she purchased the title of count where it could be bought. When she was about to turn fifteen, the Princess Malanya was also given in marriage to Count Sensibili; soon our fellow countrywoman, after adopting all the Italian customs, even forgot about the existence of a place called Russia. Ten years passed after her marriage, and she was experiencing hypochondria; also, it seems, she was suffering from the tedium of her conjugal state. She went to Vienna to distract herself, and then to Carlsbad. There I paid her particular attention and showed her that Russians could love just as tenderly, powerfully, and passionately as Italians and Frenchmen, thus reconciling her to her homeland. She even began to study Russian and found that the word *lyublyu*[8] is extremely tender and pleasant to the ear.

"Countess Sensibili was obliged to travel to Venice and join her husband. I begged Countess and Count Tsiterin to leave and spend the winter there. I had passed the time very pleasantly, visiting the lovely Countess Sensibili every day as her Russian teacher. I didn't want to enter her house under my own name, since then I would've had to introduce Count Sensibili to our dance family circle, together with the countess, and that might upset our friendly quadrille. I also met Countess Sensibili in the home of an old female friend of hers and at all the local amusements, of which there were quite a few in Venice. I'll say a few words about this city.

"The once proud Venice, after having been removed from politics and the whims of the aristocracy, and having lost its power and wealth, had not been deprived of its passion for amusements: on the contrary, it had become a focal point for dissipation and enjoyment. In Paris and London people are distracted from sensual pleasures by politics, the sciences, the fine arts, and clever conversations.

"In Venice, except for the music, which predisposes the mind for tender sensations, people don't know other pleasures, except for flirtation and amorous intrigues. Love is the atmosphere of Venice, and foreigners come there from distant lands to breathe in the air of this new Paphos.[9] Nowhere do women enjoy such freedom as they do in Venice.

---

8. I love (Rus.).
9. A coastal city in southwest Cyprus. In ancient times it was a center for Aphrodite's cult.

With only a light covering they daringly enter coffeehouses and casinos and mix with the crowds on the square of San Marco, in the monastery of San Giorgio, or on the new embankment. Women are escorted not by their husbands but by *cavaliere-servente*,[10] who perform the same service for Venetian ladies as do smart adjutants for the young wives of elderly generals; that is, a serving cavalier must be in constant attendance on the lady from morn until night, if she doesn't consider it proper to take another companion for a certain amount of time. You know that Venice is built on sandbars in the sea, that it has canals instead of streets and open boats or gondolas instead of carriages. These gondolas are floating temples of love and graves of conjugal fidelity. The celebrated jealousy of Italians burns out before Hymen's lamp and changes into smoke and vapor, which becomes a thunderstorm only when the wives' behavior threatens to affect the husband's pocketbook.

"There's no concept of hospitality in Venice. There all the inhabitants meet only in the casinos, coffeehouses, and on the square or in the theater; they treat one another only to ice cream, chocolate, and, very rarely, dinners; they send their visiting cards to various houses. In general, Italians are created neither for quiet conversation nor for unpretentious family life. The greatest blessing for them in life is to do nothing (*far niente*); pleasure itself, as well as a nice promenade, they call work. It's unnecessary for me to say there's no rule without an exception.

"I lived in Venice as if in paradise, for almost a year, when one day . . ."

Suddenly the voice of Arsalan-Sultan rang out, and I was summoned to him; Milovidin had to interrupt his narrative.

---

10. In Italy, a man who attends a lady, especially one who is married, with fantastical devotion.

Chapter 17

The Resolution of the Kirghiz Elders Concerning My Reward. The Continuation of Milovidin's Tale. A Duel. The Flight. The Apostate Yid. Arrival in Constantinople. What Is Pera? Betrayal. Slavery. Liberation.

"My dear Ivan!" said Arsalan-Sultan. "We've decided your fate in a council of elders. I know that you're longing to return to your fatherland; if you stay here among us, it's due only to your love for me. So, go with God, Ivan! Here's what we've decided."

From his bosom Arsalan removed a piece of paper, which had been wrapped in several handkerchiefs, as if it were a great treasure. He read the following: "(1) The prisoner of the invincible, free, and illustrious Kirghiz people Ivan Vyzhigin is being set free for his great service to the outstanding tribe of Baganali-Kipchak and for saving the precious life of Arsalan-Sultan. (2) The free Ivan Vyzhigin has been declared a son of the noble and excellent branch of Baganali-Kipchak. If the abovementioned Ivan Vyzhigin should gain the ability to see things with eyes of wisdom and should he ever think of returning to the blessed and best country in the world, the Kirghiz steppe, every father of a family must receive him into his yurt as if he were his own son, every Kirghiz warrior as his own brother, and every Kirghiz maiden as her bridegroom or husband, as Ivan Vyzhigin wishes. (3) The entire excellent tribe of Baganali-Kipchak is obliged to feed and clothe Ivan Vyzhigin and heat his yurt until such time as he has grown children or until he himself declines that privilege. (4) All of the plunder belonging to Ivan Vyzhigin, as well as his horses and camels, the elders take upon themselves to sell at the first opportunity in Orenburg or on the frontier in Russian fortresses, and to send the money wherever he orders. Meanwhile a thousand gold coins have been collected and awarded to him for his journey, along with twelve bales of the most valuable merchandise, which shall be delivered to him at once. (5) Ivan Vyzhigin has the right to take his Russian slaves with him out of the steppe and will receive a military escort to the border."

"Are you satisfied with our resolution?" asked Arsalan. Instead of an answer, I rushed to embrace him and burst into tears. At the mere mention of my fatherland, Russia, all my self-importance disappeared like smoke, and I decided to set off immediately.

"When do you want to leave?" asked Arsalan.

"Tomorrow," I replied, lowering my eyes, as if embarrassed by my own lack of gratitude.

"So I will get everything ready for your departure," said Arsalan and immediately summoned some of the elders. So as not to interfere, I went back to my yurt.

When I told Milovidin that we would leave for Russia tomorrow, he almost lost his mind from joy: he wept, laughed, leaped, sang, and finally, after he calmed down a bit, thanked God with tears for his deliverance and called me his benefactor.

"Vyzhigin!" said Milovidin, clasping me to his chest. "You've restored my homeland and my freedom to me, but this heart of mine will always belong to you. I'm yours forever!"

The retired soldier was no less overjoyed that he was liberated from the infidels, and he begged me to take him along as my servant, because he had neither house nor home in holy Russia.

After a breakfast of mutton roasted over some coals and a drink of home-brewed beer, I asked Milovidin to finish his tale.

Milovidin continued, "One time when I left home accompanied by a servant to take a gondola ride along the shore, a young boy handed me a note and then vanished. I thought it was a love letter and hastened to read it. But this time I was deceived in my hopes. The note was written in Russian and contained the following: 'If you have even a drop of Russian noble blood left in you and if your honor is not completely besmirched by a career of debauchery, come at twelve noon tomorrow to the Sun Tavern, on *terra firma* along the shores of the River Brenta, with a pair of pistols, without telling anyone at home about it. You'll recognize me on the spot where one of us will surely perish.'

"Although I was unable to figure out who could have sent this challenge, I decided to appear at the appointed hour and immediately went to see one of my friends, an Englishman, to ask him to serve as my second. After crossing in my gondola to the square of San Marco, I entered a coffeehouse under the arcade, hoping to find my friend there, and there at the door I received another note written in French with the following: 'One of us must perish, so that the other can be happy. I shall expect you tomorrow at 3 p.m. with a sword on *terra firma* at the Sirena Tavern along the shore of the River Brenta. We're well acquainted, so there's no need to sign my name because when we meet, you'll recognize me.'

"Two duels in one day is no laughing matter! In spite of the fact that I can handle a sword and that I was considered one of the most skillful marksmen in the regiment, I still couldn't overcome the anxiety caused by suddenly receiving two challenges at once. Think what you will, but it's very unpleasant to be killed or to kill! I guessed that my flirtations had drawn me into this unpleasant situation, but I couldn't figure out what episode had incited an unknown countryman against me. The Englishman not only agreed to be my second but rejoiced that he would witness two murders. He confessed to me that the national English malady, melancholy, had already begun to torment him, and on that account, he'd undertaken travels around Europe, so he could have more opportunities to become acquainted with death and had come to hate life.

"I spent that whole day with the Englishman. He tried to quench his melancholy with wine, while I wanted to drown my sorrow. We returned home very late. The next morning I hurried to the Englishman with my weapons, and we set off to the meeting place, to have time to eat breakfast before dying.

"Around twelve noon, we were proceeding along the main road, expecting our opponent. A pleasant-looking Italian approached and inquired which of us was named Milovidin. After that he proposed a stroll in the park where my opponent was waiting for me. At the end of a grove I found my fellow countryman, who was pacing in haste around a small meadow. I went up to him and, tipping my hat, said, 'Dear sir! I don't have the honor of knowing you; consequently, I couldn't have offended you intentionally. It seems to me that it would be reasonable if we talked first.'

"'That's completely unnecessary,' replied my countryman. 'The offense you committed is of such a nature that it's impossible to make amends. And there's no need for you to know my name. It's enough to say that I'm a Russian nobleman and officer, and I've come here on purpose to fight a duel with you. Please take up your position and fire. But remember that if you wish to play the role of a generous man, you will be committing suicide. The terms of the duel are as follows: our seconds must measure fifteen paces and, at a given signal, we're free either to fire at once from there or one of us, allowing the other to fire, can advance one step and fire at his opponent, aiming the pistol at his forehead.

" 'That's not a duel, but murder!' I cried.

" 'What, do you have cold feet already, you profligate!' said my opponent menacingly. 'But if you're thinking of avoiding punishment by cowardice, I'll blow your brains out at once!' Like a madman, he threw himself at me with his pistol, and if the Englishman hadn't managed to grab him by the arm, he probably would've killed me right then and there. My blood was boiling.

" 'I'll show you who's a coward!' I shouted and immediately took up my position.

"The signal was given. I aimed and pulled the trigger—my opponent fell, covered in blood, before he even had a chance to fire. I ran to help him, to learn his name and the reason I'd incurred his hatred. But he shouted at me to go away and not spoil the final moments of his life with my presence. His second didn't want to answer my questions either and asked us to leave. The Englishman and I returned to the tavern, mystified by this incomprehensible occurrence, and resolved to wait for the time of my next duel without returning to town.

"Around the agreed-upon time we left for the other tavern, where we found a second. He led me into a room where, to my great surprise, I found Count Sensibili.

" 'Your Russian lessons,' he said, addressing me, 'have made such an impression on my wife that she decided to take her share of our property and our children and set off for Russia. Therefore, I've decided, Mr. Professor, to give you a lesson of a different kind. I could hire and arm mercenary assassins, as other husbands do in such a case; but, being in military service myself, I have different rules and wish to have the pleasure of repaying you myself for this insult. I know everything!'

" 'Not a word about the offense,' I replied. 'But if you assume that I prompted your wife to leave you and set off for Russia, I swear to you, that you're mistaken, and this is the first time I've heard of it.'

"'Enough, sir, enough,' replied the count. 'Don't embellish your double deception with a lie: your wife and . . . But I didn't come here for explanations. Let's go into the garden.'

"It was impossible to refuse, and I had to cross swords with the unhappy husband. At first I tried merely to defend myself and inflict only minor wounds on my opponent, thus ending the fight. But the count attacked me so mightily and tried to do me in with such zeal that I myself got angry and began attacking him in turn. He tried desperately to grab my sword and threw himself at me with great force. But the sharp point of my sword pierced his breast, and he fell to the ground.

"The Englishman and I carried the wounded man to the tavern, summoned a doctor, and leaving the count in the care of his second, we hastened into town. Upon arriving home, I met my wife, who said that Count and Countess Tsiterin had locked themselves up in their room and were deeply distressed; the count was even refusing to see the lovely Petronella, while the countess had declined to receive me and asked us to move to another apartment. My wife learned from the valet that the count's son, a former captain in a Hussar regiment whom we didn't know at all before, had secretly arrived in Venice, was mortally wounded in a duel, and lying at death's door. He had written a letter to his parents that was so disturbing that his mother had fainted three times while reading it and suffered hysterics and a nervous paroxysm as well, while the count experienced a severe attack of the gout and a kind of paralysis. I guessed immediately that my irreconcilable opponent was the count's son but hid this from my wife. Half an hour later, I received a letter from Countess Sensibili in which she reproached me for the death of her children's father, called me a monster and a murderer, and forbade me to appear. In despair I ran to my friend the Englishman and there found out that the authorities were looking for the killer of Count Sensibili and a foreign traveler, and if I didn't get across the border by evening, I'd be arrested and thrown into jail. I returned home, gathered all my money and valuables, wrote a letter to my wife in which I informed her what had happened, and advised her to return to her father's house and wait for me there. After this I hired a gondola and set out for the shipyard. A Genoese ship was pulling up its anchor and planning to set sail for Constantinople to take advantage of the favorable winds. The captain, whom I had treated just the other day in the coffeehouse, agreed to take me with him, without asking to see my passport. At nine o'clock in the evening I was already sailing on the open sea. Tears flowed from my eyes at the thought of my unfortunate wife, whom I still loved and whom—by my own flightiness and, to tell the truth, my own depravity—I had led to this catastrophe! But there was nothing to be done, and reluctantly I resolved to bear my misfortune with steadfastness. I was tormented by repentance and swore to reform.

"Among the passengers was a Turk who spoke French and Italian well; seeing my pensiveness, he tried to divert me with his conversation. He was around fifty years old, had traveled a great deal around Europe and Asia, had been to Egypt, and had acquired much information through reading and observation. He confessed to me that he was a Yid from Hamburg, had studied medicine in Leiden, and when he was thirty, during a trip to Constantinople, he'd converted to Islam from pure conviction, not for any other reason. Not being accustomed to arguing about religion, I didn't begin questioning him on that score, but noticing that he was beginning to talk about his faith more frequently, praising Islam, I asked him decisively not to go on about that if he wished to enjoy our conversation. The apostate complied with my wishes and, after this, confined himself to praising the Turkish government, which I listened to patiently, simply to become acquainted with the rights and customs of the Turks. Most of all he praised the honesty of the followers of Mohammed, describing how they kept their word, and noting how Islam had cured him of the innate propensity of the Israelites—who, in his opinion, still hadn't stopped worshipping the golden calf, now in the form of money.

"Our voyage was successful, and we soon arrived in the Constantinople harbor. I moved into a house in Pera,[1] where an Italian kept a sort of inn. Upon unpacking my suitcase, I almost fainted when I found neither my money nor my valuables. In despair I ran to the ship's captain and reported the theft. He vouched for his crew but couldn't answer for the passengers.

"'If you'd handed over your money and valuables to me for safekeeping, this misfortune would never have occurred,' he said. 'You have only yourself to blame. I myself am not rich, and I can't help you very much. But here's a little money for you. You'll pay me back when you can.'

"With heartache I returned to the inn; along the way I chanced to meet my new acquaintance, the apostate, to whom I related my misfortune.

1. A fashionable district in Constantinople where the inhabitants are referred to as Perotes.

"'Mohammed orders us to help those in need, not only those who share our faith but all good people,' he said. 'I consider you a good person and can offer you room and board in my house free of charge. However, if at any time you have the resources to repay me, I won't refuse. But there's no need to talk about that now. Take your things from the inn; I'll escort you to my house.'

"I didn't know how to thank the apostate for his magnanimous offer and took him up on it immediately.

"At that time the Porte[2] was at war with Russia, and we had no ambassador in Constantinople. I didn't tell anyone that I was Russian: I said I was a Slav from Bocas de Kotor.[3] In the coffeehouses of Pera I became acquainted with several Christians living in Constantinople, which afforded me some distraction and even subsistence. I hardly saw anyone in the apostate's house; he spoke with me very little and was always occupied with some sort of business. They brought my food to my room, but the bread of charity was not only bitter but also too meager. They allotted me as little rice pilaf as a doctor would have prescribed to keep me from dying from hunger. If I hadn't had some help from the Greeks,[4] I'd absolutely have wasted away from lack of nourishment.

"Life in Constantinople could hardly please an educated and sensitive man. Europeans have almost no direct dealings with the Turks, who in their pride and ignorance despise all Christians and favor them by receiving them into their society only when they expect some advantage to accrue from pursuing their acquaintance. Besides, the Turkish way of life keeps them away from Europeans. A Muslim, if he's not engaged in some form of government service, spends most of the time in his harem and knows no other enjoyment except smoking a pipe, drinking coffee in coffeehouses, staring at the end of his nose, and listening to the nonsense of babblers and storytellers, who constitute a class of their own. Turks are very frugal with words, and they're talkative only when they're abusing the Franks—that is, Europeans and all Giaours,[5] especially the Christian subjects of the Porte. Sometimes the sultan himself is subjected to Muslim abuse, especially if he undertakes some sort of innovation, which is always considered a violation of Islam. In the

2. The government of the Ottoman Empire.
3. A bay in Montenegro.
4. Orthodox Christians living in Constantinople.
5. A derogatory word for non-Muslims, especially Christians.

coffeehouses, under the gates of the seraglio, they also mightily abuse the sultan, who could cut off their heads if he so wished, just as in Europe we abuse ministers writing in so-called opposition journals. However, the monotonous life of the Turks and their ignorance can't provide the European with pleasure in their company; and if travelers sometimes seek to become acquainted with them, it's merely out of curiosity, to fill their notebooks with tales that are only half true.

"All the business of Constantinople, political and commercial, is managed by the residents of the district called Pera, which constitutes not just a separate town but a separate kingdom, a separate people! It's where the descendants of Europeans reside: Italians (mostly Venetians), Illyrians, and other South Slavs, Armenian Catholics, a small number of Frenchmen, and an even smaller number of Englishmen and Germans. The Perotes can pride themselves that their forebears were on an equal footing with the founders of Rome during the time of Romulus, with the difference being that the founders of Rome gained their subsistence by force of arms and open robbery along the main roads, while the forebears of the Perotes used the same means, only stealthily. The Perotes have the distinction over the Romans that they didn't alter the customs of their ancestors.

"The carelessness of the Turkish police in regard to Europeans attracted captains of industry and bankrupt businessmen of all nations to Constantinople; they began to settle in Pera under the protection of the standard of Mohammed. The language of the Perotes is Italian with a mixture of Turkish, Greek, and Slavic words, with a unique pronunciation. Their ignorance when it comes to the arts and sciences is on a level with that of the Turks, but their cunning replaces all good qualities, and their knowledge of many languages constitutes all of their wisdom. Their children, as soon as they begin to babble, learn Turkish, Greek, French, and Italian. This knowledge of languages leads the Perotes to riches and honors, putting in their hands all the diplomatic affairs of the Porte, because it is from them that dragomans or interpreters are selected for European missions. One can easily guess with what loyalty they serve the Europeans when they become convinced that a Perote believes that nothing in the world is better than his own dirty Pera, nothing more majestic than a Turk, no one wiser and mightier than the sultan, and that there is nothing worse than all other nations and people who don't profess Roman Catholicism or don't have the honor of being Muslims. The Perote's ambition is no greater than to become a dragoman, and his only goal in life is to accumulate money. They also take on the calling of European trade consuls and brokers; after growing rich, they manage to become bankers by dishonest means.

"The Perotes hate the Greeks and try to harm them wherever they can, fearing their influence on social affairs. For that the Greeks pay them back in kind. As a result the Greek Orthodox don't like the Roman Catholics, merely because their religion is shared by the Perotes. Among the Greeks, to call someone a Perote is the same as calling someone a Jesuit among us. European travelers and officials from various embassies have warmer relations with the Perotes because their way of life is closer to the European model and because one can communicate with them without knowing any Eastern languages. Women play the main role in Perote society. Their entire occupation consists in sitting on a sofa all day long and, in the winter, next to a tandoor oven. A tandoor oven is a kind of low, square table covered with a padded blanket and a green cloth. There's a brazier under the table with burning charcoal, which provides warmth to the honorable company seated on small sofas arranged around the tandoor, hiding their feet under the table and covering themselves up to the waist with the blanket. As you may know, there are no stoves and chimneys in Constantinople. They play cards while seated around these tandoors, exchange gossip, sing the sultan's praises when he cuts off the heads and appropriates the wealth of his subjects who don't have the honor of being Perotes, and carry on amorous intrigues, passing love notes under the blanket. Perote women are famous for their propensity for amorous adventures, and most of them support their husbands, brothers, and fathers in matters of promotion, enrichment, and the discovery of political secrets. As a result of the absence of educated European society, foreign ambassadors invite Perotes to their balls and dances; these ladies constitute the high society of Constantinople, depending on their wealth and connections.

"A Greek acquaintance introduced me to the Perotes; since I had no money and didn't want to try my luck in love, I was received coolly. I myself didn't especially enjoy any conversations, from which I derived no pleasure for the mind or the heart. I found greater sincerity, more intelligence, and more civility among the Greeks than among the Perotes. Almost all Greek women are beauties; on the contrary, among Perote women beauty is rare. The wives and daughters of Greek nobles or the descendants of ancient Greek families are distinguished by their intellect and kindness, but they don't appear in European society because the Perote women do all they can to keep them at a distance. The Armenians are engaged solely in trade and the exchange and transfer of money; they stick to themselves and live by their own customs. The Yids, as everywhere, are old clothes dealers, barbers, shopkeepers, deliverymen, and scoundrels, except for a few rich jewelers, who are distinguished by the fact that they deceive on a grand scale, wholesale. The Turkish police keep a sharp lookout for anything relating to trade and civil order, having a large influence on the harmony and needs of a Muslim's life. They don't pay the least attention to the affairs and actions of the Franks until a complaint is made concerning duplicity or murder. But even then the police allow the accused to buy themselves off. That's why there's no place in the whole world as beneficial to swindlers as Constantinople. It's their fatherland, and the most astonishing thing of all is that besides European embassy officials and travelers, the most honest people in Constantinople are the infidels—that is, the Turks.

"I spent four months in Constantinople feeling very bored, not knowing what to take on, when suddenly the rumor arose that the plague was spreading in certain quarters. Knowing that a poor man, and a Christian at that, would have trouble taking precautions against infection, and not wishing to become one of its victims, I intended to depart from Constantinople for the islands of the Greek archipelago or for Russia. A friend of mine assured me that since I was a son of the Orthodox Church, I would be well received on the islands, where they adhere to Eastern Orthodoxy, but they advised me not to seek refuge among the Greek Roman Catholics. I declared my intention to my landlord, but he strongly opposed my plan.

"'You don't know the Greeks,' he said to me. 'Profit is their only god, which they worship constantly; discord and disagreement are the only things they know in life. Without money you'll be received as a beggar, even though you're endowed with all the talents in the world. Listen to me: I've been looking after your fate for some time and have finally found a position for you. There's a Persian merchant living here, one of the wealthiest men in the East. He's in need of a European clerk for his trade. Cast aside your noble status for a while and serve this merchant. In five or six years you'll be a millionaire yourself, you'll return to your own country, assume your noble status again, and live according to the customs of your caste, pouring water through a sieve for a lifetime.'

"After a little thought, I agreed to the apostate's proposal; the next day we agreed to visit the Persian.

"The Persian could speak a little Russian and had been to Moscow and Petersburg several times.

"'I need a person who knows French and Italian,' he said, 'but it's even better that you also know Russian. Be prepared to depart with my caravan tomorrow. If you behave yourself, you'll have a good life with me.'

"I wanted to know what terms the merchant was offering for my services. But the apostate forbade me from asking, saying that I would spoil the whole affair by the appearance of greediness.

"'In all countries not educated by Europeans,' he said in French, 'merchants don't pay a set annual salary to their clerks; they share their profits instead. You mustn't show your avarice; on the contrary, you must rejoice at your master's success, as if you were unconcerned about your own. Then the merchant will award you a share, and you will become his partner. But until he gets to know and like you, you must work diligently, like a slave, as is the custom in the East between masters and servants. If you, my dear friend, make up your mind to put up with mild unpleasantness, it will guarantee your happiness for the rest of your life. You yourself told me that you have no capital in your own country and no hope of acquiring riches. It's impossible to live at someone else's expense, and it's best to be indebted to yourself for your comfortable life.'

"The apostate's words, 'it's impossible to live always at someone else's expense,' forced me to decide, whatever the cost. I joined the Persian at his caravanserai that very evening and set off on the journey with him the next day.

"I'll describe neither the towns, nor the countries through which we traveled, nor the customs of the various Asiatic tribes which I observed along our way; that would take too long. I will describe everything we saw in a very few words. Ignorance, cruelty, and rude manners constitute the primary traits of these peoples, with the difference being that in the Asiatic towns where trade is flourishing, the inhabitants' languor and faintheartedness replace love of knowledge, the arts, and refined luxury; on the contrary, the nomadic Asiatic tribes are distinguished by reckless bravery and ruthless aggression. Dear friend! Among Europeans there are people who cry out against enlightenment. Let them look at Asia Minor and compare the condition in which it remained under the rule of the wise caliphs, lovers, and defenders of enlightenment with its present position. Ignorance reduces humanity to the state of a senseless animal, and the most dangerous type of animal on earth is a half-enlightened people who, having advanced beyond their initial ferocity, have learned to recognize merely the letters in the *great book of enlightenment* and mistake words for things and things for words. Only selfish culprits wish for ignorance to take advantage of darkness to deceive their imitation goods and counterfeit money in exchange. But, dear friend, I can't give you a better illustration of the use of enlightenment than to relate an anecdote that has remained in my memory since childhood.

" 'What's your intention in establishing academies and schools, and why do you propagate the sciences?' asked Vizier Mussafer of Caliph Harun-al-Rashid. 'Don't you think, Sire, that an enlightened people will obey you better?'

" 'Undoubtedly,' replied the caliph, 'an enlightened people will better judge the fairness of my laws and the integrity of my intentions.'

" 'But will they pay their taxes better?'

" 'Of course: in their enlightenment they will find more ways to enrich themselves and, in addition, they will understand that I'm not demanding anything unnecessary.'

" 'Will your warriors fight your wars better?'

" 'Much better, understanding that the happiness of every family depends on the well-being and renown of the fatherland; besides, they will fight more successfully under the leadership of competent commanders.'

" 'But won't your wise men, your philosophers, decide to meddle in the affairs of state? Won't they search for mistakes in your administration?'

" 'Let them search, find them, and tell me: I'll be more careful in the future and act better.'

" 'What! You'll allow, oh, light of the world, your wise men to speak boldly about anything that occurs to them?'

" 'If I didn't do that, they couldn't enlighten us.'

" 'But can't the wisest man fall into error? Can't they mistake error for truth?'

" 'One person might make a mistake, but another would notice and correct it.'

" 'Sire, I must reveal everything to you at last: from the moment the people began to be enlightened, some arrogant people even dared condemn the actions of your favorites, trusted with your confidence, and even of me, me myself!'

" 'I understand,' said the caliph, and he left the room.

"I would order this parable to be inscribed in gold letters on some public monument to expose hypocrites and cheaters wishing to spread ignorance so they can fish in troubled waters. It's desirable that all legislators have before them the example of Harun-al-Rashid, who by extending enlightenment among the crude population of Asia gained strength, wealth, and fame. Once enlightenment declined in Asia, the caliphs' monarchy did, too.

"A large number of merchants and travelers joined us for their own safety, for in ignorant countries there's no other way to travel than with protection from armed guards. We hired them as we proceeded from town to town. My new master commissioned me to oversee the caravan; he treated me very courteously, as if I were his equal. But when we arrived in Persian territories, he declared that I was his slave and that he'd purchased me from the apostate Yid. In vain I tried to persuade him that the apostate had no right to sell me, because I'd never been taken prisoner but had arrived in Constantinople voluntarily, as a traveler, under the protection of the laws and the rights of nations. The Persian explained to me that there was an ongoing war between the Turks and the Russians, and the apostate knew that I was a Russian; consequently, every Turk was permitted to take a Russian captive, wherever he found him; besides that, I owed the apostate so much for my board and lodging that it would take my whole life to repay.

" 'You did not bargain with the apostate,' said the Persian. "Therefore, he's free to demand a million sequins from you!'[6]

"To convince me completely of my legal slavery, the Persian showed me a piece of paper, which he said was a bill of sale, witnessed by a *cadi* in Constantinople.[7] I was obliged to keep silent and obey! After traveling through the famous Persian towns of Tabriz and Teheran, at last we reached the town of Astrabad, where my new master had his regular residence, and where he conducted a large trade with Bukhara, Khiva, and Russia. In general he didn't employ me in his trade but used me as a language tutor for his son, a lad of around twelve years of age; he announced that any attempt to escape from my slavery would be punished by death, while subservient obedience would be rewarded by decent remuneration and courteous treatment. As a matter of fact, I was treated rather well in the house, just as our landowners, when in a good mood, treat their sons' tutors or their parish teachers.

"Once I was in the master's room when a merchant came to buy some luxury goods. My master laid out on a table a bunch of rings, earrings, and European necklaces; I was extremely surprised when I saw

6. A gold coin minted by the Republic of Venice from the thirteenth century onward.

7. A civil judge in Arabic, Persian, or Turkish countries.

some items among them that had been stolen from me on board ship. When the customer, after examining and bargaining for them, left the room, I said to the Persian: 'Master! Among these things, I notice some that belonged to me. I can't suspect you of theft since you were not on board the ship where my things were stolen. But tell me please, how did you acquire these items?'

" 'I bought them in Constantinople from your former landlord, the apostate Yid,' replied the Persian.

" 'So that's the kind of honesty the Yid learned when he converted to Islam,' I cried involuntarily.

" 'Friend!' replied the Persian. 'The faith isn't to blame; the person is. I will give you some advice: always beware the homegrown wolf and a person whose religious conversion occurred because of base forms of self-interest.'

"I spent more than three years as a slave and at last decided to escape, in spite of the threats that were made to kill me. I made the acquaintance of a Bukharan merchant and promised to pay him a high ransom if he would escort me to Russia. Fortunately, this man had been to Russia and knew my uncle, who'd sold him several shawls for his housekeeper. The Bukharan took me with him from Astrabad and joined the caravan heading to Russia across the Kirghiz steppe. You already know the rest. I'm obligated to you for my freedom. When I return to Moscow, I intend to locate my wife and to purge myself completely of two unfortunate weaknesses: flirtatiousness and prodigality. I will return to the service, and by my labors I will earn a poor, but honest, living."

"Amen!" I said. "I salute your intention, but now it's time to prepare for our journey."

Chapter 18

Departure from the Steppe. The Police Chief Once Again! Collectors of Transit Dues. The Officials' Feast.

I won't describe how we took our leave of Arsalan-Sultan, his family, and the entire village. I can only say that tears fell much more sincerely from the elongated brown eyes of the Kirghiz than those which adorned our clothes with a badge of mourning; although neither the fond farewells of Abélard and Héloïse, nor that of Hector and Andromache, nor the friendly declarations of Orestes and Pylades have been translated into the Kirghiz language.[1] Still the simple-hearted expressions of the good Arsalan and my comrades, his horsemen, touched me to the depths of my heart. To tell the truth, the lovely Kirghiz maidens were somewhat angry with me for deciding to leave the steppe adorned with their charms, but at the last moment, all was forgotten. The old men consoled the others, repeating, "He'll come back to us; you'll see that he'll return. It's impossible that such a fine youth will like anything better than our Kirghiz steppe."

Milovidin and I rode on horseback. The retired soldier, Nikita Petrov, whom I had taken in service, led three camels with our luggage.

1. A reference to the famous twelfth-century Parisian love affair between Peter Abélard and Héloïse d'Argenteuil; Hector is one of the major characters in Homer's *Iliad*, and Andromache is his loving wife; Pylades was Orestes's cousin and intimate friend in Greek mythology.

Thirty bold horsemen constituted our escort and followed us at a certain distance. The weather was warm, and our journey was extremely pleasant.

A man of the world with a kind heart and sound mind learns the true value of society only when he's separated from it. Everyday cares, connections, acquaintances, and the search for adventures distract one's mind from important things; only a stroke of misfortune or solitude tears away the hypnotic blindfold from his eyes.

"Now I fully feel the insignificance of all that I considered true blessings," Milovidin said to me once. "And I thank Providence that it rescued me from the edge of the abyss of vice by means of the misfortune I deserved as a result of my frivolity or, better to say, my bad behavior. Here I am, all alone on the face of the earth, with no wife, no relatives, without friends, without any fortune, and I don't even have the right to arouse pity for my situation and be consoled by memories of my innocence. A bitter fate! What might I have been if I'd continued to serve, used my abilities for the general good, and tried to gain the attention and respect of decent people, true sons of the fatherland? I was searching merely for pleasure in life, for distraction, and wasn't worried about the future, or even about the present. What's left from these empty acquaintances, from relations based on depravity? Desolation in my heart and repentance in my soul. I ruined my wife, whose only fault was her frivolity. I could have turned her into a good and happy wife, an adornment to her sex. Dear friend! Let my example serve as a lesson for you. In my youth I didn't have a reliable guide—that's the reason for all my misfortunes! My lively imagination and passionate character knew no restraints. No one thought about providing me with any rules to govern my life. In my youth I considered morality and boredom synonymous. Vyzhigin, you're now in exactly the same situation as I was when I was your age. You've also been taught everything except what's essential for you to know. Beware of people who'll seek your friendship only to pursue pleasure in your company. Never follow their first suggestions, and consider the means before you set about achieving your ends. You're a handsome lad. Beware of women. . . . But you're yawning, Vyzhigin! I see that moral education has a greater impact on you by example than by precept."

As a matter of fact, not having the habit of listening to lectures on morality, I almost dozed off in the saddle while Milovidin was pouring forth his feelings from the bottom of his soul.

"Dear friend!" he added. "Like it or not, I'll have to be your guide in society. If not my past morality, then my experience, a desire to reform myself, and my love for you convey that right to me."

I gave him my hand; clasping it, he said, "Forever!"

An hour before we reached the first Russian outpost, we said farewell to our Kirghiz escorts. When we saw the Russian guard, our hearts started beating faster and we prayed through our tears, blessing our dear homeland. One must be separated from it to feel the joy of returning to it. The first moment you cross the frontier is genuinely thrilling. The future appears in the most attractive form: all shadows disappear, and each person who speaks your native language seems to be a friend, a brother!

The commander of the outpost, a Cossack officer, received us very courteously, but then he declared that since we didn't have any passports and were returning to Russia with brand-new items, he had to present us first to the local authorities, where we'd receive certificates of residence; and second, to the customhouse, where they would examine our goods, charge us duty, and affix stamps. The next day we set off, accompanied by an orderly and six Cossacks.

After arriving in the district town, we appeared before the police chief. Mikhailo Ivanovich Shtykov had been a major in an infantry regiment; retired as a result of his wounds, he accepted an appointment as police chief in his homeland at the request of the nobles. He was about forty years old. His face expressed a certain dejection and importance. It was obvious that from his habits of command and obedience, he demanded submission from those he considered his juniors. When we set foot in his presence, he barely rose from his seat; in response to our bows he merely nodded his head. Then he took the piece of paper from his orderly; when he read that Milovidin was a retired lieutenant and I was a minor from the gentry, he rose slightly a second time and bowed politely, although very matter-of-factly, from on high, as they say. Then he sat down and, pointing to a row of chairs along the opposite wall, drawled, "Be so good as to take a seat."

In the meantime his clerk appeared, stood at attention, hands at his sides, looked his commander in the eye, and waited for orders.

"Dear sirs!" said Shtykov. "There have been cases when fugitives from Russia, even criminals, have hidden in the Kirghiz steppe, then returned from there under different names, even posing as people of high rank. To stem this abuse, we now have orders to cease providing passports to Russian travelers until we have proof that their statements are true. And so, forgive me for having to detain you here in our town until we receive a reply to my documents from Moscow and from the district town, which I am sending off by post today. I know that if I were to wait for a decision from the court of law to the question of your passports, your hair would turn gray from anguish and old age. But I'm allowing myself several deviations for the common good. I will write directly to the governor and then to a friend of mine in Moscow. If I become convinced of the truth of your statements, I shall see to all the formalities as quickly as possible. Now I ask one of you to withdraw to the next room, so I can take a statement from the other."

The attendant led me to the next room, through the hallway; from boredom I began to examine the little pictures in wooden frames hanging on the walls, stained with black oil paint. Above all, my attention was drawn to the inscription under glass that was written on parchment in letters consisting of human figures in various positions, legs raised, on their knees, crawling, and so forth. The inscription declared, "Such is the world today!" Further on were some prints finger-painted and engraved with a nail: *Four Seasons*, *Four Parts of the Globe*, *The Adventures of Genevieve of Brabant*,[2] and in the place of honor, above a large chair, a portrait of Peter the Great. In a small bookcase with a glass door stood several dozen books, among which I noticed the Bible and the New Testament; *The Core of Russian History* by Khilkov;[3] Tatishchev's *Russian History*,[4] *A Book of Laws*; the *Works* of Lomonosov,[5] and an address-calendar book. In a quarter of an hour I was summoned into the police chief's room, where I had to answer various questions. I said merely that I'd left Moscow from my aunt's house with Vorovatin to travel to Orenburg, that I'd fallen ill there, and when I came to, it turned out that I was a captive of the Kirghiz, not knowing how that came to pass. I didn't want to share my guesses regarding Vorovatin and Nozhov or to say how Arsalan-Sultan had rescued me from the hands of the monsters that wished to take my life. That would've taken me too long and might have involved me in a criminal act. Milovidin advised me to remain silent until we learned more details or until we met Vorovatin. When

2. A heroine of medieval legend, whose story is a typical example of the widespread tale of a chaste wife falsely accused of adultery.

3. Andrei Yakovlevich Khilkov published his history of Russia in 1770.

4. Vasily Nikitich Tatishchev was a prominent Russian imperial statesman and historian, best known as the author of the first full-scale Russian history (1768).

5. Mikhail Vasilyevich Lomonosov (1711–1765) was a Russian polymath, scientist, and writer who made important contributions to literature, education, and science.

the interrogation ended, the police chief demanded that I turn over all my money to him for safekeeping; he said that he had located inexpensive and quiet quarters for us where they would give us ample credit.

"I'll return your money when I receive answers from Moscow or from the governor," he said.

At these words Milovidin couldn't restrain his rage, and he cried, "How dare you rob us?"

"Rob you?" repeated the police chief, turning red from anger. "My dear sir! I've taken towns by storm, seized provinces, but I've never robbed anyone. Thank your lucky stars that your situation and my office don't allow me to settle this matter any other way. I'm acting according to the law. Do you understand: according to the law! You have no passports; I don't know who you are; therefore, I can't leave this money with you and have you destroy all the safety measures I've taken on your account. It would be the same as handing the keys to the powder magazine in the fortress over to the Turkish prisoners. Please go to your lodgings!"

Remembering Savva Savvich and thinking that all police chiefs were birds of a feather, I said to him, "Listen, Mr. Major; let's settle this amicably. Take two hundred gold coins and let us go back to Moscow today without further fuss."

The police chief blushed once again, fixed his large eyes on me, and fell silent.

"If that's too little," I said, "take an extra hundred and free us from all further claims."

The police chief flared up and after tossing out three dozen or so curses, not directed at any specific person, which were sometimes repeated by us in a sort of a whisper, he cried, "Young man! Shut up or I won't be able to restrain myself. How dare you offer me money? Obviously you spent your youth with rogues or . . . ." He was unable to finish his sentence from exasperation.

I replied coolly, "Excuse me. I've known police chiefs, judges, and even prosecutors!"

"The devil take them all, and you, too!" cried the police chief. "Hand over your money and off with you!"

There was nothing to be done; I gave him the sack with all my gold coins. The police chief counted my money in silence, gave me a receipt, and ordered an invalid to take us to our quarters, saying that this man would remain with us as a guard of honor. After we got out onto the street, Milovidin said, "What do you think now, brother? We've gone from the frying pan into the fire! This Mr. Police Chief is no better-mannered than the Kirghiz horsemen. Our money will disappear into thin air. Gold will melt like butter as it passes through the hands of these officials. Damn that police chief!"

"Don't be angry, dear friend, and don't rush to judgment," I replied. "It's true that this police chief is rough as a wild horse, but you saw how angry he got when we tried to bribe him."

"This is all merely a trick," Milovidin demurred. "Long ago I stopped believing in the integrity of officials; I'm prepared to wager that we'll never see your money again! You won't be able to wheedle any money out of his pockets even by firing a cannon. Why should he take just a part of it, when he has the whole sum in his power? You know the axiom of mathematics: a part can never be equal to the whole."

"What about the receipt?"

"What's that receipt on a scrap of paper worth if even a legal document in a clerk's hands will burn up as if on coals? They'll ensnare you so much that you'll renounce all of your property to save your own body and soul."

"We'll see!"

"We will!"

They rented two clean rooms in a merchant's house for us; he traded in wines, sugar, tea, and spices. We found several customs officials already waiting for us, circling our goods like foxes around a henhouse, while our retired soldier, like a faithful mutt, was guarding our property, sitting on one bale, glancing all around him. As soon as we entered the room, the officials approached us: one with customs stamps, a hammer, and string; another with writing paper; and the third with a large book under his arm.

"Excuse us, dear sirs, for disturbing you," said one of them with a kindly grimace.

"But we'll soon be done," replied another.

"And we'll finish as you wish, relying on your word," said the third.

"Our duty involves many unpleasantries," said the first, "but among honest and educated people, there are ways and means to shorten and hasten this tedious, disagreeable process. Especially in the present case we must be lenient: you're not merchants, and you didn't know that you must present a declaration, submit a list of your goods, indicate their value, record and sign a variety of official documents."

"I'll take all that upon myself," said the second official, rolling the papers into a tube and bowing politely.

"Then there are the customs stamps and the valuation," said the first.

"That's my part," said the third, also bowing.

"Last, there's the payment of duties: my business," said the first, raising his voice and looking imposingly at the other two.

"Gentlemen!" I said. "Do what you must. We don't understand a thing about it, but seeing your politeness, we hope you won't harm us."

"God forbid that we harm you!" all three cried together.

"Now let's get on with the business," said the first. "We ask you to be witnesses, because we don't engage in any threats and don't want to arouse any suspicion in such honest men."

We all went out together under the awning where the merchandise was stored. Several guards began untying the bales, while I stood there, not knowing what was in them, overjoyed to see whole piles of silk fabrics, Bukharan shawls, and even one bale of Turkish shawls of excellent quality. I noticed that the customs officials blushed when they saw these goods. The first of them took Milovidin and me by the arm, led us to one side, and said, "The duty on these goods will cost you a great deal, almost half their worth. But we'll make it so the wolf will be satisfied and the sheep will remain whole. However, in order to value the goods, let us take home several pieces: it's not possible to price them in the presence of others, you understand, and do anything to your advantage."

I looked at Milovidin; he smiled and shrugged his shoulders.

"Do as you wish, but do it as quickly as possible," I said. The official bowed politely, returned to the piles of goods, whispered a few words to his colleagues, and began to lay some items aside. Meanwhile the second official wrote something down, and the third attached stamps. The work proceeded like clockwork. At last it started to grow dark and the customs officials departed, leaving their guards to watch over the merchandise. When it was completely dark, a driver came in through the back gate and took away the items in a cart that had been put aside and went away. All for the valuation!

The next day at dawn one of the customs officials appeared with a stack of papers that I was supposed to sign. At last he presented his valuation and the amount of duty I had to pay. I wrote a note to the police chief, asking him to pay the duty, which he did at once; he came to our quarters, locked all the goods in a warehouse, fixed his seal to it, and said, "Your goods are subject to the same fate as your money: you'll have the right to dispose of them when I receive answers to my questions."

When this entire operation was finished, our host, a respectable old man with a white beard, entered our room and said that if we needed anything, we should turn to him. I told him to go to the customs officials and ask them to return our goods, which they'd taken home for the valuation.

"There's no use crying over spilled milk!" the old man said with a smile. "Nevertheless, they charged you twice the regular duty on your goods. These gentlemen forget neither themselves nor the treasury."

"That may be called knowing how to combine the practical with the pleasant!" said Milovidin. I wanted to get angry, to complain, but the merchant calmed me down and prevented me from making any such attempts, saying that it would be to no avail because I'd already signed the official receipts.

"You must submit patiently to circumstances when it's not possible to avoid them, dear sirs!" said the merchant. "For example, if the doors in a house are low, everyone who wishes to enter must bow his head, so as not to bang it. If one board on a bridge is higher than the others, every carriage must be jolted as it crosses that bridge. So it is in certain human affairs: there are always abuses born from the ease of committing them; neither time nor laws nor force can eliminate them. Even in the days of the Apostles, excise collectors were infamous for accumulating wealth in spite of people's censure. To this day the collectors of duties in all countries of the world brilliantly maintain the relic of their origin; as their worthy descendants, they imitate their distinguished forebears. Today you experienced this for yourself, gentlemen, but I've been experiencing it all my life. However, dear sirs, don't judge everyone by the behavior of a few. Everything has its right and wrong side, and among today's excise collectors you'll find people worthy of your respect. But unfortunately, such is the way of the world that where there are more opportunities to sin, there will be more sinners. A blacksmith can't avoid burning his fingers, and a fisherman can't keep from getting wet. You understand me, gentlemen!"

Our first task was to dress in the European fashion, because we didn't have any clothes besides our Kirghiz apparel. Having some money, I wanted to dress stylishly. While our landlord was procuring some cloth, we spent several days indoors, looking at the passersby through the window. The house stood on a square where a German tavern was also located. It was filled with a crowd of officials and gentry who arrived in town on business or from idleness. We wanted to discern what the fashion was, but we couldn't make either heads or tails of it: in a provincial town every young man dressed in his own style, in the full sense of that expression. Young men sported terrible side-whiskers, mustaches grimy from tobacco smoke, and Spanish-style beards. Their bristly heads were covered with peaked caps or service caps. Their jacket—that is, frockcoat—adorned with laces in the Hussar style or their Cossack cloak, their long velveteen or nankeen trousers, and a black tie constituted all the apparel of a local dandy. Coats were reserved for important occasions, balls, weddings, and invited dinners. Each landowner had purchased a supply of clothes in the capital when he had to go there to ask for money from the Opekunsky Council[6] or had ordered clothes through his friends in the provincial town. Hence there was no prevailing fashion in this provincial town, and it was impossible to know which of the older fashions was the most recent. Besides that, fashionable coats and vests were often passed from hand to hand through bartering, with the assistance of fifty-two colorful leaflets, and therefore a person's clothes didn't always fit him well. In a word, we were so unfortunate that in the course of six days we failed to see even one person fashionably dressed, and the three local tailors with whom we conferred disagreed among themselves. At last the bailiff of one grandee who arrived from Moscow solved the matter for us. We took him for a model, ordered our new clothes at the first chance, and started to venture out of the house.

The principal figures in town were the mayor, the district lawyer, the treasurer, and members of the district court: the last, however, didn't have much influence on society because they lived on their estates and came to town only when the court was in session. Their representative was the secretary, who united in one person all the functions of a court of law in its judicial and social aspects. Although the police chief had considerable significance in the district, in town his power was second to that of the mayor; therefore he was neither the first nor the second but equal to the mayor; consequently they were natural rivals. The larger social world was reflected in this small circle (with all its intrigues, caprices, and eccentricities), "like the sun in a drop of water!"

At the end of two weeks, the police chief was satisfied with our modest behavior, and he appeased his rage and made his sister, the district lawyer's wife, invite us to a name-day party. We arrived in time for dinner and found a large group of people already assembled. The

6. A bank connected with a famous orphanage.

ladies—dressed in light-colored caps, ornate dresses, and Turkish shawls and adorned with pearls and diamonds—were sitting by themselves and chatting. The young girls made up a separate circle and whispered, their eyes lowered. The hostess didn't attend to the guests herself but scurried from room to room, bustling and fussing. Her light-colored cap had been somewhat discolored by kitchen smoke, and her curls had loosened as a result of the heat. As soon as a new guest entered the room, the hostess's little daughter informed her mother; her face bright red, she would run hurriedly from the kitchen, greet the new arrival, show him to his place, and hasten back to the kitchen.

Other female guests would eagerly inspect the newly arrived friend from head to toe, seeming to strip off her clothes with their eyes. The men, most of whom were officials, were all wearing uniforms: they were strutting imposingly up and down through the rooms, pausing frequently next to a little table with vodka and hors d'oeuvres. Everyone knew about our adventure, my money, and my merchandise, and therefore everyone treated us quite politely but with a patronizing air, because it still wasn't known if I'd become a petitioner in court or was free from any legal proceedings.

I wanted to hear what the provincial officials' wives were talking about; pausing in the doorway of a small living room, I heard the following, "Ah, my dear, what a lovely cap you have! Did you really get it at the fair?"

"No, my dear: straight from Moscow, Kuznetsky Bridge,[7] from a Frenchwoman."

"And your dress, madam, was it made here?"

"Lord have mercy! I've had enough of those homegrown seamstresses patronized by the wife of the marshal of the nobility! They can cut and sew, but they can't replicate the styles from the latest fashion journals."

"But the journals are all in French!"

"So what? Matryona Ivanovna sits around reading French books all day long. She could explain it to her seamstresses."

"But it's tailors who write for seamstresses, so not everyone can understand when the workers start talking in their language."

"That's true: recently Andrei Kuzmich's son read me a description of a fashionable dress; I can wear it, but it's too complicated to understand!"

7. A fashionable street in Moscow with many fine shops.

"Don't tell me about it; the French are odd people. How do they come up with words for every stitch, hook, and hem?"

"But, my dear, you haven't shown off your new shawl. It's magnificent!"

"Where did you buy it?"

"My Sidor Yermolayevich brought it back from his business trip."

"God grant him good health!"

"And where was your brooch purchased, my good woman?"

"In Petersburg."

"I saw it on the tax farmer's wife."[8]

"My Karl Karpich got it from him in payment of a debt and at a high price, my dear."

"How can a tax farmer be in debt?"

"After all, a lawyer would never be in debt to a tax farmer!"

"That's true, my dear."

"Ah, by the way, did Akulina Semyonovna Padcheritsyna come to see you? There's an inquiry underway about her husband's business."

"She did."

"She came to see me, too."

"And me."

"Ah, my dear, what a woman! She should have been born an official. She scatters decrees around! She's always complaining of her poverty, her straitened circumstances, but what shawls she wears, what pearls!"

"They say she would never forget about herself when her husband occupied his position."

"How could she? She's no fool!"

"The two of them are a perfect match for each other!"

"Have you heard the anecdote about the large pearls which hang around her neck like a horse's collar? God forgive me!"

"No!"

"Tell us, please do!"

"When her husband was in office, the secretary dared not write any decision without asking Akulina Semyonovna; the petitioners were supposed to appear first to her, before they went to court. Once a little old woman wearing a kerchief and a shoddy fur coat approached her to petition on account of her grandson, who'd been selected as a recruit

---

8. The Russian state transferred the right of tax collection to private individuals called tax farmers in exchange for a certain fee.

for the army.[9] After bowing to the ground, the old woman gave Akulina a small box and said, 'Take it, my good woman: if it doesn't suit you, it will suit your daughter.'

"Akulina Semyonovna thought that the old woman had given her a little box with tobacco; she got angry and shouted loudly so that the landowners who were in the next room would hear all about her impartiality, then gave the old woman a slap on the hand. The little box fell on the floor, and pearls were scattered all over. What a fuss! Akulina Semyonovna threw herself down on the floor to gather the pearls, meanwhile shouting to her daughter Ashenka to help. Ashenka came running from the next room and forgot to close the door so the gentry could observe the entire comedy. One of them questioned the old woman on the street and spread the news throughout the entire district."

"Ha, ha, ha!"

"There's a lesson for you not to reject trifles. It's not for nothing that Karl Karpich always repeats: 'Every donation is a blessing, and every gift is perfect.' "[10]

Just then we were summoned to dinner. The ladies were seated on one side at the upper end of the table, while the men were seated separately. I took a seat next to the police chief. Dinner began with a huge fish pie, which would have been large enough to hold our esteemed hostess for a nap. Liqueurs of all flavors and colors accompanied the pie and were gulped down in large quantities by the guests to keep them from any harmful effects of eating the half-baked piecrust and the half-cooked fish. Cold dishes followed the pie: a suckling pig with horseradish, jellied meats, ham, and so on. The cold dishes needed to be warmed, so once again they turned to the liqueurs and to the Madeira, which sparkled pleasantly in beer glasses. Tasty Russian cabbage soup had to be diluted in the stomach with Madeira, and so by the time we got to the first dish after the soup, the foreheads of the esteemed guests were covered in a fine sheen and their noses were as red as cranberries. It was here I understood the full meaning of the Russian proverb: "The first goblet is like a stake; the second, a falcon."[11] The difference is that goblets were flying, not falcons, as well as tumblers and bottles. While

9. The normal term of service in the Russian army was twenty-five years.

10. A paraphrase of James 1:17.

11. The proverb continues, "And the third, a flutter of little birds." The meaning is that drinking becomes easier with each additional glass.

several dishes with sauces circulated before the roast appeared, all the guests (except the police chief, Milovidin, and me) were in such a disposition that they were prepared to mount a military battery. The wine softened the officials' hard hearts, and a new candor arose in its heady fumes and settled on their tongues.

"Martynych!" cried the secretary of the district court so loudly that the windows in the house shook. "Martynych! You betrayed me, you wretch: you let the bear out of my trap. I would never have forgiven you if it weren't for your wife, the godmother of my child."

"Enough, don't be angry, Karpich," replied the local attorney. "If you skin the bear yourself, we'll end up with hardly a tuft of fur. There's no doubt about it; you're a master at fleecing petitioners, Karl Karpich, but I, too, have a wife and children to feed."

Everyone started laughing.

"What's there to say? You're a master swindler, Karl Karpich," the guests cried on all sides. The secretary proudly wobbled on his chair, stroked his head and belly, and said grandly, "A master at work."

"Honored gentlemen!" cried a thin, bald, swarthy clerk from the other end of the table in a thin, clear voice. "All human wisdom is inscribed on a Dutch banknote. All the Latin I learned in seminary isn't worth that one inscription: *Concordia res parval crescent*, that is, 'Union makes small things grow.' That means that if the gentlemen of the court wish to accumulate money, they must live in harmony, peacefully, decide matters unanimously, and listen to their secretary. The knight depicted on the coin is none other than a secretary, and the bundle of arrows in his hand indicates that he should keep all the judges and their affairs in his hands."

"Bravo, Klimych, bravo!" cried the officials in ecstasy.

"In his hands," repeated the secretary, "and rule them with a rod of iron!"

In the meantime a hamper of champagne was brought in, and toasts began. After drinking to the health of the hostess, the host, and finally every guest and his wife separately, his children and servants, they started drinking, as though it were their job, emptying all the bottles in succession. When they had finished the hamper, they stood up from the table and somehow managed to toddle into the living room.

Up to now I haven't mentioned my neighbor, the police chief. He took no part in the drinking or in the conversations of the honored company; he was silent during the course of dinner. The guests didn't address any speeches to him either because, knowing his ways, they were afraid that he might tell them the cruel truth to their faces, which is usually called rudeness. After dinner the police chief invited Milovidin and me into the garden next to the dining room, where, among various assorted fruit trees, there were sunflowers, poppies, and peonies. We sat down on a turf bench, and the police chief said, "It's a pleasure to see that you're not inclined to drain your glass following the example of my worthy colleagues. You can readily judge my pitiful position," he said, turning to Milovidin, "seeing the kind of people with whom an old officer has to spend his life. But 'necessity wears down a stone.'[12] These official leeches would've smothered me if, fortunately or unfortunately, I hadn't become a relative of theirs by the marriage of my sister with one of their gang and wasn't in favor with the governor, my former general. It's difficult to swim against the tide. It's enough that I've been able to fence off my part of the administration from their influence. The gentry elected me and allotted me my salary, which is barely enough to live on. If you stay here, you'll hear more about Shtykov, and I implore you not to form an opinion about the whole district from what you've seen and heard. There are honest and decent people living here among the landowners and elected officials, but unfortunately our gentry doesn't study the practice of Russian law, and not many of them have gotten used to putting pen to paper, while those who have been working in the civil service refuse to run for office and have retired to the country to live in peace. It follows that the lawyers control affairs. They constitute a special breed in Holy Rus',[13] which lives like a moth on the dust of edicts. I advise you to go home so as not to witness even greater temptations. It may happen that these guardians of justice will start pulling each other by the hair, when it comes to further discussions."

The police chief stood up, and we followed his advice. Meanwhile many of the guests made their way out to the garden, holding hands and singing songs. On returning to the room to locate our caps, we saw that some men were already playing faro at one table and, at another, playing a different card game. A pile of banknotes began passing from hand to hand.

After arriving back home, we asked our landlord to explain several things that we didn't understand. "Tell us, please," I said, "what sort of strange fellow the police chief is."

12. The Russian saying is actually "A drop of water wears down a stone."
13. The old name of the country.

"He's known as an eccentric," replied the landlord. "As a matter of fact, Mikhailo Ivanovich Shtykov doesn't resemble his comrades, and that's why he seems so strange to everyone. He comes from the petty gentry of the local district. He entered military service when he was a young man, and at the death of his parents, he gave away a part of his inheritance to some orphans, the children of his late sister, who had been married to an honest but impoverished official. You know his other sister. After he achieved the rank of major and retired as a result of his wounds, he lived here in my house on his small pension until the nobles offered him a position as police chief.

"Mikhailo Ivanovich declared decisively that he could not and would not accept bribes and didn't wish to learn to do so; therefore he didn't want to accept a position where there were additional expenses. The gentry begged him to accept the post and offered to provide him with an extra sum for office expenses and travel, with permission of the administration. It's now been ten years that he's served as police chief, and all honest people bless him. All local assessments, road repairs, billeting of men are organized among us with great precision, by rotation, and in accordance with the number of souls a landowner possesses.

"The collection of taxes and arrears takes place without any indulgence, but with the greatest leniency for the poor. Fugitives and idlers dare not show their faces in our district; peasants—knowing that their capture can please their good police chief, whom they refer to as their father—have given up harboring them, immediately bringing the fugitives to court. Investigations are carried on without any threats and blows but with strict justice. Mikhailo Ivanovich doesn't take any money from merchants at fairs for permission to trade in contraband or to deceive the unsuspecting by offering poor goods, but he enforces order, looks after weights and measures and the quality of the merchandise. During the levy of recruits, the village elders and delegates of small rural districts dare not try to go out of order or deprive defenseless parents of their last support. The bailiffs of private estates, whose landlords live in the capitals, can't oppress peasants and deceive their masters. Even vicious and wicked landowners, who, thank God, are very rare, can't treat their own serfs in an illegal fashion. In a word, Mikhailo Ivanovich works day and night to prevent abuse, defend the truth, and enforce the laws. True, his manner is rude; he doesn't like to waste words and doesn't know how to temper bitter truth with sweet speeches or to carry out his duties with nice compliments. He's strict with offenders, implacable with the wicked, and lenient with some weaknesses but only in his deeds, not his words. Long ago he would have fallen prey to lawyers' intrigues and the schemes of those who abuse their power if he hadn't been supported by our governor—an honest man with good intentions, also retired military, who knew him from their days in the regiment. All honest people like and respect Mikhailo Ivanovich; the evil ones hate and fear him like the plague. However, he doesn't interfere in the affairs of others and demands only that people refrain from interfering in his administration. That's what our eccentric is like! He's treated you somewhat rudely, but he didn't harm you, and he won't confiscate your property, like our customs officials."

"Agreed," said Milovidin, "that bitter medicine is better than sweet poison."

Chapter 19

A Business Conversation at a Russian Merchant's. A Tempestuous Man. The End of a Villain.

Our landlord invited us in to have tea. We found him with the parish priest and a decently dressed middle-aged man of pleasant appearance, whose behavior and manner showed that he was used to living in good society. The landlord introduced us, calling him Pyotr Petrovich Virtutin. We sat down around an oak table, sipping our tea, and began discussing subjects that seemed extremely important to me, since this was the first time I was hearing a conversation about society affairs.

"Wouldn't it seem strange to you, even incomprehensible, gentlemen," said the merchant, "if in all French ports there were only Germans and Dutchmen, and in English ports, Spaniards and Italians engaged in foreign trade, and that Frenchmen, like camels, merely lugged merchandise on their backs from the interior to the seashore, so that foreigners reaped enormous profits without labor, trouble, or responsibility, only because on the doors of their lodging was a brass plate with the word *Office*?"

"I'd say decidedly," replied Pyotr Petrovich, "that if the natives worked like dogs, allowing foreigners to make mincemeat of them—that is, natives work to enrich outsiders trading on their labor—then these locals must be lacking in the intelligence, money, or even honesty to become merchants themselves."

"That's too harsh," replied the priest. "I would say that probably some other ruling passion diverts the locals from foreign trade, and it puts all its advantages into the hands of anyone and everyone."

"Both of you have the right to those opinions," said the merchant, "but fortunately, Father, you're correct. I'll clarify the matter. I'm talking about our beloved fatherland. Isn't it strange, isn't it humiliating for our national pride, that in Russia almost all foreign trade is handled by foreign offices and trading posts, located in all Russian ports and even in the two capitals, as if Russia were China or Japan? Foreign merchants and manufacturers have contact only with their offices, while we Russians must look these clerks in the eye, give them what they want for export abroad, and purchase foreign goods from them at whatever prices are set by their general council.

"These gentlemen—the foreign clerks, whom we call negotiators—consider Russian merchants to be no more than contractors or porters, and as though for the love of Christ, they share with us only one hundredth of their profit. Tell me, gentlemen, will this order of things continue forever, and, with regard to trade, will we always remain in the same position as we were in the time of Richard Chancellor, who discovered the port of Archangel during the reign of Tsar Ivan Vasilyevich?[1] It seems that we have all the means to establish a respectable commercial class. Foreigners themselves praise the intelligence, shrewdness, and resourcefulness of our people. Our honesty in trade is no less than that of our benefactors, the foreign clerks, and as far as capital is concerned, we always have the advantage, since we have in our hands the raw materials of our land and our Russian merchandise. On the contrary, at the beginning, the clerks have nothing more than the brass plate on their door with the inscription *Office* and several bankers' letters of recommendation."

"A few bankers' letters of recommendation! That's the point," cried Pyotr Petrovich. "Tell me, dear Sidor Yermolayevich, whom would you trust more? A local old-timer, whom you've known for a while as a good fellow, or a foreign merchant, of whom you know nothing?"

"Of course, I'd sooner trust the old-timer," replied the merchant. "But allow me, Pyotr Petrovich, if this comparison applies to our

1. Richard Chancellor (1521–1556) was an explorer and navigator, the first Englishman to penetrate the White Sea and establish relations with Russia. Tsar Ivan Vasilyevich (also known as the Terrible) lived from 1530 to 1584.

discussion, it seems that Russian merchants could be compared to the old-timers."

"It may seem so, but not in reality," Pyotr Petrovich retorted. "You, Sidor Yermolayevich, have been trading for fifty years or so, and you know all the best merchants in Moscow and Petersburg. Can you please name me half a dozen families that are known in the trade since their great-grandfathers?"

"I confess, I don't know even a single one," replied Sidor Yermolayevich. "Here as soon as a merchant grows rich, he either declares bankruptcy because he ceases keeping company with his brethren, neglects his business, lives like a nobleman, and gives his daughters away in marriage to penniless princes and counts, or else he becomes a heavy drinker, from pride and joy, leaving his estate to be robbed by dishonest clerks and his prodigal offspring, who are already embarrassed to be merchants and lust after higher ranks; or, last, they themselves may attain noble status by various circuitous paths, under the disguise of his fervor and his service! It's true that we don't have any old mercantile houses, and there's hardly one eminent firm in Russia that can trace its origin further back than the reign of Empress Catherine II."

"Trade is supported by credit, and credit by the reputation and antiquity of a family," said Pyotr Petrovich. "In England, France, and German Hanseatic towns, in Holland, Sweden, and Denmark you'll find mercantile houses whose firms have been known for centuries and inspire more confidence than princely coats of arms. But in Russia merchants are like birds of passage in trade. A Russian merchant appears on the scene, grows fat, moves up in the world, and then either falls or struts around, having powdered himself with the dust of heraldry."

"That's true, too true!" added the merchant, stroking his beard.

"I'll mention one more circumstance," said Pyotr Petrovich. "Among us there are only a few merchants who get rich from trading on the stock exchange; they make their money primarily in government contracts. Contractors and tax farmers, in my opinion, can't really be called merchants or, as they say, *négociants*, because they produce benefits to the trade of their native countries only if they trade abroad and facilitate the sale of our goods in foreign parts. And so, wealthy foreign mercantile houses and manufacturers, like it or not, must carry on their business in Russia by means of clerks recommended to them by venerable old merchant families whose clerks were previously their bailiffs. How is it possible to conduct large transactions with Russian merchants when they appear from God knows where and then somehow disappear from the field of action?"

"That's also true!" said the priest. "But don't blame the merchants too much. There are many circumstances which force them to leave their profession at the first convenient opportunity. In the first place . . ."

Suddenly there was a noise in the entranceway. The landlord was about to rush out there, but he'd barely jumped off his chair when the door opened with a crash and a large mastiff ran into the room with a loud bark. Then a gentleman arrived, dressed in traveling clothes, sporting a pipe in his mouth; behind him followed a footman and a policeman. While the dog sniffed around the corners of the room, the gentleman took off his coat without any fuss, and the policeman announced, "Here's a guest for you, Sidor Yermolayevich. His Excellency has come from Petersburg on official business, and you're very fortunate that he's chosen to lodge in your establishment."

"For pity's sake, there are already six officials boarding here," replied the landlord. "Besides, the police chief has ordered me to house these two gentlemen."

"Be quiet, you long beard!" said the official, with a threatening glance at the respectable old man. "I don't care about your police chief, and I'll remain here because it suits me."

The landlord turned to the policeman and said, "But the neighboring houses are empty . . ."

"How can you compare your house with the neighbors' houses, Sidor Yermolayevich?" replied the policeman. "These official gentlemen are men of high rank; you know that the governor and prosecutor stay there . . . Enough, enough, Sidor Yermolayevich; if we don't have merchants answering for everyone, then we wouldn't have any order. It's the strong man who should shoulder the burden, and you are the richest of all."

The policeman went out and the official said, "Move it, old man! Clearly you men are so spoiled that you even dare to argue."

"I'm not arguing, sir," replied the merchant, "but my family and I have only three small rooms left, and I don't know where to put you."

"I'll take two of them, and you can have the third," said the official. "And if you're too crowded, you can use the pantry. Note, please, what airs this peasant gives himself!"

"I'm not a peasant, sir. I'm a merchant."

"Isn't it all the same?" retorted the official with a grin. "If you're not a nobleman, you're a peasant!"

We left the room, and the landlord followed us.

"Gentlemen!" he said. "We enumerated the reasons why merchants don't like to remain in that rank. Here's a small example of the respect paid us by other classes. But you haven't seen even a thousandth part of our irritation; when you do, remember the good parts of our character and don't reproach us!"

The priest shrugged his shoulders and, without saying a word, returned home; the landlord had to stay to accommodate his new lodger; and Pyotr Petrovich and I went to have a walk around the outskirts of town.

"It's the same among us as it is everywhere," said Pyotr Petrovich, "until enlightenment spreads to all classes. Only when enlightened can the educated man be aware of his obligations and relations toward others and respect all classes. The enlightened man knows that in a well-organized state every class is respectable and as necessary as all the strings in a musical instrument are to produce a harmonious sound. Ignorance erects a barrier to a close relationship, and just as the Turk regards a Christian subject of the Porte not as a human being, the same way our proud ignoramuses despise everyone who isn't related to them and who can't offer them ranks and honors. For example, isn't your landlord a reputable man in all respects? Why is that so? It's because he's intelligent and educated. It's a pity that he didn't receive a systematic education in his youth; then he'd be a hundred times more useful to his fatherland. Sidor Yermolayevich comes from the poorer class of peasants. He was left an orphan after his parents' death, went to work as a clerk with one of his distant relatives, a merchant, and by means of his hard work, diligence, and good behavior, he earned himself a considerable fortune. He educated himself by reading and through contact with clever people, as well as by reflection and experience. He's educating his sons at the university, convinced that his first task on earth, his first requirement of a mortal, is enlightenment. You've seen that decent priest, Father Evgeny. He can also serve as an example that enlightenment is no hindrance to the fulfillment of the clerical duties of his profession: on the contrary, by raising his spiritual worth in the eyes of the people, he confirms them more in their faith and morality, powerfully demonstrated by the church pastors and reinforced by the example of their virtuous lives."

In the course of our conversation on various subjects, we came to the circumstances of Pyotr Petrovich Virtutin's own life. We were extremely surprised when he told us that he wasn't a native of the place but was living here against his will. We asked him to explain the reason for this strange circumstance, and he told us the following tale.

"My father was a poor nobleman and lacked all means for his subsistence except his small salary. He married the daughter of a wealthy merchant and received a dowry of some fifty thousand rubles. My mother passed away after giving birth to me; my father left the service and devoted himself to my upbringing. I had teachers to instruct me in the sciences, but my father himself was my tutor in regard to morality. He inspired unlimited devotion to the throne, with the conviction that capacious Russia, consisting of diverse tribes, couldn't be happy or powerful except under the rule of an absolute monarch. From an early age my father instilled in me that in the whole world there's nothing nobler than morality—as expressed in the precepts of the Gospel. He allowed me to read all sorts of philosophical works, but often repeated, 'My son! The Apostle Paul says in his Epistle to the Thessalonians: "Prove all things; hold fast that which is good."[2] In the works of the philosophers you will find much intelligence and even more ingenuity, but nowhere will you find such rules for life as in the Gospels. In the works of the philosophers you'll also find advice about virtue, but nowhere will you find such higher morality, such astonishing truths as in the teachings of the Apostles. All morality developed by the philosophers in thousands of books is included by the Apostles in just a few words: "And just as you want men to do to you, you also do to them likewise."[3] "But love ye your enemies and do good."[4] Dear son! Obeying these two rules, you will fulfill all your obligations.' My father was neither a bigot nor a hypocrite but a genuine Christian, and the example of his own life reinforced the rules he taught me.

"After completing my education, I entered military service. As I left for the regiment, my father blessed me holding the icon of the Savior, with an inscription from the Apostles: 'Wherefore putting away lying, speak every man truth with his neighbor.'[5]

2. 1 Thessalonians 5:21.
3. Luke 6:31.
4. Luke 6:35.
5. Ephesians 4:25.

"With the passage of time, I grew more confirmed in the rules planted in my heart by my worthy parent and more convinced in the truth that man was created on earth only to help his neighbors by all means at his disposal. Every injustice done to anyone made a powerful impression on me: unfortunately, I couldn't restrain my tongue and protested loudly against those abuses. We were quartered in the fertile Ukraine: the wealthy landowners shared their food with our good soldiers, who, during their free time, assisted them with the fieldwork. The farmers didn't want to accept government provisions, and I insisted that they always be sold to benefit the soldiers. At the accounting of expenditures for ammunition and artillery, and on the day salaries were paid, I always took the soldiers' part. It's not easy to wrap the truth in tender, gentle forms, and I was frequently compelled to utter bitter truths, argue, and complain when they didn't listen to me. I gained the reputation of a tempestuous person and was forced to retire.

"My father, who was old and weak, wanted me to live with him. I entered the civil service in the capital, in the judicial branch, so as not to lose a chance to serve the fatherland. It was there that an extensive field opened up for my activity.

"'You've done your duty—here's your reward and consolation,' he said, embracing me. When I was just about to begin my new job, my father called me into his study and pointing to an open copy of the New Testament, he ordered me to read a section of the Apostle Paul's Epistle to Timothy, chapter 5, verse 20, 'Them that sin rebuke before all, that others may also fear.' Then he pressed me to his bosom, gave me his blessing, and said, 'May God be with you as you fight for the truth!'

"It was like a watchdog in the temple of justice: I barked at unscrupulous lawbreakers, didn't allow powerful villains into the inner sanctum, and defended the unfortunate widow and orphan from all robbers. Chicanery and usury rebelled forcefully against me. Businessmen, without whom their superiors couldn't function because they didn't know the business themselves, declared that they couldn't live with such a tempestuous man as me. I was forced to withdraw.

"In the meantime my father passed away, and I was left all alone on the earth with a considerable estate. My father hadn't tried to multiply his capital, assuming that my mother's dowry would be sufficient for me and he would use his funds to help the poor. I followed his example and shared my income in a brotherly fashion with those in need and in suffering, and at the same time protected them from oppression by those more powerful. I couldn't refuse to give advice to the unfortunate and even wrote petitions myself for the defenseless and those who didn't know how to repel chicanery and coercion by the strength of their eloquent and judicial skill; I myself intervened on behalf of the poor and sometimes frightened the most inveterate usurers with my doggedness. I had to bear a thousand unpleasantries every day, but after spending a day at work, I consoled myself with the idea that I was carrying out my late father's wishes and that my bitterness was balanced by the comfort of sufferers. I was happy! Several good friends, the sciences, and literature sweetened my existence, which evil people tried to poison with their slander.

"Clouds are formed from water vapor; rain consists of droplets; misfortune arises from slander, denunciations, and instigations; malicious words in totality compose the thunderstorms in the moral world, which hurls its lightning bolts at the innocent. I didn't host dinners, assuming that it was better to feed the poor with any extra funds than to gratify the voluptuaries; I didn't lend money to spendthrifts, so I was called stingy. I went to pray in ordinary churches together with the people and didn't wear my uniform in the domestic chapels of dignitaries—and I was called an atheist. Knowing that a monarchical state can have no other goal than the well-being of its subjects, I never complained about the government but protested loudly against those who abused their power—those who regarded their positions as farms on lease, thinking about nothing but increasing their own wealth and promoting their own relatives—and they called me a *troublemaker*. With my heart I lavished praise on dignitaries and honest officials who deserved it; when I held them up as examples as opposed to the evil and selfish, I was called *scheming* and *biased*. Often, unable to maintain control of my indignation, I declared the truth in no uncertain terms, in petitions written by me for other people, and I called things by their right names—I was called a *slanderer*. All these qualities ascribed to me were comprised in one name: *tempestuous man*. I was banished and sent to live in this town under police surveillance. I confess that at first I was distressed, but the good priest Father Evgeny consoled and comforted me.

"'You labored not for this world but for your soul,' he said. 'Consequently you will find your reward within your soul. Remember what the Apostle Paul says: "But love ye your enemies, and do good, and lend, hoping for nothing again; and your reward shall be great, and ye shall be the children of the Highest: for he is kind unto the unthankful and to the evil."[6] Don't be disheartened by your misfortune and don't slacken on the path to goodness, remembering the words of the Apostle Paul: "Now no chastening for the present seemeth to be joyous, but grievous: nevertheless afterward it yieldeth the peaceable fruit of righteousness unto them which are exercised thereby." '[7]

"Now I'm peaceful and happy, because happiness is within the heart of everyone, and there's no place on the face of the earth without good people. I take pleasure in my friendship with the police chief, the priest Evgeny, and the merchant, your landlord; I spend time reading and walking, and I perform as many good deeds as my means permit. Don't think my story is for self-promotion. No! That vice is alien to me, and I have declared the truth to you for your edification, merely because you demanded it. There will come a time when the truth will surface, like oil in water, sooner or later, but it will always triumph over malice and falsehood."

After returning to town from our walk, while passing the local prison, the esteemed Pyotr Petrovich proposed that we drop in to sow some seeds of solace in that dwelling of misery, as he expressed it. I had several coins in my purse and gladly agreed to stop by to ease the fate of the unfortunate. This prison was no more than a simple wooden hut surrounded by a stockade. Because of the small size of the structure, it was impossible to separate the inmates according to the nature of their crimes, and therefore it happened that a silly lad who'd run away from his master as a prank was placed on a bunk next to an experienced thief or robber and was imperceptibly infected by the rules of crime. As a result of lack of space, it was impossible to maintain cleanliness. The soldiers on guard stood in the hallway, and the convicts were housed on both sides of the two huts, like herrings in a barrel. I felt ill from the stuffiness and the strong impressions made by brutish faces. I asked my comrades to go out quickly into the fresh air. All of a sudden we heard piercing moans and terrible groans coming from a small cell. Curiosity led us there, and my eyes confronted a dreadful sight. In a dark corner, lying on a straw pallet, was a half-naked man, dried up like a skeleton and chained by his arms and legs. As soon as light had penetrated his den, he raised himself, sat up, and directed his terrible gaze at us. Our eyes met, and my entire body started to tremble, as if from the hostile look of a basilisk. The black hair and beard of the wretched man were

6. Luke 6:35.
7. Epistle to the Hebrews 12:10–13.

disheveled, his face was deathly pale, and his eyes, bloodshot from lack of sleep and suffering, shone like two burning coals. After a brief silence the unfortunate wretch raised his fettered arms first to his forehead, and then to his heart, and said quietly, "Fire, the fire!" Then, opening his mouth, he whispered, "Water!"

The noncommissioned officer gave him a wooden cup; then, after drinking, he pushed the officer away and exclaimed loudly, "Away, away, blood, blood!"

Suddenly his hair stood on end, his features moved violently, his eyes were fixed, and foam streamed from his mouth; he gnashed his teeth, raised himself up, and exclaimed, "I'm Nozhov—take me!"

"Nozhov!" Milovidin and I cried out together. It was the villain Nozhov, whom I didn't recognize at first in such an awful condition, but once he uttered his own name, I recognized his features immediately. Meanwhile the unfortunate fellow fell down on his pallet and howled in a terrible voice, "Don't burn me, don't burn me; kill me with one blow!"

My legs almost failed me from horror. Blood rushed to my heart, and my head started to spin, but I stood still, expecting that Nozhov would recover from his outburst and tell me the name of my enemy, the countess. The criminal fell silent again and closed his eyes; then Milovidin called him by name. Nozhov opened his eyes and seemed to be listening.

"Nozhov!" said Milovidin. "Vyzhigin forgives you for all the evil you did to him."

Nozhov sat down on the straw once again; looking around, he said, "Where's Vyzhigin? He died in the steppe. I myself threw him into a pit. The countess didn't want him murdered . . ." At these words Nozhov fell down again, closed his eyes, and snorted horribly. I couldn't stand this awful scene any longer and left the prison.

"You know this villain?" asked Pyotr Petrovich.

"Unfortunately, I do!" I replied. "Tomorrow I'll tell you the details of my acquaintanceship with him, but now I'm so distraught that I can't gather my thoughts."

Pyotr Petrovich accompanied us home. I spent the whole evening in my room and that night went without sleep, impatient to learn from Nozhov the secret of my persecution. The next morning I went to the prison to inquire how the unfortunate wretch was faring, but they told me that he'd given up the ghost in extreme agony soon after we'd left.

Pyotr Petrovich, to whom I'd related a part of my adventures and who'd heard of Vorovatin, advised me to be very careful about revealing my secret, so as not to incur any greater disaster.

"You won't gain anything by taking Vorovatin to court," he said, "because you don't have any witnesses. Vorovatin can say that the Kirghiz took you prisoner by force. Besides, if you were to involve any family of rank in this affair, you'd never be rid of trouble. Best of all, procure some information stealthily; if you can only learn the name of your persecutor, the secret will come out all by itself. You saw by Nozhov's example that audacity in vice and obduracy in crime end on a sickbed at the moment when the hope of a better life shines brightly for a virtuous sufferer and sweetens his last moments. The villain is beset with pangs of remorse and the worst tortures of hell. Vorovatin, at the first attack of violent illness or at the first real danger, will show just as much trepidation as all villains do, and he'll reveal the truth to you. There's an end to inveterate vice—firmness is characteristic only of virtue."

Chapter 20

A Landowner—the Kind We Need More of in Russia. Judge the Flock by Its Priest.

By our conduct and representations of the good Pyotr Petrovich we gained the approval of the police chief, who sometimes visited us, invited us to tea, and allowed us to take excursions out of town. Once when we were there with Pyotr Petrovich, the conversation turned to the subject of how difficult it was for the district police to keep order in such a large territory, a sparsely populated country, intersected by impassable swamps and forests.

"I ask you to arrest a vagrant," said the police chief, "if a landowner and the peasants choose to hide him! You need several thousand troops to catch one man in the forest, which covers a hundred or so miles!"

"Landowners have great responsibility before God, the tsar, and the fatherland, for everything that happens on their estates," said Pyotr Petrovich. "The happiness of the peasants depends on the landowner—their morality, their education and prosperity, consequently, all the morality, education, and prosperity of all Russia. The government spares no effort to reveal all paths to enlightenment and well-being to the nobility. No affectionate father cares more for the upbringing and happiness of his favorite son than the Russian sovereign cares for the Russian nobility. But should the Russian nobility really become like the man in the Gospel parable who hid in the ground the talent he had received from his master in order to increase his wealth?[1] The nobleman who receives must share his talent, must instill in people devotion to the throne, love for the fatherland, and by his own example, impel them to morality."

"It's all fair," said the police chief. "Otherwise, the nobleman will resemble the barren fig tree mentioned in the Gospel in Luke, chapter 13.[2] The nobleman, as the favored son of his affectionate father, should all his life be in the service to fulfill the will and the good intentions of the common father of Russia. The nobleman, living on his estate, should see himself as much in active service as if he were sitting in the State Council or as if he were commander in chief of the military. The nobleman is the primary policeman on his estate, the collector of state taxes, the controller who oversees the fulfillment of duties, the justice of the peace among his peasants, the guardian of their health, the protector of their property, and the head of the parish school."

"Splendid, splendid, Pyotr Petrovich!" cried the police chief, and he rushed to embrace Virtutin, adding: "That's as it should be! Then the local police would be what it's supposed to be: the executive power, which could enforce law and order at the request of the landowner in those cases when persuasion has no effect!"

"That's how it will be in the course of time," said Pyotr Petrovich, "when the fruits of enlightenment ripen, the seeds of which are so constantly sown by our wise monarchs; when we'll have a sufficient number of excellent Russian teachers for the education of our youth in the Russian manner, and not in the English or French style."

"These Russian foreigners have long been a bone in my throat!" said the police chief. "I have more respect for a French chef or coachman than I do for a Russian princeling imitating lords and marquises in their whims and eccentricities. Not long ago there was a young featherbrain who thought that he'd been passed over in the service, inasmuch as his supervisor had told him that he wouldn't be promoted or rewarded because he couldn't write three lines logically and grammatically. Prince Slabogolovin, after reading a few French brochures about politics with the help of his tutor, and since he subscribed to several English newspapers, imagined himself a great politician, born to be a legislator in his country. Along with the aroma of champagne, he filled

1. A talent was the heaviest or largest biblical unit of measurement for weight, equal to about seventy-five pounds. See Matthew 25:18.

2. Luke 13:6–9.

the heads of his immature companions with the rules of philanthropy and the wisdom of Voltaire's *Philosophical Dictionary*,[3] and he became known as a liberal, an orator, and a defender of humanity. When, after stumbling on the path of ambition, he came to his estate—then, do you know how his philosophy ended?"

"No doubt he began to establish country schools and to work for the good of his peasants," said Milovidin.

"Not on your life!" exclaimed the police chief with a loud laugh.

"The government—which looks after the well-being of its subjects, not just in words but in actual deeds—was compelled to take charge of the eloquent orator's estate because of the cruel treatment of his peasants and the wasteful management of his own estate. Listen to all the loudmouths during a sumptuous dinner or at an evening gathering, in a crowd of young people: they howl about the well-being of humanity and about laws, but at home or in other places under their control, they want to be treated like autocratic pashas. A true friend of humanity doesn't shout, doesn't cry out against laws and the established order. But when he's conforming to things as they are, he does as much good as he can, and much good can always be done everywhere, if only there's a will to do it. Among us the practice of good may and should be pursued, before thinking about any theories. Do you know what, Pyotr Petrovich? Take these gentlemen to our friend Aleksandr Aleksandrovich Rossiyaninov. You'll see what sort of people we have living in out-of-the-way places. I'll lend you my horses. Off you go, gentlemen; you've been in our little town for too long a time."

The next morning we set off on our visit to Mr. Rossiyaninov, who was living on his estate some fifteen miles from town. After traveling about ten miles, we observed the astonishing difference in the cultivation of the fields. Everywhere trenches had been dug to drain excess water from the tilled land. The fields were carefully measured and fertilized; the meadows were cleared of mole holes and useless brush. On a pasture along the bank of a steep stream, a slope was paved with stones so that the cattle could drink without getting stuck in the mud or sullying the water. The road on both sides was planted with trees, the little bridges were in good condition, and the marshy spots were anchored with fascines.

3. The *Dictionnaire philosophique* is an encyclopedic dictionary published in 1764. It represents the culmination of Voltaire's views on Christianity, God, and morality.

"Did you notice," said Pyotr Petrovich, "that we've entered the territory of a decent man?"

After arriving in the village, Milovidin clapped his hands with admiration and exclaimed, "This is what all of Russia can and should be like!"

Sturdy wooden huts were constructed in rows along both sides of the road. The window frames were carved with various designs; the courtyards were enclosed with high fences and handsome awnings. The houses were built at some distance from each other, to prevent the spread of fire. There were little gardens with fruit trees between the houses. Behind the peasants' courtyards were vegetable gardens, and further on, threshing barns. At the end of the village stood a fine stone church, surrounded by tall linden trees. The priest's house was distinguished by its clean and neat appearance. Several attractive little buildings stood near the church for general use. In one of them there was a hospital and an apothecary; in another, an almshouse for orphans, the infirm, and the aged; and in the third, the village storehouse and shop with goods needed by peasants, as well as the basic necessities of life; in the fourth building, the village school and the local courtroom. At the end of the village there was a blacksmith's shop, and in the middle, a large well. The peasants of both sexes had a healthy look, and the young women were distinguished by their beauty, because external beauty is an indication of contentment. We encountered neither dirty children on the street nor women in tatters nor drunken men. The peasants' horses and cattle were of excellent breeds, and the gear and agricultural implements were in good order. We entered one peasant's house to see his domestic arrangements. The house had a cellar and was divided into two halves: a bright half and another part without a chimney, the smoky part. In the first half, consisting of three sections, the landlord's family lived; in the other half they baked bread, prepared the food and the water for the cattle, dried wet clothes when they returned from work in nasty weather, and so on.

"I know some landowners," said Milovidin, "who, smitten by foreign fashion, built German houses for Russian peasants and demanded of them the same kind of cleanliness as in Germany. That's simply impossible in Russia, and not only doesn't it guarantee the peasant's happiness but it even constrains his life. Our climate and local conditions demand different construction for our houses than in Germany and England. It's not possible to build spacious stone houses for village dwellers in Russia because we don't have building materials for it; the upkeep for such houses is very expensive; our peasants don't live in large families and therefore have no need for so many rooms, which must be heated for eight months of the year in some parts of the country. The Russian peasant couldn't live without the smoky part of the house in our cold, damp climate in the northern regions; without this he won't have any place to get dry. The desire to do good often brings no reward if it is carried out without knowledge of the location. But this Mr. Rossiyaninov, apparently, is a master of his trade."

We saw some peasants' *lapti* in the hallway.[4]

"This has a taste of barbarism," said Milovidin. Pyotr Petrovich looked at the footwear with more attention and said, "These aren't *lapti* but *shmony*.[5] The use of *lapti* would not suit because they require a great deal of wood."

"When do your peasants wear *shmony*?" he asked a peasant. "I see that they all wear boots on the street."

"When they go fishing, my dear, in wet weather on the meadows, and in forest work; after all, you can't wear boots there, and you won't keep your feet as comfortable in a boot as you can in a pair of well-tarred *lapti*."

"You see, they wear these shoes only for work, and they're much more comfortable than the wooden shoes of French and German peasants. If a Russian peasant is well-off, and hasn't given up using his *lapti*, that's a sure sign they find them useful and comfortable."

Around the peasants' courtyard there was a shed containing carts, sleighs, ploughs, and harrows. That was where the horses were stabled temporarily. At the end of the courtyard stood a cattle shed and stable, and behind the house was a bathhouse. I asked the landlady how they lit the hut during the winter.

"Our neighbors," she replied. "Peasants belonging to other masters burn wood splinters, my dear, but we light the hut with night-lights burning hemp oil. You see, we don't have to buy our hemp oil, my dear; every woman among us presses oil from the seeds."

"Do you have a tavern in the village?" asked Milovidin.

"Heaven forbid, my worthy fathers!" the peasant woman replied. "In olden times, when our former landlord was still alive, there used to be a tavern: our peasants would get drunk on holidays and be hung-over on work days. Today, thank God, that's no longer the case. Our priest,

4. Sandals made of bast fibers.
5. Regional footwear made from hemp.

may God grant him health, teaches us in church that it's a great sin to drink spirits, our doctor's helper says that you won't live long if you drink, and our master forbids us to drink and doesn't like drunks; so our men no longer get drunk. Because of that, our money doesn't run out so quickly. Easter is another matter, or a wedding or a christening: then we brew our own beer, and the master himself provides the wine. During our autumn work or in the winter, our master orders our workers to drink one glass of spirits each, but no more. May God grant him health, he's a real father, and not a lord!"

Some three miles past the village on the tall bank of a river stood the manor house, built of wood on a stone foundation, painted green with a red roof. Behind the house, in the direction of the river, stretched a large garden. Around the courtyard were various domestic outbuildings. The symmetry of the parts showed the skill of the architect; the lack of adornment was compensated for by the simplicity and solidity of the building. A servant met us on the porch; he was dressed neatly but very plainly. He said that the landlord himself had gone into the fields and that the mistress was supervising her daughters' lessons. In the room we were met by the landlord's eldest son, a young man of about sixteen; he asked us to wait patiently until his mother finished her task. The youth's tall figure, his rosy cheeks, and his skill showed that as much effort had been devoted to his physical education as to his moral education. Pyotr Petrovich, who was an intimate acquaintance of the family, proposed that we take a look at the other rooms and the garden. The landlord's son, Alyosha, agreed to be our guide. After passing through three living rooms and a hall, which were notable for their unusual neatness, we entered into Mr. Rossiyaninov's study. This was a spacious room with enormous bookcases holding books in Latin, Greek, French, German, English, Italian, and Russian. There were three tables in the middle of the room; on one of them lay recent journals and newspapers; on another, various papers; and on the third, newly arrived books. In a room attached to the study, there were shelves full of physical instruments, chemical apparatus, and models of various machines; globes stood on the tables; geographical maps were hung on one wall. A small case contained samples of various minerals.

"It smells of Europe in here," said Milovidin.

From this room we went out into the garden. There were no manmade ponds contaminating the air with harmful gases, no expensive bridges over dry land, no whimsical gazebos designed in barbaric style, and no new artificial "ruins." The garden was filled with fruit trees and various berry bushes, all planted with unusual artistry. Groves of nut trees and linden provided pleasant refuge on hot days, and a large alley around the entire garden shaded by tall trees served for strolls. There were swings and other amusements on the lawns for children. At the end of the garden, on the south side, was a greenhouse, small but very well built.

"What luxury!" said Milovidin.

"Luxury which is not only excusable but even beneficial," replied Pyotr Petrovich.

"What could be more pleasant for a northern resident than enjoying the tender products of more favorable climates? The very sight of the diversity, richness, and abundance of nature elevates the soul and draws a person nearer to his Creator. Among these plants of foreign lands, one's thoughts take flight around the earthly globe. I'll say even more: why should we deny ourselves the pleasure of sometimes tasting the tender fruits denied to us by northern nature? This is not the satisfaction of shameful gluttony but the comforting of excusable curiosity. However, it seems to me that it's much better to engage in the cultivation of plants than to raise a multitude of animals in captivity and to hunt weak creatures."

We suddenly heard a voice behind us. We saw a man with a cheerful and healthy countenance, wearing a morocco cap and a green camlet frock coat, hastening toward us. It was the landlord himself.

"Hello, friend!" he said, extending his hand to Pyotr Petrovich, who introduced us to the landlord and in a few words related our adventures.

"I've already heard part of it," said the landlord. "Here you often get to hear things you don't want to hear. Spoken newspapers are more common than printed ones. If anyone wants to know the truth, he should believe only one hundredth part of the provincial news he hears. I was told that two Russian noblemen arrived from India through the Kirghiz steppe, where one had been a reigning prince and the other his minister, and that they brought with them barrels of gold coins and whole loads of shawls. I'm sure that if this news ever reached another province, one of you would have been promoted to the great Mogul, and the other one into a terrible warrior; the treasure would have multiplied into millions of gold coins and barrels full of diamonds. But please come in. It's dinner time."

Upon entering, the worthy landlord introduced us to his wife and two daughters, the elder fourteen and the younger twelve. The younger son was ten years old. To our astonishment, the lady of the house addressed us in Russian, and she was not all dressed up, although she was receiving guests reputed to be millionaires for the first time. The host also introduced the children's tutors: a Frenchman, Monsieur Instrui, and a German, Herr Gutman, whom he referred to as his friends. It seemed strange that Mr. Rossiyaninov, whom Pyotr Petrovich described as a great patriot and enemy of foreign upbringing, would employ two foreigners for the education of his own children. Pyotr Petrovich noticed my astonishment from my sidelong glance at the foreigners and relayed my observation to the host. Mr. Rossiyaninov led Milovidin and me into another room and explained, "Don't be surprised, gentlemen, that I employ foreigners to teach my children. To turn our young people over completely to foreigners is our greatest absurdity, which has been the source of great trouble for the Russian gentry; as a result it has practically become a foreign colony in Russia, hardly speaking our native language, knowing neither our customs nor our history but taught from infancy to love everything French and English and to despise everything Russian. But one can and should employ foreigners under parents' supervision, selecting teachers of respectable moral character and education, and not adventurers or charlatans. Without knowledge of foreign languages, a person can never be educated like a decent European. Other nations have surpassed us on the road to enlightenment, and they have more means in keeping ahead of us in their knowledge of the sciences. It's impossible to translate all that seems important and curious in foreign countries. To conceive on our own of everything that's already been discovered and invented would be ridiculous, and so it's necessary to adopt the easiest means of acquiring the immense kingdom of knowledge, and this means comprehending foreign languages. Knowing many languages, you become a citizen of the world: you'll agree that first you must become a *man*, and only later a Russian or a Frenchman. I love Russia more than my life; I wish it well more than my own children and am ready to sacrifice my life and that of my children, my property, and all the blessings of my life, but it doesn't follow that I shouldn't like foreigners and not take advantage of the results of their intellect and industry. This would be barbarism worthy of Turks, the Chinese, or the Algerians. The first subjects in the education of my children consisted in learning their native language, history, and statistics of Russia; my first and primary task consists in inculcating in my children a limitless attachment to everything connected to their homeland. I do this myself. With all of this, I don't conceal from them the fact that we haven't achieved the level of education found in other nations; on the contrary, I inspire in them a desire to raise the level of their own country by propagation of everything that is good and useful. Now the domestic education of my elder son is complete, and I plan to send him to university next winter." We were summoned in to dinner, and Mr. Rossiyaninov concluded his explanation.

Dinner consisted of four courses prepared with good taste and in abundance. There was no excess of wine—beyond measure, as they say—but after each course everyone (except the children and the ladies) received a large goblet of excellent wine. Besides that, pitchers of water stood on the table, as well as lager, kvass, cider, and a tasty beverage made of mixed berries, which made an excellent drink and sparkled and foamed in the glass like champagne and seemed to me to be even tastier than wine. For dessert they served lovely ripe berries. Besides Mr. Rossiyaninov's family, the two teachers, and us, there were two elderly soldiers, retired because of their wounds; two little old women, the landlady's distant relations; and the parish priest. I noted that all the guests and family, without exception, were served the same dishes, and everyone was offered the same wine. That is not always the case with landlords who give places to humble people at their dining tables. Mr. and Mrs. Rossiyaninov, in contrast, treated them with unusual courtesy, and the landlord didn't sharpen his wit at the expense of those poorer guests who shared his hospitality.

Conversation at the table was of a general nature. After dinner we all went out into the garden, and as we waited for coffee, we sat in the shade of thick linden trees. All of a sudden Milovidin's eyes filled with tears. Everyone turned to look at him with sympathy, and the host and hostess were disconcerted.

"Do you feel sad?" the landlady inquired.

"No, madam, these are tears of tender emotion, not sadness. I'm delighted by your family happiness, the well-being of your peasants, and the orderliness of your estate, and I rejoice that you are Russians!"

The landlord squeezed Milovidin's hand and said, "You are right: we are, or at least I am, happy with my family."

Mrs. Rossiyaninova, in place of an answer, kissed her husband tenderly; his children threw themselves around his neck, crying, "Papa, you make all our happiness, all our joy!"

One of the retired officers shook Mr. Rossiyaninov's hand, while the other raised his eyes to heaven and crossed himself; the teachers rushed to kiss the hands of the worthy couple. The old servant who'd brought the coffee shed tears in silence. Mr. Rossiyaninov was deeply touched.

"You can see now whether I'm a happy man," he exclaimed. "Can there be greater bliss than being loved by good creatures? Don't think, however, that this happiness cost me great effort. No! It's the kindness of Providence, which I never stop thanking. I have merely tried as best I could to fulfill my obligations—nothing more. If you're curious, I can relate my history to you in a few words.

"My father served in the navy, married for love, and lacked any supplementary means to support his family except for his salary. He remained in the service until he achieved the rank of general; as a result he was unable to provide my two sisters and me with an outstanding education. He acquired riches by means of his bravery, earning several rich prizes during the Turkish war. His ravaged health prevented him from further service; he retired, purchased this estate consisting of some five hundred serfs, and settled down in the country. My sisters married as soon as my parents were in a position to provide them sufficient dowries. I entered the Guards but had the misfortune of hurting myself by falling off a horse; on my doctor's advice, I had to retire once again. I was only nineteen years old at the time. I was advised to spend several years in a warm climate, to fortify my strengths and to take advantage of the mineral waters. I used this time to educate myself and attended lectures at the University of Bologna, then completed my reeducation in Paris. Upon returning to my fatherland with restored health and new knowledge, I wanted to be of use to my country in the civil service. At this time I had the misfortune of losing both my parents and I remained alone in the world. After serving several years in an unremarkable position and seeing that neither my efforts nor my zeal—and I dare say my abilities and higher learning, which were above those of my colleagues—proved of any use in singling me out from the crowd, my zeal for the public welfare began to cool. My father's old acquaintance, to whom I was complaining about my situation, led me out of my delusion, and pointed out to me the true road to happiness.

"'Dear friend!' he said to me once. 'You have no relatives, nor do you belong to those fortunate few whose entire worth consists in their name; consequently, you will always be condemned to carry upon your shoulders and rescue from the dirt other people's incompetence, so that it may succeed due to your services. You must await some extraordinary opportunity, one of those miracles noted in the calendar when the rays of the sun penetrate the thick atmosphere of nepotism and shine on you, a gentleman with no family connections. There are examples, I won't argue, but it requires iron patience, which you lack. What are you looking for? To be useful to the sovereign and to the fatherland; isn't that true? The means are in your hands. You have five hundred serfs. Devote yourself to their happiness. Believe me, you must wait a long time before the happiness of five hundred men and, very likely, women will depend on your will. You've studied well, read a great deal, traveled widely, and therefore you have many capabilities for managing your estate, to make your peasants happy, and what's more, to be an example to other landowners. Estate management is not a difficult thing, and your village elder, with his knowledge of local conditions, will be of much greater use to you than a course in agronomy. The main thing is to keep your expenses below your income and to use the entire surplus to improve your estate and the condition of your peasants. If you limit your needs, deny your whims, you'll have surplus funds; employ the surplus on the useful, and it will bring you satisfaction, serenity, and happiness!'"

"Like a person blind from birth, who, when he recovers his sight after a successful operation, rejoices and is astonished by the objects he sees, about which he's formed the wrong impression, I recovered the use of my intellect through the words of my true friend."

"This is his daughter!" said Mr. Rossiyaninov, indicating his wife. "I married, retired, and settled in the country. My father, being old and infirm, at that time moved to the country, could no longer engage in estate management, and left his estate to me in the same condition as he had acquired it. The fields were badly cultivated, the peasants poor and in a primitive condition as far as morality was concerned. In twenty years, with God's help and the painstaking efforts of my wife and me, we managed to bring the estate to the state in which you see it. I didn't have any capital and carried out my improvements solely using my income, gradually, making progress without haste, engaging first with the most important matters. God blessed my beginnings. Today all the young people on my estate know how to read and understand their obligations to God, to the monarch, to the landowner, and to their peers. If they are illiterate, gentlemen, it's impossible to plant morality in the people or to instill in them a genuine conception of their duties conducive to real happiness. It's impossible to instruct people by word of mouth and by habit, as poodles are trained. It's necessary for a person to be able to *read*. Only then will he remember; and besides, time spent on reading is not lost, because a large majority of people turn to depravity from idleness. My good peasants soon understood that I wished them well, and they set about helping me diligently. For this

I am grateful to our esteemed priest, who, in spite of his own poverty, behaved in such a way that the peasants had to respect him. He didn't participate in their banquets or amusements but hastened to visit them when they required spiritual succor, advice, admonitions, or to perform his clerical duty. The esteemed pastor earned his bread by the sweat of his brow and worked his small plot of land, but he never took anything from the peasants in addition to his legal due. He settled arguments, never providing any cause for dissatisfaction, and he wouldn't permit any improper jokes to be told in his presence, nor did he give occasion for any to be made. In a word, Father Simeon was and is just what a parish priest should be: gentle, abstemious, humane, and dignified in his behavior. You saw him at dinner, gentlemen. Now his condition has improved, along with that of all of us. I consider it the first duty of a landowner to raise a priest to such a state that he can live independently, without having to borrow anything from the peasants: only then will he be respected by his parishioners and be able to influence their morality.

"Following my father-in-law's advice, I began to manage the estate not in the English or German style but in a manner suited to our climate, soil, and customs. No innovations were implemented on a grand scale until they had been tested many times. At last we finished all our construction, improved our fields, and now the only thing that remains is to maintain that which we've accomplished."

We spent our time in the company of the good Mr. Rossiyaninov and his family in a most pleasant manner and by the sunset headed back to town, although our host and hostess tried to delay us. I hastened to return to town because the post was due to arrive the next day, and I impatiently expected a letter from Moscow. We promised the worthy Aleksandr Aleksandrovich to come again another time and stay for a few days, and we departed with sadness in our hearts, as if from our parents' home, When we drove out of the gates, Milovidin crossed himself and, raising his eyes to heaven, he said, "Lord, bless Russia and give her more such landowners!"

Chapter 21

The Audacious Landowner—Sila Minich Glazdurin

We proceeded along a different road to shorten the journey. After leaving Mr. Rossiyaninov's estate and nearing a grove, we heard the sounds of hunting horns, the barking of dogs, and the calls of the hunters. Suddenly from the edge of the woods a fox appeared and went running across a field of grain. Soon he was pursued by a pack of borzois and a dozen men on horseback. One of them galloped ahead: he was a man with a cap, with tousled hair, a long mustache, and was shouting like a madman, "Tally-ho, tally ho." He whipped and spurred his horse on. The fox, to evade inevitable destruction by a change of course (which people often attempt), suddenly turned onto the wide road; the dogs and the hunters rushed after him, catching up with the exhausted animal. Finally, the fox, after jumping across a ditch, threw himself directly at the feet of our horses: the dogs went after her and caught her. The frenzied hunter, like a whirlwind, flew across the ditch; seeing that the dogs were tearing into the fox, he began beating them with his whip, shouting terribly. Our horses were frightened and began to rear up as the sounds of squealing and gnawing continued. But when the hunter hit their legs with the whip, they rushed to one side, our carriage was overturned, and we fell into a ditch.

Fortunately we weren't hurt but merely sank into the mud up to our necks and couldn't get out from under the carriage. We lay there, like flies caught in an overturned glass. Around us we heard shouting and laughing. Milovidin was terribly angry and kept saying that he would split open the head of the rascal who was the cause of our unfortunate misadventure. I cursed the hunt and the huntsmen, while Pyotr Petrovich remained silent. Finally the carriage began to move above us. The hunters pushed it to one side, and we crawled out wet and dirty, like crayfish. Around twenty hunters were gathered on the main road, and one of them, the one who was in the lead, approached us and with a loud guffaw, said, "Forgive us, gentlemen! My borzois are to blame. I wouldn't be Sila Minich if there were dogs anywhere in Russia equal to my own Zalet and Vintovka. The accursed fox threw himself at your horses' hooves, but my dogs would have snatched the prey even if was held in a wolf's fangs!"

Pyotr Petrovich whispered to Milovidin that he shouldn't get angry and shouldn't abuse the jovial owner of Zalet and Vintovka, while I regarded this eccentric with wonder. His round, red face was covered in plenty of sweat and dust. Between his long, red nose and thick lips was a long, light brown mustache, like two squirrel tails. His disheveled hair was covered with a small, crumpled green leather cap. He was dressed in a short, green cloth jacket and brightly colored trousers. A pipe stuck out of one of his outer pockets; a hunting horn hung on a belt over his right shoulder, while on his left was a small flask covered in leather. In his left hand he held a whip; he extended his right hand to Pyotr Petrovich and began speaking again. "Give me your hand, brother, and don't be angry. What a great misfortune that you fell into a ditch! But there's not a ditch or a pit for some twelve miles around here that I haven't fallen into, chasing rabbits and foxes. But you, brothers, why are you staring at me as if I'm a wild beast?" he said, glancing at Milovidin and me. "Don't be angry! Is it my fault that you ended up in a ditch? For my part, I'd have rather thrown you into a bowl of punch. To err is human."

With these words, Glazdurin, taking out his flask, drank from it, and then took it off his shoulder strap, handed it to Pyotr Petrovich, and said, "Drink, brother, it's tasty anise vodka! It will revive you."

Pyotr Petrovich gave the flask back to him and on behalf of all of us, said, "Kind sir! Your carelessness was the cause of our unfortunate mishap. But since you didn't do it on purpose, we gladly forgive you and ask that, as compensation for what we suffered from your passion for the hunt, you allow us to change our clothes and set off for town in your carriage without delay."

"With pleasure, my dear fellow," cried Glazdurin. "I'll lend you my Moscow carriage and my six Kirghiz wild horses. My house is only two miles from here; mount my hunters' horses, and we'll leave right away. But have some more to drink; it's excellent anise vodka."

"We don't drink spirits at all," said Milovidin.

"What? You don't drink spirits? Ridiculous!" cried Glazdurin. "Shame on you! After all, you're not pretty young ladies!"

We refused again; then Glazdurin began to offer the drink to his comrades, introducing a dozen or so members of the local gentry to us one by one, calling each by his first name and patronymic. Afterwards he asked us, "With whom do I have the honor of being acquainted? May I know your rank, first name, and surname? And where do you come from? You seem not to be from around here."

Pyotr Petrovich, fearing that Milovidin would be angry and might say something unpleasant to Glazdurin, decided to reply for all of us. "These gentlemen [he called us by our surnames], have come to our town on business of their own; and I've lived here for three years and am astonished that you don't know me, nor have I had the honor of seeing you up to this time."

"Don't you ever frequent the tavern Schnapps, owned by the German?" asked one of Glazdurin's friends.

"No, but I'm known in many houses," replied Pyotr Petrovich.

"We don't drive about from house to house in town," replied Glazdurin. "Our agents manage our business affairs, and we meet with our brethren at bear hunts or wolf hunts and at the elections. But brothers, drink some anise vodka; it's very tasty!"

After our repeated refusal, Glazdurin exclaimed, "You wait: I'll treat you at home to such liqueurs that are impossible to find in the whole province. My wife makes them herself. She was brought up in Petersburg, and at first she used to faint at the smell of spirits and tobacco smoke, but I finally trained her so well that now she almost smokes with me and all day long she makes cordials and liqueurs for me. But it's time to go home. Hey, lads! Wipe the mud off these gentlemen with grass. Filka Sivolapy, Senka Kosoy, and Mitka Ryzhy, go home on foot.[1] Lavrushka, you little imp, run into the woods and sound the bugle. Gather the dogs and head home! Let the peasants also go on home, and tell them all to be in the field at first light on the day after tomorrow.

1. Three descriptive nicknames for these peasants: "Gray-pawed," "Cross-eyed," and "Red-headed."

We must surround the grove that's beyond Sidor's field and let the dogs loose. Petrushka saw fresh wolf tracks three days in a row. Bring the horses. Now, gentlemen, let's go!"

The rear wheel and axle of our carriage were broken. The hunters attached a pole and dragged it to the blacksmith's. We rode with Glazdurin on the hunters' horses. One of the guests proposed going by way of the field.

"What sort of manager are you, Anisim Stepanovich?" said Glazdurin. "It's one thing to gallop through a field of grain in pursuit of a wild animal—there's nothing wrong with that—but it's another when there's no need to do so. No, we'll go by the road, and in the meantime, my lads will entertain you. Hey, lads, belt out the song, 'In the Meadow!' "

As soon as the hunters finished singing, Glazdurin stopped, and we all followed his example.

"Safron, give us some fresh anise vodka!" he said. One of the hunters untied a flask from his saddle and handed it to his master, who, after drinking some, passed it to his comrades.

"Hunters must drink," said Glazdurin, addressing Milovidin. "Vodka fortifies you and *invigorates* the blood."

"On the contrary, it seems that spirits enflame the blood and weaken the constitution," retorted Milovidin.

"Nonsense, brother, nonsense!" cried Glazdurin. "That's also what the German doctor says, but we don't listen to him. Monsieur Vasserbrod never takes a drop, and he's puny and cold, like an emaciated horse; Sila Glazdurin drinks a bit like all sinners and is as healthy and strong as a three-year-old bear. Don't believe the Germans, brother. They want to get rid of their wares, and that's why Monsieur Vasserbrod wants me to drink his potion rather than vodka. Yes, Sila Glazdurin is very shrewd. Blow your horns; off we go at a gallop!"

When in Rome, do as the Romans do. We galloped after them. As we were approaching a little village, we met an emaciated-looking flock of sheep returning from the field. The borzois, which were running off-leash, fell upon the sheep and tore apart a pair of them at once. The shepherd dared not drive away the master's dogs, and the hunters stopped to enjoy this spectacle, which just delighted Glazdurin.

"Bravo, Zalet! That's the way, Vintovka! Get him, get him!" he cried with all his might. When this torment was finished, we proceeded at a slow pace to Glazdurin's own village.

The first thing that met our eyes was a tavern, in front of which a crowd of peasants was gathered.

"Do you allow a tavern to exist on your estate?" asked Pyotr Petrovich.

"What a question!" cried Glazdurin in astonishment. "The tax farmers pay, and so, in my opinion, let them have a tavern under my nose!"

"That's convincing logic!" Pyotr Petrovich said to me.

Glazdurin's village was in stark contrast to Rossiyaninov's. Here the shacks were half in ruins, the courtyards were only half fenced in, and the thatch roofs let in the light in several places. The street was impassable because of the mud. Half-naked children, upon seeing us, scurried crying into the shacks, afraid of the dogs and the whips. The men were ragged and had a gloomy, unpleasant look; the women were in tatters; as a result almost all of them seemed unattractive. It's true that there were some pretty faces peeking out of the windows, and a few lovely girls, dressed rather well, ran out to the gate as we approached to welcome Glazdurin, who greeted them rather familiarly and with a smile shook his finger at them. After leaving the village, we saw the manor house on one side. Glazdurin ordered the horns to be sounded and commanded us to gallop: we set off as fast as the horses could carry us. Upon entering the courtyard through half-ruined gates, we stopped, but with an abundance of spirit Glazdurin leaped on horseback onto the wobbly porch and rode into the hallway. A crowd of tattered servants met us at the door. It was hard to guess what color their livery was, and what metal was used to make their galloons, which appeared to have adorned their rags as fringes in days gone by.

Glazdurin had hardly crossed the threshold when he raised a ruckus and began complaining to everyone that the table wasn't set for dinner. He threatened to banish the butler to the stable; he gave the footmen a few kicks, and treated his wife to several coarse expressions, which have yet to appear in print. The house sprang into action: servants and dogs bustled noisily about the rooms, doors slammed, chairs broke, and amid this commotion Glazdurin's abuse could be heard, just the way a sea captain's voice can be heard during a storm at sea.

At last the table was set, and a belated hunters' dinner was served. The guests gathered in the hall, and Mrs. Glazdurina, a lovely young woman, appeared with her two daughters, between the ages of seven and nine. The landlord didn't bother introducing us to his wife; he merely dragged everyone to the table, where there were decanters of vodka, and recommended that we all have some of his beloved anise liqueur. We ourselves went up to the hostess and told her how we happened to be guests in her house, prudently letting her know that we didn't belong among the number of her husband's friends and had made his acquaintance on the main road. Mrs. Glazdurina had just managed to say a few words when Virtutin exclaimed, "What, don't you recognize me, Anna Lvovna?"

"That's you, Pyotr Petrovich!"

Explanations ensued, and we learned that Pyotr Petrovich was a friend of the hostess's father and had carried her as a baby in his arms. The lady was extremely glad about this meeting, and she even shed a few tears at the recollection of her past life, which Virtutin had witnessed. Glazdurin, instead of showing any tenderness or politeness, grabbed Pyotr Petrovich by the arm, pulled him over to the table, and said, "Come on, drink some anise liqueur, you old friend of my father-in-law."

After they were asked to take their places at the table, all of the guests hastened to the end of the table where the host was seated, avoiding the company of the lady, as if it was a nuisance. Even though we were not hungry, we sat down next to the hostess. The table was surrounded by servants standing in a row, two for every guest. They hastened to clear away plates on which there was any food left and carried out the guests' orders very slowly. The dogs crowded under the table and around the guests to chomp on any bones tossed to them by the hunters. The table was set with various liqueurs that were fervently recommended to the guests by the host and which he himself drank with even more zeal to set an example for his friends.

The conversation was very interesting and heated. Each guest praised his own dogs, horses, guns, and hunters, narrating curious anecdotes about hunting hares and foxes and about notable victories gained over wolves and bears. Each boasted of his prowess and fearlessness, enumerating the dangers that occurred during their hunts. But Glazdurin, if he didn't out-argue them, certainly out-shouted them all and was the winner of all arguments. But since one of the guests didn't wish to concede, affirming that his dog was better than Glazdurin's Zalet, it was proposed to play cards after dinner to determine who would be the owner of both dogs, in order to settle the argument once and for all.

After getting up from the table, the guests went into the large room next door, where coffee and tobacco pipes were brought. Suddenly the door flew open noisily, and in rushed a crowd of Gypsies with balalaikas, playing and singing, "Aye, Burn, Burn, but Speak!" Without waiting for orders, half the Gypsies began dancing, while the other half, standing in a circle, began singing a dance melody, accompanied by balalaikas, shouting, and whistling. The guests, reclining on sofas with their pipes, praised the skill of the dancers and the beauty of the Gypsy women, but Glazdurin was proudly strutting around the dancers and shouting, "Splendid, splendid, great, wonderful, faster, faster!"

Pyotr Petrovich, Milovidin, and I went into the living room, where the hostess was sitting alone.

"Excuse the indiscretion," said Virtutin, "but I really don't understand how you, with your education much more suited to a quiet life and to the higher circles of society, can tolerate this raucous tone of your guests and boisterous behavior of your husband."

The landlady blushed, and after a brief pause, she replied, "It's true that my husband is a bit noisy, but he's not a bad man, and his way of life is the result of his upbringing and poor examples. He was left an orphan at a young age and became a ward of his uncle, who was convinced that a nobleman needn't know anything more than how to sign his name and be a good hunter with the hounds; that not only the earth but the heavenly lights were created for a nobleman's pleasure; and that to live means to eat, drink, and be merry. One time, the governor, displeased with him when he was serving as a judge at the elections, asked him while they were at the Council of Nobles: 'Tell me, Frol Timofeyevich, why was man given a head?' 'To wear a hat and to get drunk,' replied my worthy uncle with a serious demeanor. By this you can judge what sort of upbringing my husband had under the aegis of such a guardian and tutor. An extraordinary occurrence, or better to say, fate, united me with Sila Minich. You know that my father lived on his salary alone, and that my mother was the one who undertook my education. Upon the death of my parents, my aunt, a widow, took over my care and loved me tenderly, like a mother. She had insufficient means and, after the death of her husband, lived in a small village in this district. Her late husband owed my husband's uncle a sum of money that she would never have been able to repay, and she would have been deprived of her last refuge for her old age if my husband, who had received a promissory note as part of his inheritance, had decided to prosecute her. While visiting my aunt, he fell in love with me and offered me his hand in marriage. I . . . but why should I drag out the explanations? I accepted his proposal, and the promissory note was cancelled. Having secured serenity for my benefactress, I'm happy. However, my husband loves me, and it's my duty . . . to tolerate patiently his little weaknesses. We all have our faults!"

Glazdurin entered the room.

"Ashenka!" he said. "Go fetch two thousand rubles from the wardrobe. We've been playing cards. I just lost a thousand rubles to Travlin, but on the other hand, I won his wonderful dog Vikhor from him. He's in despair, and I intend to celebrate this event. Now I own the two best dogs in all of Russia! Make us some punch, Ashenka, as strong as possible. But you, gentlemen, why are you sitting here like models of piety? Don't you want to have a good time? The pot is considerable—sweeten it!"

We thanked the host and asked him to permit us to retire for the night. We had dined very late and, feeling exhausted from the day's adventure, we intended to go to bed to escape the host's pestering us and so as not to become witnesses to the noisy merrymaking. We were shown to a room in a wing of the house.

"Glazdurin and his friends are like weights which restrain Russia's progress on the road to enlightenment," said Pyotr Petrovich. "One benefit derived from them: they can serve as an example. It's exactly like a public dining room in Sparta, where a drunken Helot was paraded around the table to show youth the vileness of this vice.[2] We must look at Glazdurin and his ilk to divert people from a similarly meaningless life, people who haven't yet become beasts on an endless hunting expedition and whose blood has not yet turned into alcohol."

Songs, noise, and shouts could be heard all night in the rooms. When the Gypsies got tired, Glazdurin ordered the hunters themselves to sing songs and the maidservants and country lasses to dance. He lost several thousand rubles at cards during the night, as well as his carriage in which he'd promised to send us back to town and six of his horses. But he was extremely cheerful and satisfied, having won Vikhor, and he celebrated that acquisition more splendidly than he did the birth of his first son. With sunrise the house became quiet.

We wanted to leave without saying goodbye to the host, but our carriage was still not repaired, and we were forced to wait against our will. Glazdurin woke up around noontime, and we met him at the stable while we strolled around the estate. He summoned us in a hoarse voice and pulled us forcefully into the stable, where we had to listen to a lecture about the quality of each horse and be witness to his kissing and beating them with his switch one at a time. Then he led us into

2. Helots were an enslaved people in Sparta. Plutarch states that Spartans compelled them to drink undiluted wine and led them into public halls, so that the children might see what a drunk looks like.

the dining room for breakfast, where we found all the guests pale with blood-shot eyes. With trembling hands, they each took a drink of flavored vodka along with salted snacks, and soon the strength of the spirits revived their weakened nerves. Since it was already too late to ride out on a hunt, they decided to go on a horse race before dinner. The host and all his guests (except for the three of us) bet one hundred rubles each, and the total would serve as a reward for the guest whose horse won the race. In a general meeting it was resolved that he who received the prize would keep the bank at faro after the race. In the meantime our carriage was repaired, and we departed without waiting for dinner, which wasn't ready on time because the cook, who was the lead singer in the domestic chorus, had moistened his throat too carelessly during the night's festivities and that morning could barely stand on his own two legs. When he set about concocting something for dinner, he was so muddled that he added to one pot something that should have been added to another and spoiled, burned, or didn't cook it long enough; as a result, he was confined in the cattle yard and the housekeeper had to prepare another meal.

After returning to town, we learned from our own host that the official who'd arrived from Petersburg had turned everything upside down in the offices, wanting to uncover the neglect of duties by the police chief, against whom the steward of an important person had lodged a complaint. The esteemed Mikhailo Ivanovich Shtykov had punished this steward for imposing illegal taxes on the peasants. But all of the police chief's papers were in order. The investigator, in a bad mood as he left the court, asked the crowd of townsmen assembled at the door: "Are you content with your supervisors?"

"No," came the answer from the crowd. "The police treat us badly."

"What exactly do they do to you?"

"They demand cleanliness!"

The official couldn't help from bursting out laughing when he heard this complaint against the police. Seeing at last that he would get nowhere here by accusing the police chief, as usually happens, he took his side and accused the steward, for in order to show his diligence, it was necessary that he find someone to blame, or else the investigation would be considered unfinished. The interrogator suddenly changed his mind and became very polite to everyone, even to his host the merchant. The police chief's friends decided to reimburse him for his travel expenses, which he'd bitterly complained about, pointing out that his income was very small. But all of this was kept secret from the police chief, who, if he'd found out about his friends' intention, would probably have argued with them, perhaps even gotten into a fight with the investigator.

The next morning the police chief came to see us and brought our passports, an order for post horses for the trip to Moscow, and my money. We rushed to embrace the kind Shtykov, who himself was extremely glad that the affair had concluded successfully. One thing disturbed me: I had written to my aunt several times but had received no reply. Sad foreboding weighed upon my heart, and I could only find consolation in the good Milovidin's friendship.

At last, after taking leave of the police chief, Pyotr Petrovich, the priest, and our host, and after writing a farewell letter to Mr. Rossiyaninov, we set off for Moscow with post horses in a carriage we had bought, and the goods were sent with carriers.

Chapter 22

A Retired Soldier's Story. Arrival in Moscow. My Aunt's History. I Find My Mother. The Seducer. Murderers.

On the road sometimes the most unsociable people become close to their servants. Milovidin and I, however, considered Petrov more like a comrade in our misfortune than as a servant, and we treated him very courteously and amicably.

"Where were you born, Petrov?" Milovidin asked him on one occasion.

"In the Polish Ukraine," replied the retired soldier.

"I never would have guessed that you're from there," replied Milovidin. "You speak with a real Russian accent."

"And you have no accent whatsoever."

"That, your honor, is because from my youth I was apprenticed to a hairdresser in Petersburg and entered the service early."

"And so, you come from house serfs?"[1]

"Yes, sir."

"What was your master's name?"

"I was the serf of a wealthy Russian lady who settled in the Ukraine a long time ago."

"How did you come to be a soldier?"

"I'll tell you if you wish."

---

1. As opposed to field serfs.

"Do tell us."

"My father was a house Cossack."

"What does that mean?" I asked.

"Rich landowners in the Polish Ukraine had the habit of dressing some of their house serfs in Cossack style and using them to run errands, conduct searches, administer corporal punishment, and so on. Our mistress had a troupe of some fifty Cossacks under the supervision of my father, who was called the *esaul* or Cossack captain. These house Cossacks, our old folks report, were attired just the way Ukrainian soldiers used to dress in olden times: wide Turkish trousers, tight jackets, and sheepskin hats. Cossacks shave their heads and wear a long lock of hair on their crowns, wound behind one ear. They call this lock a topknot. They also shave their beards, leaving a long mustache. They usually select the most efficient and handsome men to be house Cossacks. In spite of the legal prohibition, they sometimes arm them with pikes, sabers, pistols, and always with whips. My mistress's extensive holdings were all rented to various small landowners, while the inns and taverns were leased to Yids.

"Ukrainians are a kind people but stubborn. A Ukrainian peasant doesn't endure insults as patiently as a Lithuanian or Byelorussian. On my mistress's estate, the peasants often opposed the despotic rule of the tenants and their stewards; the Cossacks were always kept busy and profited from suppressing the disobedient and from punitive expeditions, billeting charges, administering corporal punishment—that is, they enjoyed luxurious quarters at the peasants' expense, as punishment for the peasants' disobedience.

"The Cossacks also had to recover arrears from the Yids. If my father had been frugal, he could've accumulated considerable wealth following the example of his colleagues, many of whom bought their own freedom; their children, after learning to read, are now called Polish gentry in places far from their birthplace. I met many comrades of my childhood in Petersburg: a majority of them are engaged in legal work and live like Polish lords. Unfortunately, however, my father was partial to playing cards, and the fortune he made in the course of a year he usually lost at the Kievan Fair, where he went to guard his mistress's cashbox. My father had five sons. The mistress selected me along with fifty other young men to send to Petersburg to serve as apprentices in various trades.

"The steward who escorted us to Petersburg was a friend of my father and for that reason chose me to serve as an apprentice in the easiest trade, one which would allow me to become close to my master. In my master's shop I learned to cheat and deceive, which I had no idea about previously. My father had me taught to read at his own expense, but I liked card games more than books and helped my comrades to deceive our master so I could gain the means to play cards all night long. Five years passed quickly, and I was ordered to come back home. I had to undergo a test in my mistress's presence and dress the hair of one of the chambermaids in a new fashion. But I knew better how to play several card games than to curl and fluff up a maid's hair. I burned the maid's forehead with the curling iron and spoiled her lovely curls. The mistress gave me a few slaps across my face and sent me to the backyard to await her orders.

"My mistress not only had trunks filled with silver but entire barrels of it; in spite of that, she never missed a chance to make an extra kopeck and never spent even a hundredth part of her immense wealth. Although her courtyard was full of people and many servants sat at her dining table who were members of the Polish nobility and her relations, the mistress knew how to feed everyone at the lowest possible cost. Provisions in our part of the country were very cheap, and everything needed for the mistress's table—chicken, goose, turkey, butter, eggs, mushrooms, and so on—was supplied by the peasants in the form of levies, called *gifts*. The mistress also never had to buy wine, sugar, tea, coffee, and all sorts of spices for cooking: the Yids had to provide those items whenever they received a lease for a tavern or an inn. Our mistress did nothing but receive and count her money, check her accounts, and inspect her trunks. She took particular pleasure in receiving eggs from countrywomen. For this task she had a special device, a kind of wooden cup with no bottom, through which she would drop the egg into a tub of water. If the egg didn't fill the measure, the peasant woman had to replace it with another one.

"Of the requisitions and income from the estate, all of which I don't recall, and some of which I don't even know, one source was conceived of by our mistress herself and provided a great deal of money. Every peasant household had to provide a horse's tail at least once a year, and every peasant girl at least once in her life had to cut off her braid and hand it over to the mistress. Russian merchants bought horses' tails; they would send a man to Moscow and Petersburg to sell the braids to hairdressers for making wigs, hairpieces, and artificial curls. Since the mistress was unaware of any other of my faults except my lack of skill in hairdressing, after a while I was employed to shear these so-called two-legged sheep and take their hair to the capitals. For several years I carried out this task very well, but once I fell in with some gamblers and lost several hundred pounds of the best hair, including some red hair, which was then very much in vogue. Not daring to return to the mistress, I spent a long time wandering around Petersburg, finally fell into the hands of the police, since I had no passport, and was shipped back home to my mistress.

"At that time there was a levy for recruits, and they sent me into the army to be a soldier. Service cured me of my vice and, as I matured, I became wiser. I served very well for ten years and was promoted to the rank of noncommissioned officer. Our regiment was stationed at the edge of the Caucasus, where I received a severe wound in a battle with the mountaineers and was forced to retire. I thought of going to Moscow and taking up the trade of a boot maker, which I had learned in the service. At the Makaryev Fair[2] I was recruited to serve a merchant from Bukhara, who promised me piles of gold, but on arrival in Bukhara, he sold me as a slave to an Uzbek, a nobleman of that country. I had to work like a horse in the fields, even in the hottest weather; my fatigue was chased away with sticks, and I was fed worse food than the domestic livestock. At last I fell ill from starvation and exhaustion, and my master traded me for a bull to another merchant, who upon my recovery took me with him to drive camels in the Kirghiz steppe. I'd already traveled with a caravan several times heading to Russia, but the Bukharan merchants leave their Russian prisoners in the steppe with their Kirghiz acquaintances and take their slaves back to Bukhara with them. As a result it would be very hard to escape by running away, and no doubt I would've ended my days among these infidels if they hadn't quarreled among themselves, like dogs over a bone, and if His Excellency Ivan Ivanovich hadn't been living among the Kirghiz. It's true that there are good and bad people everywhere, and in Bukhara I've seen good masters, while in Russia there are some men no better than my Uzbek master. But that leveler death will come, and then the roll call and sorting will occur according to the official list: some get gold-braid galloons, others the stockade. He who has taken part in battles and campaigns knows that everything on earth is vanity and doesn't mean a thing! On bivouacs the same amount of firewood warms a soldier as warms a general, and to sleep, no more ground is required than a

2. The greatest fair of all, the largest in Europe, was a huge fair held at Nizhny Novgorod, which took place from July 15 to September 10 every year. It attracted many foreign merchants.

man's full length. Whether it's a dry rusk or a tasty pie in the stomach, it makes no difference, a person will be full, and when it comes to treating someone to leaden nuts,[3] all get equal shares. The main thing is to have a clear conscience, a strong constitution, and a passport in one's pocket. There's enough bread and work in Russia!"

At last we caught sight of the bell towers of Moscow and embraced each other in silence. I was behaving as if in a fever. When the city gates appeared before us, tears burst forth from my eyes. We stopped at an inn; since it wasn't very late, each of us, taking a cab, went in search of our friends. Milovidin burned with impatience to find out what had become of his wife, the Count and Countess Tsiterin, and his uncle. I went in search of my aunt. At her former apartment nobody knew where she'd moved or what had become of her. I couldn't find Vorovatin either in his previous lodging. The landlord told me that after he'd returned from Orenburg, he'd sold all his belongings and left Moscow for an unknown destination. He advised me to inquire about my aunt from the police. I returned to the inn extremely sad and found Milovidin even sadder. Count and Countess Tsiterin had died; their son, the captain, who Milovidin thought was murdered, had only been severely injured, had recovered and inherited his parents' entire estate. Milovidin could learn nothing about his wife's whereabouts, except that she hadn't returned to Moscow after her time abroad. His uncle had finally retired from the service, having become tired of writing *A faithful copy of the original*, and had settled in Kiev with his housekeeper, who'd become as attached to him as a chronic illness. Her daughter had married one of those suitors who from their youth begin to search for a bride among the *wards* of wealthy people or the *housekeepers* of old bachelors. Milovidin had no money and no hope of obtaining any. I offered him my purse and in the first instance gave him one hundred gold coins. This consoled him somewhat in his grief. The next day I went to the police and found an official who took it upon himself to locate my aunt's residence. Inquiries were sent to all police offices to find out where Mrs. Baritono lived. Reports were received that "In such and such a precinct, the said Baritono does *not* reside." The next day, after receiving these reports, the footman from the inn, whom I'd also commissioned to search for my aunt, informed me that she was living only about twenty paces from our inn in a house belonging to the police captain's wife,

3. That is, bullets.

next door to the captain who'd submitted a report that "Mrs. Baritono does not reside" in his precinct.

I rushed to my aunt's house. I climbed a dirty staircase and went into the gallery or, better said, went under the awning of the second floor and could barely manage to reach its end, making my way among tubs, vats, buckets, iron pots, and jugs. I opened the door into a dark kitchen; an old woman in tatters looked at me in astonishment and bowed deeply.

"Does Adelaida Petrovna Baritono live here?"

"Yes, master."

My heart sank, my legs trembled: I opened the door to the room—*My God! What a sight!* In a small attic space with one window, on a dirty bed, lay a woman with a swollen face covered with red spots. She was lying under an old cloak, and her head was wrapped in a faded kerchief. She looked at me with motionless eyes, raised herself up, and opened her mouth as if to say something, but didn't speak.

"Auntie, is that you?" I cried, and rushed to her, but she fell back on her pillow and closed her eyes. A tremor ran through her body, a cold sweat broke out on her face, and her mouth was distorted with nervous agitation. I thought she was dying, and in my despair I didn't know what to do. The footman from the inn was with me, waiting for me in the gallery. I ran to him, ordered him to summon a doctor at once, and went back to help my aunt. Meanwhile the old cook ran to the house of a neighbor, the police inspector's wife, who came running in with smelling salts; by her efforts, she brought my aunt back to her senses. She burst into tears and that relieved her heart.

"Vanya," she uttered at last. "So, you haven't forgotten me!"

I answered only with my tears.

"I thank You, good Lord, that You've permitted me once more in my life to embrace someone who's dearest to me in the whole world," said my aunt. "Good Vanya, you've found me in poverty and illness: I've deserved this and don't blame Providence. It's been kind to me in bringing you back there. Now I can die in peace!"

The good neighbor left us and, recovering somewhat, I looked around this refuge of poverty. The walls of the little room were as black as in a blacksmith's shop. The one window was made of fragments of different kinds of glass and patched in several places with wrapping paper. One table made of fir, two chairs, and a small trunk constituted all the furniture. A votive light burned in the corner before an icon. On the windowsill stood an earthenware teapot without a lid, a white pottery cup, a glass, a pitcher containing some beverage, and a tallow candle in a bottle. After glancing around at all these things, I pressed my aunt to my bosom; I don't recall what I said to her, but I wept bitterly. At last, after calming down a bit, I went off to find some appropriate lodging for her, leaving her my purse to pay the doctor and for medicines.

That evening my aunt moved into a clean, well-furnished apartment and found in the chest of drawers everything she might need for the near future. In addition, she had a clean bed, cooking utensils in the kitchen, table service, silverware, and a clever maid, a skillful cook, and a nimble footman. For the time being I remained at the inn with Milovidin, who shared my joy and had helped to locate and furnish an apartment for my aunt, purchasing what was needed (naturally with my money). He was very experienced, having been insolvent several times and having had to set up house again.

In two weeks my aunt had recovered from her illness, and the doctors declared that the danger had passed. She could even walk around the room. At first I refrained from telling her about my adventures, for fear of upsetting her further. Finally, when her strength returned, I related everything that had occurred since the date of my departure from Moscow and ended my tale with the request that she explain to me the cause of Vorovatin's questions and suspicions about my father and the persecution of the unknown countess. My aunt fell to thinking, and at last threw herself around my neck and began weeping.

"Vanya," she said. "I want to reveal my soul to you, which contains the secret of my entire life. Don't despise me, but pity someone who's been so unfortunate. I'm a victim of thoughtlessness and vanity. Listen!

"You may not know that in Byelorussia there are settlements or *slobody*,[4] where many people live who've moved there from various parts of Russia, largely Old Believers,[5] seeking refuge from the risk of persecution in former Poland.[6] One Russian *sloboda* is located some six miles from Mr. Gologordovsky's estate. There was a prosperous peasant there named Pyotr Sevastyanov, nicknamed Krutogolovy. By transporting and trading in bristles, linen, and flax, he managed to accumulate considerable wealth. He was a widower. His sister Aksinya administered

4. Settlements exempt from normal state obligations.

5. Russian believers who maintain the liturgical and ritual practices of the Orthodox Church as they were before the reforms of Patriarch Nikon of Moscow in the mid-seventeenth century.

6. The territory of the Russian-ruled Polish state was known as the Congress Kingdom of Poland (1815–1874).

his estate. He had two children: a daughter Dunya, aged sixteen; and a son Vasily, nineteen. That Dunya was me!"

"What? That was you, Auntie?" I cried in astonishment. "With your education, with such agility! It's hard to believe . . . So, I also come from a peasant family,' I said, blushing and dropping my eyes. "But I'm your nephew, son of your sister, yet you say that you didn't even have a sister. How can that be?"

"Be patient and listen," my aunt said, "and don't be ashamed of your origins. We're not free to choose our parents; but it depends on you to ennoble your family; listen patiently to my story until the end: then you can say and do as you wish.

"A Hussar regiment was stationed in our neighborhood, and in our village there was a squadron commanded by Prince Miloslavsky, the captain. He'd just come from the Guards and astonished not only us but also the landowners by the splendor of his carriages, the beauty of his horses, and his spending habits. The prince was a handsome man, young—only twenty-five at the time—affectionate with everyone, and a great ladies' man. He presented all the girls in the village with ribbons, beads, and tasty treats; he greeted everyone politely, enjoyed folk dances, treated the peasants to vodka, and paid for everything in cash. Everyone in the village loved him, both old and young. I was the only one who wouldn't take any gifts from him and never talked to him. I was fearful, and the prince seemed timid only with me. Every day he went riding or walking past my windows and dismounted intentionally, as if to fix something, or else he stopped to talk with my father, but the real reason was to take a look at me. However simple country lasses may be, they can read the eyes of a lover as if reading a book, and they don't have to be experienced to guess the intentions of a man looking at them. I couldn't doubt that the prince came riding or walking past our house just to see me, because if I moved away from the window or hid behind the gates, he'd circle our house twenty times merely to glance at me. But I was annoyed that in spite of his friendliness he never said a word to me. To tell the truth, at the time I didn't understand what love was all about, but I felt happy when I saw the prince and very bored when several days had passed, or even one morning, without seeing him. I dreamed about him frequently with his fair face and black mustache, and when it happened that he kissed me in my dream, which I really desired, I was cheerful and content for the whole day. In our village there were many beautiful girls and comely young men, but all of their faces seemed unbearable to me, and I took pleasure in looking at only two faces, my own in a little mirror and the prince's. It wasn't only my little mirror that told me I was pretty. All our young peasants, all the officers, and landowners' sons who stayed at our house while going hunting, repeated one and the same thing, and for thirty miles around I was known as the *beautiful peasant girl.*

"My father was very strict and glum; he was a zealous Old Believer and would have rejected me if he'd known that I dared to look at a man who was not a member of his sect. He said this to me several times. The prince was aware of my father's strictness and his intractable prejudices, and that's why he avoided meetings with me, contenting himself with looks alone. Half a year passed in that manner: the prince abandoned all his acquaintances, his pursuits, and never left the village, finding all the pleasure in life in getting to see me several times a day on the street or through my window. I thought only about him, and his image lingered before my eyes day and night. Summer arrived. My father left for town on business; I was left alone under my aunt's watch; I asked her permission to accompany my girlfriends into the woods to pick berries. We dispersed in the woods, and I, singing a mournful song and thinking about the prince, was busy picking berries, when suddenly I heard a rustling noise among the bushes; I cried out from fear and wanted to run away; the branches separated—and the prince appeared, and I stayed there reluctantly.

"'My dear Dunya, I love you!' he said to me, and drew near. I remained silent, stood motionless, casting my eyes down, but I felt my knees were shaking and my cheeks were burning.

"'Dunya, I shall die if you don't come to love me!' I remained silent.

"'Just look at me,' said the prince. I raised my eyes, looked at him, and had to wipe my eyes with my sleeve, feeling them fill with tears.

"The prince took me by the hand, sat me down next to him on a tree trunk, and began talking to me. I don't recall what he said and how I replied. My hand, held by the prince, sent flames through my veins, and my heart beat so loudly that I could hear its pounding and felt feverish. The prince spoke with me for a long time, caressed me, and at last when he dared kiss my face, my eyes grew dark: I thought that I'd die on the spot from fear, and then I threw myself into the prince's arms. . . .

"We weren't oblivious for long; days flew by, and our joy did, too. I soon realized that nature had intended me to become a mother, and almost at the same time the regiment received its orders to commence a campaign against the Turks. Where could I hide my shame? How could I evade my father's strictness? One day the entire village was suddenly astonished to learn that the lovely Dunya had disappeared from her father's house. I behaved so cautiously that no one suspected me of voluntary escape. Rumors even circulated that I'd been abducted by force and murdered. They suspected the prince as well as many of the surrounding landowners. My father didn't search for me; other people talked about it for some time and then fell silent.

"Some thirty miles from our village, in a forest hamlet, there was an inn. In the neighboring town the Yids had recommended the owner of that inn to the prince: they said he was an honest man, modest and obliging, reliable for all things. The prince placed me there and entrusted me to an old woman, who called herself a midwife. He gave me a case with his valuables, including two portraits of him and ten thousand rubles in banknotes. The prince ordered me, as soon as I'd recovered from giving birth, to leave for Moscow with my child and await his return. He left his address in Krechetniki in the parish of John the Baptist. The prince set off on his campaign, promising to provide for my future happiness, and never to abandon my child. In bidding farewell to the prince, I thought my life was ending.

"I had a separate room in a secluded part of the house. The old woman, who was assigned to me, lived in a small storage room. The entire family of the Yid attended to me with great diligence. The landlord himself was known as a doctor and took care of the local gentry in the neighborhood. At last I gave birth to a son . . . . Vanya! You are my son, and your father is Prince Miloslavsky!' "

I jumped up from my chair.

"So you're my mother!" I cried in a strong rush of feelings. She sat motionless and, covering her face with her hands, wept. I threw myself into her arms, and our tears mingled.

"My son," said my mother, "don't reproach or despise me. I followed nature's lead; all the blame rests on the one who by the strength of his intellect and character could have restrained me from committing a crime. But he's no longer alive . . . let's respect his memory. His head was to blame, but not his heart!"

After we'd calmed down somewhat, my mother continued her story. "You already know that you were born with a growth on your left shoulder, which was cauterized by my landlord, the Yid doctor. Otherwise, you were strong and healthy. I had already begun to recover from my illness and was intending to leave for Moscow as soon as possible. A terrible event separated me from you.

"The woman who was assigned to me as my midwife, in spite of her helpfulness and affection, had something about her that I couldn't abide. Her face, covered with wrinkles, expressed malice and envy. Every time our eyes met, a tremor ran down my spine. I tried to avoid her presence and spent all my time alone with you or with a portrait of your father in my little room. One autumn evening I had a headache and went to bed early. But, suffering from a high fever, I got up and went out to get some fresh air. Leaning against the wall of the house, not far from my landlord's window, I heard my name uttered. I approached the window and overheard a conversation which almost made me faint.

" 'I've examined that young woman's entire trunk,' said the midwife, 'and found indescribable riches. Whole bunches of banknotes, piles of gold coins, and a handful of precious stones!'

" 'Well, take them and run away; we'll cover for you,' said the Yid.

" 'Impossible,' replied the midwife. 'I have family in town, children, and grandchildren. The girl will find someone to write to the prince; he's a friend of the marshal, the mayor, and even the governor: there'll be trouble!'

" 'Well, get rid of the girl,' said the Yid.

" 'That would be best of all,' replied the old woman. 'This place is empty and quiet. We'll dispatch the girl to the next world, give the child away to someone, divide the money and the jewels, and no one will know the difference. Let the prince come back: we'll say that she left for Moscow; let him look for her there. The dead tell no tales!'

" 'Splendid, Vasilisa, splendid!' said the Yid. 'When do we start?'

" 'Why put it off?' answered the old woman. 'She's sick today and now asleep. Take an axe, smash her head, put her body in a bag, and throw her into the lake.'

" 'Right: there's no reason to delay. You go to her door; I'll bring the axe and dispatch her at once.'

"You can well imagine my state of mind, hearing this hellish conversation. Despite the cold, damp weather, I ran off into the woods almost unconscious, in the darkness of night, and managed to hide myself among the bushes. Feeling exhausted, I lay down under a tree and there came to my senses. I reproached myself for leaving you in the hands of the murderers; after some thought, I calmed down. I was almost certain that they wouldn't dare murder you after I'd escaped their clutches. I decided to go into town, tell the governor, who was a friend of the prince, everything I'd overheard and ask him about the return of my child and about sending me to Moscow. I was wearing a large kerchief on my head and a sleeveless jacket. After praying to God, I fell fast asleep under the tree."

Chapter 23

The Conclusion of Adelaida Petrovna's Story. Marriage. Reeducation. The Free Life. The Fatal Consequences of Negligence. I Enter the World. Paying Visits.

"I woke up at daybreak from the cold and continued to wander in the woods without finding any road. I was tormented by thirst, but strong moral shock made a sudden change in my illness. After drinking some rainwater from a puddle, I felt stronger and bolder than before. But remembering that you were left with no one to provide for you, I wept bitterly and committed you to the care of Him who takes care of weak fledglings and unfortunate orphans. After taking several rests and continuing my journey as far as my strength would allow, I managed to reach the main road by noon. Fearing pursuit, I dared not travel along that road but proceeded along the edge of the woods. All of a sudden I heard the sound of a bell. I hid in the bushes, and I saw that in a carriage drawn by four horses sat a gentleman with his footman; I ran out to the road, threw myself down on my knees, and clasping my hands, I cried, 'Save me, save an unfortunate woman from her death!' The carriage stopped; the gentleman climbed out, came up to me, and began to question me. I told him my whole story and, falling at his feet, begged his assistance and protection. The gentleman was touched by my youth and misfortune: he sat me next to him on the carriage, and we sped off into town.

"My savior was an Italian by birth and was named Baritono. He had been a music teacher and conductor in the home of a wealthy landowner, and after spending six years in the provinces, he was on his way back to Moscow with some money to resume his life in the capital giving music lessons. Baritono was already middle-aged, around forty, but he had a nice appearance and a cheerful disposition. He spoke Russian fairly well and consoled me as best he could. After arriving in the provincial town, he went to see the governor and related my adventure to him. The governor was a worthy and just man. He wanted to meet me himself; just like Baritono, he was taken by my appearance and was touched by my misfortune. He immediately dispatched an official with orders to arrest the Yid and the midwife and to retrieve my son and all my belongings. But most likely, as a result of the indiscretion of the cabman in whose presence I had related my adventure to Baritono, news of my rescue had also reached the Yid. The official found the inn empty. The Yid's family and the midwife had disappeared together with you and all my things: I didn't hear anything more about you!

"Baritono brought me to Moscow and treated me the way a tender father treats his own daughter. He wrote a letter to the regiment of Prince Miloslavsky, but instead of a reply, we received his own letter back with the news that the prince had been killed in battle.

"Baritono didn't want to part from me. He named me Adelaida, hired teachers for me, and he himself taught me music. Within five years I learned to read and write in Russian, speak Italian and French, dance, sing, and play the piano. Nature has been so generous to the Russian people that it didn't take great exertion to educate me. I came to love reading and soon grew acquainted with everything that a society woman should know. Baritono was delighted with his creation; all his friends were surprised by my cleverness, understanding, and talent. I had many admirers but was attached to my savior by my gratitude. He offered me his hand in marriage, and I gladly consented to become his wife, so that my love might repay my benefactor somewhat for all the care he'd lavished on me.

"Baritono was a good man and loved me dearly. I couldn't be in love with him, but I was attached to him and fulfilled all the obligations of a wife with great zeal. Meanwhile, my husband, weary of running around town for concert tickets, was tired of quarreling with his pupils and their parents about receiving the fees for his lessons; he also felt that his health was growing weaker, so he decided to open a toys and trinkets shop and to give up teaching. He spent his entire modest capital on establishing a shop and purchasing goods; but since he had insufficient credit and, being a novice in trade, lacked knowledge of commercial subterfuge, his business soon died a natural death. As a result Baritono was so embittered that he fell ill with a nervous fever and died.

"My situation was extremely unpleasant. I was left with one thousand rubles that I had saved from our entire capital, with no hopes for the future, without friends or protector. The circle of my female acquaintances was limited to a few foreign women, shopkeepers, and actresses. I didn't know any men, except for a few musicians and my husband's fellow countrymen. But every admirer of the fair sex knew me, followed me in crowds on the sidewalks, never took their eyes off me in my box in the theater, and continually passed by my window. I had a multitude of secret admirers. Several of them, even when Baritono was still alive, had written letters to me, which I turned over to my husband without even opening them; others, through some of my female acquaintances, declared their love, but from the first mention of it, I silenced my obliging friends, and in that way I was justifiably known as a modest woman—something that rarely happens. After Baritono's death, my women friends and my husband's male friends all came to me with their advice or, better said, their instructions that I accept the good offers provided by these generous people who were burning with love for me. Not seeing anything better in reach and having heard anecdotes about illustrious ladies who were enjoying a considerable reputation in society, I thought that all this was in the natural order of things and consented to accept the offer of Prince Chvanov, who was not demanding my love at all but only requesting permission to love me, and for that he would shower me with gold. You knew this kind old man. He spent all his money on women due to his vanity, so he would become known as a ladies' man! Despite all his weaknesses and eccentricities, he had a good heart and, if he were still alive, I wouldn't have been reduced to the extreme state in which you found me.

"Knowing neither the value of money nor the lack of it, I spent all that came into my hands. After receiving the money, I considered it my duty to spend it at once, and I knew of no other expenses except for those for my apparel and for showing off. I thought I could hide the secret of my behavior by the elegance of my dress; and the respect which was shown to me by strangers thanks to my apparel and equipage consoled me for the small unpleasantries that I received from proud married women who, protected by their husband's name like a screen, condemned in others what they themselves were adhering to in secret.

"Lacking any acquaintances whom I could visit, I formed a circle of male friends among the most pleasant and delightful people in the capital. You were a witness to our musical evenings, Vanya; therefore I won't describe them to you. Being still young, I was unable to limit myself to Prince Chvanov's semi-platonic love; consequently I searched out attachments of the heart, first for amusement and later out of habit. Semyon Semyonovich Plezirin promised to marry me as soon as Prince Chvanov fulfilled his promise and secured my fate. But Prince Chvanov's affairs took a turn for the worse: a part of his estate was mortgaged, and another part was being contested in court; thus, in spite of his good intentions, he couldn't guarantee my fate. Semyon Semyonovich introduced me to Grabilin, that wealthy minor official, whose rudeness and affection made my life intolerable. After your departure for Orenburg, I categorically declined his friendship and was even intending to marry a hardworking artist, who was desperately in love with me, when suddenly a harsh illness compelled me to take to my bed. I came down with smallpox, such a severe case that my entire body was covered with scabs. I suffered from fever and delirium; the hardhearted official Grabilin used this opportunity to embezzle the rest of my property. Semyon Semyonovich was one of those minor officials who were always looking for women with connections to people of wealth and high rank, to win their patronage by promising to marry them; Semyon Semyonovich was the first one to leave me destitute. Another friend, Abbé Pretatout, also renounced our friendship, and I would have died without any assistance if it hadn't been for one Russian lady, who was angry with me because her husband used to attend my evening gatherings but didn't take revenge on me with a good deed. My landlord didn't want me to stay in my apartment without paying him, and during my illness I was transferred to the room where you found me and thrown on the mercy of fate. That Russian lady, having learned of my situation, sent me some money and her doctor; she hired a woman to look after me; but since she herself wasn't wealthy, she couldn't do very much for me. In this misery Providence sent me aid and consolation in you, my son! I have lost all my beauty and with it my vanity and foolishness, which together were the reasons for my actions. From now on I will follow the road of repentance and love of God, and I shall fill the emptiness in my heart with love for my son. Vanya, my son, nothing can be more unfortunate than a woman who considered her beauty as her only virtue and made use of it as something to trade for momentary gratification. I now feel that in full measure. What would have become of me now if God hadn't sent you to me?"

My mother, after finishing her story, threw herself on her knees before the icon and began praying with tears in her eyes. Her prayer relieved her heart; she calmed down.

"Dearest mother," I said. "Let's forget about the past and think about the present and the future. In your tale I didn't find the key to unlocking the secret of my persecution. I haven't done harm to anyone. Who is this countess who so fervently wishes my destruction? Did you have some female enemy?"

"Many high-ranking women could be angry with me," replied my mother. "But I don't think that any of them wanted to take revenge by causing my nephew's ruin. The secret of your birth was known only to me. Not one of my former friends had even guessed that you were my son. I don't understand the cause of the countess's enmity against you. Perhaps it was a mistake."

Two more months passed, and my mother recovered completely. But her beauty had disappeared: her face was covered with deep scars and pockmarks, her hair had suddenly turned gray, her eyes had lost their liveliness, and even her splendid body had changed. My mother seemed ten years older than she really was. The loss of her external qualities set her on a path of inner wisdom. She became pious and dressed in black from head to toe; she spent all her time in churches and reading sacred books.

In the meantime my merchandise arrived in Moscow, and I sold it immediately. I received almost forty thousand rubles altogether. I rented a small but clean apartment divided in two parts: my mother lived in one, while Milovidin and I lived in the other. The retired soldier Petrov stayed with me as my valet. We spent our time rather modestly. Milovidin continued writing letters to all corners of Russia to find out what had happened to his wife, about whom he had heard no news at all. I searched for Vorovatin to learn the name of my enemy, the countess. We took walks, read together, philosophized, and made plans for the future, and, to tell the truth, felt bored. Milovidin had been accustomed to a lively social life, while my soul craved some sort of activity. Several acquaintances recognized Milovidin and discovered where he was hiding; seeing him so well dressed, spending money in coffee shops and taverns, they began to pay us visits. Stories of their former connections to society aroused in Milovidin a desire to return to his previous circle of friends.

"Listen, Vyzhigin," Milovidin said to me once. "You want to enter the civil service, to acquire some sort of standing in society. That's commendable! In this country a decent man without rank is almost the same as being in a foreign country with no passport. But it's difficult to gain anything like that without patronage. Where men have power, women wield it; and where women have power, men wield it. You must look for it among women, my dear friend! For entering society you have two important qualities: money and a pleasant appearance. You know more than is needed in the great world. It would be enough if you knew French and dancing, but in addition, you're a musician and you're good at playing games of skill. All of this constitutes the highest degree of wisdom among a large circle of people to whom the path of ambition is open to reach the first levels in the government. You're only lacking the kind of agility and self-reliance which are obtained by visiting the highest circles. But you can acquire these qualities quickly, with intelligence and boldness, of which you have no lack. So listen to me and enter society. I'll introduce you to two dozen of my aunts and cousins and to several heavyweight legislators in society; you'll become acquainted with young people on your own. Agree with everything the old men say, play cards with the old women, never get angry while playing, and never ask to collect debts; give treats to young people and share their pleasures; don't argue but always agree with the majority in a group of your comrades, with the master of the house, and with each individual you meet. Don't give rise to any scandal and don't slander anyone, but listen to all rumors and gossip patiently; repeat what you hear cautiously, always omitting all names; amuse the company with your inventiveness and never, ever worm yourself into people's favor by telling the complete truth; praise everything others have and always belittle your own; call all chatterers clever, all officials efficient and hardworking, all judges honest, all rich men benevolent, all elderly ladies kind, all young women and girls beautiful, all children lovely and smart. Know by heart all the name days and birthdays of your acquaintances, and don't stint in paying visits. Learn how to laugh until you cry when someone tells you a boring story on the pretense of its being amusing, and know how to frown when someone shares his grief with you. When you're moving ahead, always make it seem that you're standing back. Ascribe every one of your successes to others and thank everyone. Tolerate small insults with patience, and let others exact revenge for you. Make requests on behalf of others, and let others do so for you. Don't ever refuse anyone anything; promise everything to everybody and then ask forgiveness for the impossibility of delivering, pretending that you did everything that depended on you, although you really hadn't even begun. Remember all my instructions, and believe that if you follow them exactly, you'll surpass all other gentlemen and will receive whatever you might desire."

I revealed the secret of my birth to my friend Milovidin. My heart wanted to be relieved of my burden by sharing it. We conferred with my mother, and she blessed me upon entering a new career. "You may perhaps meet your relatives in society," said Milovidin, "but since you have no proof that you're Prince Miloslavsky's son, and since your father left you nothing, it won't help you at all, and it might even result in some unpleasantness. I shall introduce you into society as a Russian nobleman, having property that was granted you in the Byelorussian provinces. In general, Russian families who have settled in newly acquired provinces have few connections in the capitals; they will believe us. Those people who consider you Adelaida Petrovna's nephew and saw you in her house are aware neither of your origins nor hers. Without doubt they'll find out that now she lives like a recluse and that you support her at your own expense. That will confirm them even more in their opinion of your rank. Besides, dear friend, it's only in the middle class that people are so inquisitive and demanding in wanting to know about others. In higher circles people think only about themselves and don't worry about others unless they block their path."

At last came the day scheduled to begin my visits. I hired a carriage with four horses, dressed my footman in livery with galloons, and off we went. Along the way Milovidin said to me, "Let's begin our visits with Countess Protrubina. She's the one who leads the singing of Moscow old ladies, dozens of screeching women who howl at her command; and this chorus determines the reputation of young people, especially young couples. Here's her house. You see how many carriages there are in front of the porch? It's not as dangerous to offend the government as it is to offend these harpies, who for the least neglect are ready to tear the good name of a decent man to shreds."

"She's receiving guests!" said the porter, who was busy mending boots in his little room. We entered the hall, which had been painted about a half-century earlier. Enormous chairs covered with strips of colorful canvas stood around the walls; in the corner stood a large Dutch clock in a carved wooden case.

"Please come in!" the valet proclaimed, opening the doors into the living room. We entered. The countess, an elderly woman, was sitting hunched up on the sofa, supported by pillows embroidered by her nieces and her wards. There was also a large embroidered pillow under her feet. A small dog was resting on her lap, sticking out his head from under her shawl. In front of her on a little table stood small porcelain cups with visiting cards, a snuffbox, and a little bell. Several ladies and gentlemen were sitting in armchairs arranged around her.

"Greetings, auntie," said Milovidin, after kissing her hand.

"Where are you coming from, my good man?" asked the countess, raising her head and staring directly at Milovidin.

"From distant lands, auntie; I considered it my duty to see you first."

"Thank you for not forgetting me."

"Allow me, auntie, to recommend for your patronage a friend of mine, a Byelorussian landowner, Ivan Ivanovich Vyzhigin, to whom I am greatly indebted."

The countess looked at me and nodded her head; I bowed to her.

"I'm glad to meet you: we're always glad to meet good people. Please have a seat. Are you by yourself in Moscow or with your wife?" she asked Milovidin.

"By myself, auntie; my wife remains abroad because of her weak health."

"It's better that you're alone. But where are you serving?" asked the countess, turning to me.

"I'm only now intending to enter the service," I replied. "Up to now I've been furthering my education."

"Ah, you're one of the scholars. I understand," said the countess, taking a pinch of snuff. "Do you have many serfs?" she asked.

Milovidin didn't let me answer. He said, "Fifteen hundred."

"How many children do your parents have?" the countess asked.

"He's the only one and his own master," replied Milovidin.

"Not bad," muttered the countess, taking a bit more snuff.

I looked at the other guests and noticed that mothers were whispering to their daughters and that their daughters were now sitting up straighter and raising their eyes. They cast sidelong glances at me and dropped their eyes, leaned their heads gracefully on their shoulders; those who had good teeth smiled.

"Fifteen hundred serfs for one person is not bad at all," the countess said to herself, rubbing her snuffbox.

"Excuse me, what was his surname?"

"Ivan Ivanovich Vyzhigin," Milovidin repeated loudly and slowly.

I noticed again that all the visitors moved their lips, as if repeating my name to remember it.

"I have dinner at home every day," said the countess, "and, except for two days a week and on special occasions, I receive guests every evening.

It will be a pleasure to see you in my house, Ivan Ivanovich, and you, Aleksandr, there's no reason to invite you: you're family here, until you take off again."

Milovidin kissed the countess's hand once more, and I uttered such a skillful compliment that the countess even nodded her head as a sign of agreement and doubled the snuff she took as a sign of her pleasure.

"We're done here," Milovidin whispered to me. "Now everyone will sing the same song."

And that's what happened.

"Aleksandr Ivanovich," a plump, elderly woman, heavily made-up and wearing a huge cap which almost covered her eyebrows, said to Milovidin. "Is it recently that you've gotten so conceited that you don't recognize your old acquaintances?"

"Have mercy on me, madam," replied Milovidin. "I bowed to you when I came in but being engaged in conversation with Her Excellency, I didn't have the chance to address you and bear witness to my esteem for you, intending to fulfill that obligation in your own house."

"Precisely," said the plump woman. "I beg you not to leave us as you did before. Please visit us with your friend."

I fired off another compliment, and the plump woman grimaced; probably some flatterer would have called it a pleasant smile. Milovidin knew all the guests. Introductions began, and we were invited to dine at every house and to a party *every* evening. Within half an hour I'd made eleven new acquaintances.

"Much has changed since you left Moscow," the countess said to Milovidin. "Your cousin Ashenka married a wealthy official. Your cousin Polina has separated from her husband, who lost his position as the director of the customhouse. Cousin Katish almost married a colonel; everything was already arranged, but Kukushkina's annoying rumors ruined the deal, and Katish palmed off her affected young niece, who has nothing except for money, on the young man. But you know that a decent, well-brought-up man doesn't marry for money," she added, regarding me.

"Isn't that true, Ivan Ivanovich?"

"Financial calculation in marriage is the sign of a despicable soul," I replied.

"How clever you are!" said the plump woman, regarding her daughters.

"Sensitive and witty!" cried the skinny lady, next to whom sat four overweight girls.

"You kept saying that my grandson Koko will come to no good," the countess said to Milovidin, "but we set him up decently. He is on special duty to Prince Svyazin in Petersburg and is already a titular counselor. Just this year he received a small cross in recognition of his trip to Moscow with some secretary or prosecutor. It's a pity that he came here after the conclusion of the investigation, otherwise he might have been able to grab something else. We predestine him to become a gentleman of the bedchamber.[1] Prince Svyazin is now in power and is our *own* man. In several days I plan to send him my grandson Jacques—son of the unfortunate Blagorodov, who is said to have lost his mind from reading books and has settled in the country and refuses all ranks. Jacques, thank God, doesn't take after his father. He's a splendid young man who wants to serve in the College of Foreign Affairs, and he knows his business. For my name day he composed two sheets of French couplets, which were sung by my three granddaughters. At the last ball he surprised everyone as he danced the mazurka; besides, he's very well educated. They say he knows orthography and mythology! He'll become a man yet! However, they speak ill of his aunt, Countess Nikodim. I don't like to repeat bad news, but they say that she has connections . . . do you understand? She's stopped visiting me: forget about her! And the former governor, your relative Dobrodelov, has also stopped paying me visits. Although his friends keep proclaiming his honesty, not everyone believes that. People who have stopped coming to my house probably feel guilty for some reason. I don't like to tell tales, but I do know a thing or two!"

The countess took a pinch of snuff and continued to tell me all about her relatives and acquaintances, but Milovidin took advantage of the momentary pause: he stood up, and we left the room.

"God save us from this woman's tongue," said Milovidin as he was getting into the carriage. "She's assumed power over a quarter of Moscow society, and she treats anyone who draws back from her or who won't genuflect before her as a deserter; she tries him in her old wives' court, passes sentence, and punishes him by depriving him of his good name. By her tongue and her connections she has made herself fearsome to many people who hold important positions, and they must fulfill her wishes to avoid slander and all sorts of intrigues. She must

1. A rank in the Table of Ranks—a formal list of positions and ranks in the military, government, and court introduced by Peter the Great in 1722.

be flattered; then she'll obtain a position for you. The fifteen hundred serfs and the Byelorussian nobility I granted you will have their effect."

We stopped in front of a large house, and Milovidin said, "Now I'll introduce you to one of the ringleaders of the *old men of Moscow*, whose name is pronounced with as much respect as the oracle at Delphi in days of yore. At one time Antip Yermolayevich occupied an important position, and although during his leadership events took the same path as always, he's certain that since he retired the sun shines less powerfully on Russia, the moon isn't nearly as bright, and our homeland is on the verge of ruin. He condemns everything done both inside and outside the government, and he says that he would have advised to do it better—although, unfortunately, he didn't do anything good in his life except for retiring. According to him, besides his late friends and protectors, there never existed any capable people in Russia. If he weren't giving dinners and balls, no one would listen to him, but since he loves to gather a crowd around him in his house, then, as they say, he carries weight. He might be useful to you."

We were received. Antip Yermolayevich was in his study, sitting in a large armchair, wearing a green velvet dressing gown decorated with two stars, trimmed in sable.

"Ah, my old friend, where have you been?" he said to Milovidin.

"I've been traveling and, on my return to Moscow, considered it my first duty to pay my respects to Your Excellency."

"Thank you, thank you, my friend."

"Allow me to introduce to you my friend Ivan Ivanovich Vyzhigin, a Russian nobleman who has an estate with fifteen hundred serfs in Byelorussia."

"Welcome. Where did your father serve, and what rank did he hold?"

"He was a colonel in the army," replied Milovidin.

"Was it under His Highness?"

"It was," I replied, stuttering.

"Those were the times, weren't they?"

"True, Your Excellency," we replied in unison.

"But where do you serve?"

"I'm hoping to find a place now."

"What is service nowadays?" cried Antip Yermolayevich. "They have thought up civilian posts everywhere so that a decent man can't find a place to take cover. Isn't that so?"

"Exactly, Your Excellency," said Milovidin, and I repeated the same words after him.

"But even now there are positions for special assignments," added Milovidin.

"Yes, that's true, but under whose command should one serve on these special assignments?" asked Antip Yermolayevich. "There were quite some grandees in our time, but today? Isn't that the case? It used to be that you would visit a grandee, and he'd be stretched out in a dressing gown on his sofa; he turns over, and there standing in front of him is a line of princes, counts, and generals, awaiting a signal whether they should laugh or cry. Isn't that true? But today the grandee himself dares not take a seat before inviting others to sit down; he even receives petitioners in uniform and addresses his subordinates formally or calls them by their first name and patronymic. Isn't that true? Well, what sort of times are these? What good can come of it? Right? It used to be that a grandee would abuse you worse than he could his own footman, sometimes giving you a shove or throwing papers in your face, but where there was rage, there was also kindness. Isn't that true? Just imagine to what degree our morals have been spoiled today! I was telling my nephew an anecdote about one grandee who recommended his secretary for a reward of two hundred serfs. His recommendation was rejected at headquarters, so the grandee gave his secretary two hundred of his own serfs. What do you think was my nephew's reaction to this gift? He replied that if he'd been in the secretary's place, he wouldn't have accepted the two hundred serfs from the grandee, because he serves the emperor and not the grandee and would accept a reward only from the emperor. That's what we have today. And that secretary was none other than me. Oh, what times, isn't that right? Today people are all for politeness, but what's the good of that? 'There's many a slip twixt cup and lip!' When I served in a lower rank, I needed to request a leave of absence. One day I submitted a petition to that effect and went to see my superior officer, hoping for a favorable reply; he had a large number of guests present. Do you know how he greeted me? 'You're a fool, Antip Yermolayevich, a blockhead,' said the superior officer. 'Yes, sir, Your Excellency.' He repeated, 'You're a fool, Antip Yermolayevich, an ass, a blockhead.' 'I'm to blame, Your Excellency,' I replied, bowing. 'You requested leave for two months?' 'Yes, Your Excellency.' 'How come you didn't request your salary for those two months? You're a fool, my friend! Here's your leave of absence, and here's an order for the paymaster to provide your salary.' I kissed the hand of my kind superior officer and left after bowing and blessing my benefactor. But now they come and say *bonjour* and leave with *bonjour*. Isn't that true? What do you think my nephew says to all this? He says, 'Better to give nothing, but treat your subordinates humanely and not like a horse.' That's how it is nowadays. Isn't it so?"

"Since it's not possible to return to that golden age," I said, "we must submit to circumstances, and I beg you, Your Excellency, to take me under your patronage."

"We'll see, we'll see. People who were once my clerks now fill important positions. What's the good of that? However, we'll see. I'll see them and will have a talk about it. But today some sort of *style* has become fashionable. They're demanding that official papers be written smoothly, like songs; besides, they're to be short, clear, and intelligible. Isn't that right? But that's absolutely impossible. Right? But what sense can a man make out of these bits of paper? It was a different matter when they could toss you a case consisting of three thousand pages about a stolen hen or a broken window, so you'd rack your brains before reaching a conclusion. You involuntarily train yourself to do it. Isn't that right?"

At this time a footman announced that the police chief was asking permission to enter.

"Tell him to come in! Nowadays I'm without a position because I'm incompetent," said Antip Yermolayevich with a sly smile. "I'm incompetent! Do you understand? But there is no business about which clever people don't confer with me. Now the police have ordered that my neighbor's fence be painted. So everyone comes to me for advice—what color should it be? Antip Yermolayevich is incapable! Isn't that right?"

We took our leave and departed, after receiving permission to return *every day* to dinner and to spend the evening.

"What a silly old man!" I said to Milovidin in our carriage. "He's like a broken clock with a repeater mechanism which constantly chimes the hour where the hands stopped."

"May God prevent you from telling anyone in Moscow that Antip Yermolayevich is a silly old man! They'll consider you a schismatic or a freethinker. Keep silent and listen. These old men can do you a great deal of good and a lot of harm."

"Set me free! That's enough for today."

"No, one more visit, but this one will be pleasant. I'll take you to meet my cousin, with whom all of Moscow is in love, and she really deserves it."

"Ah, *mon cher* Aleksandr!"

"Ah, *ma cousine* Annette!"

They embraced and kissed; Milovidin, after sitting down on the sofa with the hostess, began to whisper. They whispered to each other and forgot all about me. Finally the cousin remembered.

"Ah, *pardon*!"

"Dear Anyeta," said Milovidin, "I want to introduce and recommend to your special favor and patronage my friend, benefactor, savior, and whatever you like, Ivan Ivanovich Vyzhigin, who, in addition to being handsome, as you see, is also clever and kind, like you and me, and has fifteen hundred serfs."

"*Charmée*."

"Enough, my dear, let's not stand on ceremony," proclaimed Milovidin. "Remember that it's as if you were doing it for me. Listen, the point is that I want to find a place for my friend in the service and to introduce him to the best Moscow society. You have a large circle of friends, my dear cousin. Please talk him up for a week or so. You can confidently assure everyone that he's just like me, and at one time you were convinced that I was an extremely nice man."

"You're just the same scatterbrain now as you always were," she replied.

"But where's your husband?" asked Milovidin.

"He's constantly traveling to his tax farms and factories; now he's in Petersburg. I have to take care of his business here, and I confess I find that unbearable."

"My friend and I will try to console the fair Ariadne!"[2] said Milovidin, kissing the hand of his cousin Anyeta. "But don't expect me to put you in a heavenly constellation: no, you're too lovely for the earth."

"*Toujours volage and amiable*,"[3] she said.

"Meanwhile, farewell, my dear," said Milovidin. "We're so exhausted by the two difficult visits we paid to the ringleaders of your Moscow society that we're hurrying home. Good-bye!"

The cousin also invited us to dine with her *every* evening.

---

2. In Greek mythology, Ariadne fell in love with the Athenian hero Theseus and helped him to escape from the Labyrinth after he slew the Minotaur, a beast half bull and half man.

3. "Always fickle and agreeable" (Fr.).

Chapter 24

A Picture of High Society. Meeting with a Kind Enemy. Oh, Human Weakness!

What would you say, dear readers, if you were shown four men and four women who gathered daily merely to satisfy their hunger and thirst, to talk about trivialities—mice at home, smoke from chimneys—and to occupy themselves with nonsense, then to hop on one foot from boredom, twiddle their thumbs, and make faces behind someone's back? You would say they were crazy. Don't judge so harshly, but pay attention to how some people in so-called high society spend their whole lives. Listen to what they talk about; look at what they do! Make a list of all their words and deeds, and soon you'll be convinced that this list will tally with that of the activities of the four pairs presented here as an example, whom you were just about to call crazy!

> One's first duty in society is to pay *visits*: what does that mean? Tell me: isn't it strange to drive, run, or hasten to show oneself for a minute in one place, to say nothing of importance or to utter vulgar nonsense; after that, to bid farewell and hurry to another place, a third, a fourth, and so on? Time is lost, the mind is blank, the heart is empty, the body is tired, and several rubles have flown out of one's pocket, money which might have fed a poor family. Meanwhile, visits are an important activity: a society man knows

no other obligation, no other occupation in the morning than to devote several hours to his nails, teeth, and hair (and signing promissory notes), then galloping from one end of town to another, paying visits!

Another important affair is *dinner*. Of course, this matter is important in the literal sense, because it's impossible to live without nourishment, and consequently it's impossible to think. But in society people think about only one thing: how and where to eat. It's great luck to dine at a table where turkeys, hens, and grouse will be consumed by people of consequence—that is, people who can serve plenty of turkeys, hens, and grouse at their own table but who are even able to provide pleasure to others who can also enjoy their turkeys, hens, and grouse. Think about it as much as you like, but this is the real truth.

What do people want? Positions, rank, and favors. Where does all this lead? That a man, with all of the above, will mean more—which is to say, will live better. What does it mean to live better? To have more rooms in one's house and be in a position to feed others. So, as I was saying, people struggle to have more turkeys, hens, and grouse, with all the trimmings. You'll start talking about Camillus, Cincinnatus, and Fabricius.[1] Ancient history, ancient fairy tales! Nowadays these men would be considered insane. Different times, different customs—and if nowadays some military commander like Cincinnatus were to pick up a plow[2] or, like Belisarius,[3] go begging, the district police would arrest them both (and rightly so) for violating civil order and for vagrancy. Our age is one of dining, although nothing is more amusing than to see people make an ostentatious scene out of the need to eat—the simplest and crudest activity common to all animals. They assemble all dressed up, listen to the sound of music amid the glare of gold and silver—all to fill their bellies! To invite someone to partake of this majestic operation means to pay him an honor. Say what

1. Three Roman statesmen and soldiers: Camillus was chosen dictator five times, honored with the title of Second Founder of Rome. Cincinnatus was a leader who became a legendary figure of Roman virtue. Fabricius was a statesman known for his incorruptibility and austerity.

2. According to the Roman historian Livy, Cincinnatus was plowing his field when first approached by a delegation from Rome.

3. Belisarius was a military commander of the Byzantine Empire who was instrumental in the reconquest of much territory belonging to the former Roman Empire.

you will, but in this case wolves are much smarter than we are. They gather when there's prey to be had or to propagate the noble tribe of wolves, and they eat together only when they've procured the prey together. It seems to me that it would be much better if it became the custom for people not to *eat* together but rather to *sleep* together. Sleep is also one of the most essential human needs, just like eating; consequently, there's no reason to be offended. Sleep is even nobler, because it's said that a man can exist without eating for nine days, but he can't exist without sleep for more than three days. The advantages accruing from this custom, if it were introduced, would be incalculable. In the first place, this entertainment would be less expensive; in the second place, fewer stupidities would be uttered in sleep than when awake, especially during a dinner complemented by wine; third, a person would not be so exhausted and would not ruin his health at a sleeping party as much as at a dinner party; finally, we wouldn't see the baseness of the host who overspends or ruins poor merchants only to pay honor to an important person—by providing pleasure to his palate and upsetting his digestion.

After dinner comes another important affair—*playing cards*. Just imagine that beings, created in the image and likeness of God,[4] sit down at little tables covered with green felt, hold in their hands slips of glazed paper decorated with grotesque figures violating all the rules of art, and amuse themselves by collecting more points or guessing which slip of paper will fall in which position. Those who guess correctly or the lucky ones or simply the cheaters, who know how to take advantage of this sort of amusement, win money, which is either stolen from the peasants or earned through the sweat of their brow or acquired by the sale of his conscience, through inheritance or a dowry or money which belongs to his creditors.

At last the evening arrives—another important affair! One must *jump* to the beat of music. It's true that sheep do the same, but only when they're content. But people in society jump like monkeys on ropes, sometimes with tears in their eyes. It's an obligation; it's their duty! The host wants it to be said tomorrow that there was a gala ball in his house. And so the guests not disabled

4. Genesis 1:26–28.

by gout or from over-eating at dinner, or whose limbs are not crippled by old age, must jump; and by doing so, they must pay for the honor of being invited to other houses.

Finally, the last important affair—*supper*: the second volume of dinner and the necessity of sleeping a few hours to wake with a severe headache, an ashen tongue, and exhaustion in all of one's limbs. The same thing the next day, the third, and the fourth, and so on until youth and life pass by: a decrepit body is destroyed and the soul departs leaving no trace of its existence; one's name remains for some time in a broker's ledgers and a merchant's accounts and finally disappears in the abyss of obscurity; meanwhile thousands of other similar creatures aspire to follow the same path of insignificance and to vanish from the face of the earth like oysters. I ask: isn't the life of a Merino sheep more useful? During its existence on earth, it clothed and enriched many people with its wool, harmed no one with its tongue, slandered no one, refrained from intrigues to acquire a position for which it had no aptitude, deprived no one of his honor or property, and didn't show off in front of other sheep of lesser breeds simply because it was born a Merino?

In high society you'll find not only grown-ups but even children who speak several languages. The whole difference is that some speak more fluently than others. But what do they talk about? I'm really too embarrassed to repeat it. In the family circle, among people of both sexes, united by mutual advantage (which is called friendship), in heartfelt utterances, their favorite activity is criticizing, which blossoms in society under the name of candor and clever observations. Eavesdrop on their conversations in small circles. Here's their essence: so and so doesn't know how to dress; this one is a flirt, another is spiteful, and that one's a fool; so and so is a spendthrift, another is an intriguer, that one is unbearable, another ridiculous, clumsy, or simply stupid; this one is self-absorbed, another is favored beyond what he deserves, and that one is deservedly in disgrace. It was boring there, while over there it's very merry, even though the hosts are unbearable. Tomorrow we should expect that it will be pleasant in one place but very boring in another. On the other hand, there will be important people in attendance! What do they talk about in larger gatherings? Today is colder than yesterday. So and so procured a good position, while so and so received a decoration; this

> fellow has lost his post, another has just arrived in town, and that one is about to leave. In fashionable shops such and such new items appeared; such and such a seamstress makes nice dresses, while that hairdresser does fine work. A certain important lady is unwell; the daughter of so-and-so is getting married; this one has been appointed a maid of honor, this one gave birth to a son, and that one's daughter has died, and so on and so forth, etc. etc.!
>
> My God, is this why man has been endowed with the gift of speech? Is it for this reason that he is distinguished from all other creatures by an immortal soul, with a rational and creative intelligence, so he can fill the air with meaningless sounds similar to those of crows and magpies? Thought and feeling flee from high society as larks and nightingales fly away from the barren sandy steppe. The sluggish raven is attracted to a lifeless corpse: that's his food. The nightingale hides in the bushes, while the lark soars in the sky!
>
> One's entire life, from childhood to old age, is to be a slave to so-called social norms, a machine for bowing and running one's mouth; to speak without thinking, to think and say nothing, to listen to stupidities and reply with foolishness, to be in constant motion and never to forsake the circle of nonsense—and that's what is called living! Ah, my good Arsalan-Sultan, you were right, absolutely right! Long live the Kirghiz steppe! There, at least, there's some sort of goal—here there's none at all.

This is what I wrote in my notebook after spending two years living in high society. If I'd wanted to describe these two years, I could have written some fifty volumes of nonsense, as much alike in various ways as two *grandes dames*: one Parisian and one Russian. But even without me, so much foolishness has already been written, and I don't want to exhaust myself by writing a *history of monotony*. In those two years, instead of becoming smarter, I barely avoided losing whatever brains I had. Following Milovidin's instructions literally, I secured a position through patronage and was awarded three ranks, although to this day I don't know where the office is located or even what it's called: I remember only that it had something to do with construction. During these two years I managed to become the confidant of some old women and the favorite of some old men, formed many friendships with some young people. Among young ladies I also had many friends, who found me pleasant, nice, kind, and obliging. But my soul was created for activity, for strong sensations; social life, instead of being a field of action, is nothing but a restless sleep.

My mother continued to live her devout life. Milovidin, who received some ten thousand rubles from an honorable man, assumed a promissory note when he was still living with his wife in Moscow. He went in search of his dear wife, Petronella, after he learned that she was living in seclusion somewhere in Poland. I was alone in Moscow and feeling very lonely. My heart thirsted for something; I was looking for enjoyment but couldn't find it. Many women smiled at me; many young women chose me as their partner in a cotillion and in *petits jeux*,[5] touched my pride with unequivocal signs of preference. But I wanted neither to become a slave to quickly passing feminine whims nor to enter a deceitful marriage. Women could like the handsome Vyzhigin without his being a nobleman and without his owning fifteen hundred serfs, but before marriage to a young woman from a good family he would have to explain himself more completely. I was so sensible that I thought about neither love nor marriage. But this wisdom resulted from the coldness of my heart, not from my reasoning. To set off the landmine of passions in my heart, there was lacking only a spark. Nothing except the cold fumes of calculation penetrates the icy surface of high society. Some people due to their simplicity mistake the reflection of the rays on this block of ice for a flame. Deception! Pure deception! There's no warmth there, only the glare of light.

Living in the uninterrupted dissipation of high society, I searched for more dissipation. But among us there's no midpoint between boredom and debauchery for a man of society. The arts and sciences merely sprout, but much that blossoms in society never produces ripe fruit able to nourish a soul slumbering in indolence. Besides, the arts and sciences in Moscow constitute an occupation for a particular class and reach high society only by hearsay. There's one public amusement: the *theater*. I was an ardent admirer of the theater, because lacking the time to read on my own, I was glad for the chance to hear actors reading to me in public. I was able to satisfy my own taste as well as my social obligations.

One day it was announced in the newspapers that a newly arrived provincial actress would make her debut in the capital playing the role

5. Charades (Fr.), literally "little games."

of a coquette. Milovidin's cousin, my sincere friend, begged me to take her to the theater.

"I'm so bored by watching our modest women," she said, "that I would really like to see a genuine coquette."

I wanted to say that all she had to do was to look in a mirror, but I held my tongue and went to the box office to purchase tickets. We went to the theater together. The curtain went up: no new actress. Cousin Anyeta and I exercised our wit at the expense of the unfortunate players, who, as it's said, bent over backward to please us. I was in a most jovial mood. All of a sudden, the new actress appears; people in the stalls applaud her with approval; she curtsies, bows, approaches the orchestra, and begins speaking, but I could see and hear nothing.

"What's happened to you?" asked Cousin Anyeta, who wanted to say something about the dress the new actress was wearing. "For heaven's sake, what's happened? You're pale, trembling, and you look ill!"

"I don't feel well, not well at all!" I said in a low voice and ran out of our box. In the person of the new actress I recognized—Grunya!

Was I in love with Grunya? I don't know. I'd been very young when I met her, and at that time my soul was incapable of strong feelings. Passions could only smolder but couldn't flare up in my heart. Grunya's beauty had made a strong impression on my imagination then, but not on my heart. Before and after my unfortunate trip to Orenburg, I found many women more beautiful than she was; but as soon as I reached the age when passions begin to stir, in spite of Grunya's betrayal or the evil I'd experienced as a result of her treachery, I was convinced that it would be hard to find a woman *nicer* than Grunya. Her look and the sound of her voice always produced in me an effect that was hard to explain. It seemed that if I were blindfolded, I could have recognized her voice from among a million others. It penetrated right into my heart, while her looks had some sort of bewitching power to attract and hold my eyes. From the time of our last meeting, I had tried not to think about Grunya at all, but I remembered her involuntarily whenever love cast its nets out for me in high society. There were many fine women there, but not one pleased me. *Ah, why isn't Grunya's soul as nice as her looks?* I wondered frequently, and once again tried not to think about her. Now she'd appeared before my eyes once again!

I caught my breath at the buffet and then went outside to wander around the neighborhood of the theater. I couldn't account for the fact that I suddenly felt ill at the sight of Grunya. I ascribed it to my fright or to the awful recollection of the danger I'd experienced in Orenburg, to Grunya's betrayal, which caused my illness. But this wasn't fear and wasn't horror! Grunya appeared in my imagination not in any terrible form but in the full splendor of her enchanting beauty. *How pretty she is*, I thought, *how she's filled out, how she's grown. But I won't see her again, I mustn't.* Thinking like this, I found myself back in the corridors of the theater again and happened to return to our box. *I could still see her in public*, I thought, to excuse my weakness. Must I really cease going to the theater because of this frivolous woman?

"Are you feeling better?" asked Cousin Anyeta.

"A little."

"Ah, the new actress performs so capably," she said. "Such agility, what a noble voice! How well she understands her role! Besides, she sings so sweetly and is extremely good-looking. In truth, she's a fortuitous acquisition for our theater: this pretty Madame Primankina will turn the heads of our Moscow youth."

I remained silent and glanced at the poster to read the name that Grunya had chosen for herself. After skipping two acts, I watched her in the third act. She performed superbly and surpassed all expectations of the admirers of dramaturgy. There was no end to the applause. At the conclusion of the play, she was called back on stage. I was ablaze all during her performance. I followed her every word in my soul, her every gesture; I was afraid for her, trembled for her, and almost wept for joy when loud applause rumbled through the hall. I think I would have died on the spot, if Grunya hadn't been such a success!

After escorting Anyeta to her carriage, I declined the pleasure of accompanying her home and spending the evening with her. I returned to the stage door almost automatically. Wrapped up in my cloak, I intended to get a closer view of Grunya. She came out, but I'd forgotten to hide my face.

"Vyzhigin!" she cried.

"Grunya!" I said, and was unable to say any more.

She looked at me closely, then boldly took me by the arm and pulled me after her. They brought her carriage around; she got in and told me to get in and sit next to her. I obeyed. The carriage set off along the pavement, and I kept silent, not daring to raise my eyes and fearing an explanation, which might offend Grunya. She herself rescued me from this unpleasant predicament.

"Vanya, my dear friend, Vanya! You have a right to be angry with me. I'm guilty, but not as much as you think. I was too young, inexperienced, lacking in willpower, and had to submit to my mother. When you find out everything, my heart says that you'll forgive me and come to love me as before, love me as I love you. Tell me, Vanya, how was my acting today?"

I kissed Grunya's hand, sighed deeply, and said, "Your acting was splendid, incomparable, but I'm not surprised by that. Nature created you to be an actress. Your acting led me to the brink of ruin, and now you want to take away my happiness, my serenity. Grunya, you're too charming. I'm afraid of you! Let me out of the carriage, and let's say farewell forever!"

I uttered the last words in such a pitiful manner that even Grunya was moved. I was almost gasping for breath in my attempt to restrain my tears: I was so distraught.

"You're afraid of me, Vanya; you want to run away from me, yet you find me charming. Your words wound me, yet at the same time they afford me the greatest pleasure. Believe me, my friend, I love you truly and have never stopped loving you. All the time we were separated, you never left my heart or my mind. If I was guilty before you, I have atoned for my guilt by my sincere repentance and suffering. Vanya! Love me—or I shall die from despair." With these words Grunya burst into tears.

I was in ecstasy and don't recall what I said to her: I felt so good and was so happy! When the carriage stopped at her door, we were closer friends than we were before the journey to Orenburg. We joyfully climbed the stairs, holding hands, and upon entering the room, we embraced like old friends who'd never quarreled. The table was already arranged. Grunya ordered another place to be set, the best wine opened; taking me by the hand, she led me through all of her rooms.

"Look, my friend, this is my little household," she said. "You must become the master here. Here's my living room. It's not large, but I don't intend to receive many guests. Here's my dressing room. Here's the dining room; here's my study. And here's my bedroom. Isn't it true that my bedroom is very tasteful?"

"All of your rooms, dear Grunya, are furnished in good taste, very decently, and without extravagance; from this I must conclude that you're being paid a sizable salary."

"What sort of salary do we receive, my friend?" replied Grunya. "All my hopes rest on benefit performances. I brought about three thousand rubles with me but have spent almost all of it on necessities; in addition, I've yet to pay the three thousand rubles I owe for my furniture. God is merciful, somehow we'll pay off the debt; meanwhile, you must agree, dear friend, that a young woman, an actress, with my small talents and rather pleasant appearance, mustn't live like a tightrope walker. But it's time for supper."

After supper with Grunya, I stayed until long after midnight and still didn't have time to inquire what had led her to a career as an actress. She began to tell me ten times, but I interrupted her ten times to talk about love! In the first instance I found out only that she'd lost her mother and all her property. She invited me to dine with her the next day and promised to tell me her story. It was time to part. I went home madly in love, repeating constantly, "Grunya, dear Grunya, she loves me; there's no doubt that she's innocent of deceiving me."

In the morning I thought that Grunya must find it unpleasant having no money and being in debt. I dispatched Petrov to give her five thousand rubles.

In spite of the fact that I lived decently, owned a carriage, always dressed in the latest fashion, treated my friends, shared small gifts with ladies on their name days, and bought candy and toys for all the spoiled children to please them, purchased lottery tickets with cash (which never won), paid my gambling debts to the older women, and never took a kopeck from them; in spite of all these expenditures, I never touched my capital. This may seem surprising to many people, especially when I tell them that I employed no unusual means to acquire money. But if fortune smiles on a person, money seems to fill his pockets from all sides; and if, on the contrary, fortune begins to betray him, neither strongboxes nor locks can hold on to a kopeck or keep money from slipping through his fingers. I played games of skill honestly but expertly, cold-bloodedly, attentively; I sat down to play, wagered large amounts, and would almost always win. Having no idea about dishonest play, I thwarted all plots against me by my luck alone. When we played faro, I would suddenly place some cards in the middle of the deck: if I won, I took my money and went home. If I lost, I didn't continue playing and never tried to win back my money. I acted this way on the advice of Milovidin, who was very good at giving advice, although he himself was incapable of following his own wise rules, because he would advise me cold-bloodedly, yet he always behaved passionately. Not being attached either to the game or to money, I played, as they say, by calculation, and since fortune favored me, and I wasn't a real gambler, I lived by the game. In two years I won almost twenty-five thousand rubles in cash, and I was owed at least the same amount. But since I sent all my cash to Grunya, leaving myself only a few hundred rubles for everyday expenses, I would have to break into my capital if there were any unforeseen expenditures. It's true I didn't want to do that, but when I would send money to Grunya, I thought only about her, not the money. She gave one hundred rubles to Petrov, who was in ecstasy over this *kind beauty*, as he referred to her after their first meeting. She thanked me in such a tender letter that as I was reading it, I was ready to give her my very last kopeck. If someone were to say to me that while being in love, he was also thinking about money, I would tell him that he wasn't really in love; he was merely calculating.

Love is an illness, a body's feverish condition that clouds the mind. A man in love doesn't think rationally. Otherwise, how could a clever man kill another in a duel because a beautiful woman prefers him? How can he deprive himself, and sometimes his entire family, of nourishment just in order to satisfy the whims of his beloved? How can he sacrifice his peace of mind, freedom, and time for his beloved object? How can he neglect the duties of his service, his obligation to his country and his fellow citizens, out of love for a woman? Let them say what they will: love, passionate and burning love, is like an illness—even a dangerous one, often sending the unfortunate victim to his grave but more often leading to the loss of his estate and his reputation. There's only one means of salvation from this ailment: reason, tenderness of feeling, and a noble way of thinking of the beloved man or woman. But the person in love is blind and deaf. He loves even the faults of his beloved and finds a particular charm in them. Frequently, even extremely often, it happens that people in love come crashing down into an abyss, being completely innocent, distracted only by character, and not thinking at all about harming each other—on the contrary, mutually adoring each other. One of them, the man or the woman, does foolish things: the other one doesn't see that and perishes just as in a plague; the doctor perishes by getting infected by the patient, a healthy person by getting infected by the doctor. I repeat: love in an ardent, passionate soul is an illness. But let's return to the events.

CHAPTER 25

Grunya's Story. Friendship with a Clever Actress, or The Shortest, Surest, and Nicest Path to Ruin.

I didn't fail to appear at dinner. Grunya received me with open arms, laughed, cried, and repeated a thousand times that there was no one in the whole world happier than she was after she became convinced of my love. At the table I told her in brief about my adventures in the Kirghiz steppe. After dinner we sat down on the sofa, and Grunya began her own narrative.

"My father, as you know, left behind considerable property, but my mother, who'd managed the estate during my childhood, squandered it all and, in addition, accumulated debts. You saw how we lived. All the devotees and professors of card games used to assemble at our house. Everything my mother won while playing she shared with real gamblers, but when she tried her own luck, she lost to them and had to add some of her own money in the process. To complete her misfortune, she fell in love with one young scatterbrain, who promised to marry her, borrowed a large sum of money from her, and then up and married . . . another woman. The situation before our departure to Orenburg was the most desperate: our house was mortgaged, we had not even a single kopeck left of our capital, and we had incurred debts twice the value of our whole estate. My uncle died at this time, and we hastened to Orenburg to receive the inheritance, hoping that our affairs would improve.

"I'd scarcely left boarding school, where I'd acquired the usual knowledge—that is, to sit up straight and to chatter in French—when my mother decided to complete my education and teach me coquetry to attract wealthy young men to our house with my beauty and my courteous manners. You yourself saw how I would draw cards from the deck for a hot-blooded gambler and advise him to stake a large pile of money, trusting my good luck. For this purpose I would always choose gamblers who were not indifferent to my beauty and who would obey me readily. Needless to say, the cards I chose would always lose because other gamblers would whisper into my ear which cards to play and when to play them. I found my role revolting but had to submit; in addition, I was making eyes at them, smiling affably, and listening to the vulgar sweet nothings uttered by the gamblers who were in love with me, and whom I had to flatter in the hopes of arousing their reciprocal affection. I swear by my word of honor, that it was with the greatest repugnance that I flirted, until I met you.

"I was ordered to lure you to our house. That was the most pleasant commission for me since my leaving boarding school. There was no need to pretend, because I really did fall in love with you. Remember that I didn't try to entice you into playing cards; I even tried to keep you away from the games. My mother often scolded me for that, but I told her in no uncertain terms that only if I didn't have to lure you into gambling would I agree to deceive the others, as she wished. On this score she left me in peace.

"In Orenburg another misfortune befell us. The court had scarcely decided to award us the property left by my uncle when some new heirs appeared: half a dozen female students with a will drawn up and witnessed legally. The estate had been acquired by my uncle, and therefore it was useless to contest; besides, the students were quite lovely and enjoyed strong patronage. There was nothing to be done. My mother opened her house to gamblers once again: she summoned some experienced players from Moscow and once more forced me to play the role of a siren, luring mariners toward the enchanted Scylla and Charybdis!

"Business went very badly until winter. We were living almost in debt. Particularly at first we were lacking money. At this time an adjutant of a certain Petersburg general arrived in Orenburg on government business: Captain Count Lovkov, a good-looking young man, son of wealthy parents; he had a cheerful disposition and was extremely obliging. He took me out for a stroll, fell in love, introduced himself at our house, and began to visit us every day. My mother, threatening me with her curse, ordered me to employ all possible means of temptation to attract Count Lovkov. This amorous game is much more dangerous than gambling on cards, and very frequently it happens that the party spreading its nets to capture its victim suffers the loss. Count Lovkov lost money in our house, but to compensate, he exerted his rights and captured me unfeelingly in the same snares I set for him. Listening patiently to his declarations of love, I grew so accustomed to them that I felt bored if I didn't hear them; finally, to carry on this pleasant amusement and keep the count dependent on me, I confessed that he was dear to me. The count was a man of the world and experienced beyond his years in such matters. Soon a close friendship was formed between us, as well as a familiarity, of which you were the witness. . . .

"You were still alive in my heart, but I confess that your respectful, timid love seemed like child's play when compared to the passionate, sincere ecstasy of the count. When he learned from Vorovatin that you'd arrived in Orenburg as a result of your love for me, he swore that he'd destroy you; so, to save you from danger, I resolved to renounce you and even to slander you. Of course, this remedy was not very pleasant, but at the time I thought that I'd done a good deed. Your sudden appearance put me in such a distracted state that I was beside myself . . . I didn't know what I was saying. Your intention of diminishing me in the count's eyes drove me into a rage. . . . Dearest Vanya, forgive me!"

Grunya started weeping; I swore a solemn oath that I forgave her and that I didn't harbor the least bit of indignation in my heart over what had happened in the past.

"Be sincere, Grunya," I said. "All is forgotten, and all is forgiven; I love you more than ever."

"I wanted to find out what happened to you," she said. "I was told you'd fallen ill, that Vorovatin had rented a new apartment the next day, and that some unknown person came to fetch you with a cart and to transport you to your new lodging, yet the landlord of the new apartment never set eyes on you. Several days later Vorovatin left Orenburg without saying good-bye to us, and I didn't know what had become of you. A secret voice inside me reproached me for your misfortune. I was frequently bothered by terrible dreams: I saw you dying and your ghost threatening me with revenge. I thought you'd died; I wept and prayed; at last, little by little, I calmed down and, if I didn't forget you completely, at least I began thinking about you less often.

"Dear friend! Spare me from having to relate in detail my adventures together with my actions, which I feel in full measure and which I truly repent. The count, after representing to me in a deceitful manner my unfortunate situation in the gambling house and promising to marry me after the death of his old and sickly father, persuaded me to elope with him secretly to Kiev, where his regiment was stationed, and where he had been ordered to appear, after giving up his title as adjutant. It wasn't long that I was so deluded. The count was affectionate, tender, and polite like all seducers until their schemes are completed; but afterwards he became rude, capricious, and cold—eager to rid himself of his gullible target. Not one day passed without quarrels, mutual recriminations, and tears. The contempt with which I was surrounded tormented me, and the inconstancy of the count, who sought diversion in other attachments, was driving me to despair. At last he declared to me that his father had died and that he had to leave for Petersburg immediately. I reminded him of his promise. He was silent. I begged him to take me with him; he claimed that it was impossible. At last he departed, and a month later I learned that his father was still alive and that my seducer had married a wealthy young woman from a noble family.

"You can imagine my anguish. I intended to return to my mother, who'd moved back to Moscow, but in answer to my letter, I received the news that my mother had died. I was left an orphan in the world, without a protector, without money, and without a good reputation.

"The count commissioned one of his friends to settle with me and proposed to pay me a pension on the condition that I'd leave him in peace. I spurned his offer and wrote a letter to his wife in which I depicted all the vileness of the count's actions. I hesitated for a long time as to whether to continue living or to throw myself into the river. At last my youth overcame my despair. I calmed down; not knowing how to earn my livelihood, I decided to work as a servant. Just at this time a troupe of traveling actors was visiting Kiev; it was composed of half-educated schoolboys, expelled seminarians, semi-literate actresses, and serfs who'd been granted their freedom or were living there legally. I suddenly got the idea of becoming an actress. The manager of this horde, a retired stage prompter, after assessing my abilities for the theater, was so pleased with me that he awarded me a place in his troupe at once, as the primary singer, the leading actress for both comedy and tragedy, and the principal dancer. I didn't want to perform in Kiev, where the officers knew me. We departed to work at the fairs in Little Russia,[1] where I acquired renown and attracted spectators to our

1. The old Russian name for Ukraine.

performances. I was the main support of the troupe and therefore was respected by everyone, even more than the manager. Even the women loved me because I didn't interfere with them at all, behaved modestly, didn't wish to have adoring admirers, and was even said to be hard-hearted. I had no respite from suitors; some of the smaller landowning gentry even asked for my hand in marriage, but I loved my free life and didn't want to bury myself in some small village. Applause became my necessity: I dreamed of fame!

"Lack of money followed us everywhere like a guilty conscience. Arriving in any town, we lived in debt until we collected enough money to pay our debts and move to another place. We clothed ourselves on the proceeds of benefit performances, and we had money for room and board from the general fund or the generosity of the manager. The division of the profits was always discussed as we arrived at each new fair, but it always seemed that there was nothing left to divide. However, we lived modestly but merrily; we didn't worry about the future and enjoyed the present.

"Once we were passing through a small town and the manager announced that our coffers were so depleted that we couldn't continue our wandering. We stopped at an inn, set up a theater in the barn, made chandeliers out of barrel hoops, hung up our paper scenery, and plastered the street corners with written announcements. Several days passed, but no one came to our theater.

At that time a wealthy gentleman stopped at the inn; he was on his way from Petersburg to his estate. After seeing a poster that our company intended to perform Sumarokov's tragedy *Dmitry the Pretender* and Fomin's opera *The Miller*,[2] and was merely awaiting spectators to show off their splendid abilities, the traveling gentleman, for his own amusement, ordered a show for himself; for fifty rubles he sat alone in the theater with his poodle. In spite of the fact that the poodle interrupted our performance, barking stridently as soon as our Dmitry began to rant and rage, and in spite of the fact that the candles attached to the hanging hoops either blew out or fell on the actors' heads, and that in the whole orchestra there wasn't a single violin with all its strings intact, we completed our performance successfully; the wealthy gentleman had noticed abilities in me, which he was pleased to call great talents. Out

2. Aleksandr Sumarokov (1717–1777) wrote his most famous tragedy in 1771, based on historical events. The early Russian opera *The Miller Who Was a Wizard, a Cheat, and a Matchmaker* by Yevstigney Fomin (1761–1800) was first performed in 1779.

of pure generosity he presented me with a gift of two hundred rubles for my travel to the provincial town, where one admirer of the theater had established an acting company. I took his advice, left my colleagues in the traveling troupe, and upon arriving in the provincial town, made myself known to the theater director. After my debut I was awarded a benefit performance on the condition that I perform several times to profit the theater. My benefit performance was brilliant, because it coincided with the elections of provincial magistrates and I managed to please the public. With the money I collected and with letters of recommendation, I set off for Moscow and found a position as an actress in a local theater; on the basis of my debut, you can form an opinion about my limited abilities and about the success that awaits me in this choice of career."

"Dearest Grunya," I said. "You see only pleasant experiences in your calling as an actress, but you haven't thought about possible reverses that you might encounter. Listen to me: leave the theater. I'll marry you, and we'll leave for some remote town: with my capital we'll enter a trade or I'll engage in farming. Happy hearts need so little in life!"

Grunya thought a little while, then put her hand on my shoulder, looked at me tenderly, and said, "Vyzhigin! Your Arcadian dreams would be good in vaudeville but not in reality. Is it really possible that at the mention of *fame*, your heart can remain so cold? Is it possible that your Grunya's splendid success doesn't affect you? Vanya, dearest Vanya! If you only knew the sweetness of hearing applause, the pleasure of attracting public attention, of seeing your name in print, of reading words of praise in journals; then, in loving me, you wouldn't want to deter me from my profession, but you would be twice as happy, enjoying my love and my good fortune! No, Vyzhigin, I can't renounce the theater at the very moment when it's affording me a reputation, a means of existence, and the greatest pleasure; furthermore, it reconciles me with the world which, so to speak, I deserted. Wait a bit, let me enjoy myself, and then—I'll be yours forever."

I wanted to argue, to reason with her, but Grunya begged me to end the conversation.

"Fame and love!" she exclaimed. "That's the maxim of a good actress. Accept things as they are—or I shall be unhappy!"

I had to submit—or, better said, I didn't have to, but I wanted to submit—and I kept silent. A month passed, and Grunya became the object of adoration of all the admirers of the fair sex and dramatic art, the object of envy of all coquettes. She triumphed; I was suffering and kept silent. Little by little in my house a small circle of the patrons of dramaturgy formed, of those humble and obliging actresses who trail in the wake of any of their sisters who have become the latest thing in order to catch a cast-off admirer or to distribute their tickets to a benefit performance, and of some theater officials, indispensable for the success of the actress, just like wooden struts erected for supporting stage scenery. But Grunya conducted herself admirably. She behaved proudly but politely with her wealthy and devoted admirers of dramaturgy; she received them only on certain days and at certain times, and only all together, in the presence of other women; and she didn't allow any liberties either in their words or their actions. She knew how to treat the theater officials in such a way that they themselves invariably anticipated her wishes. Grunya was known as a phoenix of intelligence and virtue among other actresses. In higher circles no one was talked about more than this Russian actress, a beauty who spoke French fluently. This last circumstance drove the aging devotees of the fair sex crazy. "A Russian actress who speaks French? *C'est charmant! C'est charmant!*"[3] repeated the old philanderers. "What a pity she's so virtuous! Virtue in an actress is an extravagance, and even one that shouldn't be tolerated!" That's how the old flirts reasoned, but Grunya laughed and loved only me.

Once I found Grunya very sad. Her eyes were red, her face was pale; it was obvious she'd been weeping. I was horrified.

"Dear Grunya, what's happened to you? Tell me, for heaven's sake."

"Ah, Vyzhigin, I'm so unhappy! They've given me the leading role in a new opera to spite that stupid and lifeless creature Maskina, who prides herself because she can do anything as she squanders the property of Count Zhalkin and appears on stage in gold and diamonds. She'll perform the secondary role in the opera; I arranged this in spite of the intrigues perpetrated by the count's party. I even had to listen to a foolish declaration of love by a scatterbrain who works behind the scenes. . . . Don't worry, Vanya! Your eyes are already wide open, and you're losing heart; I only listened to his declaration and forgot it at once. Meanwhile, the leading role belongs to me. What do you think this wicked Maskina has decided to do? She's supposed to play my rival, an old widow, but she ordered a splendid dress embroidered with gold thread on velvet, and she wants to appear wearing all her diamonds,

3. "It's charming!" (Fr.).

alongside me, while I, in the leading role, will be wearing some worthless thing and only glass beads!" Grunya burst into tears.

"But we can fix that," I said, stammering. "Don't cry; let's confer about it calmly."

"What's the use of conferring? Out of one hundred debauched old men I could find one easily who'd agree to ruin himself for my sake. But for a million rubles I don't want to have anything to do with those lifeless bodies. Every woman has her own way of thinking: I'd never agree to say *I love you* to anyone for whom *memento mori*[4] would be more appropriate. Handsome young men, however, are either poor as church mice, or so preoccupied with themselves that they imagine their looks are finer and dearer than diamonds. What do you advise, Vanya? I love you alone and would rather perish or burn in shame than betray you."

I kissed Grunya's hand and said, "Dear Grunya! Your acting will eclipse the splendor of Maskina's apparel."

"How can I perform well when that doll with all her arrogance will sparkle before my eyes?"

"How much would a dress cost?"

"Fifteen hundred rubles."

"That's not a large sum, but the diamonds . . ."

"The diamonds could be rented, but we must have something to pledge in return. For myself, I need only a pair of diamond earrings and a pearl brooch; all the rest can be rented. But let's forget all this. Come sit with me, Vanya, and we'll mourn together."

"Excuse me, Grunya, I can't stay here with you any longer. I ask you one thing: don't torment yourself, and don't take any action before dinner. I'll come back then, and we'll confer. Who knows, perhaps I'll be able to help you!"

I left Grunya and was in a state of strong agitation. *She loves me*, I thought. *She avoids all other contacts out of her love for me and sacrifices even her female vanity for me—and her self-love. Oh, precious Grunya! I must reward you for your fair-minded love and return at least a part of the pleasure provided me by your love*. With these thoughts I raced home, got the receipts from the Treasury, took them to the Board of Trustees, withdrew ten thousand rubles, and rushed right to the jeweler. I chose a pair of splendid earrings and a pearl clasp for six thousand rubles and rented a diadem, necklace, and bracelets worth twenty-five thousand rubles, leaving my

4. "Remember you must die" (Lat.).

pledge, and returned to Grunya just as she was planning to sit down to dinner, assuming that I wouldn't be returning. She received me tenderly, but with a sad face.

"You know, Grunya, I'm afraid of dreams?"

"What of it?"

"I dreamed, Grunya, that during dinner something unexpected would happen. Humor me, my dear, and go into the kitchen to see if everything's all right. You know that recently in a certain house the maid carelessly sprinkled the tart with arsenic instead of sugar that was being kept in the same cupboard for poisoning rats!"

"My goodness, what strange thoughts you have!" said Grunya and left the room; in the meantime, I laid out on a small table the jewelry I'd purchased and two thousand rubles for a new dress. As soon as Grunya came back, I took her by the hand, led her to the small table, and said: "Don't be sad: your wish is fulfilled!"

Grunya looked at the items, then cast such a look at me that I nearly melted on the spot; she threw herself into my arms, cried out, and fainted.

I carried her over to the sofa, called her maid, bustled about, sprinkled her face with water and scent, and finally managed to bring her around.

"Vanya," she said, "I don't know how to thank you: my heart, which belongs to you, feels deeply, but my tongue is too weak to express my feelings."

After such depression, Grunya was experiencing such joy that I was afraid she might lose her wits. She shouted, laughed, sang, and repeatedly tried on the diadem, then the necklace, and finally the bracelets. I made her sit down at the table, but she kept jumping up to look in a mirror and to rearrange the jewels according to her taste.

"Grunya," I said. "You're so clever! Surely these splendid toys can't be so valuable in your eyes that you forget about everything else?"

"No, my friend," she replied. "It's not the things that are so dear to me but the imminent triumph over my arrogant rival, a triumph she doesn't expect, and which will be all the nicer for me since you're the person I owe it to."

In the meantime the date of the performance approached, and Grunya revealed to me that Count Zhalkin's friends were hatching a plot against her.

"Dearest Vanya," Grunya said to me, "our close intimacy is unknown to society, and so it's necessary for you to form a party in my favor.

I could do this easily myself, but I don't want to excite your jealousy, and I don't want to wound your sensibility. Take several dozen tickets and tell your friends that you won them on a bet and give them away as gifts. Host a dinner or a lunch for the most fiery, irrepressible, and audacious mischief makers, and instruct them whom to support, to express their approval in applause, and to call me back onto the stage, while they hiss at Maskina."

I wanted to object, but Grunya sealed my lips with her lovely little hand, kissed me, and demolished all my philosophical arguments with a smile. I was obliged to submit—that is, I wanted to.

At last the day of the performance arrived. That evening I gave a dinner for my friends, the brawlers, at an inn near the theater. Once they were all tipsy, I proposed that we go to the theater to support the right person, and I distributed the tickets. We entered as a crowd, and my friends were waiting for a signal to hiss or to clap. Meanwhile Grunya did not appear from her dressing room until it was her turn to step out on stage. When she finally emerged, Maskina almost fainted at the sight of the diamonds and Grunya's splendid costume, and the entire behind-the-scenes crew had decided that it was impossible to be dressed better or richer than she was. Grunya was beside herself with joy, and this mood had such a powerful influence on her performance that as a matter of fact she surpassed all expectations, while Maskina, in despair at her rival's triumph, forgot her lines and spoiled the performance. Count Zhalkin's friends tried as best they could to support his mistress, but the hissing from our party drowned out their weak applause. Grunya, delighted by the praise during the performance, was called back on stage, but Maskina, covered with shame and mockery, quarreled with Grunya backstage and, after arriving home, had a fight with the count.

Grunya received me with great enthusiasm. She had invited a party of guests for supper, but I felt so troubled by all the day's emotions, I was feeling unwell and went right home.

In proportion to Grunya's success in her dramatic career, and in proportion to the extent of her fame, it was incumbent on her to dress better than others or at least as well as the other actresses, to have more appropriate lodgings, and to keep her own carriage. I couldn't agree that Grunya should appeal to other people to fill her needs, so I myself provided everything for her that she needed. She didn't own a shawl but never asked me for any; when I invited her to go for a stroll outside of town or asked her to wear her diamonds for an evening out, she would refuse with a smile, because she had no shawl, and it would be impossible to go for a stroll or wear a fine dress. Naturally she had to purchase a few shawls for herself, because those that I had brought with me from the steppe had all been sold.

At last three new productions, two relocations of lodgings, provision of a wardrobe and winter clothing, the equipping of a carriage, one celebration of her name day and one of her birthday, all in the course of one year, relieved me of forty thousand rubles and put me in debt for another ten thousand. I repeat that Grunya never asked me for anything and I lacked the least desire to buy love or anyone's favor with money. Neither Grunya nor I knew how it happened that we spent such a large sum of money! She wanted to *own*, and I had *what it took* to acquire; my money was disappearing and finally ran out completely. So I was left without a kopeck and without any means to acquire more; meanwhile I was still obliged to support my poor mother. . . . After reflecting on my situation, I fell into despair but didn't have the heart to tell Grunya about my plight. I even thought about shooting myself or running away to the Kirghiz steppe, but my mother's condition restrained me. For several days I didn't even go to see Grunya but sat locked up in my room, considering ways to stay afloat in society. I told my mother that I was not feeling well. I couldn't come up with any solution; all I had left was fifty rubles. Once I even wrote to Arsalan-Sultan via Orenburg, but I didn't receive any reply: now I wrote again to him and the Kirghiz elders, informing them of my place of residence and asking them to send the rest of the money from my share from the sale of the booty. The silence of my friends in the steppe was not a good sign. Meanwhile I was afraid that my friends, patronesses, and creditors would learn of my ruin. Thousands of projects were born and died in my head, when all of a sudden, on the sixth day, my door flew open and in rushed Grunya.

Chapter 26

Deliver Us from Evil! A Lesson in Daytime Piracy. Advice from an Old Soldier. I Come into Money Again.

"What does this mean, dear friend? Have you abandoned me?" asked Grunya. "Is it so terrible that you've squandered all your money?"

"How's that? How do you know already?"

"Of course, I do," said Grunya. "Your own Petrov reported your grief to me."

"The traitor!" I cried.

"Don't get upset; he's your true friend. After seeing that you'd lost your good cheer and had given up all your usual habits, he guessed that your supply of money was suffering from depletion. Finally, when he noticed that you'd begun to examine and handle your pistols, the good Petrov couldn't endure it anymore; he came rushing to see me with the request that I come to your rescue. Why don't you say something?"

I glanced at Grunya sullenly, in shame and embarrassment, and observed her expression, which was cheerful and smiling.

"Don't lose heart!" she said. "Aren't you, a Kirghiz warrior, ashamed to mourn the loss of your booty when you yourself are safe and sound? Haven't you referred to me many times in the past as your treasure and your good fortune? Here I am in front of you, and you're grousing about the loss of your money!" Grunya sat down on the sofa, ordered me to sit next to her, and said, "Well, how much have we squandered this year?"

"More than fifty thousand!"

Grunya burst out laughing.

"Splendid! Very nice!" she exclaimed. "Yet it seems that we've been very thrifty! Now, judge for yourself. Is it worth grieving over money? Is it worth tormenting yourself because of it? It's merely dust that's moved about and blown away by the wind."

"That's a consoling philosophy! But it's not possible to exist without money," I replied. "The most tender love and the most unselfish friendship can fill only the heart—"

Grunya interrupted me.

"Ah, how clever you are when you're broke!" she said. "But enough of this, dear Vyzhigin! Nothing in the world is more boring than the reflections of a penniless philosopher! Well, how much do you have left?"

"Less than nothing."

"How so?

"That is, I have debts and no way to pay them."

"Great! Listen to me, Vyzhigin. I've come to rescue you from this unpleasant situation. Be firm and fearless. One of my mother's old acquaintances, Yakov Prokofyevich Zarezin, has asked me to keep the faro bank in my house. . . ."

"Grunya, you're resorting once again to dishonest means, which led your family into ruin!"

"Since I was born I've never played cards, and I certainly won't start now; consequently, I won't lose any money. Zarezin is giving me an equal share in the winnings, with no loss, simply for permission to play in my house."

"That is, to win for sure, to steal, to destroy absolutely!"

"What's it to us, dear friend?" Grunya said coldly. "Everyone is given reason and willpower; if someone's unable to use them, he must learn how; and, you know, you have to pay for lessons."

"Your philosophy, although it's less boring than my impoverished one, is something like an order for post horses all the way to Siberia."

"Enough, no more nonsense; look at what people who are received and respected in high society live on. One person becomes wealthy taking bribes, another by robbing the Treasury, a third by guardianship over an orphan's property, and a fourth through unjust lawsuits. 'No man is a thief until he's caught,' says the proverb; rich rogues raise their heads high, are proud that they've managed to gain wealth. You haven't had dealings with merchants. Try it and you'll see how your best friend fleeces you for ten times the price; and after you leave his shop or his office, he laughs at your gullibility. Even with all my respect for humanity, I believe that almost half the town's residents are gamblers for sure. The difference is in the game they play: one person plays in politics, another in commerce, a third in administration, a fourth in law, some at faro, and others at whist and other card games.

"Grunya, my dear Grunya," I said, kissing her hand. "You're a real demon, a demon in a beautiful form; I can't argue with you, but please don't force me to become dishonest by taking advantage of my weakness! I love you so much that I can't refuse you anything. I can only implore you, 'Lead me not into temptation!' "

"I'm not proposing that you should start gambling," said Grunya. "You'll merely be my deputy with Zarezin: you'll observe and make sure he doesn't deceive me, that he behaves *properly*—that is, he doesn't become conceited—and that he practices his skill with moderation. For that purpose you'll need to know all the tricks of gambling."

"I don't know a single one. I've heard about some, but I don't know how to perform any."

"Zarezin needs a croupier and a *moitiant*,[1] who's yet to become known and who, as they say, has a presentable appearance. For that purpose he couldn't find anyone in the world more suitable than you. You're modest in your behavior, skillful, and have a pleasant façade, dear. . . ." At these words Grunya smiled, patted me on the head, and kissed me. I felt faint.

After talking further about peripheral subjects, Grunya left Zarezin's address for me and told me to visit him the next day at ten o'clock in the morning, saying that he was already informed and would be expecting me. She left, wishing me more good cheer, firmness of spirit, and—philosophy!

For the thousandth time since I had become involved with Grunya, I exclaimed, "Oh, human weakness!" For the thousandth time since then I repeated in prayer, "Lead me not into temptation!" and remained just as I was before.

My mother observed that for some time I had seemed altered; I'd become thoughtful, serious, and irritable. In high society, which

1. A partner in a casino (Fr.).

I always visited but not as frequently, I was just as courteous as before, but a man as a guest and a man at home are two different people. Sometimes a domestic tyrant, a tormentor of servants and family members, is considered to be the most amiable of men in society; and sometimes a man who makes people in society laugh heartily with his cheerfulness has arrived from home in tears and returns to the same. To learn to recognize a man's character, it's necessary, in the first place, to observe him as a citizen of his country, then in his family life. A bad father with good children, a bad husband with a good wife, a bad son with respectable parents can never be good members of society; and not only wouldn't I entrust a district or a department to such people, I wouldn't even entrust them with care of my dog; I'd be afraid to spend a night with such people in the forest without a weapon.

I told my mother that rash financial deals had ruined my fortune and that now I had to work to gain a livelihood. My mother didn't reproach me and didn't get angry. She begged me to allow her to retire to a convent where the mother superior, her acquaintance, had already offered her serene refuge. I agreed, and that day my mother made up her mind to move into her new lodgings, securing a promise from me to visit her there every day, or at least three times a week.

Meanwhile I set off, according to our agreement, to see Zarezin. His servant led me into the living room, very smartly furnished, where I found him pacing the room. He was not very tall, about forty years old, pale, thin, with a penetrating gaze, making some sort of grimaces, similar to those footmen employ to imitate their master's looks. In line with my ideas about physiognomy, his eyes and mouth indicated cunning, shamelessness, and cowardice. It was his custom to wear a green eyeshade, although he was gifted with such extraordinary powers of vision that he could see the smallest speck on a playing card with his naked eye, as if looking through a microscope. His fingers were extremely long and thin. On his right hand his index finger and thumb were bound with black taffeta. He was constantly shuffling and cutting a deck of cards even when he was talking with me, so as not to waste any time, as he would say, and gradually perfect his movements. Yakov Prokofyevich Zarezin was dressed in a peculiar manner: his cravat was tied tightly around his neck, his frock coat with wide sleeves hung upon him as if on a peg, his short undergarments and knee-high boots made his legs look like the twisted pillars of Gothic-Arabian architecture. He rarely looked into the eyes of the person with whom he was speaking, and then only when he was talking not about *business* but about some peripheral subject.

"I beg you to be seated," said Zarezin, indicating a place on the sofa. "I'm very glad to get to know you: Agrafena Stepanovna (Grunya) has informed me that you were acquainted with my dear friend Luka Ivanovich (Vorovatin). He's much esteemed, the kindest man! He and I have worked together a great deal. It's a pity that I can't find out where he is now."

I was silent. Zarezin began speaking again. "I've heard that you've gambled a lot and used to win a great deal of money. Allow me to ask. Were you keeping the bank or punting?"

"I was punting, but largely in games of skill."

"I understand, sir: with *your own* cards and your own partner; and at faro you were probably playing with *your own* people, *for sale*?

"Neither one nor the other. I played honestly."

"So much the better, but Agrafena Stepanovna didn't tell me that you played *honestly*."

I looked Zarezin in the eyes to express my astonishment and lack of understanding of his statements.

"You don't understand the meaning of the word *honestly*? It means with skill, dexterity."

At these words Zarezin moved his fingers as if he wished to snap them.

"No, you haven't guessed correctly," I replied. "Agrafena Stepanovna told you, and I repeat, that I don't know much about cards and that if you want me to be of use, you must initiate me into the mysteries of your art."

"Of course, one must know something," replied Zarezin. "Would you please *be so kind* as to follow me into my study? I'll give you your first practical lesson and show you the tools."

From the living room we proceeded into a cold room where there were a variety of objects in total disorder. Painting, porcelain, bronzes, equestrian items, meerschaum pipes, and a rich assortment of other items was spread out on windowsills, chairs, tables, and the floor. In addition, there were trunks and cases of wine, and so on. Everything was covered with dust and dirt. In another room, or study, all three windows were shaded by green blinds. Under the windows there were small tables covered in large sheets of paper, while in the middle stood one large table wrapped in green cloth. Zarezin went up to one small table and lifted the paper: I saw several decks of playing cards and, on a plate, powder for blue and red ink and several crow quills.

"I suppose you can guess," said Zarezin, "that this is the *pictorial part* of our art—that is, marking the cards. The best ones for marking are those whose backs are dotted with spots. Placing one extra dot in a given place is enough to know the value of the card, as if the deck lay open. Cards are marked in the center for shading the dots. You don't know such a game?"

"No, sir."

"Allow me to demonstrate: you deal your own marked cards, and in betting you always know what's on top, and as a result you avoid any loss by the first bets. This is the most innocent play, used only against experienced gamblers. The advantage here is no more than ten percent. These cards with dots on the edges are used to avoid losses on the first bets. A sure and sharp eye sometimes sees the fourth card in the dealer's deck and then, farewell to the pot! Here are the dealer's cards with the dots on the corners—so that seeing that the stake is high, one can *switch the cards* in the dealer's deck." While saying this, Zarezin pulled open a drawer in the table, pulled out a snuffbox, and handed it to me.

"Do you see anything special about it?" he asked.

"Nothing, except that it is very heavy and well crafted," I replied.

"It's heavy because its center is gold while its surface is platinum, and its weight is very important. Do you see its bottom is encircled by a small ridge or frame, and in the very center of the bottom is a flower decorated in matte finish. Now have a look. Let's say I'm the dealer."

At this Zarezin sat down at the table, took the cards into his hands, and continued his explanation. "Now let's say that the second card would win a high stake for the punter. I place the cards on the table, cover the deck with my snuffbox, as if out of caution to prevent the other players from seeing them; I take out my handkerchief, wipe my nose, open the snuffbox, take some tobacco, pick up the snuffbox, and continue to deal: sure enough the seven, which should have been on the left, turns up on the right."

"How did this happen?" I ask in astonishment.

"Here's how! There are two bottoms in the snuffbox, one of gold, and the other of platinum. The gold one is thin and flexible, and in the platinum bottom the flower is on a spring and the point has been smeared with wax or glue. When I take some snuff, I press the center with my finger, and the uppermost card sticks to the flower on the bottom and holds it firmly in its frame, and now the next card is on top. Now comes the other card, which I need to place on the right. In exactly the same way I place the snuffbox on the cards, press the bottom with my finger, and the card is now released from the flower and sits on top; the card which should have won in the first round is now a losing card in the second. Isn't it true that this is all very nice?"

I nodded my head as a sign of agreement.

"This is a new Petersburg invention created by a bosom friend of mine, and it works well with cardsharps who can't be deceived easily. You see, skilled gamblers can't be caught except by the simplest means. I also have a favorite black frockcoat, which I wear during card games. In the right sleeve there's a mechanism for concealing cards. It's a miracle, not an invention: I'll show it to you later. All you have to do is rest your arm on the pack, and the card vanishes, the same as with the snuffbox."

We moved over to another small table and, after removing the paper cover and pointing to a deck of cards, Zarezin continued speaking. "Here are the rigged cards. That is to say, a certain number of cards are cut wider in such a way that when they're shuffled with the rest, the wide ones are collected by their value. There are lots of them, all arranged in different patterns. There are some where the first thirty cards lose—that is, when the punter doesn't take a single trick. There are cards with a large number of *pliés*[2] and with a false *routier*.[3] Bent cards can be used only with inexperienced players. These days the world has grown wiser! Here are the various cuts of the deck, arranged for the hands to shuffle. For this, one must have unusual dexterity in one's fingers, more so than required for today's popular piano players, and this skill must be acquired over time and with hard work. You see that my fingers are wrapped: observe, the skin on these fingers is so filed down with a rasp and the skin has been so softened with ointment that during a game I can guess which card it is simply by touch, and my joints are more flexible than any springs. But you won't reach this stage for many years: it's the fruit of twenty years of experience and incredible effort. You'll be my croupier, and therefore you need to pay attention to the punting and to observe the players during the game. I can't watch them because I'll be preoccupied with the *deeper contemplation of the art*, in order to put into action my banking experiments; and meanwhile,

2. Bends (Fr.).
3. Suit (Fr.)

you'll make sure that our false brothers don't cheat us, worming their way into the game in the guise of simpletons."

We moved to a third table, and Zarezin, after removing the paper as before, and showing me various cards, continued his story. "You see this three. Look again! Now it's a two; look once more! It's an ace!"

Zarezin merely took the card from the table and on the card, as a matter of fact, the spots on the card actually changed at his command.

"Do you know what this is?" asked Zarezin.

"How should I know?"

"It's a Russian invention, although it has a French name, and therefore it's not so terrible a machine as its name suggests. It's a *guillotine*. Please observe: I unglue the card, and the cut pips are attached to this watch spring. The spring is secured in the center while its end protrudes from one side. Moving that end with one's finger, the spots appear and disappear at will. The guillotine can be made out of all cards except the picture cards. But I have picture cards in reserve, or *masks*. Note: here on one card is a king and queen; on another, a jack and king, and so on. This can be done with figures which have two heads. The painted card is unglued, cut in two, and the heads are exchanged. This is good for the *obscure ones* and *sleepers*. These cards are more complicated. You see I'm placing a seven; the six will win, and my card immediately changes into a six. These are *powdered marks*. A mark or pip is made on the card with glue and is sprinkled with black powder from burnt bones. Naturally, the card is *dark*, and if my card wins, I turn it over and take the money; if another card wins, I wipe a mark before turning over my card, and once again I win and take the money. Here are the *sacks*: you'll note that this card is unglued in the middle, and I've left an empty space where the *banknotes* can be hidden. If the card loses, the punter removes the card from the table and leaves several notes; if the card wins, then the punter skillfully shakes the banknotes from the sack, and the banker sometimes pays ten times over, especially with a triple bet. You keep glancing into this drawer. Here are the instruments: a wolf's tooth for polishing the dotted cards, *cherry glue*; *brass plates* of different sizes for cutting the cards with this tiny *pair of scissors*. And here on the cupboard is a *press* or *vice* for squeezing the cards that have been unsealed and then sealed up again. Would you like to know what that large table under the green cloth is for? Prepared cards. But this is enough for your first lesson. Let's go have lunch and chat about your forthcoming campaign."

Lunch was already on the table, but there were neither place settings nor any wine. Zarezin took his keys out of his pocket, went into the next room, called his footman, and returned with wine and table settings. After the footman had left, I observed, "Your footman must be badly behaved and that's why you don't trust him with the silver?"

"I haven't noticed anything untoward in the course of ten years," he replied. "But, sir, I have the custom of not trusting anyone, for that's the best means of preventing dishonesty. Besides, 'Lead us not into temptation!' Why furnish a man with an opportunity to engage in stealing?"

I made no reply but inwardly cursed my beloved for having made me enter into a connection with such a fiendish creature.

"You see," said Zarezin, "that Agrafena Stepanovna is a very kind young woman and my old acquaintance, but she's a bit frivolous, a bit capricious, and she loves to throw money around. We shouldn't trust her completely with all our affairs and financial dealings. She's ready to warn someone if she likes him, and if she knows the exact amount of our winnings, and if she's in need, she's capable of demanding more than her fair share. Do you understand me? I have the habit, when I play jointly with someone, to stash part of the money from the bank in my boot: when I make a wry face at you and say, *My boots pinch*, you should do the same. Afterwards we'll go home and settle our accounts."

"We'll see!" I said and hastened to leave Zarezin so I could go see Grunya.

"You've set me up with a genuine bandit!" I said to Grunya.

"You don't think I'd choose an honest man to swindle swindlers? Stop acting like a child, Vanya: you're boring me with your schoolboy virtue. We won't rob anybody of their money but will take it from those who are looking for a chance to get rid of it. However, if you don't want to do it, so be it! But then you have to renounce your unbearable jealousy."

"I've decided!" I exclaimed almost through tears. I returned home to escort my mother to the convent, promising to see Grunya in the evening. Zarezin was supposed to open his first session that evening.

After escorting my mother, I returned home with an aching heart and lay down on the sofa. Petrov came into the room; standing at attention in the doorway, he said, "Would you, Your Honor, allow your devoted Petrov to say a word or two?"

"Speak."

"We're broke!"

"If so, then go find a position where they have some money."

"God forbid! You're my benefactor, Ivan Ivanovich, and I won't leave you until my death. A solider doesn't need much: a coat on his shoulders and a rusk in his pocket. I can work for the neighbors for a daily ration and will always be ready to serve Your Honor. That's not the point."

"What is it then?"

"Agrafena Stepanovna is very pretty."

"I know that without your telling me."

"She's affectionate as a bunny rabbit, chatty as a swallow, and sweet as a lark!"

"And so?"

"But, sir, she spends more money in one day than a whole company of grenadiers spends in a month."

"What's that to you?"

"Necessity, Your Honor, because I love you more than I love my own father, as much as I love my company commander, may he rest in peace: he died from his wounds in my arms! Do you think I don't know how your money slipped through Agrafena Stepanovna's tender, white fingers?"

"It's none of your business."

"It's not my business, but it's my sorrow! Your Honor, Ivan Ivanovich! I would be glad to lay down my life for you, but it sickens and grieves me to see that because of Agrafena Stepanovna, your aunt has left your house, and that you yourself will soon have no place to go in the whole wide world. If a young man is to perish, better it should be from a cannonball or a bullet, and not from a woman's whims. We will come to no good with these Moscow beauties. You should enter military service, and we'll go to the Caucasus. Here, sir, one needs carriages, furniture, twenty suits of clothes, and God knows what else; there a young officer needs nothing but his sword and his courage; you have both. As for life there, it's full of good cheer! Every heavenly day there's a skirmish, and with what young men, with what marksmen, what horsemen, who, except for the Russians, have no fear even of the devil himself. Excellent wines, delicious mutton, good bread, and the girls, what girls: Georgians, Circassians, splendid! They say that the Turkish sultan in his own Tsargrad wishes for nothing better.[4] The one misfortune for Russian soldiers is that they can't always get to drink kvass or eat a bowl of cabbage soup, but for you, that's no great sorrow. Hey, Your Honor, listen to an old soldier! You'll see that in the lofty

4. Tsargrad is the Old Russian name for Constantinople.

Caucasus your heart will be cleansed of love. The Circassian horsemen will preoccupy you more than Agrafena Stepanovna!"

I really liked Petrov's proposal, but my love and my debts kept me in Moscow. "Thank you, brother, for your advice, and even more, for your love. I'll think about what you've said; in the first place I want you to know that I am not at all against doing battle in the Caucasus. Meanwhile, give me my coat: I have to go out."

The evening at Grunya's was magnificent. She'd invited several beautiful actresses and a large number of wealthy supporters of dramatic art, who worship art neither in books nor in productions but embodied in the form of beautiful actresses. At first we engaged in conversations and music; then, as if to clear away old scores, Zarezin and I sat down in a corner room to play cards. Grunya, as if in jest, invited one of her wealthy guests to split the bank in two with her, adding that she was very lucky in picking cards for punters. Several female servants begged Grunya to draw cards for them. The game began on a small scale, but it grew large, and Zarezin managed to empty everyone's purse. The game continued until six o'clock in the morning; when the guests finally left, we divided the winnings into three parts, and each one of us took away around eight thousand rubles. However, Zarezin was very displeased with me because I'd asked him if his boots pinched, and he was obliged to take them off in my presence and there I found two heaps of banknotes and a pile of gold coins. To console Zarezin, I told him I'd done that only to win Grunya's trust; she'd noticed how he was stashing money in his boots. The swindler didn't believe me, but he pretended to. In this way the least departure from a path of honesty results in a multitude of vices. After becoming involved with a gambler in order to cheat others, the first day I myself became a liar in order to deceive Zarezin, imagining that it was permissible to become a swindler when dealing with a swindler. This easy acquisition of money turned my head and lulled my conscience to sleep. I returned home very cheerful. I tossed the money into my cabinet and, after giving Petrov twenty-five rubles, said, "Things might be good in the Caucasus, brother, but they're better in Moscow. Let's enjoy ourselves here first, and then we'll see!"

Chapter 27

False Gamblers. A Letter from Milovidin. He Located His Wife. Petronella's Repentance. Sequestration in Poland, or Check and Mate to Creditors. The Death of Mr. Gologordovsky. Mr. Pochtivsky, His Other Son-in-Law.

The profession of a deceitful gambler combines all the vices that humiliate humanity. There's no baseness of which a dishonest gambler is incapable in order to lure a passionate gambler into his nets. Dishonest gamblers, like real demons, rack their brains simply to create every means of temptation to deprive a man of his property and his good name, to drag him into a quagmire of vice, and to ruin his entire family. And these people are received in decent society and enjoy rights accorded by birth and merit! A poor little thief who's stolen twenty-five rubles, sometimes just because he needs it, is punished like a criminal, while these ordinary thieves proudly ride around in grand carriages, are on intimate terms with grandees, regard with disdain a poor but honest man from whom they can steal nothing, and even dare criticize the weaknesses of other people. Oh, poor humanity, with your habits! Who is to blame? Laws condemn a dishonest gambler with disapproval and punishment, but according to *custom* it's considered inappropriate to expose these ordinary thieves and haul them away to face justice; meanwhile it's considered worthy to catch a little thief pilfering twenty-five rubles and mete out a well-deserved sentence to him. What absurdity! And thus, if you're too ashamed to exterminate the wolves at your dachas, let the wolves exterminate your flocks of sheep and kill the shepherds until they get to you personally, which they will do in good time.

The gambling in Grunya's house gradually increased because the size of the gatherings grew. It's true, however, that what is gained by injustice doesn't last long. Grunya and I didn't know how much money we had and didn't know the bounds of our desires. Easy come, easy go. Our gambling den became notorious, and we were forced to admit into partnership some of the most expert players, so they wouldn't interfere with us; in the meanwhile Grunya and I squandered our money on clothing, furniture, carriages, horses, dinners, and suppers; our accomplices played furiously among themselves and lost among their own group what they had won from others by deception. Besides, among dishonest gamblers, there are no upstanding heads of families, modest or quiet members of society. In wine, riotous amusements, and affairs with debauched women, they attempt to forget their own pettiness, stifle the voice of conscience, and cover their own baseness with wealth and luxury. They live in a constant state of intoxication, afraid to come to their senses. Loneliness and quiet are the preliminary torments of a depraved mind.

Unfortunately, distinction of breeding isn't always accompanied by spiritual worth; a proverb exists in all societies: *There's a black sheep in every family*. In our society of gamblers there were two black sheep of famous families: Prince Plutolensky and Count Tonkovorin. The former, after refusing an advantageous marriage and renouncing all connections with good society, was leading a debauched life, always appearing in public inebriated and destroying all decorum by his brawling. He was still in the prime of life and could have served as the subject of a painter wanting to depict a desperate robber. His swollen red face, covered with his thick, overgrown whiskers, expressed audacity and lack of restraint; his eyes were always bulging and bloodshot, like a hyena's; his lips were swollen and opened only to eat or drink and to utter rude remarks. The latter, Count Tonkovorin, was already elderly; he'd been through fire and water, earned money and squandered it all several times, and all his life he was on bad terms with his own conscience. Finally he chose, in his own words, the most *innocent* profession, that of a cardsharp. He possessed every vice and only one attribute in common with honest people: fearlessness. But since he used this attribute only for evil purposes, he acquired the name of the *brave corsair* among other gamblers.

Count Tonkovorin lived openly and lavishly, hosted sumptuous dinners and merry evening parties; in his own home he managed to fleece not only novices but also even experienced gamblers. Zarezin admitted these two "fine fellows" out of fear that they might kill him, and, to provide for his own protection, he chose two of the most skilled players and known criminals, Udavich and Yadin.

Udavich—a middle-aged man, dark-skinned, not too tall—was crafty as a demon. He spent his time mostly among merchants and was himself a usurer. Among rich merchants it's considered a mark of good style to lavish money in society, and they're proud of their expenditures, just as in more refined society, men take pride in their witty remarks, puns, and ingenuity. Every wealthy merchant considers it his responsibility to go on a spree several times a year; tavern owners, debauched women, and dishonest gamblers lie in wait for these joyful days, to take advantage of the darkening of the rich merchant's powers of reason and to clean him out completely. In addition, dishonest gamblers are in the habit of befriending merchants' sons, who begin to squander money while their parents are still alive. Udavich loaned money at very high rates of interest, traded in promissory notes, and cheated his acquaintances, merchants who flocked to his house because there they would find all the trimmings of debauchery.

Yadin, besides his natural intellect, was rather well educated, read a great deal, spoke well, and spent his time with writers who didn't know his occupation, with actors, and in general with people who had pretensions to intellect. In his own home he engaged in gambling on a small scale; he would catch his prey *in flight*, as the saying goes, when he happened to spy a novice among his circle of acquaintances. I was surprised by one thing alone—namely, how these rogues could find such simpleminded people who believed in them when nature had placed on them the seal of an outcast. At seeing these operators for the first time, I could read signs in their faces of their diabolical proclivities. I believe, I do, that an evil soul is reflected in one's physiognomy. Skeptical readers! Merely glance into the eyes of the first dishonest gambler you meet, or the first hypocrite you encounter—and you'll be convinced!

That was the society in which I had to live, due to my blind attachment to Grunya, who'd lulled my conscience to sleep by her affectionate behavior and tenderness and had clouded my reason by her false logic. Meanwhile time kept flying by: almost a full year had passed since I'd begun sharing booty with the gamblers. Once when we weren't playing at our house, because several of the wealthy punters were away, Grunya sent me on an errand to Udavich: to discuss Zarezin's replacement, since he'd begun cheating us. There I found Prince Plutolensky, Count Tonkovorin, Yadin, two other masters, and more than a dozen merchants, among whom there were several wealthy men sporting long beards. They were all tipsy and had just returned from a tour of several out-of-town taverns. Footmen were serving champagne and Madeira; half-drunk Gypsy girls and plastered Gypsy men were strutting through the rooms; merchants were raucously and affably squabbling among themselves, rehearsing their old complaints; some women were peeping furtively through the half-open door of the back room; the gamblers in the crowd were winking and conferring with one another; a one-eyed musician was tuning his zither in the front room. I stopped, looked around, and immediately concluded that this merriment would end in something more serious. Udavich came up to me, winked meaningfully, led me into a dark corridor, and in a low voice said that I should be very cautious because a major affair was *in the works* from which I would profit, if I promised to tell no one about it, especially the other players. I promised to keep silent, mostly out of curiosity, and we returned to the other room. Udavich loosened up and began to play the role of a cordial host. He made his way around to all the guests, one at a time, kissing and embracing each, and exclaiming in a loud voice, "Gentlemen! Why have you grown so quiet; are you bored or what? Hey, more champagne! Forget the glasses: give us our forefathers' *stowps*.[1] Ivan Merkulych, have some. Semyon Pratrikeich, Foma Nazarich, come on, drink, brothers! Now you, Pafnutich, you joker, enough of your nonsense; drink and serve the others! Wine! Waiter, come here! Isn't it true that this wine is good? I ordered it myself from Petersburg from Boasonet's shop. Well, Styoshka, sing us something more cheerful; musician, play Ivan Merkulych's favorite song! And you, you mischief makers, Masha, Vasilisa, Parasha, dance some lively Gypsy dance to amuse these gentlemen!"

While Udavich was talking first with the merchants, then with the Gypsies, the wine flowed like water; other gamblers also treated the guests to kisses, embraces, and entreaties. When everyone was feeling lightheaded, Ivan Merkulych—a wealthy merchant with a respectable beard, father of a family, who ate cabbage soup and kasha at home all year round—would drink kvass and liqueurs, extract a few coins from

1. A smaller-sized vessel for holding liquor, sometimes also used as a drinking vessel.

his clerks, and haggle over a ruble until he was blue in the face. While in taverns, he would demolish whole cases of champagne, and when drunk, he lost tens of thousands of rubles. Ivan Merkulych, for whom Udavich had the highest regard, went up to him, slapped him on the back in familiar fashion, and said, "Why go on and on about this nonsense? Let's play cards, Klim Yegorych!"

"I'm afraid," replied Udavich. "After all, I know that you, Ivan Merkulych, are a desperate gambler and will clean out the bank in a twinkling. One must be careful with such rogues. I heard that you won sixteen thousand rubles from Sidor Sidorych."

"What's the harm in that? Sometimes I win, and sometimes I lose; don't fool around, Klim Yegorych, and let's play cards."

"All right, but for low stakes!" said Udavich with a grimace.

"No, brother, I won't play for low stakes."

"There's nothing to be done. I'll wager ten thousand," said Udavich and had the tables arranged.

A hubbub arose immediately among the gamblers. They couldn't conceal their joy and eagerness. Udavich put down his money, sat at the table, and was preparing to keep the bank. But even before he picked up his cards, Yadin cried, "Wine, some wine! Champagne!"

Several bottles of wine were produced, and Yadin took it upon himself to treat the guests who'd sat down at the card tables, while those who didn't wish to play were ushered out to other rooms under various pretenses, where Prince Plutolensky, Count Tonkovorin, and other gamblers proposed that they all go out and have fun. The merchants jumped at the proposal and the chance to enjoy themselves with princes and counts on an outing, and fortunately they all left happily. Yadin and Udavich once again set about plying the guests with wine, and soon I noticed that they were completely drunk; they played cards indiscriminately, drew them at the wrong times, and mechanically followed the directions from Udavich, who was scoring against them as he wished; he removed their wallets from their pockets with his own hands, took their money, dealt two cards to each at the same time, and, in a word, treated the punters as irrational creatures. Their drunkenness seemed strange to me, and even stranger was the impudence of Udavich, who clearly robbed his guests while they were dozing at the card tables. One of the gamblers, who probably thought that I'd been invited to assist in the execution of this scheme, took me into another room and said, "That Udavich is a devil, not a human being! He gave the merchants way too much to drink, but it's like water rolling off a duck's back!

He cleaned out their purses with no trouble at all, and besides that, he wrote down a thousand against each one, while these blockheads didn't play at all and didn't lose anything! He's clever, a criminal, a master!"

Just then Prince Plutolensky and Count Tonkovorin came into the room.

"Is the business finished yet?" asked the prince.

"It is," replied my companion.

"Well, splendid; we had real trouble getting rid of those damned shopkeepers; they wanted to come in here to have supper. Order the gate to be locked, and don't let them come into the courtyard. They should be told that Klim Yegorovich went off to see the governor for the evening and that no one's at home. We have no need of these scatterbrains now, when the game's already been snared."

Meanwhile Udavich didn't leave his spot but kept watch on the stupefied punters, the way a snake watches its prey; as soon as the gamblers observed that the inebriated guests had begun to shift in their seats, and their sleepiness and delirium were ending, Prince Plutolensky and Count Tonkovorin sat down at a table and began to punt by design.

"Well, how are things going?" asked Ivan Merkulych, coming to himself and rubbing his forehead. "I felt so much buzzing in my head that I couldn't stay awake. Let's calculate the score."

"You owe 23,327 and a half rubles," Udavich replied coolly.

"What?" cried the merchant.

"Yes, indeed: you lost all your cash; then you had me make a note of it. I'd trust you for a million, so I obeyed you."

"Lost my cash?" objected the merchant, grabbing his purse. "I had seventeen thousand rubles in here!"

"I didn't count it yet," Udavich replied coolly.

In the meantime the other punters had also recovered and began to calculate; they were all extremely surprised to find their purses empty, and besides, each one of them owed a large sum of money. One tea merchant, a young man from whom Udavich had won some ten thousand rubles, felt desperate, started weeping, and grew angry, saying that he'd have to drown himself if he couldn't pay a certain promissory note which would be due tomorrow. Udavich remained cool, but when Merkulych and others began to get heated and demand that their debts be cancelled, since they didn't remember how they had come about, Prince Plutolensky and Count Tonkovorin came out onto the stage and spoke up in turn.

"How dare you say in such honorable company that you don't recall losing? Aren't we the witnesses? We're prepared to teach you a lesson: you won't leave here alive."

The other players also objected and cursed; just then a crowd of footmen and Gypsies showed up in the doorway. The merchants lost their courage and quieted down. Peace was restored; they sent for a notary who'd been waiting in the hallway for some time. Ivan Merkulych and his comrades handed over the promissory notes; Udavich loaned the tea merchant ten thousand rubles and took a note for twenty thousand; everything became amicable again. They served supper, and the guests, from their sorrow, drank and ate their fill; several of them, including Ivan Merkulych, stayed on to spend the night in complete enjoyment, having forgotten about the money and the bills of exchange. They gave me four thousand rubles for no reason at all and once again asked me not to mention what had happened there for the time being.

Milovidin would write to me from time to time after his departure from Moscow to locate his wife: up to this point his search had been unsuccessful. After receiving no letter from my friend in over half a year, I was very worried about his fate. When I returned home from Udavich's, to my great delight I found a packet awaiting me from Milovidin. He informed me that he'd finally found his Petronella. I shall relay Milovidin's letter in full to my readers:

Like the knight of rueful countenance, I wandered across Poland, in search of my wife's place of residence. By means of some well-informed Yids, I found out that she was located in the neighborhood of Kraków, but I had trouble discovering her refuge. Chance, as it usually does, helped me more than my own efforts. Petronella had assumed the calling of a "sister of mercy"; to compensate for the sins of her youth, she devoted herself as a sacrifice to suffering humanity; she nursed the sick in a hospital. You know that sisters of mercy do not take monastic vows and can leave their calling at will, but it cost me considerable effort to convince her to accompany me back into the world, which had become loathsome to her. It was only the undoubted proof of my love, as a result of which I had been wandering the world to locate Petronella, which persuaded her to follow me. She was extremely glad when she heard about the change in your fate, and she sends prayers to thank the Almighty for your good luck, and in return, for all that you've done for me. Naturally, she's changed a great deal, but with the loss of her youth, she hasn't lost any of her beauty. Her impulsiveness has disappeared, and she's become hard on herself and compassionate toward others, contrary to the custom of women, who are liable to be guided by vanity, even after they've reformed themselves.

You probably want to know what's become of Gologordovsky and his family. My father-in-law, by living above his income, continually incurred new debts without paying off the old ones and followed the advice of the Yid tenant in his trading transactions: he finally had to declare bankruptcy. You know that in ancient Poland the nobles themselves passed laws for the entire kingdom; consequently, everything was organized for their own benefit. It seems that there was nothing fairer for all parties than to sell the estate of the bankrupt party to the highest bidder among the public and to use the proceeds from the sale to pay off the creditors. So that the owners of the property wouldn't be able to rack up any further debts, thereby raising the price of the estate, what could be fairer than to value all the property and record every debt in the public register on a guarantee of that property? That way the creditors wouldn't lose anything except the interest on their money. But in spite of the fact that there were clever people in Poland, and they had passed some wise laws, as far as the general welfare of the state was concerned and as far as the debts of the gentry, the levying of taxes, and other financial matters were concerned, a foolish veto turned all their good intentions into disgraceful resolutions. My bankrupt father-in-law declared sequestration, or the division of his estate among his creditors, on the basis of Lithuanian law. The creditors chose judges or arbitrators from among the neighboring gentry, allowing my father-in-law the legal right to choose a judge from his side. In addition, a chancellery was formed of several regents or secretaries and clerks, and each side chose a legal advocate for itself. The estate was put under the control of the court, but only on paper; in actuality it was entrusted to my mother-in-law, who, for the dowry she'd brought to the marriage and for promissory notes given to her on the eve of the bankruptcy, was also one of her husband's major creditors. At the appointed time, the judges, regents, and advocates gathered, each with his own assistants, horses, and dogs. Everyone had to be fed and entertained at the expense of the estate belonging to the creditors. The affair dragged on for a very long time, since the judges and chancellery found it pleasant to live at the expense of others in such good company. Mr. Gologordovsky, in order to entice the judges to his side, treated them magnanimously (at the creditors' expense); he invited all his relatives who had attractive daughters to the sequestration; he hosted balls, went on hunts, and lived more cheerfully than before. The judges played cards, flirted, fell in love, drank, and danced; meanwhile the chancellery worked gradually, urged on by the lawyers, who were eager to receive their own reward. At last, after two and a half years had elapsed, the sequestration was complete. The estate was divided according to a plan, like a chessboard, and the plots were assigned to the creditors in proportion to their claims. My mother-in-law was awarded the best part, which was worth three times more than her dowry; the other distinguished creditors and relatives of Mr. Gologordovsky, were assigned parcels with peasants, while the creditors who happened to be poor and absent were given swamp land, barren thickets, and sandy steppes, at a higher valuation than fields in India covered in cinnamon, cloves, and sugarcane. My father-in-law became much richer after the sequestration than he was before because he received the best part of the estate. With the barren land and at a small sacrifice he discharged his debts, which exceeded twice the value of the whole estate. The creditors, too—after paying a percentage of the debt to the judges, the chancellery, and the lawyers for the land surveyors and the government dues for the acquisition of their parcels—were completely ruined. Some of them even withdrew their claims completely, in order to be freed of the expenses, which were twice as much as the debt owed them.

Gologordovsky didn't live long after this fortunate occurrence; he died of an infected spleen, after becoming angry that a provincial marshal, whose grandfather was a poor Polish nobleman and who'd served Gologordovsky's grandfather, sat in a more prestigious place in church and was invited to dine at the governor's while my father-in-law wasn't awarded such an honor. His last words were addressed to the Yid tenant, to whom he said, "Iosel, Judgment Day is at hand. Previously thunder didn't dare strike a Polish noble, yet today the governor, who comes from Tatar stock, doesn't invite a pearl of Polish nobility to dine with him, the firstborn of the Gologordovskys." After saying this, he smiled bitterly and gave up his soul to God.

Fortunately, a certain landowner, Podkomory Pochtivsky, came from the Grodno district to Byelorussia on business. He fell in love with my sister-in-law, Cecilia, and since the Pochtivsky family was as well known and numerous in the Grodno and Vilna regions as the Gologordovsky family was in Byelorussia, my mother-in-law agreed to give her daughter away in marriage to this landowner. Meanwhile my brothers-in-law completed their education at a Jesuit college, where at least the spirit of economy was instilled in them. My mother-in-law turned the management of her estate over to her sons, while she herself went to live with her daughter in the Grodno district.

After learning all these details, we set off from Kraków to see Mr. Pochtivsky. Before arriving at the manor house, we stopped at an inn to change our clothes. To my surprise, the inn was a decent establishment with clean rooms for guests. There was no Yid presiding there: it was run by a Christian, a cabinetmaker, who engaged in his trade in one of the rooms, while his wife managed the inn and sold vodka.

"Why is there no Yid here?" I asked the landlady.

"The master has driven the Yids out of his estate and forbids them not only from dealing in spirits but even from living in his villages. As a result, in the last ten years, our peasants have become much better off, so all the neighboring landlords envy us."

"Your master probably looks after his peasants' well-being?"

"He's like a father to them, not a master. In the ten years since he became the owner of the property, he's fertilized all the fields, both his and the peasants' fields; he's increased the livestock, given horses to the peasants, rebuilt houses for them, established a school for their children, and takes better care of their health and wealth of his peasants than his own; as a result, he's loved and respected by everyone."

I was glad to hear such news about my brother-in-law, and we hurried impatiently to his house. I won't describe my Petronella's joy at meeting her mother and sister, who had supposed her to be dead. Cecilia was happy with her noble and wise husband: she had two sons already, fine little lads, and she was expecting a third child. We became friends with Pochtivsky on the first day. He'd been educated at Vilna University, and at graduation had been awarded the degree of Doctor of Philosophy. He'd traveled around Europe and, after returning to his fatherland, he decided to devote himself to the improvement of his estate, which had been badly managed by the trustees during his nonage. Pochtivsky speaks Russian fairly well, loves all Slavic dialects, and considers all Slavic tribes as blood relations, all Slavs as his brothers, who should love one another and aspire to enlighten their fellow countrymen and raise the level of literature, to occupy a respectable place in the universal republic of arts and sciences. I won't describe for you all the arrangements in Pochtivsky's house; I'll merely say that there was neither a plenipotentiary nor a commissary nor a Yid confidant; that he had neither debts nor lawsuits; in a word, the entire estate was the opposite of Mr. Gologordovsky's.

After living for two months in Mr. Pochtivsky's house, I received news from Kiev that Avdotya Ivanovna, while waiting impatiently for her uncle's death in order to make use of his last will and testament, had at last fallen prey to consumption, brought on by an excessive fit of screaming, and had fallen into the clutches of death before my uncle, who himself was in despair because there was no one left to torment him. They say that Avdotya Ivanovna's daughter, Liza, is hastening to Kiev with her husband to take her late mother's place. Following my friend's advice, I myself am heading to Kiev and will expend all my efforts to make peace with my uncle. I don't know how it will end, but in the meantime, be healthy and write to me in Kiev.

Chapter 28

The Young Nobleman. Glupashkin. An Aficionado of Dramatic Art. Disorder in the Robbers' Den. Misfortune. Grunya's Flight. Honesty in Wolf's Clothing, or Don't Judge by Appearances. The Egoist.

Young people of the best Moscow society gathered to go hunting at the estate of a young candidate for bankruptcy, who after exhausting his ingenuity on all sorts of extravagances in town came up with new ways to spend money at his country estate. He'd built a theater, organized a large hunting expedition with hounds, and opened a kind of complimentary tavern in his house. To this hunt ladies were also invited—the host's relatives, with their acquaintances. Milovidin's cousin Anyeta persuaded me to escort her to these festivities. My absence was not to last longer than a week; bidding farewell to Grunya, I set off on my journey.

We passed the time very pleasantly. The host, Faleley Glupashkin, desperately wanted to play the role of an English lord. His country house was luxuriously furnished with imported furniture, paintings, statues, and bronzes. His stable housed more than one hundred English horses, his kennel more than three hundred dogs of various breeds. Among his servants he had a great number of foreigners: Englishmen, Germans, and Frenchmen. For company he kept a Frenchman, called a *littérateur*, who served as his private secretary; he paid an Englishman a large salary to converse with him so he could perfect his English pronunciation. An Italian, an old rogue, lived with him as a sort of friend. He enjoyed a reputation of being an expert in painting, archeology, and music. The Italian traded in crude Italian paintings, mosaics, fake antiquities, and was also a usurer and love's messenger. The German, a librarian, served for a small sum, mostly out of love for catalogues, of which there were a large number in the library. Glupashkin bought an entire troupe of serf actors from a bankrupt aficionado of dramatic art, Kharakhorin, who, at the loss of his estate, consoled himself by acting in domestic theaters and managing his own troupe. Glupashkin's orchestra also consisted of peasants collected from various domestic orchestras. There were almost five hundred individuals eating at his expense and merely supplying the entertainment. It was impossible to refrain from laughing at seeing the solemn face of the beardless fool, who, imagining himself a great man, spoke about everything in definitive tones; he uttered pronouncements about politics, repeating and reinterpreting the judgments of his English companion, uttered judgments about literature in the words of his Frenchman, and spoke about art under the influence of his Italian friend. Many members of our society, having no idea of the subjects about which Glupashkin was speaking, and knowing only the names of the sciences, considered him an amazing font of wisdom; while they ate their fill at his table, they loudly proclaimed that Russia would be fortunate if Glupashkin served as a minister. He thought that himself, and in anticipation of his first call to serve in the government, he enrolled in the College of Foreign Affairs as a translator from Russian into French. To be fair, I must say that his supervisors had reason to be satisfied with him: he fulfilled his duties very well. One poor student translated Russian documents for him word for word into French for money, and his French companion reworked them and employed French turns of speech. Thus Glupashkin, executing precisely the commissions of the administration, had the right to claim rewards and promotion, and there were grounds on which he could expect to ascend to higher ranks. He wasn't the only one who managed to obtain rewards through someone else's intellect and labor; nor was he the only one who became known as a smart operator and a great politician by repeating the words of his companion.

In the mornings we went out hunting, followed by dinner; then we attended performances of tragedies and ballets under Kharakhorin's direction; finally we danced, played cards, and ate supper. It was impossible to feel bored, because Kharakhorin's own performance of every tragedy supplied laughing matter for the entire day. He was convinced that there didn't exist a better declaimer in the whole world than himself. He put on airs terribly, roared verse in a singsong voice like a wounded bear, strutted, and waved his arms like a madman. To get used to wearing clothes of the ancient heroes and marquises of the eighteenth century, he would always dress in theatrical costumes from early morning on the day of a performance, put rouge on his face, and speak to everyone, even with the servants, in his theatrical voice. It was said that once, while planning to perform in a private theater out of town, he traveled there wearing his costume. As usual, his carriage was stopped at the barrier to ask his name and rank. Kharakhorin announced his real name, but the sergeant on guard, assuming he was a fake and a clown, sent him to the nearest police station without heeding his objections; they sent him off to a lunatic asylum, where they detained poor Kharakhorin until his friends came to retrieve him, having to convince the authorities that he was simply a fool, not a madman.

Kharakhorin formed his entire theatrical troupe according to his own conception of declamation; as a result, spectators were forced to weep during comedies and laugh during tragedies. His ballets consisted of leaps, which were tolerable only when the female dancers were attractive. I would have stayed in Glupashkin's house longer, but unfortunately, I was lodged in the same room as Kharakhorin himself; he tormented me so much by reading aloud his dissertation on dramatic art based on love for the fatherland that I refused to attend these diversions; on the sixth day I ran away from him to Moscow.

Upon my arrival home, I learned from Petrov that a policeman had come every day for some time to inquire if I was at home, wanting to speak with me about some affair. I ordered tea and had barely sat down when Petrov announced that the policeman had appeared once again and was asking permission to enter. He came in very modestly and bowed politely. Although his physiognomy was unremarkable, some simplicity and good nature in his manner inclined me in his favor. His uniform was as worn-out as the pavement; his hat was a relic of the last century; and the hilt of his sword was made of burnished steel. He bowed to me and said, "My supervisor has communicated with yours, and I've been assigned to disturb you by posing several questions, which you must answer immediately."

"What's happened?" I asked with uneasiness.

"Be calm," replied the policeman. "Let's sit down and read it together."

An inkwell was fetched, and I replied to the following questions.

"Has the Collegiate Secretary Vyzhigin been acquainted with the actress Agrafena Stepanovna Primankina for a long time?"

"Since childhood. I became acquainted with her when her mother was still alive, the widow of the Titular Counselor Shtosin."

"How long has Vyzhigin been acquainted with Prince Plutolensky, Count Tonkovorin, Zarezin, Udavich, and Yadin?"

"I became acquainted with them in Primankina's house, a year and a half before this."

"Did Vyzhigin know about the intentions of the aforementioned people to cheat the Durindin brothers, who've recently come of age and who borrowed three hundred thousand rubles from the Board of Guardians, on the collateral of their estate?"

"I did not. This is the first time I hear about this intention and about the Durindins."

"Was Vyzhigin in the house of the aforementioned Primankina, when the game took place among the aforementioned people, after they had administered some poisonous drug to the Durindins, and when, as a result, there occurred a fight in which Zarezin lost his left eye, Yadin's nose was broken, Prince Plutolensky's right side-whisker was torn off, Udavich's forehead was cut by a bottle, Count Tonkovorin's index finger was broken, and the Durindins received dangerous wounds to the head and chest, as a result of which they are now dying?"

"No, I was not present. I was away at the country house of Mr. Glupashkin and just now returned, after an absence of about six days."

"Does Vyzhigin know where the aforementioned Primankina—who is accused by all the aforementioned people of having enticed the aforementioned Durindins to the house, having administered the potion, and having invited Plutolensky, Tonkovorin, Zarezin, Udavich, and Yadin, to rob the Durindins, causing the fight when the Durindins refused to pay the money they had lost at cards—is hiding from the police?"

At these words the pen fell out of my hands.

"What? Grunya's gone into hiding? She's left me?" I cried, and threw myself on the sofa in despair, covering my face with my hands.

"Agrafena Stepanovna, calling herself Primankina, has left Moscow, and her whereabouts are unknown," replied the policeman frostily. "From the interrogation of her servants it appears that you were pleased to visit the aforementioned Agrafena Stepanovna daily, sometimes more than once, and that you were living with her in a close friendship; the authorities thought it appropriate to take evidence from you, to learn if you knew anything about the events which took place or the whereabouts of the aforementioned Primankina."

"I know nothing at all, and you can see what a state I am in, having learned about the misfortune of Primankina, whom I loved and was planning to marry . . . and now . . . I have lost everything!"

"I have noted in the protocol your shock at hearing the news, and I consider this as proof that you didn't know anything about the events that took place," said the policeman.

While he was writing and getting his papers in order, I calmed down somewhat and thought it better that Grunya had escaped persecution by the police; I was consoled that perhaps this occurrence would compel her to follow my advice and turn to a path of honesty. I hoped to find her, to exonerate her with the help of my friends; in a word, my sadness suddenly changed into joy.

"Mr. Policeman," I said. "I'm prepared to swear an oath and confirm my testimony; I declare frankly that it was only my absence that saved me. If I'd been in Moscow, I would have been drawn into this affair against my will. Now relax, have some tea, and tell me all the details of this dreadful story."

"You seem to be a decent and honest man," said the policeman, "and therefore I'll be frank with you, especially since the neighbors speak well of you and during the general search they declared that you are a well-meaning, generous, and humble man. Your servant, Petrov, swears that there's no better master in all of Moscow."

"Enough, without further preface! Tell me what you know; satisfy my curiosity: I'll be very grateful to you."

The policeman stood up from his place, tiptoed to the door, glanced into the other room, then came back quietly, sat down, looked around, and finally began speaking in a low voice. "I'm an insignificant man, a noncommissioned officer, a mute facilitator of my supervisor's orders, but thank God, I'm neither deaf nor blind, and I possess both some intelligence and a clean conscience. Why are you sticking your neck out in this manner? Why are you eyeing me so strangely, Ivan Ivanovich? Yes, sir, I have a clear conscience and therefore . . ." At this he pointed to his well-worn uniform and his faded brown hat and continued. "The police knew that in Primankina's house considerable gambling was taking place in a dishonest manner, and that the main cardsharps of Moscow would gather there. But these are Glupashkin's serfs on quitrent; as a good landowner he supports his hardworking peasants, and so, in spite of my reports, the matter took its own course. The fight with the Durindins would have been relegated to oblivion if it hadn't been for the complaint from their uncle, a powerful man, who by means of money and threats compelled Zarezin to confess everything. Then Udavich proposed to his companions and to the policeman to shift all the blame to Agrafena Stepanovna, on the grounds that a different location for gambling could be found but one could not come up with such intrepid players. In the meantime they managed to hint to Primankina that she should disappear, and the affair assumed another form. But since it was essential to discover and punish the guilty party without delay to pacify the Durindins' grandfather, they contrived to sacrifice and banish the traitor Zarezin and to lock up Yadin in the guardhouse. They didn't touch the others, but their *ataman*,[1] Udavich, remained safe and sound, naturally, for the time being. Sooner or later Providence will punish the culprit.

"Ivan Ivanovich!" he said. "I know everything. Take some good advice: disentangle yourself from these accursed gamblers, who will eventually lead you to ruin. Forget the treacherous enchantress Primankina, who flattered you while at the same time she loved a Frenchman, a traveling agent for a French factory, and ran off to Paris with him."

I interrupted the policeman's speech and cried, "Enough! Enough! You're killing me!" Wounded self-esteem and deceived love combined to produce a strong shock. Fortunately, I could cry, and that relieved my heart to some extent. "And so, Primankina's gone to Paris?"

"That's correct," replied the policeman. "Her servant Katerina told me everything; she's our sergeant's fiancée. She says that Agrafena Stepanovna loves you very, very much, but that you're too tender and you torment her with your jealousy; on the contrary, the Frenchman was cheerful and wasn't jealous in the least; in fact, he takes comfort in Agrafena Stepanovna's conquests. She preferred the Frenchman and, though she was departing with him, she wept bitter tears for you."

I suffered torments upon hearing his tale, but my natural pride and the remnants of good sense fortified me. After a brief silence, I gathered my strength and said, "Why did you pose these questions to me when you know that I didn't take part in the Durindins' affair and that I didn't know about Agrafena Stepanovna's flight?"

"That, sir, was for form's sake," said the policeman. "I wanted to show my zeal and my efforts to discover the whole truth. I mixed it up with so many *names* and gathered a variety of evidence. In proportion to

1. Cossack chieftain.

the number of people interrogated and the size of the file, the validity of the investigation will be determined."

I didn't want to remain alone and asked the policeman to stay for supper with me. He agreed, and while Petrov was setting the table, I strode around the room, reflecting on my situation and Grunya's second betrayal, which had twice caused me such misfortune. The first time I lost my freedom because of my love for her; now, having forfeited my capital and almost lost my good name, I had fallen into the company of swindlers and become a participant, at least, aware of their deception. Why was I making such sacrifices? Because of love for an unfaithful woman, unworthy of this splendid, sublime feeling! *No,* I thought, *it's time to become a man worthy of my noble Miloslavsky blood. I shall begin to overcome my passions, and my very first sacrifice will be my love for Grunya.*

I reflected well and this time followed my reason because Grunya was nowhere near me. I can't vouch for what might have happened if during my struggle with my passion Grunya had appeared, in all her beautiful splendor, with her charming eloquence and tender caresses. But fortunately Grunya was far away, and I triumphed over myself. I cried a little, grew angry, became irritated, abused the world and people in general, women in particular, and to tell the truth, this time it was in vain. I went up to the policeman, clasped his hand in mine or, to put it better, his dirty glove, and said, "Thank you for your good advice. From now on, I'm a different man."

Unable to eat, I comforted myself with the sight of the policeman's appetite. As a distraction, I asked him to tell me how he wound up in the police, why he serves up to now without a promotion, and how his conscience, sailing in such stormy seas, had avoided a shipwreck. Arkhip Arkhipych gulped down some wine, cleared his throat loudly, coughed, adjusted his tie, and began his tale.

"Say what you will, but it is my firm belief that a man can't avoid what's been decreed at his birth. My father was the butler of a noblewoman, Lukeriya Semyonovna Poryadkina;[2] for his faithful service he and his family were awarded their freedom. My father had two sons; we lost our mother during our infancy. There was no one to look after us in the manor house: we did as we liked. My greatest pleasure in childhood was to fight with policemen. I tossed stones at them from behind corners, caught their legs in a loop when they passed our gate in the

2. Her surname means "proper order."

evening, splashed them with water, and played other pranks. My hatred for them resulted from the fact that they'd once arrested my father, and when he dared complain, they treated him so discourteously—that is, they beat him and fined him—all because of someone else's fault. For my childhood revenge, I keep being punished by the police all my life and, finally, I will have to die from hunger in custody.

"My father employed a deacon to teach us how to read and write; but since the deacon knew very little, he couldn't teach us very much: besides, everyone has his own talent—mine wasn't literacy. I know how to read and write, and I can more or less tell a story; at least there are some people who listen to me with pleasure; but when it comes to setting down on paper what I've just related by mouth, I'm at a loss: I struggle to keep my head above water! Nothing flows from my pen! It's no great harm that I can't cope with soft signs and hard signs, with periods and commas—our smart operators aren't able to do any better than I am—but my misfortune is that I can't write as I think and speak. If it were possible to write with one's tongue instead of a pen, perhaps we'd have more writers and I would end up a scholar.

"I didn't wish to remain in my lady's service, but I didn't know what else to do with myself after my father's death: he was an honest man, God-fearing, but he didn't leave us a kopeck, although he'd managed the lady's house for some thirty years. My elder brother entered the service as a clerk in the civil court and soon became so proficient that he was said to be an educated man. I managed to find a position in a city supply store under the patronage of the mayor, who'd known my late father. In that job I could scarcely provide for my own daily bread. Fortunately our noblewoman's elder son, who'd served in the army, was appointed police chief in Moscow. I went to see him and told him about my unfortunate fate and asked for his protection; he awarded me a position in his chancellery and assigned me special commissions.

"Sergey Semyonovich Poryadkin was an honest and truth-loving man; he wished and did good whenever it was in his power and even looked for opportunities to do so. But be he a King Solomon with a heart as large as a policeman's booth, he could do nothing without assistants, and he would end up with consumption. That's just what happened to him. 'Arkhipych,' my superior said to me, 'I'm convinced that you're an honest man. Keep watch, observe, and reveal all wrongdoings to me; your prayer will not be ignored by God, nor will your service to the tsar be in vain. Remember that the calling of a policeman, the preserver of peace and the security of our citizens, is an estimable calling, if only the civil servant operates according to the law and his conscience. Don't be afraid of anyone: I am your protector!'"

"I soon became familiar with police business and began to act. I discovered that Sergey Semyonovich's secretary was taking bribes from civil servants, tax farmers, and merchants, as if they were for his master.

"We went to the secretary at night, searched his cabinets, found money and receipts from the savings bank and correspondence with various people. We interrogated him, and since he couldn't explain or prove how he'd collected so much money in such a short time, it was returned to the office, and the secretary was dismissed from the service. I discovered that one officer was in the habit of intentionally delaying collecting debts and confiscating property as decreed by the court of law; he also used to beat the porters of those houses in which the landlords gave him no gratuities, used to take money from shopkeepers, pub owners, and butchers for permission to trade in spoiled goods and provisions. The civil servant was dismissed. I discovered that thieves were allowed to live in one place and only some were held responsible when the affair was too flagrant and it was necessary to show off a speedy search for things stolen from important gentlemen. The civil servant was put on trial; the thieves were caught and exiled to Siberia. I produced evidence that soldiers were being admitted to taverns and the only pub owners brought before the police were those against whom the inspectors of the tax farmers had a personal grudge. The abuse was stopped, and the guilty were punished. I discovered those granting asylum to thieves and the traders in stolen goods; I revealed contacts between thieves at large and those serving in prisons, thus severing what was a rich source of revenue to many people. Lastly I resolved on a desperate venture.

"As a person, the worthy Sergey Semyonovich had his weaknesses. He was in love with a certain woman who did not deserve his noble heart. She took money from petitioners, and at a moment of his weakness, she extracted from my honorable superior his consent to her requests—of course, always presenting the matter in the most favorable light. I gathered incontrovertible evidence of the falseness and selfishness of this cunning woman and presented it to Sergey Semyonovich. The poor fellow even started crying, but he overcame his passion and cast off this worthless trader on his good name. After three years he promoted me to the rank of titular counselor, gave me a medal, and made me the supervisor of the best district in town.

"You can guess that everyone looked at me as something of a scarecrow and would have been glad to get rid of me. They tried in various ways to destroy me, but as long as Sergey Semyonovich was still alive, all their efforts were in vain. I behaved like an honest man, didn't take advantage of anything, and since my salary was insufficient for my maintenance because I had to keep horses and always be well-dressed, Sergey Semyonovich allowed me to accept voluntary offerings of grateful people when I was looking for stolen property, collecting a debt, or discovering a debtor's hidden property; in addition, he gave me confiscated contraband for my own use, as well as fines levied for negligence, and so on. Sergey Semyonovich, as I said above, couldn't maintain his struggle against these abuses for long. The fervor of his character, his lack of rest, his work and stress destroyed his health. He died, and with him my good luck disappeared.

"His successor was also a well-meaning man, but he had his own trusted people, whose advantage consisted in destroying me. He didn't know me, and he believed what my enemies said. They began to undermine me. A whole gang of thieves began circulating in my district, leaving dead bodies in various places; they made numerous false accusations, started writing letters, and trapped me in a web of quibbles and cavils. It ended with my district being taken away from me; for the sake of Christ they gave me the rank of police supervisor, on the condition that I not look further than my nose, cover my ears, control my tongue, and keep my mouth shut. I've lived this way for the last fifteen years, from hand to mouth fed by the kindness of good people and hardly owning the means to cover my own nakedness, while only yesterday the wife of our local policeman (who three years ago didn't have enough money to buy tobacco), was wearing diamonds worth twelve thousand rubles and a shawl which cost twenty-five hundred rubles. 'Be patient, Cossack; you'll wind up a chieftain!'[3]

"In the meantime, my brother has become a wealthy and famous man: he holds the highest position under an important civil servant in Petersburg and manages all his affairs. I wrote him a letter and asked him to allow me to come see him in Petersburg and to secure a modest position for me through his supervisor's influence. He wrote me a reply, which I carry around with me in my wallet because I have nothing else to keep there and the letter itself is really rather amusing. Here it is."

3. A well-known Russian proverb.

Arkhip Arkhipych took a letter out of his faded wallet and gave it to me to read. It ran as follows:

Dear brother!

You wish to come to Petersburg and stay at my house. That is impossible. I'm forced to spend so much money on my large family and the excellent circle of my friends that I can't afford to give you even a kopeck for your travel. True, my lodging is provided by the government and appears to be very large, but it's organized in such a way that I can't accommodate you, *dear brother*. My study occupies one room; then there's my wife's study; the third is our bedroom; the fourth, the living room; my daughters sleep in the fifth room, and my two sons in the sixth; the seventh is my daughters' classroom; the eighth, my sons' classroom, the ninth is a hall reception room; the tenth, a dining room; our French Madame resides in the eleventh, the French tutor in the twelfth, the maids in the thirteenth, and my two clerks in the fourteenth; the fifteenth is for the footmen, and the sixteenth is a cloakroom; the seventeenth is where papers are stored; the eighteenth is a small conference room for petitioners with whom I have to meet privately. Downstairs are the rooms for the servants and coachmen, also the pantries and storerooms; in a word, there's no empty space even for a cat, let alone for you, *dear brother*.

At our dining table every day there are eight members of our household; in addition, there are my secretary, the officer on duty, and two young gentlemen entrusted to my care to introduce them into society; besides that, I have to keep three or four vacant places, in case anyone should drop in on us. These days life is very expensive, incomes are low, and although I'd be glad to share my last kopeck with you, my circumstances will not permit it, *dear brother*! My children are being brought up in the modern manner; they all speak several languages; they're acquainted with important, wealthy people; and so, the appearance of a poor uncle, a retired policeman at that, would be unpleasant and might even damage them in public opinion, *dear brother*. As to the position, which you hope to secure thanks to my patron and benefactor, *dear brother*, I can't be of use to you in this case. My benefactor doesn't like to be asked for anything, and he especially can't stand to be asked for anyone else's benefit at all. He distributes his favor one drop at a time: thus I must keep him for myself and my children, like a good head of a family and a moral man. Do remain in Moscow, *dear brother*, and put all your trust in God, whom I will continue to entreat to preserve you in His holy right hand, and to grant you all earthly blessings, which I wish you earnestly,

Your tenderly loving brother, Pantaleimon

P.S. Don't be troubled, *dear brother*, and don't write to me anymore. These days postage is very expensive, and I'm so busy with my affairs that I can't always answer you. From time to time I'll inquire about your precious health through people coming from Moscow. Our shared acquaintances blame you for not acquiring competence when you had the chance, and even more, you've made many enemies for yourself: they can harm me if they find out that I've intervened on your behalf. And so, *dear brother*, I ask you not to tell anyone that we are brothers; say that we merely share the same surname. I'm certain that due to your family love, you will do this for me until the opportunity occurs when I can be of use to you.

"A fine brother!" I exclaimed, handing the letter to Arkhip Arkhipych. He returned it to his wallet with a smile and then planned to take his leave from me. I went to my study and, taking one hundred rubles from my bureau, returned to the room and begged Arkhip Arkhipych to accept it from a friend.

He refused with the following words. "If I hadn't come to see you on business, I would have taken it, but now I can't. It's not in the order of things, and your gift would have the appearance of a bribe."

I embraced the good Arkhipych and consoled him by saying that his honesty, although late, would be rewarded. Arkhip Arkhipych raised his index finger and said, "That's where my hope lies!" He wiped away his tears and left the room.

Chapter 29

My Intention to Marry. Official Arithmetic. Acquaintance with a Wealthy Tax Farmer. A Feast in the Home of the Merchant Moshnin. His Family. Domestic Theater.

After visiting my mother in the convent, I was extremely surprised that she knew about the recent events at Grunya's house, about my close friendship with her, and even about my own behavior. She implored me tearfully to be more careful in my contacts and to earn my living in a less dangerous manner than associating with gamblers. I promised to change, and promised it sincerely. Unable to repress my curiosity, I asked her how, in her seclusion from the world, she'd learned how I'd acquired money and about my relationship with Grunya.

"News travels through the air like odors, dear Vanya," my mother replied. "Our elder nuns visit many pious women living in town; they also come to see us, so it's impossible for town news not to find ways to scale these convent walls."

I was extremely worried that rumors of the events with Grunya where my name was mentioned had spread through town. With a feeling of unease, I left my mother and went to spend the evening at the home of a retired grandee, whose son occupied a high position in Petersburg, and consequently all Moscow would come to visit him. I entered the hall with fear and trepidation. The guests stared at me with curiosity, whispering among themselves as if surprised at my presence. One of my friends drew me aside and asked what had happened, and was it true that I'd fallen into a nasty situation as a result of my connection with the runaway actress? I replied resolutely that I knew nothing about it and had been away at Glupashkin's for a whole week; when I returned to town, I heard indirectly that there had been a dispute over cards in Primankina's house and that she had left Moscow in secret. I spoke in a loud voice on purpose, and soon a small circle formed around me where, wearing an artificial smile, I related the events in Grunya's house, embellishing the narrative with puns, presenting the whole affair in a comic guise. It soon spread through the whole company that I was not involved in the least, and all doubts on my account vanished. Ladies declared me innocent, while the young men even envied that I was suspected of being in a relationship with Grunya. Only Cousin Anyeta didn't believe my explanation; having found an opportunity to speak with me privately, she said in a friendly manner, "Dear Vyzhigin! I know everything and I forgive you everything, but, for God's sake, be careful: get a better circle of friends. Don't disgrace yourself. Women have done everything for you that you wished for; they'll forgive you everything except flirtation outside their own society. Remember this and mend your ways!"

I truly began to ponder how I might support myself in the world by honest means. Never having engaged in business, and being only nominally in the service, I had no hope of ever reaching a level where I could support myself by written labor. Besides, at my rank it was impossible to count on receiving a large salary, and I had an insurmountable aversion to bribes. I still had several thousand rubles left and a few valuable items. I began to live with extreme frugality, dismissing all my servants, selling my expensive furniture and my carriage, and renting a small apartment; I retained only Petrov in service and was never at home to those friends who came calling to lure me into amusements and expenditures. I dined out as a guest every day, played cards for low stakes, danced at all the parties, and paid compliments to others; time passed, but I could never figure out what to do with myself.

At that time one of my friends, a ruined nobleman, married the ward of a wealthy man. This event aroused in my own mind the need to reform or, better said, to secure my situation through marriage. But where should I search for a bride? Despite all my self-esteem, I didn't dare try to make a match among those wealthy families where breeding and connections constitute the primary value of the bridegroom. Wealthy wards are difficult to find; older rich widows marry a second time more out of calculating ambition. Newer nobility seek connections with old families, and vice versa. I decided to search for a bride in the merchant class, but lacking any connections, I didn't know where to begin. One day, returning home at six in the evening, against my usual habit, I met an old woman in my doorway; she was dressed nicely, in a short jacket, with a silk kerchief on her head.

"Who are you looking for, granny?"

"Your servant, Petrov, sir: I'm his godmother."

"And what do you do?" I asked out of curiosity.

"I'm a midwife, dearie, and if necessary—a matchmaker."

"Splendid! Go in to see Petrov, granny, and afterwards I'd like to have a word with you."

Half an hour later I ordered the old woman to come into my study.

"Whose matches do you arrange?"

"Whoever wishes a match, sir: merchants, officials, and even gentry."

"Do you have any rich brides now?"

"Of course, I do! We have plenty of merchandise—if only we had buyers."

"Well, there's no harm in trying: if you find me a wealthy merchant's daughter, I'll load you down with gold."

"At your service, sir. At the moment I have two brides from merchant families; they're both very pretty and stylish, even learned! They speak all foreign languages, dance foreign dances, and dress like dolls. . . ."

"Good, very good! But do they come with large dowries?" I asked the talkative old woman.

"A hundred thousand rubles each in cash, plus fifty thousand in silver, gold, pearls, precious stones, and all sorts of finery."

"Superb! Who are these cherished young ladies and their venerable parents?"

"The father's name is Pamfil Merkulovich Moshnin, from our Poshekhon area, registered in our town. The mother, Matryona Yevdokimovna, is an excellent housewife, God bless her! She's given birth to eight children: two sons, already grown, and three little boys; three daughters—two are marriageable, and the third one is a child, aged fifteen."

"What are the daughters' names?"

"The elder is Akulina, the middle one is Vasilisa, and the youngest is Lukeriya."

"Which one is the prettiest?"

"Akulina Pamfilovna is plumpest and rosiest of all, Vasilisa's next in line, and the third one is very thin, but she's still a child."

"How do I begin the process?"

"I'll talk to the girls about you, whisper in Matryona Yevdokimovna's ear, praise you to the aunts; and you, sir, should make the acquaintance of Pamfil Merkulovich: he's a generous man and loves all sorts of amusements. A large number of gentry gather at his house; he does a lot of business of various kinds."

"Fine. Here's ten rubles for your first nice words about me; God speed, and come back soon with good news. Good-bye!"

After the matchmaker left, I began thinking seriously about how to proceed with this plan. I considered one hundred thousand rubles in cash and a connection with the family of a wealthy contractor to be the greatest blessing in my current situation. There was only one difficulty: how to introduce myself in that home? Among the circle of my friends, I didn't expect to find a guide to Moshnin's house; besides, I didn't want to reveal my intentions to any of them. I recalled that I had frequently noticed at the card table in Grunya's house a secretary, who was the butt of our jokes, saying that ink spots were visible on his money.[1] Once, when I was the croupier, I noticed how he bent an extra corner of a card; I didn't want to drag him into an unpleasant argument, so I kept quiet, but after the game I told him what I'd seen. The secretary promised me he would return the favor, so I decided to visit him and ask how it might be possible for me to make the acquaintance of Moshnin, who, without doubt, he must have known.

My Petrov knew where he lived, so I made my way there immediately. He lived in a small, lovely, wooden house in a remote part of town. I hired a carriage on purpose. As soon as the carriage drawn by four horses had stopped at the door, I perceived movement inside the house; the footman opened the door with a bow and let me into the hall, where the secretary met me wearing a light woolen frock coat, red boots, and a colored scarf around his neck. He removed his cap and his glasses out of respect and asked me to enter the study, a little room, in which there were no books, no papers, and no writing implements.

"How can I help you?" asked the secretary in a patronizing but polite tone.

"Don't trouble yourself," I replied. "I have no business; I merely want to know if you're acquainted with Pamfil Merkulovich Moshnin or with any of his good friends."

1. That is, he was cheating at cards.

"For what purpose, may I ask?" said the secretary.

"I have commercial interests."

"I understand," said the secretary with a sly smile. "That depends!"

"You're mistaken: since receiving a wealthy inheritance, I have completely given up playing cards," I said, covering my face so that the crafty secretary couldn't notice my lie.

"Ah! You've received a rich inheritance, and you're no longer playing cards? That's fine, just fine. But I, like a damned fool, can't curb this accursed passion! I'm a good friend of Moshnin. I'm handling a small business matter of his right now. He promised to come here later today for a secret meeting; I can introduce you to him right away. But do me a favor. Wait here a little bit while I talk with one petitioner whom you didn't notice in the corner of the living room. I'll give you a splendid book to look at so you won't get bored: *The Works of Fyodor Emin*."[2] The secretary brought a book from the next room and a heap of papers, which he took in to see the petitioner.

They spoke rather softly, but as far as I could make out, the secretary stated various objections to the petitioner, which he answered in a rather gentle voice. At last they grew angry, argued, suddenly fell silent, and I heard only *one* . . . *two* . . . *three* . . . and finally *forty*; then a minute later, another reckoning from one to forty, and that was the end of their discussion.

"Your affair is perfectly right!" said the secretary to the petitioner. "Go home and don't worry about it!"

The petitioner bowed, and the secretary returned to me. We talked for about a quarter of an hour about the unfortunate events at Grunya's house, about her escape, and so on, when suddenly the servant came in and announced that another petitioner had arrived. The secretary left, and the same comedy was enacted once again. At first, objections, then an argument, then convincing, requests, and finally the arithmetic—counting to forty three times. And afterwards a farewell compliment from the secretary: "Don't worry about it; your case is absolutely just."

When the secretary came back in to me again, I couldn't refrain from asking him who the second petitioner was who'd argued so vehemently.

"He's the adversary of the first petitioner you saw here!" replied the secretary.

---

2. Fyodor Emin (1735?–1770) was a satirist and the author of the earliest Russian novels.

"Lucky opponents," I said, with a smile, "when both of them are right!"

"So you overheard?"

"Yes, I heard only your assurance that each one was absolutely right."

"That's the usual form of judicial compliments," said the secretary. "But we'll see who's right and who's guilty after the case is *heard* and the judgment *rendered*."

Just then a carriage drove up to the door.

"Here's our esteemed Pamfil Merkulovich!" cried the secretary and ran out to meet him.

I was somewhat flustered, not knowing how to begin the acquaintance or how to behave with this wealthy tax farmer. I was afraid to irritate him by arrogance or to lower myself in his eyes by modesty—a man who probably wouldn't trouble to discover my true worth. Like a general who on the field of battle, in sight of the enemy, carries out his intentions but in his study feels his own indecisiveness and shortsightedness, I awaited Moshnin's appearance to form a plan of attack and begin my moves. He remained alone with the secretary for about half an hour, and finally the secretary called me into the hall. I saw before me a tall, stout old man, with a long gray beard and a fresh, shining rosy face, wearing a long blue frock coat cut in a German-Russian fashion, something midway between Siberian and German style. He was smiling very kindly and made several bows even before the secretary introduced me.

"I recommend my good friend, Mr. Vyzhigin," said the secretary, "a wealthy man, intelligent, and well-connected. He wants to make your acquaintance, Pamfil Merkulovich, knowing that you keep pleasant *company*."

"Very glad, sir!" replied Moshnin, continuing to make his half-bows. "Welcome. Many persons of rank both like us and favor us, and we do our best."

I can't recall what I muttered to him about his reputation, honesty, skills, and so on, but Moshnin was very pleased with me.

"Would you do me the favor of coming to see me tomorrow, together with Anton Trifonovich?" said Moshnin, indicating his secretary. "Tomorrow is my elder daughter's name day. You're welcome to partake of our hospitality."

I thanked him for the invitation; Moshnin bid us farewell, moving backwards toward the door, continuing his half-bows, and repeating several times, "We wish you good-bye, thank you kindly, don't trouble," and the like.

After he'd left the room, the secretary said, "Well, now you're acquainted! You see I found an opportunity to pay you back for your discretion at Agrafena Stepanovna's house."

"I promise to be even more discreet concerning your arithmetic with the petitioners!" I said with a smile.

"I'm not afraid," replied the secretary cheerfully. "*A pike lives in the lake to keep all the fish awake!* Everyone knows we live by our labors."

"But the publicity!"

"Publicity," continued the secretary, "sometimes it's of use, more than uncertainty and doubt about our actions. At least the petitioner knows how to behave, and that's a great relief. Let them shout, speak, sing, write, and perform on stage! I myself will never miss a performance of *Chicanery* or *The Honest Secretary*,[3] and I always prick up my ears when the actor who plays the government official, knuckles under, and sings:

Ah, what a time this is—
We're forbidden to accept bribes!

"That, sir, is mere child's play, but things do take their own course!"

After sharing a laugh with the secretary, I bid him farewell, promising to go with him to dine at Moshnin's the next day. I asked him whether it was necessary to call on him first, or whether I could appear at the table without having made the acquaintance of the entire family.

"That's an unnecessary formality among merchants," said the secretary. "Their families are used to seeing new faces come and go in the house as needs be. Among them, acquaintance begins with dinner and usually ends when a man who's no longer of use to them asks for a loan."

"I'm obliged to you for the advance notice. Farewell until tomorrow."

The next day I spent all morning at home, reflecting on the past and the future. I was in a strange mood: I categorized and criticized all my actions. In the first place I reproached myself for using impermissible means for acquiring money; in the second for the thoughtlessness with which I squandered what I had acquired. I resolved to live a more modest life: marry a merchant's daughter, engage in business to increase my capital, and become a decent man. Avoiding high society and wealthy

3. Two early influential satires, the former, *Chicanery* (1798) by Vasily Kapnist (1738-1823), the latter, *An Unknown Marvel, or An Honest Secretary* (1802) by Nikolai Sudovshchikov (1770-1812)

acquaintances, I thought that I wouldn't have to make unnecessary expenditures on whims, which are excusable and sometimes even necessary for people in high society but are ridiculous among merchants. My wife, born and bred among simple people, wouldn't have any idea of those refinements in life, which constitute a torment for people of higher orders, amid wealth and honors. A quiet life, management of the home, the upbringing of children, and innocent pleasures—that's what should be the lot of the wife, whose husband limits himself to a small circle of acquaintances. I resolved to renounce all thoughts of ambition, to avoid intrigues, and to engage in business. Without doubt the fate of an honest merchant with moderate desires, is the most enviable. The matter was decided: I would become a merchant, relinquish all useless connections in society; if necessary, I'd even move to another town, for example, to Astrakhan,[4] and . . . but first I have to get married and get hold of a hundred thousand rubles. . . .

Engaged in such reflections and taking comfort in these hopes, I didn't notice how time flew by before dinner. The chiming of the clock informed me that it was time to get dressed. Dressing in the most fashionable style, I left for the place designated to meet the secretary, and from there we proceeded to dinner in Moshnin's house.

I still don't understand what pleasure the host experiences by inviting people to dinner who differ so much in rank, education, class, cast of thought, and life itself! In the first place he creates a great deal of trouble for himself and often dissatisfactions; in the second place he causes some unpleasant moments for his guests. With every guest the host must wear a different face, while the guest doesn't know what tone to use or with what degree of candor he should speak. I experienced all of this that day at Moshnin's. We had barely entered the hall when it seemed to me that I was at the Makaryev Fair. There were officers, civil servants, merchants of all nations, in various costumes, of all sorts from the first guild to market brokers; women in fancy dress, the height of Parisian fashion, wearing pale lace caps, others with silk kerchiefs tied around their heads, some in short jackets; in a word, a mixture of languages, a genuine *divertissement*! I cast my eye over the crowd of guests, whispering and shouting about the weather; fortunately, I didn't see a single familiar face: that heartened me, I confess. I was afraid of meeting my card-playing acquaintances.

4. Astrakhan is the largest city and administrative center of the Astrakhan Oblast in Southern Russia, located on two banks of the Volga River.

The secretary asked a footman where the host and hostess were; we were led into a spacious dining room. There Pamfil Merkulovich was working, sweat on his brow, with his better half. The footmen were unloading wine from baskets, the wine steward was announcing the quality of each, while the host was arranging the bottles, placing the finest wines in a place of honor, but the local Madeira and port were relegated to the end of the table for the more ordinary guests.

The hostess—a healthy and hefty woman aged about fifty, wearing a German dress with a silk kerchief on her head (in Russian style)—was arranging the desserts. They apologized to me for being in the midst of household chores, asked me not to stand on ceremony, and bade me make myself at home. We returned to the guests, and I asked the secretary to introduce me to the host's children. Moshnin's two sons, dressed in the latest fashions, welcomed me with French phrases and tried to appear clever, at ease—in a word, people of the best sort. It was apparent that they had adopted all the mannerisms of young dandies in high society, not as revealed in living rooms but on display in theaters, on boulevards, at promenades outside the city, and in the *corps de gardes*; as a result, at first their behavior seemed too familiar and even impudent. They'd already left the merchant class behind and entered upon careers in the civil service; that is, shopkeepers and footmen would now have to address them as *Your Honor*. I tried, from our first meeting, to win their approval, agreeing with their ideas, and asked them, *as is done in high society*, to introduce me to their sisters. The words *high society* appealed to their vanity; taking hold of my arm, they led me into the living room where a large group of young ladies had gathered, all dressed up. Several were sitting on chairs or on a sofa; others were standing and whispering next to the windows, and a few were strolling about the room. The brothers led me up to their three sisters, who, fortunately, were all sitting together in one place; they introduced me, muttering several words in French. The two eldest were dressed in the latest style, and at the same time, most ostentatiously; the youngest was wearing a simple dress. She bowed to me, according to all the rules of the art at her dancing school, and the eldest sister spoke to me in French on behalf of all three, "*Charmée de faire votre connaissance!*"[5]

If plumpness and whiteness are considered standards for beauty in China, then Moshnin's eldest daughter would have been the most

5. "Delighted to make your acquaintance!" (Fr.).

beautiful woman in Peking, and the middle one would have been second. It's only a pity that the Chinese love small feet, while in the north of Russia this is a great rarity and was not characteristic of either of Moshnin's two elder daughters. But the youngest daughter was enchanting, in every sense of that word. From the color of the eldest sister's face and a certain involuntary embarrassment, I guessed that the sharp-witted matchmaker had already managed to speak to her about me. At the same time I noticed that all the guests were looking at me distrustfully, then at each other, and beginning to whisper. I considered it improper to continue my conversation with one young lady in a circle of other silent witnesses, so I bowed and withdrew with my new friends into another room. We were soon summoned to dinner, and I was seated between Moshnin's two sons—at the proper end of the table,[6] of course. There couldn't be any sort of general conversation at dinner. The officers chatted among themselves about promotions and new developments; the civil servants talked about new edicts and changes in ministries and provincial posts; legal experts spoke about crimes and punishments, and merchants about the rate of exchange and the price of market goods. Several of the young people from the merchant class, including Moshnin's two sons, talked about horses, fashionable frock coats and vests, and about the theater, singers, and dancers. In the meantime none of the guests forgot about the food and wine: empty bottles were constantly replaced by full ones at a signal from the host, who, sitting at one end of the table like Jupiter, solely by raising his eyebrows put the entire drinking mechanism into motion. Women's voices could not be heard, except for their short answers to men's questions. My neighbors constantly drained bottles, ordering the servants to bring them better-quality wines, and when it came time for making toasts, all the guests were already quite tipsy. Half-inebriated footmen ran with fresh bottles like madmen, spilling wine on the guests and making a big fuss. They began toasting each other's health, first the name-day celebrant, then parents, children, relatives, and honored guests, each one separately, then the whole company, and so on. In the meantime the fair sex was quietly busy with dessert. The young girls pecked at the berries like little birds, and in spite of their corpulence shoved fruit and small sweet morsels into their mouths with pleasant affectation. Although I was extremely disposed to enjoy myself, I found it unpleasant to hear the

6. Opposite the host.

young Moshnins make fun of their parents. The dear little lads laughed at their mama's and papa's every ineptness, covering their mouths with their napkins and winking across the table at their elder sisters. The sons called their father a stingy old clerk and their mother an office drudge; they even made jokes in French at their expense. The good parents, failing to understand what they were saying, were pleased to hear their children speaking a foreign language. I began involuntarily thinking about the worthless nature of our educational system, in which people concerned themselves only with outward appearance, without worrying about underlying morality; while this compels us to despise the condition in which we were born and also smothers the feelings of nature in our heart by inappropriate arrogance.

After dinner some of the guests sat down for a game of boston[7] and whist; the women and girls amused themselves with conversations and snacks in their circle, while the young people, including me, gathered in the rooms of the young Moshnins to smoke pipes and drink champagne, chatting about subjects that would be inappropriate to mention here. An hour and a half later, the Moshnins' elder son asked the guests to return to the larger rooms, announcing that there would be a presentation of a French comedy as a surprise for his *maman* and *papa* (as he referred to his parents). The chairs were arranged in the dining room; the actors gathered at the buffet—that is, the Moshnin family and some of their daughters' girlfriends. At one end of the hall movable stage wings were erected, and a curtain made of several rugs sewn together was hung. Instead of an orchestra the youngest daughter's music teacher played the piano poorly. When all the guests had taken their seats in order of rank, Moshnin and his wife sat down in the first row of armchairs, with the French tutor of their youngest children between them to translate the play and explain what was happening. This tutor, by the name of M. Furet, was the author of the drama about to be performed under the title of *The Liberal Parents, or the Good Children*. Although the title itself revealed only nonsense, there was no lack of applause in approval, and the clapping resounded at every word, every couplet. The content of the play was as follows: a wealthy merchant spares no expense for the upbringing and maintenance of his children; he gives his sons money to treat their friends, to hire carriages, and so on; he gives money to his daughters for their clothes. In addition, he

7. A card game similar to whist.

takes them all on promenades, to theaters and masquerades, and he hosts balls and parties at home. At last the daughters marry princes, counts, and generals, while the sons attain the highest ranks in the service. The sons and sons-in-law, as a reward for their service, manage to procure a title of nobility for their father, who, at the theater in French, is privileged to receive the title of *Your Honor*. One had to see the ecstasy of the good Moshnins during the performance of the play. The tutor accurately translated every word, every couplet relating to the parents' honor, and tears of tender emotion flowed from their eyes. In spite of the fact that the elder sons, warmed by the wine, flubbed their lines, and the two elder daughters didn't know their parts at all, and the prompter's voice drowned out the speech of the actors—who, in addition, were singing out of tune—the performance received much praise and achieved its goal: that is, children should be denied nothing for extravagances, because that would serve to elevate the entire family. The performance ended with dancing: the Moshnin daughters performed the Spanish fandango, the tambourine, and the shawl dance, while the younger sons jumped around like monkeys. The china cups and chandeliers shook and jingled in time with the movements of the elder sisters, but the youngest daughter charmed everyone with her acting, dancing, singing, and, most of all, her beauty and modesty. I really liked her very much. But knowing that in merchant families daughters had to get married in order of seniority, I didn't foresee any hope of winning her hand, unless it might be by the forceful intervention of her brothers. That day I managed to form a strong friendship with them, and as I was leaving, I invited both to have breakfast with me the next day.

Chapter 30

Failure in Matchmaking. Letters from the Kirghiz Steppe and from Paris. Departure for the Army. War. Distinction. Return to Moscow.

I won't describe all that I went through to win the friendship of the two young Moshnins. Associating with them for several months and wishing to adapt to their way of life, I nearly became an alcoholic and almost fell into the abyss of depravity. The greatest pleasure of the rich merchant's sons, who chose not to engage in trade and merely pretended to be in the civil service, consisted of excursions outside of town, where they freely indulged in drinking, rowdiness, and debauchery, broke windows and china, instigated fights with officials and poor German craftsmen, and quarreled with, and then made peace with, the police. The Moshnins treated me like a friend and a brother and revealed all their secrets to me. I learned how they incurred debt at their father's expense; how they deceived their mother and took money from her, saying it was to buy gifts for their supervisors in the service; how they cleaned out the cabinet, which contained a stash of money, using a forged key, and so on. At last I confessed to them my love for their youngest sister; they undertook to assist me in attaining my desires. The simple-hearted girl agreed to marry me and willingly began a correspondence through the medium of her brothers. Pamfil Merkulovich and his corpulent spouse were also well inclined toward me, having heard that I was of the nobility and possessed fifteen hundred serfs; they were extremely eager for me to make a *good beginning*—that is, by marrying their eldest daughter. It remained to overcome one obstacle—namely, to persuade the parents to allow me to make a good beginning by marrying their youngest daughter—when suddenly one day all my plans and hopes of the last few months evaporated like smoke.

The sly secretary found out that I had deceived him and hadn't received any inheritance, and that I refrained from playing cards because I was afraid of landing in trouble. Being acquainted with a clerk, originally from Byelorussia, who'd been expelled from the legal ranks for his chicanery, the secretary found out from him that there wasn't a single noble family by the name of Vyzhigin in all of Byelorussia. Over a glass of punch, when he was in a most communicative mood, he relayed this to old man Moshnin and described me in the darkest of colors. He was joined by Ivan Merkulovich, the same merchant who was defeated and robbed at Udavich's in my presence, who also testified that I was a gambling swindler. Old man Moshnin warned his sons not to associate with me. But if I'd really been as bad as described to the old man, I still would have been the best person among the friends of the young Moshnins. They told me everything and encouraged me to present proof of my nobility and the deed to my estate to their father. Naturally I had no choice other than to cease my visits to the Moshnins and lose out on the hundred-thousand-ruble dowry and the lovely young girl. I regarded this as righteous judgment for my connections with the gamblers, and I patiently submitted to my fate. A man who experiences a severe loss and failure surrenders to despair only when fate subdues in him the flame of the ruling passion but doesn't extinguish it. It is easy to be consoled In misfortunes where reason prevails, and not the heart. Having weighed all the advantages and disadvantages of the proposed match, I congratulated myself for having escaped a connection with the young Moshnins—I gave up receiving them at my house and soon ceased meeting them at all.

One day I received two letters, one from Orenburg and the other from Paris. My former medical assistant, Baksa Temir-Bulak wrote to me from the Kirghiz steppe. His letter follows.

To the highly respected, illustrious, brave Mr. Ivan Vyzhigin, from his faithful friend Baksa Temir-Bulak, greetings, and best wishes for your health and well-being!

Since your departure from our blessed steppe, Mohammed, sitting in the ninth heaven, has been angry at the distinguished tribe of Baganali-Kipchak, and his sacred mare El-Borak has waved her tail and brought misfortune to the village, which was prospering under the rule of the wise and brave Arsalan-Sultan. Fatal omens in heaven and on earth aroused our caution: the moon hid her brow behind Mohammed's sacred robe and appeared murky, like an antelope in the mist. Insects were found in the entrails of sheep, and Arsalan-Sultan's best mare gave birth to a dead foal with two heads. I predicted misfortune, but Arsalan-Sultan, having imbibed in Russia bookish light-mindedness, believed neither my dreams nor my divinations and didn't listen to my advice to join with the Great Horde to avoid the conflict of two strong tribes, those of Chizlyk and Dert-Karik, whose chief, Arsalan-Altyn, had fallen by a stroke of your powerful arm, oh brave Mirza Ivan Vyzhigin. These two tribes, after summoning their allies, unexpectedly attacked us, and although they didn't conquer us, they killed our best horsemen. The courageous and still undefeated Arsalan-Sultan, sharper than the Prophet's sword, the glory of the steppe, fell in the ranks of the enemy, like a wolf among a herd of sheep, as a punishment for disregarding the wisdom of the mullahs and disbelieving Baksa's prophecy. Our flocks and herds became prey for the enemy, our villages were sacked, and our beautiful women were led away into captivity! In the general commotion, the surviving warriors saved themselves by flight and joined the Great Horde. I received your letter in Orenburg, at the barter market, where I'd been sent by the khan on his business. And so, Mr. Ivan Vyzhigin, do not count on receiving your property, which had been kept aside in the yurt of Arsalan-Sultan himself and fell into the hands of the victors, together with his treasures. The successor of the brave sultan, your friend Gayuk, is so poor that he drinks his koumiss as a result of the generous bounty of the khan of the Great Horde and serves as commander in chief of his bodyguards! However, the khan has heard so much about you that he would be glad to see you and probably would award you an honored place in his horde. Farewell, and don't forget your friend Temir-Bulak, who prays to God for your happiness and asks Him to instill in you a desire to return to the beauty of earthly beauties, a preview of paradise—the Kirghiz steppe.

Tears flowed from my eyes as I read the news about the worthy Arsalan-Sultan's death and the misfortune which had befallen my old comrades. My hope for help from the steppe vanished. My situation became even more difficult.

The other letter was from Grunya. With trembling hands I tore open the seal and read it several times, struggling with various feelings. Here's what she wrote:

My friend, dear to my heart, Vyzhigin!

You probably already know the reason forcing me to leave Moscow and Russia. I love you so much that I didn't want you to fall subject to misfortune, which united my bitter fate with yours. But since it's difficult for a woman to exist in the world without the protection of a man, I chose as a defender M. Sansouci, a cheerful and kind Frenchman who loves me as fervently as I love you! It was noted in his passport that he was traveling with his wife, but since Madame Adèle remained in Russia as a governess, I took her place and arrived safely in Paris.

Ah, my dear friend, what a city Paris is! Our quiet, gloomy Moscow is like a pond to a waterfall in comparison with the capital of France. During the winter in Moscow, it's deserted and still by twilight, and only the sound of carriages reminds you that you're not living in the forest. But here there's perpetual life, unending motion; there's no difference between day and night, only a change of scenery, the replacement of natural light by artificial. I'm surprised that I didn't suffer an apoplectic attack from the delight I experienced when I first saw Parisian fashion shops! Ah, my friend, what a sight! Novelties don't show up here after months or weeks, but every day, every hour, every minute. This is the temple of taste, the legislative power of fashion, the concentration of all inventions. Here life is reckoned not in years but in the number of pleasures; everyone hastens to live like a sailor, who hurries to arrange his affairs onshore, even after the sails on his ship have already been raised.

Paris is the hotel of the entire world. Seekers of wisdom, pleasure, and happiness from all the ends of the earth are gathered here and as a result, everyone here lives according to his own taste, without constraints, as they would in an inn.

Dear friend! If you only saw how our ladies, who won't take a step without a convoy of two dozen footmen and who require a carriage with four horses to cross the street in Russia, stroll all on their own through the winding lanes of Paris, the illuminated garden of the Palais Royal, under the arcades, and who ride to the baths in a simple cab! This incognito provides them with a thousand pleasures: if anyone dared mention them in Russia, he would be called an ignoramus, a brute, and an impudent fellow! Here there are offices open for everything; there are agents for every desire. One can even buy and sell a heart and a mind. It was only here that I discovered any conception of social life. No matter how high the level of our education, you will agree, dear friend, that in our middle class we still have much that is Asiatic; and women, although they rule over men as they do everywhere, even in Asia, are still confined by old-fashioned customs. Here everyone has total freedom. Decent women visit taverns and coffeehouses, travel alone in stagecoaches and post chaises, and often have their own connections and acquaintances, about which the husbands know nothing and don't concern themselves. Every Frenchwoman is the full mistress in her own house, and the duty of a husband is to engage in business outside the house. Foreign gold makes its way to Paris through various sources, and all the cares of Parisians consist in making use of this golden rain.

The designation of foreign traveler is the most honored only if he comes to Paris to enjoy himself spending his money; however, every foreigner is awarded a title of count, prince, lord, and baron, granted not by rank but by the size of his purse. I'm also called a princess, though I'm having a good time not on my own money. Refinement in entertainments and pleasures is taken here to the highest degree, and the human intellect seems to have exhausted itself in inventing comforts in life. Amusements are divided into two groups: public and private. In the first category belong the theater, concerts, society balls, promenades, and country holidays. Everything that in other capitals amuses the public only in large celebrations and on special occasions occurs here every day and always attracts crowds of fans. I won't tell you about the theaters, which constitute the ruling passion among the French; I won't describe all the amusements partaken of *incognito*, and I will keep silent precisely because I want you to come to Paris and enjoy yourself in person and not on paper.

I'm still not able to come to my senses: my head is constantly spinning. M. Sansouci is a very kind man and doesn't trouble me with his demanding love. I've made the acquaintance of several foreign women and my fellow countrymen who are in search of diversion as I am; we live an extremely happy life. Take pride, my dear, in my love! Even in Paris they call me the *lovely Russian*, and if you saw me in Parisian fashions—you would fall at my feet together with a dozen lords, German princes traveling incognito, and our own wealthy Russian compatriots. At home our seamstresses and shop attendants don't know how to dress us well, and all they think about is trying to sell off their rags. But here they work for fame and for money.

Come to Paris, my friend; only leave behind your jealousy and your philosophy: there's no place for them here. Ask for me at the Palais Royal, in the fashion shop at no. 113.

I saw from this letter that misfortune had not reformed Grunya and that flightiness and vanity remained her dominant passions as before. I didn't even want to reply to her letter, knowing that my advice wouldn't help.

In the meantime war broke out between Russia and Turkey,[1] and, recalling the good Petrov's advice, I decided to enlist in military service. I revealed this to my good friend Cousin Anyeta, with whom I'd been living like brother and sister. She praised my intention and undertook to obtain by petition a transfer for me from the civil service to the military. Oh, omnipotent women, I am obligated to them for so much in life! Cousin Anyeta set in motion all her friends, aunts, and cousins. Notes were written, meetings held, consultations, petitions, and recommendations sought. My supervisor, with whom I played whist twice a week and dined every Sunday, provided me with the best testimonial of enthusiastic and flawless service, even though I had never set foot in his office. Two months later I was designated a cornet in the same Hussar regiment where my late father had served.

When I appeared in full Hussar dress to Cousin Anyeta, she cried out in astonishment and confessed that I was born to wear a uniform. My supporters rejoiced at the success of their petitioning, and I nearly exhausted myself dancing the mazurka out of gratitude with all their daughters and nieces. Petrov was ecstatic and tormented me with requests to hasten to join my regiment. My kind cousin Anyeta loaned me several thousand rubles and, collecting the remnants of my property, I said farewell to everyone and left for Little Russia, where my regiment was stationed, and there awaited my first orders to get on the march.

I didn't tell my mother about my intention and appeared before her in full dress uniform the day before my departure. She almost fainted at the sight. I looked so much like my father wearing the same uniform

1. Russo-Turkish wars were fought between Russia and the Ottoman Empire in the seventeenth to nineteenth centuries. The wars reflected the decline of the empire and resulted in the gradual southward extension of Russia's frontier.

that my mother couldn't get her fill of gazing at me. After crying a little, as is usual in such circumstances, she blessed me, loaded me with good advice, and wished me good fortune. The next day I was on my way to Kharkov.

The regiment had already begun to advance, and I caught up with it on the move. When I presented myself to the colonel, he took one look at me, clapped his hands in surprise, and cried, "My God, what an astonishing resemblance! If I myself hadn't witnessed the death of my friend, Count Miloslavsky, I'd think I was seeing him before me."

He summoned the regimental quartermaster from the next room; he'd been the sergeant major in my father's squadron, and asked, "Who does Cornet Vyzhigin look like?"

"He's the spitting image of the late Prince Ivan Aleksandrovich Miloslavsky!" cried the old man and his eyes filled with tears.

"Did you ever hear about the prince?" the colonel asked me.

"No," I replied.

"I know that my former friend was a bachelor," he said, "but it often happens in the world that . . . that is, there occur strange resemblances! I hope that you, my dear comrade, also resemble the prince in spirit and courage, and since I have no reason to doubt it, I will give you one piece of advice to start. Try to get to know the battlefield: without that the best person will remain a bad officer. We have many recruits from whom I've formed a junior squadron, and I must train them as we advance. I appoint you to the guards, and for the time being, so that you get to know how things are done, I place you under the command of the training squadron of Captain Bravin, an old soldier, whom I encourage you to love and respect like a father, because he deserves it."

It's not appreciated when someone enters a regiment from some other regiment with seniority or, as they say, as an officer in command. Although I was ranked as the youngest cornet, my comrades received me extremely coldly because I'd transferred from the civil service. In spite of my polite behavior and my efforts to win the favor of the officers, I was nicknamed "the clerk," even though I swore that from my birth I had written nothing except for love letters, and that I hated pettifoggers more than the Turks we were going to fight. Jokes didn't diminish and were even repeated more often, and I started to get angry. Captain Bravin, who came to love me dearly, advised me to teach the jokesters a lesson. I fought two duels with sabers and one with pistols in the space of a single week, wounded two of my opponents, and received a slight bullet wound to my left arm. The colonel arrested all of us and announced a reprimand as punishment; as soon as I recovered, I treated my comrades to lunch, inviting my opponents to attend, and declared to everyone that if someone wanted to be sure that I had never been and would never become a scribe, I was prepared to present proof with my saber and my pistol. My comrades liked my frankness and boldness, and, amid the clinking of champagne bottles, I was declared to be a spirited Hussar.

"Vyzhigin!" said Lieutenant Zastrelin, the man who had wounded me. "You've washed away ink with your blood; now you're one of us, and if anyone is against you, they're also against us. Give me your hand, brother! We need Hussars like you."

The colonel, who called me to join him, gave me some fatherly advice. "I punished you as my duty that I owed the service, but I have no reason to be dissatisfied with your behavior. You were compelled to fight, but now that you've entered into comradeship with the senior officers, avoid all quarrels. A good officer must demonstrate his bravery in fighting the enemy, not in duels. Captain Bravin informs me that you know the protocols of fighting at the front, and that you could take command of a platoon. Be so good as to present yourself to the commander in chief of the light squadron: I've ordered him to give you the third platoon."

I don't know if an experienced general who's received command of an entire army would have rejoiced as much as I did upon being ordered to command the third platoon. My good Petrov jumped for joy.

I didn't tell anyone about my time in the steppe with the Kirghiz, so that they wouldn't give me another nickname, and I didn't show off my horsemanship, which I practiced frequently even in Moscow, riding outside of town in out-of-the-way locations. However, I purchased a hair lasso and bought myself a mountain horse so that I would be prepared if the opportunity of using my skills ever presented itself.

Dear readers! If you get a chance to hear the tales of cornets and ensigns about plans for a campaign, about the whole complex of military actions, mistakes made by generals, or the reasons for success or failure in warfare—listen out of politeness, but believe only half of what they say or, even better, don't believe it at all. An officer serving at the front can see nothing more than what happens there and can't make judgments about military plans other than by hearsay, and by putting together the multitude of circumstances and opportunities that come to light after a campaign. And so, I don't wish to talk about military actions, especially since I don't intend to write the history of the war, but I will speak only about my own experiences. I'll mention the war as far as it has to do with me personally, not out of vanity, but to carry out my design to record my own life history.

After crossing the Danube River, our regiment joined the vanguard of the main army. Since we didn't take part in several battles—that is, victories—which had been won before crossing the river, we joined the vanguard with our full complement of men—that is, "fresh," as they say.

Once I stood with my platoon at an outpost on the Turtukai.[2] It was in June, but the night was bitingly cold. I was lying next to a small campfire wrapped in my overcoat and waiting while Petrov heated the teapot. All of a sudden a Hussar came galloping up from the outer chain and informed me that he'd heard a noise in the bushes at the edge of the plain, where our mounted sentries were posted. I ordered my Hussars to mount at once and, leaving them in place under the command of my sergeant, I myself advanced with two men and with Petrov, who never left me, to corroborate the sentinel's report. The night was dark; thick clouds covered the moon, and a mist hung over the valley. I dismounted, put my ear to the ground, and really did hear rustling and a slight noise in the bushes. Was it really the enemy? How was one to tell in the darkness? Before I took up my post, I had surveyed the surroundings for a mile or two around and discovered that from the side where the noise was coming, there was no road at all and the valley was bordered by hills, which adjoined a forest. Our last patrol had discovered an enemy party at a distance of about twenty miles in the other direction, so I couldn't expect an attack from that side. While I was reasoning with myself, the moon suddenly peeked out from behind the clouds, and rifles started gleaming in the bushes where some men were only half concealed. Judging from what I saw, I concluded that there were about one hundred men there. What was to be done? I followed my first instinct, sent one Hussar back to our camp to inform the others of the enemy's presence, and advanced to attack them with my platoon. We fell upon the Turks with such speed that they were thrown into confusion; they fired some shots and began to shout *aman*[3] and to throw down their weapons. We gathered the Turks into a group, disarmed them, tied them up with ropes, and drove them back, covering our retreat with half the platoon. I had a Tatar translator who

2. A city in Bulgaria on the Danube River. It was formerly the site of a Turkish fortress that guarded a convenient place for crossing the river.

3. "Peace" (Arabic).

interrogated a captured officer and learned that the Turks, after receiving reinforcements, had advanced to attack us in the morning. The hundred Arnauts,[4] whom I luckily managed to take prisoner, were sent to one side as a foraging party; but their guide, a native Bulgarian,[5] betrayed them: he led them into the forest and escaped from them at night. Lost in the forest, they came across our outpost and, not knowing where they were, assuming they were in the middle of the Russian army, they cringed in fear and decided to surrender to the attackers, who, in their opinion, must have been strong, since they were brave enough to attack them during the night, without knowing how many of them there were. These Turks confirmed a remark made by our colonel, that if someone wants to win a battle, he must be the first to attack; if he waits to be attacked, he will suffer large losses.

I sent a patrol forward; the Hussars trotted several miles ahead and reported that there was no sign of the enemy. I halted and waited for the return of the man I had sent to the detachment with news of our meeting with the enemy. In a short time we heard the sounds of horses' hooves from one side of our camp; soon two hundred Don Cossacks came galloping up under the command of a volunteer from a distinguished family. He'd been sent from Petersburg to seek distinction in the army, which was under the command of his great-uncle. I delivered the prisoners to him, and he returned to our camp; I myself remained at my post until morning.

After I was relieved and had arrived back at the regiment, I received congratulations from my kind colonel and from my comrades. "Splendid, Vyzhigin, splendid!" cried the officers. "You do honor to your brave regiment." The colonel invited us all to breakfast—that is, to eat roast mutton and to empty a keg of Moldavian wine. They drank to my health: right then and there a report was drafted to the commander in chief of the brigade, in which it was stated that with 30 Hussars, I captured 112 armed Turkish soldiers. In a separate letter the colonel asked that I be given a reward. My laudable reputation was established throughout the regiment.

The volunteer who received the prisoners from me was named Pustomelin. This young man, educated by a retired French drum major, considered himself a military genius, and he was continually talking

---

4. A native or inhabitant of Albania or of one of its neighboring mountainous regions, especially one serving in the Turkish army.

5. That is, a fellow Slav.

about tactics in the society of fellow officers, about great operational plans, about the campaigns of Turenne, Montecuccoli, Prince Eugene, and Frederick the Great.[6] He criticized all our military movements and plans and judged everything and everybody arrogantly and stubbornly. We sometimes made fun of his general knowledge; more often, we didn't listen to him at all and accepted him into our company only because it's impossible to hide from wearisome chatterboxes on a bivouac. Pustomelin, on taking the prisoners to the barricade of wagons, didn't show up again in the vanguard and stayed in the headquarters on account of his illness. Soon we received an order in the regiment in which it was said that Pustomelin was to be awarded an honor for capturing 112 Turkish foot soldiers, with the assistance of Cornet Vyzhigin, to whom the esteem of the commander in chief was to be extended.

The officers were indignant, while I was furious. I galloped up to headquarters and hurled abuse at Pustomelin, calling him a dishonorable coward, even shook my fist at him, and challenged him to a duel. I was placed under arrest, and they wanted to court-martial me but released me solely through the intervention of my fellow officers and the colonel, who congratulated me again and consoled me with the Russian proverb, which had already been repeated by me several times: *A prayer for God and service to the Tsar will not be lost.*

"Rest assured, Vyzhigin!" my kind colonel said to me. "You fulfilled your duty. You showed yourself to be a brave and efficient officer and won the respect of your comrades: that's the greatest reward for an honorable man! Injustices and errors occur everywhere: but that shouldn't deprive you of your zeal to serve. Be patient. The truth will emerge in its turn; however much people attempt to entangle and ensnare it in webs of intrigue, the truth will always come out."

Several weeks later our army halted in a position facing the entire force of the enemy, which was entrenched in a fortified encampment, defended by their advantageous location. It was proposed to launch a full-scale battle. The commander in chief moved to the vanguard just as the Turkish horsemen flanked our Hussars and Cossacks. Our whole cavalry vanguard was in battle array, while the infantry was under arms;

6. Turenne, a renowned French military genius, was named Marshal General of the King's Camps and Armies in 1660. Montecuccoli was an Italian-born professional soldier who served the Habsburg Monarchy. Prince Eugene was a field marshal in the army of the Holy Roman Empire and of the Austrian Habsburg dynasty during the seventeenth and eighteenth centuries. Frederick the Great was king of Prussia from 1740 to 1772. His most significant accomplishments included his military successes in the Silesian wars.

everyone was looking at the single combat of Turkish horsemen with our Hussars and Cossacks as a dramatic spectacle. The commander in chief, with his entire staff and a number of foreign officers who were serving as volunteers, paused to enjoy this genuinely enthralling scene, where agility and bravery had such an extensive field for distinction. One must pay one's due to the Turkish horsemen: they outshine almost all other cavalrymen in their horsemanship, their handling of arms, and in single combat, although their fervent bravery can never withstand our own steady courage and resolution in general attacks. One Turkish horseman distinguished himself more than the others, arrayed in his rich attire and riding his white horse. With astonishing bravery he attacked our men on the flanks and had already managed to knock several of our best Hussars off their horses. The commander in chief was annoyed by this triumph of Asiatic skill in the presence of foreigners, and he said to our colonel in annoyance, "Don't we have anyone to match that daredevil to punish him for his arrogance?"

After hearing those words, I climbed on my mountain horse, let out my Kirghiz lasso, and asked my colonel's permission to engage the Turkish horseman. He agreed, but I noticed in his eyes his concern mixed with his love for me.

"Vyzhigin!" he said. "I know that you're not a coward; but artistry is required here; you couldn't have learned horsemanship in the civil service. I feel sorry for you!"

"You'll see!" I said, replacing my Hussar shako with a service cap; I spurred on my horse and rode off.

I really wanted to take the horseman alive. First I fired my pistol at another Turk, then I rode up to the Turkish horseman, fired my other pistol at random, turned my horse, and threw myself to one side, as if I were going to reload my pistols. The Turkish horseman, seeing that I was separated from my countrymen, rode right up to me, approaching me on the left to cut off my head with one blow of his sword. Just at this decisive moment I ducked under my horse; the Turk lost his balance from the exertion of his powerful swing and reeled back in his saddle. I jumped back into my saddle and, coming up behind the Turk, threw my lasso around his neck, pulled, and the Turk fell to the ground. This unexpected fall on his back at a full gallop took his breath away. The reins of the stallion were thrown back into the rider's hand over his shoulder, and the steed was stopped short by the fall of his rider. I jumped down from my horse, disarmed the Turk and tied him up with my lasso; lifted him off the ground; threw him, unresponsive, on his stomach over my saddle; jumped on my horse; took the reins of the Turkish stallion; and galloped back to my regiment. A crowd of Turks ran forward, shouting, attempting to rescue their leader, but our commander in chief ordered two squadrons to trot out and the Turks turned their horses around. When I reached the regiment, there was a great noise and much banter among the ranks. The commander in chief rode up to me with his suite, dismounted, and ordered me to approach. I jumped down from my horse, took my prisoner, untied him, and presented him to the commander in chief, who kissed me, shook my hand, and said, "I thank you for this gift, and in return I grant you this present."

With these words he ordered his adjutant to undo an Order of St. Vladimir with a bow,[7] and he fastened it to the strings of my dolman with his own hands.

"I won't forget you!" said the commander in chief and moved off.

The officers of our regiment surrounded, congratulated, and embraced me; every single one of them rejoiced as if it had been his own achievement. My colonel pressed me to his heart and said, "Thank you for maintaining the honor of our regiment!"

I was in ecstasy. Never in my life had I experienced such joy.

"Give Petrov my Turkish stallion and order him to bring my frontline horse," I said to the sergeant.

"I'm here!" said a voice behind me. Tears flowed from Petrov's eyes, but he had a smile on his face. He wanted to kiss my hand, but instead I pressed him to my bosom. Petrov was unable to utter a word; he was touched to the depths of his heart. Accepting my booty, he went off slowly along the front, crossing himself and moving his lips. The good Petrov was praying for me!

Nothing else of consequence happened that day. By evening our forces returned to their position, and the colonel went to the commander in chief, who was posted with the main division a few miles behind the vanguard. An hour after the colonel's departure, a messenger arrived with orders for me to appear at once before the commander in chief. The colonel was waiting for me in the adjutant's tent, and as soon as I dismounted, he led me into the commander in chief's tent. I found there a number of generals and staff officers. Pustomelin entered after me without his sword.

---

7. An imperial Russian military and civilian order established in 1782 by Empress Catherine II in memory of the deeds of Saint Vladimir, Grand Prince and Baptizer of Kievan Rus'.

"Cornet Vyzhigin!" said the commander in chief. "Your esteemed colonel has told me about your deed, about your capture of the Turkish detachment. The recognition and reward for it were appropriated by this gentleman officer (he pointed to Pustomelin), who, unfortunately, belongs to my family. Certain people who don't know me led me into error, and I was forced to be unjust; they thought they were doing me a favor by furnishing an opportunity to reward a relative. But in the army the only family I have are the brave warriors: they are my real brothers; they are my children and my nephews! He who wishes to serve the tsar and the fatherland faithfully must be fair to subordinates and reward only merit, because nothing harms the service more than partiality, prejudices arising from family members, and connections. One injustice does more harm than a hundred rewards can yield benefits. Remember this, you commanders in chief! And so, I congratulate you, Mr. Vyzhigin; as for you, Mr. Pustomelin, you may return to Petersburg at once, under the wings of your aunts and grandmothers. Never dare show your face here again. There's enough room for you on parquet floors; but gentlemen who bow and scrape are out of place on the rugged battlefield. Farewell!"

We left the tent. I was jubilant, while Pustomelin was downcast. He seemed pitiful to me, and I was about to console him but was afraid to wound his vanity. My comrades gathered in a circle, drank to my health, and shouted my name, repeating *Hurrah!* three times!

The next day there was a major battle with much bloodshed; both sides fought with great ferocity. The Turks were more numerous, but Russian bravery, strengthened by discipline, gained the day. Their fortified camp was taken by storm; artillery, transports, a large number of standards, Cossack flags, and prisoners ended up in the hands of the conquerors. The Turkish forces were defeated and dispersed. Fame crowned the Russian forces with new laurels.

Our regiment took part in the action and distinguished itself more than others. But we suffered many losses of life and wounds doing battle with the enemy's crack troops. While we charged with our swords in hand, I grew somewhat heated and, with my Hussars, forced my way into the very thick of the enemy's ranks. They couldn't escape from us because the narrow passage was occupied by Turkish janissaries.[8] The commotion was horrific! The janissaries fired at us from both sides

8. A member of the Turkish infantry forming the sultan's guard between the fourteenth and nineteenth centuries.

of the passage and the ravine; sabers clashed desperately; it was impossible to hear commands because of the yelling and shooting; the trumpets sounded an attack, and we broke through the enemy's lines. I was hemmed in and could hardly swing my sword. Blows showered down from every side, and I slashed away to the right and left at random. But soon I felt that blood was bathing my eyes and that my left hand was unable to control my horse. At that moment someone grabbed the reins of my horse and pulled him back hard. After getting free of the crowd, I rubbed my eyes and saw that it was—Petrov.

I received two wounds to my head, one to my left arm, and another to my right shoulder. Blood flowed in streams, and I was becoming weaker and weaker. After withdrawing about a mile from the scene of the battle, Petrov helped me off my horse; took prepared bandages, compresses, and lint from his case; he washed my wounds with water and vinegar, bandaged them, and then sat me back on my horse; he sat behind the crupper, put his arms around me, and led me to the barricade, having tied his own horse to my stirrup.

My wounds were not dangerous, but they were painful. The doctors feared only that weakness from my excessive loss of blood might result in my total collapse. I could hardly move my legs and soon took advantage of the first opportunity to set off for Russia.

Petrov didn't leave me for a minute and even slept next to me. No tender mother could have taken better care of her only child, her beloved son, than this old soldier did for me. The good Petrov cooked my food, administered my medicine, changed the bandages on my wounds, and led me out on his arm to walk around. During the day when I was asleep, he drove away the flies; at night he jumped up as soon as he heard me moan or cough. He lived for me alone, and when I wanted to thank him, he would always frown and say, "When you thank me, your honor, it feels awkward and not right, as if I were ashamed of something. After all I must serve my commander. What's there to thank me for? Get well, Ivan Ivanovich, that's the best way to please me."

After arriving in Kamenets-Podolsk, I wrote to Milovidin in Kiev, intending to set off to see him, if he were still there. I addressed the letter to a commandant whom I knew; he replied that Milovidin had been reconciled with his uncle and had left for Petersburg. This news surprised me, since I had very little money left and couldn't travel as far as Moscow on what I had.

"It's not good to be left without any money," I said to Petrov.

"That's true, sir, but we have no reason to complain."

"What? I have only thirty silver rubles left!"

"A little more than that," said Petrov, who went into the other room and returned with two heavy leather belts.

"What's all this?" I cried out in astonishment.

"It's your money, sir," replied Petrov. "By my count there are fifteen hundred real Turkish silver coins and, besides that, a diamond stylus."

"Where did you get it?"

"You took it, sir, and I kept it safe. When you captured the foot soldiers at night, I relieved their commander in chief of his turban and his sash, so that no one else would take them; and when, in front of the whole regiment, you caught up with the brave Turkish *aga*,[9] I galloped up to where he was lying and took his turban, too, knowing that Turks hide their money there. Besides that, I found about two handfuls of gold in his saddle; that's what has filled our treasury. I didn't tell you before, fearing that you might want to give the money back to the Turks, and even more, because you might lose the money at cards, since you'd returned to your former dealings on bivouacs from boredom."

"Listen, Petrov. It's your money; I won't agree to accept it except as a loan."

"How is it my money, when you procured it by risking your life? Booty in battle is neither a sin nor a shame; but it's sinful and shameful to rob one's own and cheat them out of provisions, forage, and hospitals! God be with them! The money's ours! Take what you need, either as a loan or for yourself, only take it: it's yours."

I sold my horses and kept the Turkish arms and accessories as souvenirs of my victory. After purchasing a comfortable carriage, I set off to heal my wounds in Moscow, where I arrived safely at the end of autumn.

---

9. A person of high rank or social position, especially in the Ottoman Empire.

Chapter 31

Retirement. Departure for Petersburg. The Difference between Petersburg and Moscow Society. A Wicked Plan. The Unfortunate Olinka. I Am Imprisoned. It's Possible to Be Happy Even in a Disastrous Situation.

After arriving in Moscow, I immediately rushed to the convent to visit my mother, who almost fainted from joy when she saw me with a medal of distinction. But my pallor and weakness upset her, and she advised me to retire, fearing that continued military service might completely ruin my health. Peace was concluded: my good colonel was promoted to general, and the regiment was given a new colonel. I myself wanted to get some rest and enjoy life; after I gathered my testimonials, I submitted my petition and received my retirement, a promotion in rank, and permission to wear my military uniform. After I visited all my acquaintances and benefactresses, who knew already about my deeds from reports and received me favorably, I began to obtain medical treatment and stayed home for the next two months. My mother visited me every day; after I conferred with her, I decided to depart for Petersburg. Now having a right to patronage, I was looking for some comfortable position that would allow me to earn a living. Besides, curiosity was drawing me to the famous capital city, where I also hoped to find Milovidin and Cousin Anyeta, who had finally rejoined her husband and settled in Petersburg. After recovering my health and collecting new letters of recommendation, I set off on my journey at the end of winter.

I arrived at nighttime and stayed at the Hotel Demuth on the Moika River. The next day I set off for the city to familiarize myself with the layout of the streets, which I knew only from a map. The general cleanliness, order, and a certain pleasant simplicity in the midst of splendor made a favorable impression on me and inspired my high opinion of the cultural level of the residents. I didn't see any Gothic carriages, as in Moscow, nor any harlequin liveries; nor did I find any dirty Moscow alleys, nor pretentious houses with monstrous carved figures, nor grimy shops and dilapidated huts next to gorgeous and uninhabited palaces. Up to then I had no conception of what a European city looked like, and only now did I understand why the inhabitants of Petersburg refer to Moscow as a "big village." It's true that Moscow has an advantage over Petersburg in terms of location, antiquities, and historical recollections. Moscow is the heart of Russia, while Petersburg is its head. Moscow is to Russians as Rome is to the descendants of Romulus, when Constantine the Great moved his throne to the charming Byzantium.[1] Moscow is the cradle of all ancient Russian families and the might of Russia; no matter how dear Petersburg, this testimonial to the greatness of Peter and his successors, is to a Russian, his heart always beats faster at the recollection of Moscow. Like a Muslim, whose faith requires him to make a pilgrimage to Mecca at least once in his lifetime, the Russian considers it his sacred duty to visit Moscow. The view of the Kremlin and God's temples, where the desires, hopes, joys, and sorrows of our ancestors are concentrated, nourishes the soul and elevates our love for the fatherland.

I went looking for Cousin Anyeta, who was extremely glad to see me. She introduced me to her husband, a large, portly man with Tatar features, who lived in his own way, without worrying about his wife; he played whist, ate and drank for ten men and was engaged in supplying wine to the Treasury. He bowed to me rather matter-of-factly, invited me to visit him, and after leaving me alone with his wife, he set off—to eat oysters. Cousin Anyeta told me that Milovidin was visiting Petersburg with his wife and his uncle in order to cancel his spiritual testament, various deeds, and promissory notes, which Avdotya Ivanovna had made him sign when he was still in her clutches. After completing all this business successfully, Milovidin had decided to renounce high

1. In the year 330 C.E., Emperor Constantine decided to move the seat of the government from Rome to Byzantium, which was later renamed Constantinople.

society, which bored him, forever; he purchased a lovely estate in the Crimea, on the southern coast, and settled there with his uncle, who'd replaced all his old habits with a passion for *grande patience*[2] and for reading the *Moscow News*. He became a great politician, and according to the prophecies of Martyn Zadeka, Albert the Great, and *Bruce's Calendar*, he foretold great changes in the world.[3] Milovidin and his wife made it a rule to listen to him for two hours every day, and as a result, he bequeathed them his entire estate.

Cousin Anyeta introduced me into the homes of several members of high society; in addition, I had letters from Moscow addressed to many distinguished persons, and thus I soon had established a large circle of acquaintances. Petersburg society is much colder than Moscow society: in every house they try to copy etiquette and decorum from above. The presence of foreign envoys lends society a diplomatic significance and a sort of restraint, which hampers social intercourse to a great degree. Here they don't appreciate storytellers, convivial fellows, or people who amuse others by their talents, the kind who are so popular in Moscow. In Petersburg society everyone has to speak according to his briefs, proceed by plan, and appear as a guest only where he's wanted, as if in a comedy. Here every acquaintance is the object of calculation and is valued on the basis of his importance, connections, and family. Everyone regards his acquaintances as steps on the ladder to promotion or advantage and collects as many of them as he needs to reach the top. Some people are received because they're necessary, others because they serve to amuse the necessary people. Amusement is playing cards; and so, he who can gamble for high stakes is accepted in society to form a party for important people.

Petersburg is reputed to be a musical city or, to render it justice, a place where many people sing and play various musical instruments. This is true, but one shouldn't conclude from this that there are many genuine connoisseurs and lovers of music. They play cards or listen to music to avoid conversation; at dinner they talk about the weather. They don't like to converse because everyone is seeking or hoping for something, and in such a case it's dangerous to let the cat out of the

---

2. A kind of solitaire.

3. Martyn Zadeka was the reputed author of a Russian dream book; Albertus Magnus (ca. 1200–1280) was a brilliant medieval philosopher and theologian; James Bruce (1669–1735) was a scientific advisor of Peter the Great and published an almanac with predictions for the future.

bag. The candid talkativeness in Moscow, the lack of restraint in manners, and the ancient Russian hospitality are here all considered crude and barbarous.

Here they don't invite you at first sight to come to dinner every day or for an evening as they do in Moscow, but they invite you as a favor; also in Petersburg, where everyone is busy with something or nothing, it's impossible to visit your acquaintances except on set days at certain hours and at fixed times. In Moscow the language of high society is some sort of strange combination of French and Russian; in Petersburg you don't hear a word of Russian spoken; you must speak French with a pure Parisian accent; the slightest mistake against the rules of French grammar is considered a sign of ignorance. In Moscow they *sometimes* talk about Russian literature, Russian journals, and about Russian writers; but in Petersburg that's considered bad form. Higher education consists in being able to judge French literature according to the system of La Harpe,[4] by the articles published in the *Journal des Débats*,[5] and to read English novels in the original. Not one eminent writer or famous Russian artist is received in the higher circles of society if he doesn't enjoy the special patronage of some notable personage. One exception to the rule is a regard for Moscow connections: the host or hostess, introducing the new person, *unknown* in Petersburg society, will apologize by saying that he is *an acquaintance from Moscow*.

The young people in Petersburg society manifest an air of coldness in their behavior, which makes them particularly intolerable and tiresome. They make friends not as a result of any correspondence of taste or in their way of thinking, but according to the significance and connections of their relatives. Each person who's unable to do anything for them or isn't in a position to help, to facilitate the elevation of their own influence and connections, is considered unnecessary in society; they behave haughtily toward him and even shun his acquaintance. The women are nice, as they are everywhere, when they are attractive and courteous. But here women are also subject to the general attitude of ingratiating themselves, like the men, and are cold in their treatment and much too modest; at least that's the way it seems. Tenderness and

---

4. Jean-François de La Harpe (1739–1803) was a French playwright, writer, and literary critic, whose principal work—*Lycée, ou Cours de littérature* (1799)—is a monument of literary criticism.

5. A former Parisian daily newspaper (1789–1944) that was one of the most influential organs of the French press.

compassion are in fashion, like hats. Moscow ladies quarrel and behave whimsically, but when they assist, they do it sincerely. Here they sigh, talk splendidly about morality—and organize lotteries for the poor. A Petersburg ball seems to be organized by a committee consisting of a French ballet master, a Chinese master of ceremonies, a German knight of rueful countenance,[6] and an Italian scene-painter. Things are in their place, there's enough of everything—most of all, boredom. In Moscow, on the contrary, they sometimes dance out of step, the musicians play out of tune, there are tallow candles among the wax ones, sometimes the floor creaks in the ballroom; at a hearty supper there is sometimes too much champagne; sometimes there is more noise at a ball than on Red Square; however, the enjoyment results not from custom, but from a pure heart; people come to town intentionally, to dance, and to have a good time. . . . But I've gotten carried away and forgotten to say that there is no rule without an exception, and everything that's been said here is mentioned in a general sense and should be understood only in part.

I played whist for high stakes, danced, spoke pure French, sang, and played the piano at house concerts, rode in a carriage with four horses, and had connections in Moscow—that is, I could spend half an hour chatting with the hostess about her Moscow relatives and friends; as a result, I was received everywhere and invited into people's homes. But having become accustomed to friendships and the caring treatment in Moscow, I was bored in societies where the host and hostess hardly afforded me a glance and a question or two about my health and the weather. I wasn't *needed* by anyone, and therefore, in receiving me, they thought that they were doing me a *favor*. I even noticed that in society a belligerent party was being formed against me by wicked old men and young people, full of unbearable pride.

The friendship of Cousin Anyeta and a small but excellent circle of her acquaintances made up for the boredom I experienced in high society, in which Cousin Anyeta appeared only for the sake of decorum.

Summer arrived, the city emptied out, and everybody went to his or her dacha, and I still hadn't done anything for myself. Cousin Anyeta advised me in the first place to gain the favor of some notable dignitary, and then to concern myself with securing a position. Dignitaries were very gracious to me at card tables and in our conversations about the

---

6. A phrase first applied to the hero of Cervantes's *Don Quixote* (1605).

weather; but as soon as I mentioned my desire to make myself useful to my country, the dignitary's face would assume such a cold look that chills ran up and down my spine. I would sooner throw myself into a crowd of swords than attempt to extract a drop of sympathy from a frozen heart. Women would intercede only on behalf of their own relatives, so I resolved to wait for more favorable circumstances.

Once, having gone out in the morning, and returned home to dress for a dinner that I'd been invited to, I found a letter in French in a woman's hand with the following content.

I know that you are as discreet as you are polite. Come today at twelve midnight to the village of Yemelyanovka past Yekaterinhof.[7] Leave your carriage at one end of the village and proceed on foot, alone, along the seashore. There, in a solitary cabin above the window in which you'll see a wreath of fresh twigs, a person who takes a very active interest in your fate will be waiting for you. Circumstances compel her to conceal herself and to be your friend in secret. Come—you'll find out everything.

"An amorous intrigue," I thought. And so, even the local modest women, who hardly raise their eyes in the presence of a strange man, love solitary out-of-town cabins! Oh, those dachas, what a wonderful invention! One can live nearby, go for walks to the solitary cabin rented in some official's name, visit one's neighbors to have some cream, and so on. "Splendid, splendid!" I thought. "This will distract me and compensate for my boredom." I decided to go to the rendezvous.

At twelve o'clock I was at the appointed place, found the solitary cabin, knocked at the gate; an old peasant woman unlocked it, and I went into the cottage. I didn't find anyone in the first room except for a footman, who was standing next to the folding doors; he immediately locked them and went out onto the porch, as soon as I had crossed the threshold. At this moment three unknown persons came from the other room, and one of them came right up to me, asked me to sit down next to him on a bench and to hear him out. I was somewhat disconcerted by this sudden and unexpected scene but resolved to wait patiently for the conclusion.

"Ivan Ivanovich!" said the stranger. "You're in such a position now that it all depends on you whether you perish immediately or will be

7. Yekaterinhof is a historic island park that began as an eighteenth-century empress's estate southwest of Petersburg.

happy forever. By birth, although not in a legal marriage, you belong to a family that wishes to arrange your fate. If you agree to sign this paper and acknowledge here in the notary's records that you will make up for the injustice suffered by one member of this esteemed family, you will receive twenty thousand rubles in cash at once; in addition, for the rest of your life you can enjoy the patronage of some extremely important figures; you will obtain a position that you desire; you will have rank and honors; you will marry a wealthy woman; in a word, you will be happy. If not, on the contrary, your demise is unavoidable. Proof and accusations of major crimes will be brought against you, and you won't be able to avoid exile to Siberia, perhaps something even worse. You're only one man, without family and without patronage; your acquaintances will abandon you at your first misfortune; women who've helped you in your minor affairs will refuse to deal with a criminal against whom powerful, wealthy people will take a stand. Decide. Here's the paper and ink. Sign it, and God be with you! You can have the money first. Here it is!"

While one of the strangers was speaking, another placed two large pages of stamped paper covered in writing and a large book on the table; the third stranger was busy counting out banknotes. After a brief silence, I replied, "Kind sir! If your business is honest, you should put these proposals to me without any mystery. First of all I ask you to explain which family demands that I redress the injustice done to one of its members. I know that I'm obligated to Prince Ivan Aleksandrovich Miloslavsky for my birth. He died from his wounds, knowing nothing about my existence because he left my mother still expecting his child. His estate was divided into four parts among his grandnephews, whom I never met since they were educated abroad and now serve in missions. I've never been in contact with any of my late father's relatives and never had any business dealings with them. And so, let me first read the documents that you wish me to sign, and then consider your offer seriously, and finally make a decision. It's in vain that you're trying to frighten me with talk of Siberia and my crimes. You know that I'm no coward. I know my own worth and will find protection in the laws of my country."

After saying this, I stood up and went over to the table to take the papers, but one of the strangers grabbed them at once and hid them in his bosom.

"So, you don't want to sign?" asked the first stranger.

"I don't sign anything without reading it first," I replied.

"Is that your last word?"

"It is."

"You have yourself to blame," said the stranger. He ordered the carriage. Several minutes passed in silence; suddenly a carriage with four horses appeared at the porch steps. I glanced through the window and saw that a young woman was sitting inside. The three strangers took the book, exited from the cottage, got in the carriage, and departed. I was left alone in the house.

The peasant landlord and the old woman, his mother, entered the room and asked me if I wished to spend the night there.

"Who rents these lodgings?" I inquired.

"I don't know, sir," replied the peasant. "The house has been empty all summer; yesterday some gentlemen arrived, rented it for a single day, had dinner here, and off they went. I think you should be the one to know who they were."

I left the house and hurried to my carriage, reflecting on this unusual adventure. Going down to the seashore and passing some bushes, I heard a rustling. I glanced around and just then a shot rang out; a bullet whistled past my head. It was a night clear as day; all of a sudden a person emerged from the bushes, and I recognized—Vorovatin!

He set off running as fast as he could through the bushes, loading his gun as he ran. Since I was unarmed, I dared not pursue him and ran back to the place where I'd left my carriage. But I couldn't find it; I saw marks in the sand indicating that it had turned around and guessed that it had probably been sent back to town by the conspirators. I picked up a stick from the ground and proceeded along the seashore to Yekaterinhof.

I walked quickly and glanced around frequently, fearing pursuit or an ambush. Halfway back I heard a rustling in the forest. Gathering all my cold-bloodedness, I resolved to advance toward the danger, which it was impossible to avoid, knowing that at the decisive moment bravery always triumphs over deviousness. Raising my stick to my shoulder, I plunged into the forest and there I met—a woman!

"Have mercy on me, spare me!" she cried. "I'm unhappy enough already!"

I stopped as if thunderstruck. I recognized that sound in my heart; it affected me and set my blood into action. It seemed to me that I was hearing Grunya's voice. I took the woman by the hand, led her out of the forest in silence, looked her in the face; our eyes met, and a sudden chill ran up and down my body. A young woman in the very bloom of youth, lovely as an angel, was standing in front of me, her hands clasped on her bosom, her eyes begging for sympathy. I looked at her but was unable to utter a word. Her dark brown hair was disheveled and hanging randomly over her shoulders. Her long eyelashes were dripping with tears; her dark blue eyes, reminding me of Grunya's enchanting eyes, expressed both fear and hope; her charming mouth was half-open and seemed about to beg for mercy. She was wearing a white dress and covered by a dark cape.

"What are you doing here in the forest all alone at such an hour?" I asked at last.

"I was running away from deceit, treachery, and debauchery, and I don't know where to hide; I'm afraid to return to town alone; I have no place to lay my head."

"Come with me; I'll be your guide, your defender. I also met with betrayal, treachery, and cutthroats."

Without waiting for an answer from the lovely woman, I took her by the arm and pulled her along after me. Her hand trembled in mine; she kept glancing at me nervously and kept hurrying after me. I stopped.

"You're afraid of me," I said. "I swear to God and by the honor of a Russian officer, that I have no evil intentions against you. I'm ready to sacrifice my life to defend your honor, and while I'm alive, no one will dare touch you."

"I believe you," the young woman replied. "Be my guardian angel; I'm unhappy, very unhappy."

I was in a state of such confusion that I could say no more and went on in silence, holding the young woman by the hand. At the end of the village bordering on Yekaterinhof, I saw my carriage. My hired footman was sleeping on the grass; the coachman and postilion were dozing in their seats. I woke them.

"Why did you leave the spot where I'd ordered you to wait?" I asked the footman.

"I was ordered in your name to set off for Yekaterinhof."

"Who ordered you?"

"Some footman in livery with galloons."

My suspicion was confirmed. I asked the young woman to get in the carriage. She obeyed in silence.

"Where are you taking me?" she asked, bursting into tears when she heard me order the carriage to drive into town at a full gallop. "I told you that I have no refuge. I'm a poor orphan, cast by fate on the world, without shelter."

"Rest assured, I'm a bachelor and won't dare bring you back to my lodging. I will arrange sanctuary for you with a respectable lady, but I ask you not to keep secrets from me and tell me all about your misfortune."

"Undoubtedly, I will tell you all that's happened to me, but give me your word not to pursue the people who are responsible for the position in which you found me."

"I give you my word!"

"And so, listen to me. My father was a staff officer and a member of the lower gentry. He served as secretary to an official married to a wealthy widow; she had a daughter from her first marriage, and this daughter was my mother. The secretary loved his superior's stepdaughter and was loved by her in return. The two lovers, having no hope of winning the agreement of her proud stepfather, were married in secret. I'll say it in a few words: the marriage was discovered; the daughter was driven from the house and deprived of her inheritance; the money was assigned to the children of his second marriage. My father was expelled from the service.

"My father, who earned his living through hard work, died five years ago. My mother took control of my education, taught me foreign languages, music, women's pursuits; she earned her living by the work of her hands and gave lessons in a girls' boarding school. It's been two years since she passed away, leaving me a homeless orphan!" With these words, she burst into bitter tears. "The boarding school in which my mother taught no longer exists. I knew no one in town except for a Frenchwoman who ran a dressmaker's shop, where I used to take my mother's work to sell. I went to see the Frenchwoman in tears and begged her to give me a job in her workshop. She granted my request and gave me a place of honor among her seamstresses; she caressed me, dressed me very well, and in general treated me better than the other seamstresses. I wrote to my grandmother in Moscow, described my unfortunate situation to her, but received no reply. I spent two years in that shop working in peace. Yesterday I turned sixteen.

"The mistress gave me a new dress as a birthday present, caressed me more than usual, sat me down at her table for dinner, took me out for a stroll around town after dinner, and toward evening summoned me to her room. She said, 'Olinka![8] Take this box with a ball gown and take

8. An affectionate diminutive form of the name Olga.

my carriage to the dacha on the Peterhof Road where the old man who comes here so often and who's so affectionate with you lives. It's a dress for his daughter. From today on you will fill the role of my assistant and carry out my errands. Gentlemen like it when such sweet shopgirls as you make deliveries, and they pay much more than they do to women like me. Be polite, my friend, don't be shy; know and remember that you are very pretty and learn to use your beauty—youth comes but once in a lifetime.'

"Not daring to disobey my mistress, I took the box with the dress, got in her carriage, and left on my errand with the coachman. I knew the face of the old man to whom the mistress was referring, but I didn't know his name. He ordered and bought a great deal at our shop, gave the seamstresses candy, and treated us very affectionately and courteously. It was rather late when I arrived at his dacha. The footman led me into the hall and begged me to follow him into the inner rooms. Thinking that he would lead me to the young ladies, I boldly followed him and wound up in the old man's room. He was wearing his dressing gown and sitting on the sofa, in front of which stood a small table covered with fruit, preserves, and wine.

" 'Sit over here, my angel,' he said.

" 'But where are the young ladies?' I asked in confusion, not knowing the reason why.

" 'They'll be here shortly. Sit down. Don't be so stubborn!'

"I went to sit on a chair, but the old man made me sit on the sofa next to him and began plying me with fruit and wine. I refused the wine, but out of politeness I had to take some fruit. The old man started to stroke my face; I made allowance for his age, so I took no notice of it. But when he began to take inappropriate liberties, I jumped up in indignation and tried to leave the room. The old man took hold of my hand to restrain me and said, " 'Listen, my dear; don't be a child, and don't be so stubborn. Love me, and your happiness will be secured forever!'

"I regarded him with contempt and was unable to utter a single word from an excess of indignation. The old man continued. 'I have a nasty old wife, and if you wish to sweeten my life with your love, I'll give you thirty thousand rubles initially and in a formal legal transaction I'll promise to pay you ten thousand rubles a year. You're still so young; in ten years you'll find yourself a husband, and if you'll love me during that time, I promise to give you another thirty thousand rubles in the tenth year.'

"Patience deserted me.

"'How dare you propose such disgrace and debauchery to me?' I cried. 'Clearly you've never known an honest woman in your life if you think that you can buy love for money. Aren't you ashamed at your age, and you a married man trying to corrupt an innocent girl?'

"'But, my dearest, your mistress, has already sold you to me. You owe her for your clothes and your maintenance . . .'

"'My mistress is just as despicable as you are!' I said, and pushed his arm away as he tried to block my retreat; then I shoved him so hard that he had to sit back down on the sofa. 'You dishonorable tempter!' I cried, and paused in the middle of the room and picked up a knife. 'Let me go or else I'll teach you how to harm a Russian gentlewoman! You know that I'm the daughter of a court councilor, Aleksandr Uralsky, and my mother was a general's daughter, Yevgeniya Slavina. I'm equal to you in birth, and I don't even want to compare myself to you in terms of sensibility. Let me go, you villain!' As soon as I named my parents, the old man covered his eyes with his hand and exclaimed, 'My God!' and he ran off into the other room.

"Unable to open the door and unwilling to enter the room where the old man retreated, I opened the window, jumped out into the garden, and from there unlocked the gate and ran out onto the road. I asked in the next dacha who lived in the house I'd escaped from and found out that my tempter was Grabilin, my grandmother's husband and the man who'd deprived my mother of her inheritance."

"Grabilin!" I exclaimed. "I've known that debaucher since I was a child. My God! How strange fate is!"

Olga continued, "In terror and indignation, I didn't know where to hide. I didn't want to go into town, fearing that the villain might pursue me, so I proceeded in the opposite direction. Seeing a road to the right, I followed it, without considering where it might lead, and finally wound up in the forest. I needed to rest. I sat down under a tree and started weeping bitter tears. That relieved my heart. I didn't know where to go and was afraid to walk alone on the road in the middle of a forest, so I waited until some kind man came by. Several carriages passed along the road, but no one else appeared. I began to despair and decided to spend the night there, when all of a sudden you showed up and walked directly toward me. I was afraid, but when you looked me in the eye, my fear disappeared and I felt—I don't know what, not fear but something terrible and consoling at the same time. I was afraid of men, but my heart whispered to me that I had found a magnanimous defender. I could see from your eyes that you wouldn't hurt me."

"Your heart guessed right, Olga Aleksandrovna. From now on I'm your father, brother, and defender! You may rely on God and on me for all things. As long as I'm alive, you won't need anything, and I won't demand anything from you, nothing but the favor that you believe I'm prepared to sacrifice my life for you without any hidden intentions. Do you believe me?"

She squeezed my hand and said through her tears, "I believe you, oh, noble man. God will reward you!"

I ordered the driver to drive to my good cousin Anyeta.

It was already three o'clock in the morning. Everyone was asleep in the house, but I demanded to wake the mistress. She came out to see me, trembling from fear, thinking that something extraordinary had happened to me. I said nothing about my adventure in the lonely house because Cousin Anyeta didn't know the secret of my birth, but I did relate Olinka's adventure. The kind, good Anyeta received her joyfully into her house and thanked me for bringing the unfortunate young woman to her, as if I had done her a favor. What a noble woman! I returned home in state of complete distraction.

Of course, I couldn't sleep. I was in love. Olinka had aroused my love—not that fiery all-consuming passion ignited by the enchanting Grunya but a tender, sweet love that knows no other desire than the happiness of the beloved person and doesn't produce even one single earthly thought when thinking of her beauty. Olinka seemed to me to be a bit like Grunya, but it was as if Grunya's portrait had been made showing her as an angel with an expression of modesty, which she lacked completely. Grunya's beauty was dazzling—Olinka's was touching. Grunya's glances devoured the heart and set the blood racing feverishly; Olinka's looks flooded the soul with soft delight. It seemed to me that I fell in love with Olinka so deeply because she resembled Grunya a little, but I felt that if she were completely like Grunya, I couldn't love her so passionately. Olinka seemed to be the ideal of beauty, one which had long existed in my imagination and which my heart was seeking. Hadn't I fallen in love with Grunya because she resembled somewhat the ideal in my fantasy—which I had finally found in Olinka?

Completely worn out, I fell fast asleep and was troubled by strange dreams. I dreamt that enormous serpents tried to devour me. I woke up at four in the afternoon, feeling alarmed and agitated; my heart was pounding forcefully. Just at that moment Petrov came into the room and announced, "Your Honor, some police officers are here demanding that you get dressed at once. Here they are."

One policeman explained to me that he had orders to seal my papers and take me to the local prison.

"Have you been told what I am being accused of?"

"No, but you'll soon find out."

Guessing the source of this blow, I dressed hurriedly and, leaving the two officers rummaging around in my apartment, ordered Petrov to set off for Cousin Anyeta's house to tell her what had happened and to wait for me there until this event was over.

I was assigned a separate cell in the prison and told that if I had sufficient funds, I could live as I pleased, but I had to remain confined to quarters. Cousin Anyeta and Olinka appeared an hour later. Petrov was with them. They were allowed to see me in a receiving room, in the presence of the police. Anyeta's face showed her state of mind; Olinka couldn't restrain her tears; Petrov was gloomy and grave.

"What did you do?" Anyeta asked me.

"It's an infernal plot of my relatives, which I don't completely understand, but I can guess somewhat. I swear to you on my honor that I'm innocent. Let's have patience! They won't imprison me without a trial, and then I'll learn what I'm being accused of, and undoubtedly I will clear my name."

I took some money from Petrov and asked Anyeta not to visit me in prison, in order not to endanger her own good reputation.

"You don't know women when you talk that way," replied Anyeta. "A woman's friendship begins where a man's friendship ends: that is, in misfortune, in danger. Modesty restrains a woman only in the usual course of society life, but when it's necessary to save someone, console, and assist, then rules of propriety vanish, and a woman's heart flies to the heart of the unfortunate person. No, dear friend, I won't abandon you."

"Nor will I!" said Olinka through tears. "You're my savior, my benefactor." She could say no more; sobs prevented her from speaking.

We had to part to spare the attendant the painful task of witnessing this outpouring of affection.

"Your Honor!" said Petrov. "I didn't abandon you on the battlefield, and I never will leave you, whatever happens. Let your enemies sound the alarm—Petrov will stay with you until death do us part! A Russian soldier does not desert his watch during a time of danger!"

I spent three weeks in confinement, together with both guilty and innocent men. I observed both the degradation of humanity and unfortunate virtue; I saw vices and weaknesses, and I don't want to describe them. May the dark veil cover a refuge of sorrow. I don't want to rub salt into the deep wounds of my recollections and the enumeration of crimes and vices, which, like venomous poison, corrupt the moral nature of man. I leave it to a man with a heart, tempered by experience, with a soul, cooled by contact with vice, to present a living picture of the inside of a prison. A faithful depiction of morals of the creatures expelled from society can be instructive, but it will always be abhorrent. I don't wish to inspire anyone's loathing of mankind. I'm not in a condition to carry this out. I would be unhappier than those unlucky men whom I'd like to subject to shame. Even someone else's crime lies on my heart like a stone.

Cousin Anyeta visited me every day with Olinka. Petrov left me alone only at night. I learned that in society people were afraid even to mention my name and that they reproached themselves for having known me. Only a few kind women stood up for me and didn't want to accuse me of unknown crimes

One day Anyeta was feeling unwell and was unable to visit me, and she sent Olinka alone. The attendant, whose job it was to guard us during these meetings, became convinced that there was nothing blameworthy in our conversation, so he finally allowed us to speak alone. He would usually retire to a corner of the room, but this time he left the room completely. I took advantage of the opportunity to put Olinka's feelings for me to the test.

"Olga Aleksandrovna!" I said. "You don't despise me in my humiliating situation?" She looked at me meaningfully.

"Despise you? Call me simply Olinka; I'm annoyed when you treat me too courteously, as if we weren't acquainted."

"You feel compassion for me, dear Olinka! But perhaps we'll have to part forever. . . . I have to confess to you that I can't live without you. I will die if I'm parted from you!"

"Parted from you—never!" she said, and suddenly blushed and lowered her eyes.

"I'm being pursued by powerful and wealthy people," I said, "and I, too, am a homeless orphan, like you. They're even threatening me with exile to Siberia. . . ."

"I'll follow you. I will work there and won't desert you, just as you didn't desert me!"

"Oh, God, how happy I am! Olinka, dear Olinka! I love you more than life itself—and you . . ."

Olinka threw herself around my neck and burst into tears.

"I'm yours, yours forever!" she cried, sobbing. "Perhaps I'm doing the wrong thing by revealing myself, but I'm not strong enough to rise above my feelings: I love you!"

I have never felt as happy as I was at that moment. Prison seemed to me to be a temple of bliss. I couldn't utter a word and could only squeeze Olinka's hand and bathe it with my tears.

The attendant came in, and we were forced to part. I returned to my room, locked myself in, and didn't emerge for the rest of the day. I needed solitude for this surfeit of happiness.

At last they presented me with the points of interrogation. The first accusation was that I had run away from Russia to the Kirghiz steppe, plundered and attacked lands within Russian frontiers, and robbed caravans. To justify myself, I described everything that had happened to me since my departure from Moscow, including Vorovatin's betrayal and my illness; I referred to Milovidin, Petrov, and finally, to Gayuk himself and the whole Kirghiz village. I was accused of converting and changing my religion out in the Kirghiz steppe. I referred to the priests in Moscow before whom I had fulfilled the rituals of our church after my return from the steppe. They accused me of posing as a member of the gentry and thus receiving a rank in the civil service. I confessed that Milovidin had referred to me as a gentleman to introduce me in society, but my passport didn't specify my rank; it merely stated that I was a free man. I added that I'd been awarded the rank of nobility through sacrificing my blood, was promoted to staff captain, and had received the Order of St. Vladimir. I was accused of collaboration with the cardsharps in swindling the Durindins. I confessed that I was in contact with these people through my acquaintance with Grunya but declared that I had not participated in that affair and alluded to my absence from Moscow at the time. In conclusion, I described my adventure in the secluded cottage in Yemelyanovka and Vorovatin's attempt on my life.

A week passed after I had signed a document listing all these points, and I waited impatiently for the decision about my fate. Olinka hardly left me. I confided to Cousin Anyeta my love for Olinka; she gave us her blessing and undertook to intercede on my behalf.

Chapter 32

A Savior. It's the Crime, Not the Place, That Dishonors a Man. A Just Punishment for a Villain. A Secret Revealed. Last Will and Testament. Love and Friendship. The Lawsuit. Solicitors. Secretaries. A Visit to the Judges. There Are Good People Everywhere.

Ten days had passed since my happiness began, my declaration of love for Olinka. On the morning of the eleventh day I was pacing up and down the corridor, waiting for Olinka or Petrov, with a letter from her, when all of a sudden an attendant came running down the corridor, gasping for breath, almost knocking me off my feet; coming to his senses, he exclaimed, "Oh, it's you, just the man I was looking for! Please follow me to His Excellency!"

Without giving me time to reply, he ran downstairs, repeating, "Oh, I've had it with this cleanliness! What a pain these generals are!"

Entering the reception room, I saw a man wearing a fine embroidered uniform, a ribbon over his shoulder, and two stars. I bowed and awaited his commands.

"You don't recognize me, Ivan Ivanovich?" he asked. I kept staring at him right in the face and was afraid to be mistaken.

"You don't recognize the *agitated man*?" he asked with a smile.

"Is it you, Pyotr Petrovich?" I cried, extended my hand, and stood still. He threw himself around my neck and pressed me to his heart.

"Do you remember my words," asked Pyotr Petrovich, "that truth will rise to the top, like oil? Now you see that I've been decorated with unsought-after honors, and my slanderers have been deprived of their means of harming me and becoming rich by resorting to all sorts of meanness. But let's go to your room, where you can change your clothes and then come with me. You're free, acquitted, and the entire secret of your persecution has been revealed! Don't be embarrassed or disheartened that I found you in prison. As a consolation, I'll repeat the inscription located in a Warsaw prison: 'It's the Crime, not the Place, That Dishonors a Man.'"

I rushed to my room; Pyotr Petrovich scarcely had time to enter before I was already dressed.

"Tell me, for God's sake, tell me, Pyotr Petrovich, why are they pursuing me? What am I accused of, and how am I guilty?"

"You'll find out everything, but there's no time now. Let's go to my place, and I'll explain the whole thing to you."

Along the way Pyotr Petrovich kept asking me about my time in the service, about Moscow, and about Milovidin, but I was so eager to learn the secret that I replied incoherently and abruptly. On arriving at his house, we locked ourselves in his study, and he told me the following.

"Your case was assigned to me for investigation. No sooner had I read your replies to the points of interrogation than I guessed that this was a continuation of the intrigue against you, and that you had almost been deprived of your life in Orenburg. I had long known Vorovatin to be an immoral man, capable of all kinds of wickedness. I ordered him arrested. We found bunches of copied keys, tools for making counterfeit money, forged passports and post orders, and many stolen goods in his apartment—in a word, all the evidence of his connection and participation with villains and thieves. I ordered some of the men under arrest to be interrogated, and they confessed that Vorovatin was their protector. They were confident that he had bailed them out, concealed their tools and stolen goods, provided them with passports, post orders, and told them where to commit robbery. Vorovatin was even accused of several murders. I promised to mitigate his sentence if he would be truthful in his confession, especially pertaining to you. This villain was so cowardly that he said even more than I demanded from him. As a result he lost his rank and was sentenced to exile and hard labor. Here's what I found out about you from Vorovatin.

"Your father, Prince Ivan Aleksandrovich Miloslavsky, was an honest and honorable man. Before setting off to war, he made a will in which he left 250,000 rubles to his infant, who would be delivered by the peasant girl Avdotya Petrova. The money and testament to this are with the Board of Guardians. He named his friend Count Bezpechin as executor of his will and left it to him to seek out the unfortunate victims of his weakness. Meanwhile, it stated in his will that the legal heirs could have access to this sum of money only when they presented evidence that the infant was dead and, in that case, they must pay his mother six thousand rubles a year until her death. If, in the course of thirty years, neither the peasant Avdotya Petrova nor her child could be located, then the heirs would have the right to appropriate that sum.

"Count Bezpechin dispatched his trusted agent to search for your mother, but his efforts were unsuccessful; he didn't renew them and soon forgot all about this matter. After your father's death, his huge estate was divided among his great-nephews, two Counts Nichtozhin and two Chestinskys, children of the prince's first cousins. The mother of the Counts Nichtozhin—born in Italy, although some people say she was from Pera—protested the will forcefully but dared not break it, because Count Bezpechin was still in power and the Chestinsky family didn't want to thwart the testator's will. Much time passed before Vorovatin finally made your acquaintance. Familiar with all the details of this affair through his connections with Countess Nichtozhina, and having seen your deceased father frequently, he surmised from your resemblance to the prince that you were his son and that Adelaida Petrovna was the same Avdotya Petrova whom Count Bezpechin had failed to locate. After bribing your mother's servant, he and Countess Nichtozhina searched through all her papers and things during Avdotya Petrova's absence from home, where he found a portrait of Prince Miloslavsky and several of his letters, which confirmed the truth of Vorovatin's surmises. Fearing that you might eventually learn of the legacy, my mother decided to send you away from Moscow. Vorovatin recommended the known criminal Nozhov to the countess, who undertook to murder you and your mother. The countess, despite all the deceitfulness of her character, wouldn't agree to this crime, but wishing to take possession of your money, she promised Vorovatin fifty thousand rubles if he could secure your renunciation of your inheritance through a legal document or something similar. Vorovatin clung to you like a snake to worm his way into your heart, to gain your confidence and deceive you. He tried to instill a passion for gambling in you to corrupt you, and afterwards to procure your signature on the renunciation for a mere trifle. Your love for Grunya gave him new hopes, and when you agreed to set off to Orenburg with him, he no longer doubted his success, all the more so since you were now old enough that your signature would be valid. Nozhov was sent by the countess to assist Vorovatin and to bring her the expected news about the transaction. They were ordered to make haste, because Count Bezpechin was expected in Moscow, and they were afraid that he might somehow recognize Avdotya Petrova.

"Your sudden illness upset their plans, and the villains decided to murder you, forge your signature, and get the money from the countess. Providence saved you from death. The forged document stating you'd received the money from the countess and had transferred your right to the inheritance to her didn't succeed either. Although they managed to forge your signature very skillfully, they couldn't find a notary in Orenburg who would certify the document without your personal presence. Besides, the villains quarreled among themselves, and Vorovatin turned Nozhov over to the hands of justice, while he himself escaped his accomplice's vengeance, settled in Petersburg, pretended to lead a saintly life, and sought out the friendship and protection of a person who was equal to him in villainy, although of a different kind—Prityagalov, the same person who ruined me and about whom I'll speak later. Meanwhile, the countess went abroad and lived with her children in Italy until your arrival in Petersburg. After I heard your name in society and recognized your resemblance to the late prince, she tried once more to try and deprive you of your inheritance, which by now had grown to over a million rubles. Evil people encounter each other more easily than good people. Vorovatin sought out the countess and offered his services. No longer hoping to obtain your signature by cunning, they decided to propose to you directly to sign the document without reading it, threatened to inform on you and persecute you, and tried to entice you with money. This intention was daring and rather stupid, but villains are never exposed and punished unless they commit foolish acts. Vorovatin summoned help from some lawyers who'd been expelled from the service, found an obliging notary's clerk, and played out the unsuccessful drama with you at the secluded cottage in Yemelyanovka. When you refused to sign the document, the embittered Vorovatin, afraid you might accidentally find him out in Petersburg, decided to kill you and fired at you from the bushes. Meanwhile, the denunciation against you was already prepared and submitted by one of Vorovatin's accomplices. For the investigation of such serious crimes of which you were accused, it was necessary to take decisive and immediate measures. They arrested you, and the case was put into my hands. I didn't want to meet with you because I was afraid to create suspicion that I was prejudiced, since we'd known each other before. However, I investigated the affair with all the full rigor of the law, and you were acquitted simply because you were right, not because Virtutin, who loves you, did the investigation. If you were my own son but guilty, I would have signed your sentence. That's the solution of this riddle. The countess has filed a petition for cancelling the will, citing legal ambiguity and the fact that the money bequeathed to you wasn't acquired by Prince Miloslavsky but was received by inheritance; thus, in addition to her persecution, you're burdened by a lawsuit, which may be more difficult to endure than your imprisonment by the Kirghiz. You must defend yourself, but I advise you not to present Vorovatin's evidence, because you have no written proof to implicate the countess, and the Nichtozhin family is large and extremely powerful—therefore its honor must not be compromised. Besides this does nothing to account for the legality of the testament, and it will only cause you more trouble.

"Farewell for now; get busy with your own case, find a knowledgeable lawyer, and I will advise you at my leisure. I have so much business on hand from various commissions and committees that I hardly have time to rest; and with all my desire to be useful, I must perform the greater part of my duties superficially. It's unfortunate when someone's declared to be an expert at his business; then he's forced to work instead of dozens of dullards."

After thanking Pyotr Petrovich for all his good deeds, I hastened to my kind cousin Anyeta or, to speak more correctly, to Olinka. She already knew from Petrov about my liberation and stood at the window, impatiently glancing all around.

My secret would soon become public in the lawsuit, and so I intended to reveal everything to Anyeta and Olinka. I confess it was painful to acknowledge the faults of my parents and my mother's lineage. But Anyeta received the news in its true colors and even congratulated me that princely blood was flowing in my veins. She assured me that from the time of our first acquaintance, she'd noticed signs of a higher lineage. Olinka said nothing at all. It would have been all the same to her if I'd been the son of Prince Miloslavsky's coachman, because she loved me deeply and true love never considers one's parentage. I begged Cousin Anyeta to spread news of my adventures, my lineage, and my lawsuit in society.

"If you want this to be made public," said Anyeta, "then you should ask me *not* to broadcast it but to tell it as a secret to a few women; then the news will spread faster than by means of any newspapers. The word *secret* will compel every woman to share the news with her acquaintances also as a secret, and it will make its way around town and be repeated into every ear. Women think that a secret is nothing other than *news* that should be whispered with a formal precaution: 'I am telling you this as a secret; I heard it in confidence,' and so on. You see that I don't spare myself—that's a tribute to friendship."

Taking Petrov along with me, I returned to Demutov's Inn to rent lodgings there again. The doorman told me that some travelers from Moscow had arrived and were asking about my whereabouts and about Petrov. I sent him to find out who the Moscow acquaintances were while I remained standing at the gate. I suddenly heard a cry on the staircase. Milovidin came running out and threw himself into my arms.

"Where are you coming from, and what are you doing here?" I asked.

"I've come from home, from the Crimea, from the embrace of my wife and son, to see you, my friend, and to help you!" cried Milovidin.

He took hold of my arm, pulled me to the stairs, and said, "Let's go see your mother."

"What, is she here?"

"Of course, she is. She didn't know anything about your misfortune because you didn't mention it in any of your letters, and she didn't want to believe the rumors. . . ."

"I understand."

"But, after receiving the news from Cousin Anyeta, I came rushing to see you, drove to Moscow to visit your mother, and when I told her about your imprisonment, she begged me to take her back with me."

I shook Milovidin's hand and thanked him not in words alone for his tender part in my fate. Genuine feeling is short on words.

In the meantime we had climbed the stairs and were already in the rooms; my dear mother's tears moistened my cheeks. After weeping and rejoicing, I told her in detail all that had happened to me and explained the secret of my persecution. When I got to the last will and testament, my mother was deeply affected and said, "I was not mistaken about his soul! He thought about me, thought about the unfortunate pledge of our love. But I became unworthy of his heart and his memory. . . ."

She burst into tears, and we had difficulty consoling her. I didn't want to conceal my love and confessed everything to my mother and my friend. They didn't contradict me but merely asked that I not rush into marriage and get to know Olinka better.

Two weeks passed after my release. My mother went nowhere but church; Cousin Anyeta and Olinka visited her every day. Milovidin honored his pledge and didn't appear in society. He would spend the morning reading newspapers and journals, strolling, and visiting only

Cousin Anyeta and Pyotr Petrovich; for diversion he'd go to the theater. On Pyotr Petrovich's advice I sent his butler to Byelorussia to locate my birth certificate and to find out how I'd ended up in Mr. Gologordovsky's house. Meanwhile he assigned one of the experienced officials from his office to familiarize me with the character and behavior of every agent, from whom I selected the most distinguished and arranged a meeting, each at a different hour. I had to endure intolerable boredom from six o'clock in the evening until midnight, but this was only my first experience with the law. I didn't yet know that in this labyrinth every step was accompanied with aggravation and, as in an illness, when the body is covered with wounds, every turn, every movement produces unbearable pain.

This official, Fyedosy Savelich Kavykin, had been working since his childhood; he was familiar with all sorts of underhanded tricks and knew by heart the biography of every official and advocate. Kavykin's head contained a lexicon of chicanery. He was a man of cheerful disposition and occupied his free time collecting scandalous anecdotes from law courts. He was very glad he could show off his knowledge in this case and be useful to his superior's friend.

From the agents invited, the first one to appear was Mr. Durachinsky, a man of middle age with enormous side-whiskers and dressed foppishly. He wanted to play the role of a dandy, a clever, educated man of the world, but his curved neck, half-familiar tone of voice, and manner of expressing himself revealed his lower class origins.

"Excuse me if I'm late. I work in the service in a very high position and am busy with cases. Besides, I have private matters, connections, and acquaintances! Now I'm coming from the English Club, where there are three senators waiting for me to play whist. I'm a member of the English Club, and that's an important distinction! Only the most honorable and distinguished people are voted in, well-known people with a reputation—so you can imagine what an honor it is to be a member! I play cards in the Club every day for high stakes with important people, settle business in an informal manner in the reading room, collect a supply of news, and share a morsel or two of my own. I advise you to maneuver your way into membership. It would be very useful for you. There you will get acquainted with everyone worth knowing, be treated to champagne, invited to dinner, conduct business . . . True, I wasn't born to deal with such matters: I come from a count's family . . . but circumstances demand it!"

Durachinsky would have continued talking in this incoherent way until evening, but I passed him a brief about my case and asked him to read it when he was alone; then I went into a third room where Kavykin and Milovidin had agreed to wait for me.

"What do you think of this daring person?" asked Kavykin.

"Simply a ridiculous braggart," I replied.

"He's a member of the Lithuanian lower middle class, ennobled by his apparel," said Kavykin. "He was a boy—that is, a servant of Count Pianotti's, who taught him how to read and write, and by his special, incomprehensible kindness, was subsequently made his agent. He deceived poor Lithuanian nobles with his importance in Petersburg, and officials with his importance in the provinces; Durachinsky managed to climb out of the mud, worm his way into the service, and he continues to intercede—that is, to deceive and take money from clients and give it to no one. He's so stupid that he can't write letters in any language, but he plays whist, loses, brags that he has large estates—and as a result we tolerate him among decent people. Get rid of him without beating around the bush."

I returned to Durachinsky, took back the brief, and asked him to leave me, saying that I was busy now and would give him my answer later.

After Durachinsky, there came another little figure, the personification of chicanery: a short, grimy, withered old man wearing rags. He stood there about a quarter of an hour unwrapping his outer clothes, coughed, and finally cleared his throat; then he announced in his heavy Byelorussian dialect, that he was formerly a chamberlain in the late Polish court and his name was Pan Kryuchkotvorsky.

"If you want to win your case," he said, coughing, "take me. I have all unfair cases in my hands; if I don't win, I will drag it out so that your adversaries will demand an end to the matter and give you what you want."

I put my brief in his hands, sat him down in an armchair, and went to see Kavykin, who said to me, "He's a well-known snitch who for the last fifty years has raged, like the plague, in law courts; in his old age, he's settled in Petersburg. In spite of the fact that he's dressed like a beggar, he has considerable property and capital. Would you believe that this miser has pocketed the dowries of three wives, whom he's outlived? When he draws up his marriage contracts, he always makes an agreement with his wife that the estate will be left to the one who lives longer. Since he's had consumption for the last thirty years, of course his young wives catch the infection from him and succumb. He's like the mythical Python,[1] poisoning his prey and then devouring it. Away with him! Away, so that by his presence he won't pollute the air!"

I got rid of Kryuchkotvorsky the same way I'd gotten rid of Durachinsky.

After him there appeared a large, fat, elderly man. He burst into the room like a wild boar, darted his wolfish eyes at me, and roared his greetings in such a tone that I thought he was uttering curses.

"Well, what's the matter? Allow me, I'll tell you how to begin. The main question is, is there any money?"

I gave him the brief and asked him to read it, but he refused.

"I'm not going to work for nothing and read other people's nonsense. Money, money, here take the documents!"

I asked him to wait and went back to Kavykin. As soon as I uttered the name of the solicitor, Milovidin exclaimed, "Bah, he's Mr. Gologordovsky's renowned agent, Pan Strukchavsky Khapushkevich, a notorious swindler who has exchanged his faith several times, been exiled for polygamy, and debarred from practicing law."

"He's been banished from Petersburg several times," replied Kavykin, "and always finds his way back to the capital, like a fox to the henhouse. Out with the swindler! Out with him!"

"But tell me, please, why are there so many Polish solicitors here?" I asked. "And why do you treat them so badly?"

"A landowner with a good name and property doesn't move to a new city to live as a solicitor," replied Kavykin. "Honest and skilled lawyers in the Polish provinces have sufficient means at home not only for their own needs but for making their fortunes; in addition, they enjoy general respect. And so, only the chancery clerks, legal assistants, and adventurers of all sorts travel because it is the easiest and most profitable profession, the basis of which is lying and deceiving creditors. They take money from landowners, as if to give it to officers of the court; but they don't give it to anyone and do nothing but slander both the innocent and the guilty. These solicitors for a long time disgraced the honor of the entire Polish nation, because Russian officials, who had never been to the Polish provinces, judged everyone by these worthless examples. Now this has all changed. Many well-educated and principled

1. In Greek mythology, Python was the serpent, sometimes represented as a medieval-style dragon, living at the center of the earth.

Poles have entered the service in Petersburg, and by their behavior they have offset the poor opinion of their fellow countrymen. Among the solicitors there are also some very good and respected people (although very few), and they, poor people, must suffer for the rest! But go ahead and drive out Pan Strukchavsky."

I proceeded in the same way I had with the first two.

After him came Titular Councilor Zagadchenko, a native of Little Russia. After the initial greetings he said, "We people of Little Russia are simple, honest people; we love the truth, and we take the straight road. I'll tell you candidly what's good and what's bad."

I gave him the brief and returned to Kavykin.

"This is a man whom I don't know, nor does the devil," he said. "Some people speak ill of him; others see him as a knowledgeable and a diligent solicitor. He's won many cases."

I repeated Zagadchenko's words to him.

"It's a common trick of the people of Little Russia to assume an appearance of simplicity, Among them I know many honest and good people, who have never deceived or offended anyone, but I don't know one who would allow himself to be deceived or who would forgive an insult done to him. You know there's a German proverb that applies to clever people: *He hears the grass growing.* I won't explain, but merely state that in Little Russia they've found out *how the grass grows.* Russians, Poles, Bohemians, and other Slavic tribes on occasion like to show off their wit. Only the Little Russians brag about their simplicity and their coarseness. Whenever a man gets a reputation of being *subtle* and artful, he's no longer able to make use of those qualities. His subtlety consists in being considered simple and coarse. Remember that in Turkey wealthy Rayahs pretend to be poor,[2] in order to enjoy their riches: the same thing occurs with intelligence. But enough about this. Dismiss Zagadchenko. We'll see what to do with him later. I'll inquire about him. Perhaps we'll figure him out sometime!"

Finally came a Russian agent. Pafnuty Sidorovich Ruboperin announced definitively that he would not take the case until he had read the documents and come to an agreement with me concerning compensation for his services. I gave him the brief and returned to Kavykin, who said to me, "This fellow knows his business: he's a first-rate writer, and he is inexhaustible, but don't give him any money

2. A generic name for non-Muslim subjects of the Ottoman Empire. Though mainly Christians, Rayahs were governed according to Ottoman law.

beforehand. Settle with him when he appears on an empty stomach, because according to old custom he tends to bury his talent! I advise you to accept Ruboperin. You won't find anyone better."

I told Pafnuty Sidorovich that he should draft an agreement and power of attorney and, in anticipation of the arrival of my messenger's arrival from Byelorussia, I set to work on drafting a petition and a brief. We parted, and I was so exhausted that I scarcely had time to undress before falling asleep.

Milovidin, in spite of all my urging, didn't want to return home and decided to wait, at least until the court case began. I'd already been ordered to produce proof of my birth; I waited impatiently for the return of my messenger. Finally, two months later, Pyotr Petrovich's steward returned and brought my birth certificate and a witness, the Yid Iosel, Mr. Gologordovsky's former tenant. Iosel had been a wealthy tax farmer, had become impoverished in his old age, and taught reading and writing to the children of a new innkeeper. Smuggling had ruined him, and some of his accomplices had sent him to jail. That was how I escaped from the murderers' hands and wound up in Mr. Gologordovsky's household.

When the midwife and the Yid doctor found out about my mother's flight and learned that she'd found a protector, they gathered their belongings and ran away, taking me with them. They didn't want to kill me, assuming that in case their place of refuge was discovered, they could deny my mother's accusations, and after returning me, they could put an end to the whole matter. The Yid doctor went to see his cousin Iosel and, after spending a week there, proceeded further, without revealing the reason for his journey; instead he devised a story that some wealthy Pan had invited him to settle down as a village doctor. He confessed, however, that an officer had entrusted him with the infant, given birth to by a peasant girl who died in childbirth, and asked Iosel to give me to some peasant girl, and he paid for one year in advance. The midwife herself brought me to a Russian priest and ordered him to baptize me, giving me the name of Ivan. When I began to crawl, the poor peasant girl—my nurse, who'd lost her husband—hired herself out in another village and abandoned me, following Iosel's advice, in Mr. Gologordovsky's house. The matter was clear, confirmed by entry in the record of births, in which it was written that I was the illegitimate son of Prince Ivan Aleksandrovich Miloslavsky and Avdotya Petrova. Iosel told me that the Yid doctor had drowned along with his entire family and their midwife while crossing a river in a dilapidated ferryboat.

"Your lawsuit is just," Ruboperin said to me after seeing my birth certificate. "And you'll win it, if you try hard and make an effort. Without that, you'll fail."

I came to an understanding with the secretary by means of official arithmetic, which I'd learned in Moscow from a secretary, Moshnin's friend. The secretary embraced me, kissed me, and even started weeping from compassion, having heard about the persecutions that I had undergone. Not one science can soften hearts the way practical arithmetic does! The secretary assured me that I would undoubtedly win the case and swore on his life, honor, and children that he'd sooner agree to die on the spot than have to countersign a decision against me.

Pyotr Petrovich advised me to distribute briefs to all the judges and try to explain my case to each one. Ruboperin excelled in the composition of a brief: he laid out the matter clearly, briefly, and based on laws. After hiring a carriage, I set out first thing in the morning to distribute my documents.

Upon entering the waiting room of the first judge, I had to ask the footman to announce me ten times and could scarcely get a reply from him. The servant grumbled, saying that it wasn't his job and I should wait for the valet. In spite of my Hussar's uniform, before which Turks trembled in fear and to which brave Russian soldiers paid tribute, the judge's servants scarcely deigned to look at me and didn't want to speak with me. At last, when I declared that I would enter the judge's study without being announced, the valet proceeded unhurriedly to his master; when he returned, he said rudely, "Go in!"

The judge, Mr. Dremotunov, was an elderly man and, in the old-fashioned manner, powdered his gray hair and wore it in a braid. He was sitting in a white dressing gown in front of a mirror, and the barber, in a soiled gray jacket, was combing his hair.

"Have a seat, sir," the judge said to me. I gave him a copy of the brief and sat down.

"Be so kind as to read it to me yourself, and I will listen," said the judge. I bowed to him again and began to read in a loud, distinct, slow voice.

"Good, good, it's correct!" the judge kept repeating. "Senka, comb my crown, that's right, good, gently. Your case, sir, seems just to me."

Suddenly Senka accidentally pulled the judge's hair, and he cried, "You scoundrel! You've torn my wig off!"

Then, turning to me, his face flushed with pain and anger, he said, "Chicanery, sir, mere chicanery! All your reasons aren't worth a thing. . . . Ah, that villain Senka. What pain he's caused me!"

Meanwhile I stopped reading.

"Why aren't you reading?"

I started reading again.

"All right, Senka. That's the way, gently, now comb my right side-whiskers. Splendid, splendid!" he said, turning to me. "The case is clear, fair, and just; the law is certainly in our favor. . . . Senka, you rascal you, you're mauling me—that's not a rake, it's a comb! Tricks, sir, attempts to deceive, chicanery!" he exclaimed again, and I stopped once more. The judge pushed Senka aside; resting for a moment, he ordered Senka to continue work and me to keep reading. Fortunately Senka completed the process of combing successfully; the judge stood up, wiped the powder from his face, and said, "Leave the brief; I shall examine the original documents in court. It seems to me that your case is just."

From my joy, I gave Senka ten rubles in the hall and left the other servants to repent their rudeness. Mr. Dremotunov was one of the older lawyers who had made his fortune; at one time he was in control of everything, but in his old age he served from mere ambition and had access to the votes of several old friends.

Another judge, Mr. Formin, whom I knew from society, received me politely; but when I showed him the brief, he shook his head and said, "What use is this? We don't judge by the words of our petitioners. I've been a judge for *twenty-five years*, and I know that all petitioners spout nonsense in their briefs."

"My case is stated here with citations to the laws and the original documents," I replied. "Most likely my opponent has done the same. Please be so kind as to check our statements with the original, and our references with the laws, and then you'll see who's right and who's guilty."

"I've been handling cases for *twenty-five years*, and I know what these briefs are!" cried the judge.

"Our briefs replace the lawyer's opinions," I objected.

"It seems to me that without reading the private briefs of the case, it's impossible to understand it. You must listen to the petitioner as you do to a patient. And just as the skillful doctor, considering the words of the patient and the symptoms of his illness, learns its cause and nature, judges, after considering the evidence on both sides, learn all the strong and weak points of the case."

"Theory, sir, all theory!" exclaimed the judge. "I've been practicing for *twenty-five years*, hearing cases, and I know *everything* I need to know.

It's not the petitioners but the chancellery that states all the particulars of a case and discovers the strong and weak points."

"But the chancellery, with all of its cases, might occasionally overlook something or make a mistake; besides, there are real people in the chancellery, not angels. . . ."

"What do you mean by that?" asked the judge angrily. "I've had *twenty-five years* of experience with the chancellery, and I'm convinced that petitioners' complaints against the chancellery are baseless! But don't despair," he added, in a calmer voice. "We'll take a close look at your case."

Still I left my brief on the table and said, "Don't read it, but take it: it eases a petitioner's heart. I can't presume that you're so hardhearted as to refuse to listen to an unfortunate man. If you don't read my brief, it's like driving a beggar away from your door." After saying this, I bid him farewell and left. In the entrance I heard the judge exclaim, "For *twenty-five years* . . ."

The judge's crafty servant, after giving me my overcoat, said with a grin, "Our master's making a mistake in his calculations: fifteen years have passed since he ended his twenty years as a judge."

This judge was a good and honest man, but all his life he'd engaged in things he wasn't supposed to do. In court he thought about books, and while reading, he thought about court; as a guest he talked about cases, while in the office he talked about diversions. He always spoke well and did nothing; if he had done even a thousandth part of what he talked about so eloquently, then he would have been a useful person. He loved honest and clever people and associated with them, but he was dominated by scoundrels, whom he despised but whom he was too weak to drive away or to disobey. He was a good man but a genuine zero, which had meaning only if placed after a number.

After seeing him, I went to see Mr. Chuvashin, who was known to be a great man of business and a giant of justice. He was neither a rogue nor a fool, but thanks to his father, having attained a high rank in his youth, he'd gone crazy with excessive self-esteem and believed wholeheartedly that he'd absorbed the sum total of human wisdom. Educated with foreigners and living only in high society, gathering his knowledge of various subjects only from foreign books, he didn't know Russia and regarded it only through the prism of foreign ideas. In his old age his head was chocked full of theories, foreign laws, and legal codes, together with what knowledge he'd picked up about Russia in passing; from all this there emerged such chaos that the good old man, in spite of his best intentions, constantly committed stupidities. For a long time people in society didn't know him well and misinterpreted his good intentions as great deeds. At last they found out that he was nothing more than a bookcase of half-read books turned upside down!

He received me in a civil and friendly manner. God grant him health for that. But when I began to explain my case to him, he almost drove me crazy with his observations. According to his rules of old jurisprudence, women and children were always right even if their husband or father admitted that the case was unjust; so, inasmuch as he'd already been contacted by the Countess Nichtozhina and her friends, he could never persuade himself that I would be in the right. When I cited laws, he said that cases of this kind should be judged not according to law but according to conscience; when I was trying to prove that according to conscience I should receive the money left me by my father in his will, he assured me that according to the law he didn't support my claim. I pointed out the laws in my favor; he said that he knew the law and produced piles of quotations from Jeremy Bentham and other English legal scholars and theoreticians.[3] Wishing to demonstrate his knowledge of the law, he began to show off his memory to me: instead of edicts he offered pandects; instead of English laws he cited the Code of Tsar Aleksey Mikhailovich and others.[4] I concluded my visit and left with a heavy heart. Up to that time I'd never had any business with him and considered him to be a great man; now I was convinced that public opinion could be mistaken just as private individuals could. Chuvashin was an obvious supporter of all *family* bribe takers, and he defended them wherever and however he could. Many bribe takers got married deliberately to enjoy his protection, and for that they wrote his opinions, which he passed off as his own. Oh, people, people! Chuvashin, who had a good heart, did mischief from mere vanity and desire—to be known as a Publicola.[5]

The large majority of judges received my brief in silence and, with a nod of the head, indicated that I should withdraw. Others made me relate my adventures in the Kirghiz steppe and elsewhere and didn't want to hear details of the case. A few of them excused themselves,

3. Jeremy Bentham (1748–1832) was an English philosopher, jurist, and social reformer.

4. Tsar of Russia from 1645 until his death in 1676.

5. One of four Roman aristocrats who led the overthrow of the monarchy, and became a Roman consul in 509 B.C.E.

saying that they were busy with their own cases. Still others complained about their poverty, or the difficulty of getting a loan, and congratulated me on my claim to a million rubles. In a few places I was received very rudely, and in others—with such pride and arrogance that I lost my patience and even refused to play the onerous role of a petitioner. True, I did find noble and clever judges, who consoled me with their friendly reception and whose known candor comforted me regarding their colleagues. Within a week I'd made the rounds of almost all of my judges; I was more exhausted from this round of visits than an entire campaign against the Turks; I even fell ill from aggravation. "Dear God, if it is Your sacred will that I have to experience suffering in life, please send me illness, captivity, poverty, but save me from lawsuits!"

Meanwhile Milovidin received news from his wife that his only son was ill. I begged my friend to return home, promising to visit him right after the end of the case, which, counter to the usual situation, should conclude fairly soon since the opposing side, strong and wealthy, wished it so just as much as I did.

When my suit was ready to be discussed, the secretary secretly showed me the report he'd drafted, with the assurance that it was favorable to me, and an outline of the decision. I got caught in a noose from this unnecessary candor, but Ruboperin rescued me from that. His friend had shown him another report and another outline of the decision, favorable to Countess Nichtozhina, which the secretary was intending to show to the judges. I told Pyotr Petrovich about this, and he, with his influence, removed the outspoken secretary on the very day of the trial. My case wound up in the hands of a good person.

"Sir, I am a poor man," he said to me, "but I will not sell my conscience. Nichtozhina proposed to give me twenty-five thousand rubles. I confess, I'm a sinful mortal. I would have taken the money if her cause had been just, but I won't take a kopeck to do the wrong thing. You yourself are not wealthy now, but if God rewards you, then perhaps you'll remember my children."

Although in strict fairness, much might be said against this kind of honesty, still, considering the circumstances, I rejoiced that I had found such a good man. At last my case was to be heard.

Chapter 33

Usurers. The End of My Lawsuit. Supplement to Pyotr Petrovich's Account. The Fate of Literary Men. Trouble from Hypocrites. Persons Who Curry Favor. Marriage. The Grandee's Kindness. The Course of Affairs. The Incursion of Relatives. Retirement. All's Well That Ends Well. Conclusion.

My money had run out; I didn't want to sell the diamond clasp that Petrov had taken from the turban of the Aga I'd captured, because I considered it the property of my loyal servant and friend and planned to purchase it from him as a souvenir of my victory. I could have borrowed money from Pyotr Petrovich, Cousin Anyeta, or Milovidin, but I didn't want to burden them, so I decided to pawn the diamond clasp. Ruboperin took me to the moneylenders. We entered a small shop, no more than a few square feet, crammed to the ceiling with tattered old books in all languages, ancient and modern, covered with dust and spiderwebs. In the far corners of this shop dozed a skinny tomcat and a shopboy, side by side. Ruboperin woke the sleepy sentinel with a flick of his fingers on his nose and asked him where Tarasych was.

"Well, as you know, in the mornings he makes the rounds of courtrooms and offices, but it's almost time for him to come back to the shop."

"How can the landlord of this miserly hole have any money?" I asked Ruboperin.

"He has three hundred thousand in cash, no more and no less," replied Ruboperin. "This shop is nothing more than a front, a den for meetings and negotiations, and a sign of Taras Tarasovich Kashcheyev's residence. It's a pity that today isn't Saturday—the day of reckoning and payment of weekly debts among the merchants; you'd see how the shopkeepers and owners of rich shops and stores hang around here, and how they wink at Taras Tarasovich and invite him to visit their shops. Kashcheyev is a lenient and kind fellow: he takes only three kopecks per ruble per month on a pledge from someone he doesn't know, and for loyal customers he even lends on credit. But let's go elsewhere; we'll see how much he'll give you and how he'll evaluate your pledge."

We entered the flea market and in one booth, cobbled together from old boards, we found a middle-aged man, engaged in reading *The History of Vanka-Cain.*[1] On shelves in the booth lay old nails, brass buckles, buttons, pomade, apothecary jars, pieces of chalk, vitriol, leather straps, broken cups and plates—in a word, all the riches of a refuse pit.

"Greetings, Pafnutich!" said Ruboperin, tapping the seated man on the shoulder.

"Hello, Your Honor!"

"Well, do you have any money?"

"What money is there today, sir? Trade goes badly!"

I couldn't restrain myself from laughing upon hearing this complaint. Pafnutich repeated it, imitating merchants who continually grow richer yet complain about the decline in trade.

"Pardon me, friend," I said, "and just when were your goods in demand? Are you really also going to complain about tariffs and customs?"

"Why shouldn't I complain when wealthy merchants complain, too? After all, small-scale retail trade follows in the footsteps of wholesale trade. When wholesale advances, so does retail; when wholesale retreats, retail follows suit."

"Enough talking, Pafnutich," said Ruboperin. "Here's a diamond clasp; diamond merchants valued it at fifteen thousand rubles; how much will you give me for it as a pledge?"

"So diamond merchants valued it!" exclaimed Pafnutich. "Go try to sell it to them; you'll see that they won't give you even half that sum. First tell me how long you want to keep the money; the price of the item depends on that—that is, the percentage of interest."

"A month, maybe two," I replied.

---

1. Vanka-Cain (Ivan Osipov, 1718–ca. 1756) was a robber and a Moscow detective who became a legendary hero of thieves' adventures and daring.

"That's very short," replied Pafnutich. "I can't give you more than three thousand rubles."

I grew angry.

"You're worse than a Yid!" I cried. "You deserve to be thrown into the Neva with your tricks."

"Why are you getting angry?" asked Pafnutich calmly. "It's a free country. If you don't like it, go to someone else or to a pawn shop."

I took Ruboperin by the arm and left in annoyance.

"It's no use getting into a fit of temper," Ruboperin said to me. "It's only bargaining. If he offered three thousand at first, he'll probably raise it up to eight or nine. Moneylenders are glad to lend out more money, so that they can earn a higher percentage, but they bargain out of indomitable habit, to pretend they're giving out of their kindness alone. That Pafnutich is a devil, not a man. He's evaded criminal court several times."

While I conversed with Ruboperin, we returned to Kashcheyev's shop and found him examining his bills of exchange and receipts.

"Well, Tarasych," said Ruboperin, "Demonstrate that you're a good man. We need fifty thousand rubles; count it out and we'll give you a whole sack full of diamonds."

"Where will I get so much money?" Kashcheyev replied, sighing and looking askance at me. "Times are bad! But if you have the items, perhaps I can gather the money from friends."

"I was joking," said Ruboperin, "just joking! You always pretend to be poor. Here's the thing: we have an item worth fifteen thousand, and we need ten thousand in cash."

"That's a lot, but we'll see. Would you please come with me to my house? You know I live not far away from here."

We followed Kashcheyev to his house. He was unmarried; only an old cook and a retired invalid guarded his lodgings, not daring to venture even a step from his door. Three rooms were arranged in good order; in the bedroom one whole wall was covered with sacred images in gold and silver frames; an icon lamp was burning in front of them. An enormous iron bureau stood next to the bed. Kashcheyev begged us to show him the item; he turned it over and over in his hands, haggled for a long time, and finally gave us nine thousand rubles plus three kopecks per ruble in percentage for each month, on the condition that I kept the money for half a year. He left a pledge with the following content: "I, the undersigned, *sold* a diamond clasp to the merchant Kashcheyev for the sum of 10,620 rubles, which I have the right to buy back for that sum during the course of six months; if it's not bought back at the end of that time, I forfeit my right to redeem the item at all." At first I didn't agree to write down that I'd sold it, but Ruboperin persuaded me that this was merely a formality, and that Kashcheyev was an honest man.

"If you please, sir, don't be afraid of us. You'll incur a calamity if you get involved with other people engaging in the same business. A signed agreement is necessary to *include the percentage* and to vindicate myself in case of any complaint. It sometimes happens that when payment is due, we're charged with extortion. So you see, we must protect ourselves."

If I were angry with my readers and wanted to punish them, I'd describe in detail, filling several volumes, the course of my lawsuit, which after several months almost resulted in my falling victim to consumption, while my readers would no doubt be forced to toss the book away. I'm surprised how people endure such torments over the course of many years; and I'm even more surprised that there exist fans of lawsuits! But the strangeness of human nature is unfathomable! There are people who, despite being in good health, are treated by doctors all their lives, lose their health, and die. It's the same for people who think they will grow rich through lawsuits; they waste their last possessions and finish their lives in poverty. But a lawsuit sometimes comes unexpectedly, like an illness; then reason demands that one reject slander by means of the laws and use medicine to overcome the illness. One is in luck, if the means help instead of leading to exhaustion.

In spite of all Countess Nichtozhina's strenuous efforts and those of her friends and acquaintances, Providence saved me; the case was resolved in my favor—and I suddenly received a million rubles.

I loved society because I didn't know what to do at home. In addition, I was very well treated in Moscow, and to a certain extent I was obligated to appear in homes in which I was regarded as a regular visitor. I myself never tried to seek others' favor; Milovidin and Cousin Anyeta continued working on my behalf. But in Petersburg Cousin Anyeta, who'd already passed her prime, didn't have much influence; I didn't have my own advisor and withdrew altogether from society, partly from false shame, and partly not to seem like I was searching for patronage, which in truth I had no hope of finding. A large number of people who occupied high places in society were friends or connections of civil servants, and nothing is more unbearable or insulting to a sensitive person involved in a lawsuit, than to appear in society and be received with general coldness, which is certain to be the case at the mere mention of the *petitioner*'s name. Everyone avoids being alone with the person bringing the suit, afraid that he'll be asking for assistance or about entreaty. Everyone runs away from him as from a leper, fearing that he might start talking about his case or begin speaking ill of judges and complaining about injustice. Having seen this in other instances, I didn't want to play the role of Lazarus in society and preferred to keep away from high society. I was happy in our small circle, the adornment of which was Olinka. My mother came to love her so much that she couldn't go without seeing her even for a day. Olinka stayed with my mother from morning to evening and returned to Cousin Anyeta's house only at night.

After I won my case, over the course of three days, I received so many visiting cards and invitations to dinner and evening gatherings that it would have been impossible to satisfy all these desires in three months time and pay personal visits. On looking through the cards, I was surprised to find the name Grabilin. Every day I prepared to begin my visits, yet every day I never found the time to do so. Time passed so quickly in Olinka's presence that I had no time to spare.

Pyotr Petrovich invited me for an evening to speak privately about my hopes and plans. He already knew about my love for Olinka and advised me to get married as soon as possible, if I was certain of our mutual love.

"Dear friend," he said. "Happiness comes down from heaven like the dew; sorrow comes like a thunderstorm. Make use of the moment, which is favorable to your happiness, and refresh your soul with pure love. There is no higher pleasure in life than true love and friendship. The soul to which they belong is capable of everything good and great. But these blessings are not given to everyone, even if the person's soul is capable of feeling them. I too have loved and been loved, but death robbed me of my happiness; now I'm already old and can no longer think about love; I seek pleasure in friendship alone."

Just then the doctor arrived and, after saying a few words to Pyotr Petrovich, withdrew to the inner rooms.

"Do you have any patients in this house?" I asked. "I'm surprised that you summoned this man: although he's known in society as *skillful*, he's also considered *unlucky*."

Pyotr Petrovich smiled.

"It's my rule to confer with those doctors, who are known as both *skillful* and *unlucky*, but to avoid those who are called lucky, yet unskilled. We're in the habit of calling the first doctor at the beginning of an illness or keeping this doctor on a yearly basis for less money, and of bringing in a well-known and experienced doctor as a last resort, when we don't really need a doctor but a priest. As a result it happens more often that the best medics must be witnesses to the patient's death; meanwhile the relatives can place all the blame on the doctor."

"Who's sick in your house? I thought that you lived alone."

"I've undertaken to raise the orphan of one of my distant relatives; he's now ill. This young man is very talented, but he distresses me with his unfortunate passion for poetry and literature. He wants to be a writer!"

"Forgive me, Pyotr Petrovich, is that what's distressing you? I confess that I too have a desire to write, and I never thought that such an enlightened person as you are, Pyotr Petrovich, would consider an ability and a passion to become a writer as a misfortune! Tell me, how would governments and peoples become famous if it weren't for writers? What would become of victories, with all the wise institutions, if writers didn't preserve them for posterity? They are proclaimers of popular illustriousness, teachers of entire generations, representatives of their fatherland in the gathering of men, chosen from the entire human race to establish the rights of reason and virtue! Where are the names, where are the heroic deeds of these followers of fortune, swelled with arrogance, who during their lives enjoyed both wealth and power? They've disappeared into oblivion, while the names of writers, despised by the proud favorites of fortune in life and even persecuted—those names are preserved with respect; they have become the property of a nation, its fame. Pyotr Petrovich, count the names of all the great men who, while not writers themselves, are still remembered by posterity. You'll see that they rose to the surface of the waters of the River Lethe,[2] only because engaging in other occupations, they loved and protected the sciences, arts, and literature. That's the first condition leading to fame—for sciences, arts, and literature are gifts of the word fame. Without them fame is mute."

Pyotr Petrovich sat there, leaning his elbows on the table, sunk in deep thought. At last he spoke. "That's all true, dear Vyzhigin, but you've considered only the future and haven't peeked into the present. I myself am free to roam on a frail boat across the stormy sea, but I don't have the right to advise someone else to do it, and I must point out the danger to him. Look around; what do authors mean in society? The designation *writer* alone, especially *poet*, is worse than a bad certificate of service. A writer is a synonym for someone incapable of

2. In Greek mythology, the Lethe was one of the five rivers of the underworld of Hades, where all those who drank from it experienced complete forgetfulness.

human action; and in addition, among us it's still the custom to place the writer on the same level as comedians, buffoons, and other entertainers. If a writer is bad, he becomes the laughing stock of the crowd; if he's mediocre, he's subject to oblivion; if he's gifted with intelligence and unusual talent, he becomes the object of envy, slander, and persecution, precisely because people willingly forgive everything except superiority of intellect, to which each one has claims; the dumber they are, the more they try to claim it. A writer's duty is to tell the truth, and printed truth wounds the heart more than spoken truth. Sort through, in turn, all the writers who dared speak the truth to blinded humanity; you'll see that all of them are better known for their misfortunes than for their creations. Estranged from society, in which they're also feared, they are like schoolboys who dread the presence of their strict teacher; they're not privy to matters to which they are not admitted, for they are considered incompetent; they spend their days and nights in arduous intellectual labor, only to receive the ingratitude of their fellow countrymen and barely earn their daily bread! No one considers the income of a bribe taker but is always surprised if a writer doesn't live by begging. True, it sometimes happens that a powerful hand watches over some fortunate writers and that some of them, either through kinship or through connections completely unrelated to literature, possess independence and a voice in society, but these are exceptions, which cannot serve as examples. Even a writer significant in society, received in the highest circles, is subjected to extraordinary unpleasantness. He would like to relax in society and forget his work in his study, but no! Every ignoramus who's happened to read only one book in his life suffocates him and exhausts him with his views on literature, in order to show off his learning! No, dear Vyzhigin, I don't advise you to embark on a career in literature: it's a most slippery and dangerous path. And to write nonsense, flattery, to praise lethargy, and to pour water through a sieve, is a path unworthy of a man with intellect and a soul."

I didn't want to argue and asked Pyotr Petrovich to relate the reason for his own persecution and, finally, his release from exile. He fulfilled my wish and told me the following.

"In every profession and condition there is an exterior side and the reverse. A contagious disease rages in a career of service in all governments, which is called *a desire to curry favor*. As a result of this illness a great deal of evil occurs as well as a large number of injustices; it is manifested in false enthusiasm for one's work and unlimited *devotion to one's supervisor*. A person who's succumbed to this ailment attempts to present everything he didn't conceive of as bad and every person who stands out from the crowd by his talents, zeal, and insubordination to his way of thinking as ill intentioned. Disfiguring and blackening others, the toady thinks that he makes himself look good and embellishes himself with other people's merits; presenting everyone as guilty, he supposes that he himself will appear as right. To act more boldly, these toadies cover themselves with masks of virtue. Piety, dear friend, is the requirement of a gentle and virtuous soul; genuine piety doesn't seek out publicity, just like genuine virtue. But hypocrites, crying loudly about the quiet obligations of a Christian, use the most sacred feeling as a weapon to carry out their intentions. Of all moral monsters, the most dangerous is the hypocrite, whom the immortal Molière dimly depicted in his comedy *Tartuffe*.[3] Molière's hypocrite strives merely to destroy the happiness of one family, but there are hypocrites who destroy the tranquility of an entire civil society.

"We had a certain fellow, Prityagalov, who spent his life preaching freethinking and Jacobinism,[4] representing a model of debauchery; suddenly he declared himself a sanctimonious person and, and like the false prophet Mohammed, he strove with sword and fire or, even worse, slander to destroy all honest and intelligent people, and consequently his adversaries, in order to ascend to the heights after overthrowing them. Preaching humility, he thirsted for honors; proclaiming about heaven, he demanded earthly treasures for himself. Like those in Gehenna,[5] he gnawed on both the living and the dead; he required sacrifices, guilty parties, and unfortunately he fell upon me just at the time when, passionate and irrational in my aspirations to be of use, I was acquiring enemies. Prityagalov and his followers, fearing that I might expose their schemes and tear off their disguises, declared that I was an *anxious man*; defaming me, they managed to exile me to the place where you met me.

"By deception and simulation Prityagalov managed to blind temporarily some good and decent people, who believed in his zeal for the common good. But the triumph of the prophet was short-lived—Providence raises up the wicked, so that on the heights it can reveal more clearly

3. The play was first performed in 1664.

4. A radical political movement that was the most famous political club during the French Revolution (1789–1799).

5. The abode of the damned in the afterlife in Jewish and Christian eschatology, sometimes used as a synonym for hell.

their vileness and make their fall more striking and more instructive. Justice overtook him and punished him in the cruelest manner—that is, it took away his means of *doing harm*; this is the same as taking away a snake's venom, without which it can't exist. Prityagalov's revenge and slander turned out to benefit me: they investigated my case, found me to be in the right, even discovered my small services and the purity of my intentions, and rewarded me beyond my hopes. They gave me the *means for doing good*!"

I embraced the good Pyotr Petrovich, who, bidding me farewell, said, squeezing my hand, "Believe in Providence, my friend, and never despair of finding justice. Sooner or later it will shine upon you as the sun does behind a storm cloud. It seems that you have been convinced of this by experience. Now you'll appear in society with a million rubles in hand and a beautiful wife. It's a new opportunity for experiences. People will cling to you as the metal filings of society cling to a magnet. Be careful! Rust is apt to spread."

On Pyotr Petrovich's advice I rented a small but quiet apartment; it had a very small kitchen and an even smaller dining room. I arranged for a carriage and gave some money to Cousin Anyeta, asking her to start a dowry for Olinka. The kind Anyeta wanted to furnish part of it with her own money, but I wouldn't agree. We concealed all these arrangements from Olinka, who didn't see her own dress and jewels until the day of the wedding. She thanked us not for the items themselves but for the attention.

"My friend," she said. "You fell in love with me when I was poor, and I swore my love to you when you were in prison. Now you're rich and I rejoice in the change in your fate, but I confess that it would have been more pleasant for me to love you if you were poor."

I asked Pyotr Petrovich to give away the bride; in addition to him and Cousin Anyeta's family, no one else was invited. Anyeta's husband even skipped his game of whist at the English Club and stayed for the wedding because of the Strasbourg onion tart his wife had purchased for him to keep him home. When we were all ready to go to the church, I received a package addressed to me. I opened it and found one hundred thousand rubles in pawn tickets and the following letter.

Dear Mr. Ivan Ivanovich!

Your fiancée's disobedience of her mother compelled her, my wife, to deny her the inheritance. In spite of all my requests and representations, my wife didn't want to return her mother's inheritance to her granddaughter because we'd heard false rumors that she was behaving badly. I intentionally *tested her virtue* and became convinced that she maintained decent feelings and wouldn't wander from a path of honor. That forced me to go back to my wife with entreaties, and she finally agreed to fulfill my request. The money, which belongs to your bride is hereby transmitted, and I ask you to include me in the number of your true friends and admirers.

I have the honor of being, etc.

Yeremey Grabilin

I could hardly recover from my astonishment and handed the letter to Pyotr Petrovich, who smiled and, taking another letter from his pocket, asked me to read it. Here's what it said.

Dear Mr. Pyotr Petrovich,

The patronage and special friendship which Your Excellency manifests toward Ivan Ivanovich Vyzhigin, who is about to marry my wife's granddaughter, have forced me to intervene on behalf of your friend; I have managed to receive my wife's consent to return to his bride-to-be her mother's inheritance. Take this as a sign of my particular respect for and devotion to you and as proof that I am not *mercenary-minded* but have been slandered by vicious people, from whom you have also suffered a great deal. From no aspects of ambition or self-interest would I wish to reenter the service but only to show the world that I am not the person my enemies depict, and I want to have a chance to guide my children into a career of active service. I might prove useful by my experience in affairs and will always try to win your favorable opinion. I know that your word alone is capable of attaining my desire. I would want to obtain a modest honored position, one that yielded considerable rewards that I would turn over to the government treasury, being a wealthy and unselfish man, as you can see from my actions toward your protégé Vyzhigin.

With this I have the honor to be, etc.

Yeremey Grabilin

"The rogue!" I said.

"And a fool as well," said Pyotr Petrovich. "Only fools suppose that they can deceive everyone and hide from a clever man who has eyes to see. If they were smart, they'd be sure that it's in their own interests to be honest. Rogues have cleverness, a kind of instinct for deception, like beasts of prey, but they lack true intellect. A rogue always gives himself away. Isn't that what happened to Grabilin?"

When I told Olinka about the contents of the letter and gave her the pawn tickets, she said to me, "I don't know if I should return the money to my grandmother, even though it's my mother's property, but I would like it better if I had nothing of my own and was obligated to you alone. Take the money and do whatever you like with it; I don't need it myself if you have it."

I spent two months in perfect happiness, and I still couldn't commence any visits. Olinka decisively refused to make new acquaintances.

"Do as you please, dear friend," she said. "But the custom seems strange to me—how newlyweds spend the third day after their wedding paying visits, seeking new acquaintances to prevent future boredom, showing off their new equipage along the promenades, their diamonds and silks in society, as if this were an essential component of conjugal bliss. Let's wait. Acquaintances will come by themselves, by chance, by mutual choice; as for now, I'm content with talking to you, to your mother, and to my benefactress, Anyeta."

Pyotr Petrovich became so accustomed to being with us that he dined with us daily and spent the larger share of the evening with us. We loved and respected him like a father. Once he brought a stranger to see us—an elderly man, robust and ruddy, with a physiognomy that expressed good cheer and generosity. The stranger, upon seeing me, paused, and was about to smile, as was his habit, but suddenly pressed me to his bosom and burst into tears, saying, "What a resemblance! It's he, it really is!" Then recovering his composure, he added, "I was a friend of your father's, his schoolmate, even a distant relative. Perhaps you've heard of Count Bezpechin?"

"Are you the executor of my father's will?"

"But I was unable to carry out your father's wishes; I can only rejoice that Providence has protected you."

The count wanted to meet my wife and my mother and sat with us until late that night; he was cheerful and affectionate, and he stated plainly that I should consider him a second father and that he would visit us every day.

The count was an extremely kind man, well educated, and since his childhood he'd become accustomed to the idea that other people would be working for and instead of him, so he spent his time reading, in pleasant conversation, and in traveling; he didn't like dealing in business, although he was forced to serve, partly as a result of the disarray in his circumstances. His family, connections, long service, uprightness and honesty, and lastly, his reluctantly acquired experience in business, cleared his path to the important position that he'd come to occupy. One evening, sitting at tea, he said, "Vyzhigin! I came to see you to offer you a position as director of my chancellery."

"Forgive me, Count! I have no experience whatever in business and could do more harm than good. When I was poor, I sought a place to provide me with a crust of bread, but now I wouldn't undertake something I don't understand. If it were necessary to command a squadron, and I were still single, I could decide in a minute. But what you're proposing is as foreign to me as Chinese."

"Nonsense, friend," the count objected. "I can find more businessmen than I need. But I am looking for an honest man, one whom I can trust, who won't deceive me or be corrupted."

"And if that honest man should be deceived?" I asked.

"He also has to be smart and hardworking; then he'll soon learn the business."

I wanted to object and refuse, but Pyotr Petrovich convinced me, saying that on the whole, honest and disinterested people are needed to balance the businessmen. I agreed.

By a strange coincidence of circumstances, I took the position of the brother of the Moscow police inspector, Arkhip Arkhipych, and I settled into Pantaleimon Arkhipych's apartment, where he had been unable to provide refuge to his own poor brother. Pantaleimon Arkhipych had been expelled from the service and put on trial for a *wrongful accusation*, according to his own words. But since he had a wife and children, he had no doubt of being acquitted by arousing sympathy for a family man. He found a powerful protector in the person of Chuvashin.

Pantaleimon Arkhipych had so arranged an official residence that he occupied more than twenty rooms himself; almost thirty rooms were awarded to his favorite officials, and the chancellery was located in only four small rooms. He made use of the horses designated for carrying messages, the guards worked as his servants, and the couriers ran errands to fashionable shops and carried letters from his daughters and his wife around town, inviting people to gala balls. The officials, who had no place to work, crowded around the windows and spent their time reading newspapers and in inane conversation, discussing only interesting matters *handled* according to the instructions of Panteleimon Arkhipych. Three-quarters of the employees served simply for the honors they could receive for their connections with the director, and the last quarter did all the work to earn their crusts of daily bread and in the hope of future benefits. There were so many unresolved cases that it was shocking to look at the shelves where they were stored. It goes without saying that everything had to be changed, and a new order had to be established.

At first I intended to consult with someone who knew how to set about this matter, but I finally decided to rely on my own intelligence and began to arrange everything opposite to the way it had been done before. I designated twenty rooms for the chancellery, took six for myself, and the remainder I gave to the officials, leaving to them only as many as were necessary for carrying out official duties. I fired all those who were there just for rewards and honors, having advised them to seek what they wanted on the battlefield if they had no fondness for the pen; then I declared that before I would provide letters of recommendation, they had to complete working through all the unresolved cases.

There was one clerk in the chancellery, Sofron Sofronovich Zakonenko, reputed to be an effective man of business, who, although he hadn't been a favorite of my predecessor's, had been retained because he couldn't do without him. Once I summoned him, complimented him, and asked him to explain to me the course of chancellery work and to teach me how to devise a plan for working quickly through the huge backlog of cases, stacks of which kept being delivered to the office. Here's what Mr. Zakonenko told me.

"Only in courts of law, where decisions are made according to the form prescribed in the edict, is the secretary obliged to examine the entire case for the purpose of composing a summary and the preparation of a decision. Looking at the enormous pile of several thousand sheets of paper, it will seem to everyone that one needs to have the wisdom of Solomon and the strength of Samson to extricate oneself from this quagmire of paper. But skill is needed for all things. One only has to read the first petitions of the parties to the lawsuit; then the court's first inquest or decision; then the petition of complaint; the decision of the second instance, corroborate the references to the law—and you're home free. All the rest is superfluous and mere chatter. On the basis of the latest decision you will reach your own conclusion—what must be left in full force, what is to be annulled, what is to be added, and your decree is finished. In chancelleries which have no right to decide and are merely obliged to reexamine cases and the petitions presented to the superior, who, in his turn, sends them elsewhere for a decision or allows the decisions to be carried out, the order is quite different. Here all the skill consists in *rinsing* the paper—that is, so that the paper passes from one desk to another and emerges from the chancellery in a different form but with the same substance it had when it entered. For this to happen, the only things needed are gumption and practice to compose a report with reference or connection and, including the same circumstances of the case, shift them to another place. For this you don't even have a reason to disturb His Excellency, who, as you certainly know, doesn't really like to deal with documents. With regard to the cases about which the count must endorse his own conclusions, in that case one must proceed with extreme caution. His Excellency is a conscientious man and will not want to endorse documents which he hasn't read or decide a case about which he knows nothing; he will put it aside, and then cases begin to accumulate. As a result the count himself, you, and the entire chancellery acquire a bad reputation. Our activity and diligence are measured by the number of documents we process. And so, there's a means to mollify the count's conscience and proceed rapidly through the business by writing decisions, which neither help nor hinder the case, no matter what it might be. Here, for example, are some of these general decisions: *to make a recommendation and report in due course; to proceed according to the existing order; to dispatch to the appropriate place for clarification of all circumstances, and then to report; to present to the higher authorities for consideration; to follow the regular course; to turn to the proper place for a resolution according to the laws and to illuminate all the circumstances of the case; to demand an opinion from the place where the case originated, and transmit it to the proper place, and so on*. It's even easier to reply to private complaints, for example: *to ask in the regular manner if the petitioner has a right to what he claims; to transmit it to the appropriate place; to wait for the resolution of the case; to investigate further and then report; to seek the opinion of the local authority; to confirm the former decision*. And best of all, *for lack of valid reasons, to reject, reject, reject*. That's both short and clear!"

Due to the large number of cases, in spite of myself, I was forced to resort to the means pointed out by Sofron Sofronovich Zakonenko. The cases flew through my hands numbering in the thousands, and soon I became known as a model of promptness and diligence. It's true that I worked very hard on some of the more important cases—that is, I gave them to dependable officials to read and to put together short summaries, with a conclusion based on the essence of the case and on the laws; to maintain order in the choice of cases, I wrote down numbers on separate cards and had my wife choose them as in a lottery. Whichever number she pulled out would determine the case I took under consideration, and that gave me the appearance of impartiality. Meanwhile other documents were dispatched in correct order with the recommendations of Sofron Sofronovich.

Count Bezpechin was extremely satisfied with me and thanked me for squashing the unfavorable opinion circulating about him. He was transformed from a lazy fellow into an energetic man. To give greater weight to this opinion in public, he established one day a week for receiving petitioners; the other days he saw nobody in the mornings. The porter would always say one and the same thing: he was engaged, and the count, locking himself in his study, would lie on a sofa and read newspapers and recent novels. In the evening he visited my wife to have tea, and at the same time, he would sign legal documents. He trusted me completely because I never deceived him. If we didn't accomplish much good, at least we didn't do any evil knowingly, and we defended the just as best we could when we found out the truth unintentionally or by someone's suggestion. Pyotr Petrovich helped us a great deal, communicating brief comments about just and unjust cases, which were given to us to examine; we followed his opinions to the letter and were never mistaken.

God gave me a son, to increase our happiness, and Count Bezpechin became even more attached to our family, taking great pleasure in constantly fussing with the child in his arms; he regarded Olinka with tender emotion, feeling sorry that he'd remained single. Wicked tongues took the occasion to view the friendship in another manner, and others, those who were not satisfied with me, even believed that the count was my wife's lover; but those who knew the count better were certain of the injustice of these accusations, and I was so calm on that score that I even laughed and joked about it in the presence of the count and Olinka.

Pyotr Petrovich, making good use of his power and doing good, promoted all the honest people whom he'd known previously, and meanwhile awarded the position of governor to the kind Shtykov, and the title of commercial councilor to the merchant Sidor Yermolayevich. I followed the example of Pyotr Petrovich and rescued from an unfortunate situation many worthy people and among them some others I awarded the position of police supervisor in Petersburg to Arkhip Arkhipych, which was the single aim of his desires.

Everyone knew that I was in control of the department and that Count Bezpechin had unlimited confidence in me, and so, in spite of the wishes of my wife and myself to avoid making new acquaintances, many petitioners with their families managed to worm their way into my house to plead for their cases or for the friends of young men wanting promotion. Besides that, a large number of relatives appeared about whom I had never heard, as well as the fourth generation of my wife's relatives by her father and mother, my father's relations, including even Nichtozhin, organized a plot against my equanimity, and fell upon me like an army of family members—358 people—and referred to me as their *dear uncle*, demanded positions, ranks, honors, and unjust decisions to their cases. In addition to this number of relatives came three cousins on my mother's side, my Uncle Aleksey Petrovich's offspring, who upon my grandfather's death had settled in Vitebsk and amassed a considerable fortune. His children considered it shameful to remain in the merchant class while their cousin had become such an important man. Chamberlain Kryuchkotvorsky concocted some certificate testifying that they belonged to minor Polish nobility; they also demanded positions and higher ranks from me. In addition, all the Moscow ladies who had helped me and received me hospitably in their homes referred dozens of their grandsons and nephews to me to clear their path to honors and to make efforts that they become gentlemen of the bedchamber. I was tormented, tortured, and inundated with requests and justifications at home, in the chancellery, as a guest, in the theater, and on promenades. Even during the winter I had to leave the city in order to take a walk all alone along the highway, without daring to show my face on the streets. I spent three years in such a distressing situation; finally, having time neither for business nor for my family life, I set off on a vacation to Moscow for twenty-eight days, where I requested retirement with convincing letters to Count Bezpechin and Pyotr Petrovich, asking them to take pity on me and release me from my intolerable yoke.

While waiting in Moscow for the resolution of my fate, I learned from one of my acquaintances returning from foreign parts that poor Grunya had ended her boisterous career in the Hospital of St. Lazare in Paris. I genuinely wept over her death. Unfortunate girl! With her intellect and beauty, she might have been an adornment to her sex, if in her youth her family had taken care of the education of her heart. Here I also learned that Skotinko had lost his mind, and his children, after squandering their ill-begotten wealth, were now living in poverty. Savva Savvich went to seed in drink and died in a tavern fire. Zarezin died from wounds received in a brawl; the other gamblers disappeared without trace, while Udavich was standing trial in the criminal court. As you make your bed, so must you lie in it!

After a long correspondence I finally received my discharge. At this time I learned from Milovidin, with whom I'd always been in contact, that a short distance from him along the seacoast, a small but lovely estate was for sale in a picturesque location, with a large garden and a vineyard. I sent the money at once to purchase it in my wife's name and immediately set off with my family and my mother to Milovidin's house; Petronella received us like family, and I decided to settle on the shores of the southern coast of Tauride for the rest of my days.[6]

It's been ten years since I've been living happily in the circle of my family in the embrace of love and friendship. I have three sons and one daughter; Milovidin has only one son. We are both engaged in the primary education of our children and pass the time in pleasant conversation, music, and reading; we take strolls and cultivate our fields. We are cheerful and serene because we are not seeking anything, and we do as much good as we can. My mother spends her time with Milovidin's uncle, tells his fortune, and plays cards. Petrov looks after the children and makes toys for them; he tells the boys stories about battles and teaches them how to march.

After having experienced so much in my life, having been both a servant and a master, a subordinate and a commander, a Kirghiz horseman and a Russian warrior, a sluggard and a smart dealer, a spendthrift and a gambler from weakness rather than passion, and having experienced people both in good fortune and misfortune—I withdrew from the world, but I didn't lose my love for humanity in my heart. I became convinced that people are more frail than evil, and that for one bad man it is most likely to find fifty good ones, who are not noticed in the crowd because one evil man makes more noise than one hundred good men. I rejoice that I'm a Russian, because in spite of our oddities and caprices, which are as inseparable from humanity as physical

6. Tauride is an old name for the Crimea.

diseases are, there's not one nation in the world that is more ingenious, kind, and grateful than ours. There is not one foreign country where travel is as safe as it is in our sparsely populated Russia, with its forests and steppes; nor is there any place where the unfortunate are helped as willingly as in our fatherland, which is justifiably regarded as a model of religious toleration, hospitality, and tranquility.

Milovidin's uncle, in his extreme old age—the one who could scarcely decipher the letters in *Bruce's Calendar* or in the *Mirror of Albert the Great*—prophesizes that soon, very soon beneficial enlightenment will illuminate all corners of Russia and spread its favors onto all classes of society; that Russian grandees and ladies will begin to speak Russian, read Russian books, and laugh at their fathers' devotion to foreign things; that our literature will rise to such a degree as to rival those of England, France, and Germany; that young people will begin to study to be of service to their country, not just to receive promotions to become officers of field rank; that merchants, becoming more and more enlightened, won't seek certificates of nobility but will constitute among themselves a respectable class of society; that on the basis of time-honored enlightenment, justice will raise its head everywhere, from the lowest to the highest, and usher in a black year for all bribe takers and malefactors. These prophecies made me pick up my pen, in spite of Pyotr Petrovich's advice, and describe my adventures and to rescue from oblivion such heroes as Skotinko, Savva Savvich, and others like them, whose existence will probably not be believed in the future, just as now no one believes in the existence of *The Minor*'s Mitrofanushka.[7] If in the course of time my manuscript becomes known, then everyone who reads it carefully will be convinced that all evil in the world comes from the lack of moral education, while all good comes from genuine enlightenment. Critics will forgive my faults for the sake of my worthy goals, convinced that the bad has been introduced for no other reason than to add more luster to the good.

7. The protagonist of a satirical play titled *The Minor* (1782) by Denis Fonvizin (1745–1792).

Principal Characters

The following list includes only the main characters; many of them have "speaking names," and I have indicated the foreign roots in parentheses.

Gologordovsky	Belarusian landowner; proxy father of the hero
Gologordovskaya	His wife
Petronella and Cecilia	Gologordovsky's daughters
Kanchukovsky	Steward on Gologordovsky's estate
Masha	Servant girl
Ivan Vyzhigin	The hero of the novel; a.k.a. Vanya, Vanechka; (*vzhech* = to scorch; and *vzhiga* = experienced rogue)
Iosel	Gologordovsky's solicitor; a Jew, referred to as the Yid
Aleksandr Ivanovich Milovidin	Lieutenant stationed in Gologordovsky's village (*milovidnyi* = nice-looking)
Moishe	A wealthy Jewish merchant
Rifka	His wife
Sorka	Moishe's daughter
Yudel	His son
Skotinko	Public prosecutor (*skot* = livestock; *skotina* = swine)
Plutyagovich	Skotinko's predecessor as public prosecutor (*plut* = cheater)
Farafont	His servant
Adelaida Petrovna	Vyzhigin's "aunt" later revealed to be his mother, a widow of an Italian named Baritono
Prince Chvanov	Her wealthy patron (*chvanit* = to boast)
Semyon Semyonovich Plezirin	Young gentleman who served in Moscow (*plaisir* = pleasure in French)

Abbé Pretatout	French confidant of Vyzhigin's aunt (*prêt á tout* = ready for anything)
Herr Biersaufer	Vyzhigin's German tutor (*biersaufen* = beer-guzzler)
Herr Schmierhofen	Another German tutor (*schmieren* = to bribe)
Monsieur Felix	A French tutor
Monsieur Lebrilliant	Headmaster of Vyzhigin's boarding school
Luka Ivanovich Vorovatin	A friend of M Lebrilliant's; a troublemaker (*vorovat* = to steal)
Grabilin	A suitor of Vyzhigin's aunt (*grabit* = to rob)
Matryona Ivanovna Shtosina	A widow and friend of Vorovatin's
Agrafena Stepanovna	a.k.a. "Grunya"; Shtosina's lovely daughter; Vyzhigin's first love interest
Savva Savvich	Police captain
Nozhov	Vorovatin's accomplice (*nozh* = knife)
Arsalan-Sultan	Kirghiz chieftain
Gayuk	His son
Sofya	A Russian wife of Arsalan
Firyulkin	A general and Sofya's suitor
Avdotya Ivanovna	Housekeeper of Vyzhigin's uncle
Liza	Her daughter
Mikhailo Ivanovich Shtykov	Police chief in district town (*shtyk* = bayonet)
Petr Petrovich Virtutin	Upstanding merchant encountered in the district town (*virtu* = love of artistic objects)
Sila Minich Glazdurin	An audacious landowner (*sila* = strength; *glaz* = eye)
Anyeta	Vyzhigin's cousin; source of good advice
Yakov Prokofyevich Zarezin	An unscrupulous cardplayer (*zarezat* = to stab)
Faleley Glupashkin	Host at country house party (*glupyi* = stupid, foolish)

Pamfil Merkulovich Moshnin	Merchant and father of several daughters, one of whom (Olga, "Olinka") marries our Vyzhigin (*moshchnyi* = powerful)
Prince Ivan Aleksandrovich Miloslavsky	Vyzhigin's long-lost father, finally revealed

Selected Bibliography of Major Works in English on Bulgarin's *Ivan Vyzhigin*

This list includes the sources I used in preparing this annotated translation.

Herlth, Jens. "The News and What Is Behind it: Social Disorder and Conspiratorial Reading in Mid-Nineteenth-Century Russian Literature." In *"Truth" and Fiction: Conspiracy Theories in Eastern European Culture and Literature*, edited by Peter Deutschmann, Jens Herlth, and Alois Woldan, 36–40. Bielefeld: Transcript, 2020.

Katz, Elena. "Faddei Bulgarin's Polish Jews and Their Significance for the Russian Judeophobic Tradition." *Russian Review* 66, no. 3 (2007): 406–23.

Klier, John D. "*Zhid*: Biography of a Russian Epithet." *Slavonic and East European Review* 60, no. 1 (1982): 1–15.

Le Blanc, Ronald D. "Faddei Venediktovich Bulgarin." In *Russian LiterJature in the Age of Pushkin and Gogol: Prose*, edited by Christine Rydel, 87–100. Detroit, MI: Gale Research, 1999.

Le Blanc, Ronald D. "Gogol's Chichikov: Russian Picaro or Real Vyzhigin?" *Canadian-American Slavic Studies* 23, no. 4 (1989): 409–28.

Le Blanc, Ronald D. "Making *Gil Blas* Russian." *Slavic and East European Journal* 30, no. 3 (1986): 340–54.

Le Blanc, Ronald D. *The Russianization of "Gil Blas": A Study in Literary Appropriation*, 145–200. Columbus, OH: Slavica Publishers, 1986.

Lubensky, Sophie. "The First Russian Novel in English: Bulgarin's *Ivan Vyzhigin*." *Russian Language Journal* 37, nos. 126–27 (1983): 61–68.

www.ingramcontent.com/pod-product-compliance
Lightning Source LLC
Chambersburg PA
CBHW051211120726
47905CB00004B/1074

* 9 7 8 1 5 0 1 7 8 2 6 2 6 *